FALL OF THE
DRAGON
PRINCE

Copyright © 2017 by Dan Allen

First Edition
First Printing, 2017

Cover design by North Star Editions, Inc.
Cover image by Andrew Kiselev/Fotolia

Jolly Fish Press, an imprint of North Star Editions, Inc.

Jolly Fish Press
North Star Editions, Inc.
2297 Waters Drive
Mendota Heights, MN 55120
www.jollyfishpress.com

Printed in the United States of America

THIS TITLE IS ALSO AVAILABLE AS AN EBOOK.

ISBN 978-1-631630-86-6

Library of Congress Control Number: 2016034873

For the next great generation. May you discover greatness within yourselves, and share it.

THE FORGOTTEN HEIRS TRILOGY BOOK 1

FALL OF THE
DRAGON
PRINCE

DAN ALLEN

JOLLY
FISH
PRESS
Mendota Heights, Minnesota

CHAPTER 1

The Outlands.

Toran's warhorse pawed anxiously at the muddy earth as the rain intensified. To his left and right the line of mounted warriors extended out of sight. The horses' heads bobbed. Some stepped in place, sensing the impending action.

With his entire cavalry assembled behind the enemy lines, Toran risked everything—the fate of his own kingdom and that of his allies, the Montazi.

From the center of his line on the barren high desert of the Outlands, Toran the Conqueror surveyed the vulnerable rear flank of the enemy horde.

In the distance, blurred by the veil of dense rain, tattooed Outlanders stretched out along the lip of a steep cliff. The savage invaders were concentrated at the rim. Thousands massed on the mesa by clans, interspersed by massive coils of grappling rope, crude ladders, and black-mouthed cannons on sledges, readying their invasion into the fog-shrouded realm beyond.

Displaced from their native lands by Toran's ancestors centuries before, the inhabitants of the barren Outlands gathered each summer to reclaim their lost lands. They faced an impossible maze of deep and treacherous hazy canyons out of which jutted islands of black volcanic rock mesa—megaliths—laden with the greenery of lush forest. The broken earth was known as the Montas realm. Its defiant people were all that had ever stood between the Outland horde and the inland plains.

Until now.

The Outlanders faced two armies; they only knew about one.

Toran, sovereign of the inland realm of Erdal and leader of its ever-growing alliance, gripped the pommel of his sword hilt and ground his teeth. Curls of youthful blond hair peeped out of his open faceplate and his plate armor strained around a body of taut muscle. Everything in his bearing spoke of action.

The time for speeches had passed, and the time for action was bleeding away. He was running out of excuses.

"Largest horde ever assembled," he mused aloud. "Warrants an alliance."

Two cavalrymen behind Toran exchanged a concerned glance.

Toran's mount stamped the ground with an eager hoof. Again, he reined the animal back. His outward gaze swiveled as he angled his horse toward the sound of approaching hoofbeats.

A roan warhorse cantered into view from the right flank, shouldering a man in heavy and battered armor. The rider leaned toward Toran as his horse came to a halt. His voice was urgent. "Sire, I have personally verified the regiments are in position. We have their rear, but we cannot risk waiting any longer. If we lose the element of surprise—"

"Hold the line, Rembra," Toran said. His voice was firm as his eyes lifted to scan the clouded skies.

The captain at arms threw back his helmet visor. "Toran, what are you waiting for?"

The young king's head turned toward a shape that moved overhead in the clouds. His blue eyes widened and newborn confidence flared in them. "That."

The shadow that had appeared in the clouded sky fell through the spray of rain like a windblown tent. As it descended, its form grew into the silhouette of a winged, fanged demon—with a rider.

Horses whinnied and strained at their reins. Soldiers bent forward as the dragon turned overhead and landed behind the line, ten paces from Toran's banner.

The dragon's rider was slight, as all Montazi were, compared to Toran's husky inlanders. The rider was completely clad in thick full body leather coverings topped by a lightweight helmet, chest plate and gauntlets. His face had a brash look that perfectly complimented the hungry gloss-black eyes of his mount. The dragon's body was large enough to seat a single rider on its back. Its chest rippled with muscles. Its gaping jaws loomed just over the saddled cavaliers with pure predatory menace, twitching constantly toward the slightest movement, promising lethal speed and certain death.

Toran dismounted and strode to where the dragon crouched forward on the knuckles of its bat-like wings. The king approached the saber-fanged terror with no apparent fear, moving close enough to let the beardless Montazi champion lean over to speak into his ear.

"I left her with a seamstress in Neutat," said the rider.

"All was well?" Toran asked intently.

"Yes. Your child will be born before the day is out."

Toran closed his eyes and whispered an oath of gratitude. "Guardians be praised." He raised his head and looked the youthful rider in the eye. "May all your dragons return, Ferrin of the Montazi."

A smile played on Ferrin's lips. He snapped the reins and the fearsome beast reared back onto its hind legs, stretching its wings thirty feet across. "This shall be a great day, a terrible day!"

Toran paused as if in a moment of decision. "A fateful day." He was playing with a power he barely understood, a power that he wished he had never brought to light.

The Lyrium Compass.

It was his decision to open the sealed door that led him and his once-betrothed Tira to discover the Lyrium Compass.

He had argued against using it. But she could not resist its power. How many turning points had she discovered before she was exiled? Toran hated Tira and her cruelty. The compass had brought out the worst in her.

Would it do the same to him?

He shivered at the thought.

He was playing with fate itself. He had no choice. With knowledge of the turning points, Tira held power over the destinies of nations.

Unifying the realms was the only weapon he could wield against her.

Of the five inland realms descended from the ancient settlers, two were already under his command. Three remained.

United, they would live, or fall.

Ferrin's dragon beat its wings down heavily, rising into the downpour.

Toran gripped the reins of his warhorse and swung into his saddle. He scanned over the armored cavaliers closest to his banner. Fear and expectation weighed in their expressions.

They were Erdali, like him. They, too, could feel the millennial tide.

It rose at turning points like this, floating fate on a sea of possibility. Peace and chaos were won as easily as tipping a coin on edge. It just required a tiny push at the right instant.

When it rose, the Erdali came to arms in great conquering armies. As the tide fell, they dissolved into selfish squabbling villages.

Before the Erdali, there were others who had felt it. They built the Lyrium Compass to reveal the turning points.

Then they had buried it.

Perhaps fate wanted the compass rediscovered, Toran considered. The tide was rising on the field of battle before Toran, to sail the Montas realm and the plains beyond into a new dawn or a very long nightmare.

Toran lifted his head, his gaze hard as diamond. His voice roared. "Ready arms!"

The tide was rising. Toran knew it. He could feel it, just as he had the first time he had watched the drifting rings of the crystal compass stabilize, pointing to one place in time.

To this place where the streams of fate collided in a perfect storm, Toran had brought more than an army.

He had brought his unborn heir.

Tira won't understand what I've done, Toran said to himself with as much doubt and fear as blind hope, *until it's too late.*

Only a handful in Toran's inner circle knew what a birth at a turning point would do. The fate of the child and the realm would be bound together. While the child lived, the realm could never fall.

He drew his sword with a slick ring that echoed a thousand times over as the cavalry drew in unison.

Toran lowered his visor and raised his sword high in his powerfully steady arm.

Silence. Even the rain drew an awful pause.

His sword dropped forward through the air and his horse burst forward. For ten lonely paces, the massive steed charged alone, distancing itself from the line.

Then the wave of the cavalry, a seemingly endless row of lances, broke forward, rending the silence. The sound of four thousand charging hooves thundered into the fog-shrouded abyss in the distance.

The battle had begun.

Montazi Realm. Village of Neutat.

At the edge of the blighted Outlands where the battle raged in a crumbling rush of mounted beasts and their riders against numberless savage brutes, deep cracks between the half-mile-wide megaliths formed a labyrinth of canyon trenches, webbed at increments by rope and slat ladders, the only tenuous signs of civilization.

Torrents of rain crashed mercilessly against the volcanic rock draped in jungle. The water collected in streams that poured off the leaves of the great ivy that grew down over the edges and disappeared into the fog of the deep.

From the summits of the gently domed megaliths, the wooded stems of the giant ivy splayed out through the rain forest like snakes of enormous proportions.

Heavy rain sounded dull thumps on the roa small dugout home within a thick-wooded ivy stem. In the narrow workshop with rounded walls, a wide-bodied nurse gripped the hand of her patient—a delicate-featured young woman with her back arched against a large pillow, her jaw clenched in pain. The pale yellow glow from a few short candles illuminated the tearstained faces of both nurse and the mother-to-be.

Fear and desperation showed in the nurse's eyes. She wrung her hands and turned to face the seamstress who owned the tiny workshop. "It's breeched."

"Can't you turn it?" asked the seamstress in a voice both bothered and frustrated from where she watched at the opposite side of the workshop. Her blouse and leather vest were halfway undone to relieve the oppressive humidity.

"I . . . don't know. I've never done it."

"Just try. Surely you have enough strength."

"If I do it wrong I might kill the child," the nurse whispered anxiously, but not quiet enough to keep the words from reaching the ears of the mother who screamed again with the pain of another contraction. "I could break its neck or I could wrench the mother's liver. I only saw it done once."

"If you cannot turn it, you must take the child out with the knife," the seamstress said angrily, "or they may both die."

"Mother!" shrieked the animated voice of a young girl from outside the small home.

"Tannatha," shouted the seamstress, turning to the doorway.

"Mother, news!" cried the young child, bursting in through the beaded entry. She looked like a moving potato under her handmade dragon skin rain cover.

"Victory?" the seamstress cried, her hazel eyes desperate with hope.

"We won," the child shouted, throwing off the musky dragon hide and embracing her mother. "We won, mother. The Outlanders are beaten. The horde is gone."

"What happened, Tanna?" the seamstress asked, kneeling down and wiping water from the face of her daughter.

"A rider came to the keep to send a signal. He said Toran's cavalry went down off the Montas in the night and circled around behind the horde. They trapped them against the cliffs and cut down their archers. There was nothing to stop our dragon riders from diving on them from the skies."

"But, child?" the patient asked. The arms she leaned back on quivered with pain and exhaustion. "How many of ours survived?"

"Most of them. That's what he said."

"A miracle." The seamstress wrapped her arms around Tannatha in a moment of rapture. "The horde outnumbered ours nine to one."

The nurse leaned over to comfort the young mother in labor, "We are safe. And the inlands are safe."

A look of passive acceptance passed over the foreign face of the young woman. Her eyes closed. "Use your knife," she whispered. "It is enough. The father is alive."

"Are you sure?" the nurse asked. She pressed her hand against the pale cheek of her patient. Her beauty was both captivating and distant, her land of origin a mystery.

"If any are alive, he will be with them," the pale woman said, forcing the words out through heavy, pained breaths. "Please! I can feel it—the babe is dying. Please. Take the child!"

The nurse grimaced, eyes brimming again with tears. "I . . . won't be able to save you. I'm just an apprentice."

The woman cried out again in agony. "Save the child! Please."

The nurse fought back tears. She readied the knife, and with a scream that pierced the heavens, the child was free.

"Hold the babe," the nurse shouted over the screams of the dying mother, severing the cord and handing the infant to Tannatha's mother. The nurse frantically tried to remove the afterbirth and sew up the oversized cut, but the blood made her hands slippery. The seamstress passed the baby to her own child and pushed the nurse aside. "Let me." Her stitches were expert and swift, but the young woman's life ebbed away.

Finally, her hands fell still.

Aching moments passed in horror and doubt.

Thunderous footfalls sounded outside and the beaded curtain was thrown aside.

Bent over in the entrance was a large inlander, clad head to foot in mud-splattered armor, heavily dented and streaked with the terrible crimson of bloody deeds. Behind him, a dragon, angry at the downpour, let fly a burst of fire into the air. Its rider brought it under control with a jerk to the reins tethered to its neck spines.

The man in the doorway removed his helmet and a mane of neck-length blond hair fell out. He took a step into the room and froze.

"By the sacred plain," whispered the seamstress, backing away and bowing.

Tannatha, cradling the still-naked baby, gazed up at the man. "Are you . . . Toran? The king?"

He did not speak. His face clouded with ravished grief as he saw the mother, pale-faced, and the blood pooled on the floor. He brought his gauntleted hand to his lips. A long moment later his eyes drifted to the child whose constant high-pitched cries made the only sound in the hollowed-out dwelling.

"A boy," he said solemnly, voice softened with grief.

"Are you his father?" Tannatha asked.

"He is," said Toran, looking from the nurse to the seamstress, "the son of a rider who perished in the war. Tell him this. And tell no one of me. Swear it on your allegiance."

"I swear it," said the nurse, her voice breaking into a sob.

"I will swear," said the seamstress. "But I don't understand," she added boldly.

Toran's voice rang like a hammer on an anvil. "Say he is the son of a rider who died in the war, for it is truth. This child is to be a rider of the Montazi. You will care for him and see that he becomes a rider." His voice was imperial; his command left no margin for misunderstanding.

"But how can you do this?" Tannatha's mother asked, irked by the man's callous dismissal of his mistress's death, and leaving the child a burden for her. "Why don't you take him with you? He is your son . . . isn't he?"

Toran looked at her and then down once more at his lifeless love. "I do what I must, until the gathering is complete. Do you understand?"

The eyes of Tannatha's mother narrowed slightly. "No," she protested. "We are Montazi. This child is of Erdal."

"And she's not even from the Montas," Tannatha noted, speaking of the dead mother. Her own mother threw her a furious look that silenced the girl.

Toran's voice filled the room with power. "Hundreds of my blood-kin died to save you and all your Montazi children. You can raise one of mine!"

Tannatha cringed as Toran removed his gauntlet and took the child from her, cradling it in his hand like a practiced father. He spoke softly. "Give him a Montazi name. This child will bear your hopes on the wings of the great dragons."

"But the war is over," sputtered the seamstress. "You can go home. You can raise him in Erdal."

Toran eyes became distant and he spoke in a hushed voice, almost to himself. "You cannot conceive of the terror that is to come. No one can. What I do, what those who are sworn to me seek, is a purpose greater than just one realm."

"Yes, but—"

"There is war now in the south," Toran said, his voice growing heavier with each word. "Tira, the witch queen of Hersa, stirs our enemies against us. The Serbani are falling. I go to war again. We can only hope—" His gaze turned to the pale face of the mother, her body still and silent. The king's composure crumbled as grief stabbed through his steel armor into his unprotected heart.

He gently handed the child back and looked from Tannatha's mother, to the nurse, and said again with the ferocity of an enraged lion. "On your allegiance!"

His shoulders shook. His eyes closed tight. The pit of his grief suddenly swallowed the strength of the conquering warlord. In two steps, he moved past the silent witnesses and knelt next to the still body. His hand touched hers disbelievingly as he swept her hair from her face.

The infant's cries grew louder.

"Go find a nursing mother," the seamstress said, shooing her daughter toward the door. Tannatha didn't move. She watched as the king scooped the dead maiden into his arms. Her head lolled back as he lifted the body and her arm fell to one side exposing a palm scarred by a clan symbol: a cross and x within a circle—a compass.

Then he was gone.

The nurse knelt where the body had lain and muttered to herself, explaining away the tragedy to an audience of silent Guardians. Her ramblings melted into sobs.

"Mama, if Toran leaves will the Outlanders come again?" Tannatha asked. Her eyes filled with fear and innocent faith as she rocked the wailing infant from side to side.

Tannatha's mother smiled thinly. "Not for a long time, dear." She lifted the infant and clutched the babe to her chest. Its cries softened to pitiful whimpers. "The Outlanders won't invade while we have an alliance with Erdal. Together we are too strong for them." She looked her daughter in the eyes. "We were lost without Toran's cavalry. Remember that."

And she did. She remembered Toran—and his heir.

CHAPTER 2

26 years later. Serbani Realm. Port of Yerban.

The old courtier lifted the fired-clay mug in an air of lost refinement. His vest bore no buttons and his hat was flat and tattered on the edges, yet he spoke with conviction born of liquor and dotage.

"They say Toran left no heirs." He wagged his head, miraculously managing to keep his balance. "It's a lie. I was his cupbearer, keeper of many secrets."

The other patrons in the Musk Mink, the rankest wallowing place of the Serbani port town of Yerban, made no response, except one old sailor whose face slumped to one side where a missing eye left a gaping hole in his face. "Then where is your mark, Ranville?" he said to the old man.

Ranville snorted. Simply because Toran had not branded him with the mark of the compass did not mean he was no less serviceable or trusted by the great leader.

His social graces dulled by the stiff local grog, Ranville pursued his rant with increasing vigor. "The bringer of the great peace ruled five kingdoms. *Five* realms!"

Rising to his crooked height, Ranville rapped his cane on the wood floor. "I ask you, how many heirs ought there be?"

"Five," the bartender droned. "Five heirs born in secret to his mistresses, one on each of his campaigns—we've all heard your rant a dozen times, old man. Now what can I get you to drink?" He added under his breath, "With luck, one more pint and you'll pass out."

"Five heirs," Ranville stated with an inland plains accent that hinted at better grooming than his rags implied. "Five heirs to reunite the kingdom—may I live to see the day!"

"You know, I think Ranville's got a point there," called out a tavern rat with fewer teeth than fingers. The man's gap-toothed grin widened. "But Ranville, have you ever thought how you are going to serve five cups to five kings all at once?"

Rude laughter erupted across the room with the clatter of mugs against tables, hands slapping knees, drunkards spraying beer into the air, and old frogs wheezing into coughing fits. A few drinkers fell from their chairs, all making for a scene of comedy so desperate one might have forgotten why they were there in the first place.

Ranville turned with a tight-lipped grimace. He slogged his way through standing mockers and out of the shanty tavern.

"They mock his memory—the king who saved them all. Where was Serban's strength when the battle masters laid siege to the tower of Essen? When the Hersians ravaged the coast, who turned back the cursed corsairs?" he said to an audience of two bedraggled horses tethered at the hitching post.

Even they ignored him.

He leaned up against one of the village's few lit oil lampposts. Sighing, the old bureaucrat reached into the inner pocket of his battered waistcoat and withdrew a leather folder. He opened it with trembling, wrinkled fingers to reveal a side-bound collection of aged parchments.

"I'm the only one who can find them." His voice choked on the words. His drunken face grimaced as grimy tears pushed out of the corners his deep-set eyes. "I must not give up . . . I must not . . ."

The cryptic pages held scattered clues, the fragments of conversations, maps, names, and notes. But his dim eyes could no longer read his own handwriting. The clues he had known and clung to for so long floated just beyond the reach of his fading memory.

"I've been looking for you."

A tall man descended from his horse a few paces away. He was dressed in clean trousers and a tailored black dress coat.

"What did you say, sir?" Ranville asked, gazing at the tall gentleman.

"I know who you are, old man. You served the great king," he said smoothly, keeping his horse's reins in his hand rather than looping them over the tavern's hitching post. He had a southerly accent, and his clothes were altogether too clean.

Not a local, Ranville decided. The only irregular thing about him was a patch of pale skin on the side of his neck. *An old burn scar,* it appeared to Ranville.

"Such loyalty as you show is a rare thing," the merchant said, stepping into the yellow light of the lamppost. His face had a sallow but piercing look, born of luxury and mingled with misfortune. He had straight shoulders and straight, black hair topped by a wide-brimmed hat.

"Why do you come to me?" Ranville asked warily. His feet shifted backward until his heel bumped against the rough outer wall of the tavern.

The gentleman tucked one hand into his own coat pocket and looked Ranville in the eye with something of a smile. "It is time the children of the king take their places."

"But what can you do? How can you find them, when I myself have searched in vain these thirteen years?"

"I have resources."

"What do you want with me then?" Ranville said. "Speak to the point. If you are out to mock me like those ingrates in the tavern—"

"Time counts your paces, Ranville," said the well-to-do young man, who looked to be not much older than twenty.

Hearing his name spoken with a nobleman's elegant diction stirred a vestige of pride in Ranville. He lifted his eyebrows and straightened his posture as much as his age allowed.

"I know what you carry with you: clues to the identities and locations of the heirs," said the young man smoothly. "It is time to enlist new help, or your commission will die with you." He let the words steep in Ranville's fogged mind before continuing.

"You must trust *me* with your clues. With your knowledge and my resources, we can find the heirs." He added in a distant voice, "I have longed to see their faces."

Ranville's eyes widened with hope, as if he were being pardoned a lifelong sentence. "You will find them?"

"I have sworn to do just that," said the man, drawing his horse alongside. He quickly tore the folder away from Ranville and vaulted himself into his saddle.

His eyes shone with a look of fiery determination as they narrowed. "I will find them, one by one. And I will *kill them all.*"

Ranville's mouth fell agape. He reached for the precious notes, but in vain.

Eyes burning with vengeance, the stranger drew a saber and swung it, striking the unarmed drunk across the head with the steel hilt.

Ranville fell. Blood spilled from the side of his skull as he crumpled to the ground.

The stranger spurred his mount, galloping away with the clues to the heirs.

"Stop!" Shock and guilt closed on Ranville like a trap from which there was no escape. "What have I done?"

CHAPTER 3

Montazi Realm. Village of Neutat.

The narrow rope and slat bridge bobbed precariously as Terith raced across it. Beneath him, the shifting currents of perennial fog hid the bottom of the steep-walled canyon. In the darkness below lay a seething swamp, roiling with gas vents and hot pots where creatures lay in wait to feed in frenzies on the unlucky victims that slipped on the ivy and fell into the deep. Terith gave no thought to the deep and its terrors as his well-placed steps carried him down the curve of the gently sagging bridge and up the opposite slope.

At the end of the bridge a guard stood, seeming to appear from the mass of giant green ivy leaves that draped over the edge of the cliff. The soldier dropped his half-drawn sword back into his scabbard and gave a salute to the man half his age.

"Ho, Terith!"

"Abervall!" Terith called, recognizing the seasoned foot solder.

"Back from the southern lookout already?" Abervall asked. "That was fast."

"All clear on the south rim," Terith said without slowing. "Tell Malian to send the report once the northern watch returns."

"Because you've got better things to do," the round-bellied Abervall said with a twinkle in his eye.

Terith just smiled and accelerated up a short section of exposed black volcanic stone, shortcutting two switchbacks.

Abervall called after the young champion, "Good luck!"

Terith turned onto the main path as it leveled. He followed it toward the center of the megalith, where the great ivy sent a single taproot into the stone and siphoned water from an aquifer below the megaliths. Even in the dry season, the ivy never faded.

Terith followed the path as it ducked under one of the enormous ivy stems, crawling like a python of gigantic proportions. Tannatha's workshop was inside the root. Beyond it, overhung by the dense shade of jungle trees and broad ferns, a dozen more stems fanned out over the megalith.

Within the great wooded stems were long comfortable bed-chambers, storerooms, visiting spaces, and shadowy places where Terith, as a child, had raced through hidden tunnels and disappeared into the shaded forest at the first word of warning from an elder.

Terith bounded up a boulder and onto the top of the giant stem, before disappearing through a smoke hole into his one-room dugout home. He washed at the stone basin that flowed continuously with water from the taproot spring before shaving with an Outlander's knife he had caught in mid-throw during a raid. His hair, like that of many of the riders, was cropped short, giving his face a strong, lean appearance.

Terith breathed in the hot, moist air that drifted in through the round windows. He drank in the change of climate with a thrill of expectation.

The rains are coming.

It was time for the challenge.

Terith felt that at last his moment had come. As a foster child of the village, his lonely beginnings had foreshadowed nothing of the miraculous path his life had taken.

If his luck held for one more week, he would be the champion of champions and engaged to be married.

Thinking of Lilleth, the eldest daughter of the Montazi chief, anticipation thrummed through him as he stepped out through the beaded entry curtain onto a cobblestone courtyard.

He jogged away from the small cluster of dugout homes on the edge of the village on a shaded path.

A bloodthirsty screech ripped through the air. Terith instantly rolled to the ground. He landed in a crouch, quickly drawing two long, curved knives from the sheaths on his calves. From a place far away, beyond the horizon, he summoned the light of the Montazi awakening. His body rippled with light at the edges, a haze of pure energy.

Few humans on earth could hope to fight a dragon successfully in combat. Terith risked no chance. He drew every thread of fate tight about him. The power of the awakening coursed through his muscles and mind. The world slowed into an almost-suspended animation where Terith alone moved at the speed of his will.

Terith saw the laughing girl on top of the ivy stem and banished the euphoria of the awakening. Life came back into real motion, along with a massive headache.

"That was a very good imitation," Terith said to the giggling twelve-year-old. He sheathed his knives and rubbed his temples. "You even got the rising pitch as the dral starts a dive."

"I know," the twiggy girl said smugly. She reached down and jumped into Terith's arms. "My awakening is getting stronger all the time, don't you think?"

He caught her and then dropped the sound-casting prodigy unceremoniously. "I could have done with some warning, Mya."

The girl grinned ear-to-ear at her besting of the young champion. "You glowed so bright it looked like you were going to light the forest on fire!"

Terith let a small laugh escape through his attempt at a reprimand. He mussed her hair and started back along the trail.

Mya followed in a lighthearted skip. "Where are you going?"

"The keep."

"Wanna hear a joke?" she asked.

"Sure," Terith said. "But if it's as bad as—"

"Where is the best place to get stung by a buzzing scorpion?"

"Well, it's not the leg," Terith said. "You can't run away once your leg is paralyzed."

"Give up?" Mya said expectantly. "In the hive. Get it? If you get stung in the scorpions' hive then you get eaten faster, so it hurts less."

Terith groaned. "That . . . was the worst joke I have ever heard. Who told you that?"

"Kyet—he probably learned it from Nema. Anyway . . ." she said, drawing the word out expectantly, "just between the two of us—when you win the challenge, will you choose Enala or Lilleth?"

Terith stopped and focused his most imperial stare at the blushing girl. "That's none of your business."

Mya stared at his boots and clasped her hands in front of her. "I've already placed my bet, so it won't matter if you tell me."

Terith ignored her plea as he hurried down the stone stair to the edge of the megalith where a cavern opened toward the deep.

"Can I at least make a guess?" Mya called from a wary distance from the keep's entrance. Her voice became fainter as she continued to call after him. "Do you think Lilleth would be satisfied with someone as simpleminded as you for a husband? My mother wants to know—and if so, how come you flirt with Enala so much? And . . ."

"*She* flirts with *me*." Terith hollered back. "Farewell, Mya."

Terith turned into the torch-lit entrance of the natural cavern formed long ago by the swelling pressure of a large ivy root. A trickle of water ran out of the cave, off a cliff, and disappeared into the mist in the canyon depths.

Terith climbed farther up into the cavern to where Redif, the warden of the keep, was busy sharpening a spear on a grindstone. Endle, the apprentice, worked the hand wheel. This spear had a foot-long metal tip at the end of a seven-foot shaft, just long enough to reach through the bars to the center of the yearling dragon cages.

Redif nodded at Terith's arrival and stopped sharpening. He came alongside the young champion, his dreadlocks of tightly matted black hair bobbing.

"What of the first rides?" Terith asked.

"Two could not yet bear a rider," Redif reported. "One was imperious and refused."

"Keep it."

"And the others, Terith? Shall we dispatch them now?"

Terith looked past Redif farther into the keep and noticed Kyet, the youngest rider in the Montas, struggling with a yearling dragon. Terith nodded to Redif. "I'll take care of it. Call it a day."

Redif whistled to Endle, who bolted for the exit with nothing but dinner on his mind. Redif followed, quickly disappearing out the mouth of the cave.

Terith lifted two of the long spears and approached Kyet, considering what he was about to do. Kyet was only fourteen—as young as Terith had been when he became a rider—and unproven. Terith set one spear on the ground and leaned the other against his arm.

Kyet pulled hard on the neck spines of a yearling fruit dragon to get it to bow its head for harnessing, but the dragon merely twisted its neck and screeched at him. The fruit dragon had strong hind legs and short maneuverable forearm wings balanced by a long tail with a flattened tip. The yearling was a dull green color, with hints of a brilliant yellow and gold that would cover a full-grown queen, like Terith's Akara.

"Yield!" Terith ordered, staring Kyet's dragon in the eye. The yearling bowed submissively.

"I worry about this one," Terith said. "It gives up too easily."

"Too easily?" Kyet scoffed. "Yeah, right."

"Your will to dominate must be complete from the first moment," Terith reminded.

"A dragon senses fear," Kyet rehearsed, as if for the hundredth time.

"And it will kill anyone that fears it," Terith noted with finality. He took a weighted breath, still eyeing the weak-willed dragon. "We don't have enough room to keep them all."

"I wish we had larger varieties," Kyet said, his voice rising with expectation, "like the strythe."

The strythe were heavyset and powerful—with enormous saber fangs—and very aggressive.

"The problem is feeding them," Terith said. "Strythe hunt mountain goats. We have no prey for them out here so close to the Outlands."

"Or at least dral—why can't we raise dral instead of fruit dragons?" Kyet asked, or whined—it was hard to tell with teenagers.

The strong-armed dral were the feared predatory dragons that clung to the cliffs of the megaliths. With wings disguised as great ivy leaves, they waited for fruit dragons to poke their noses under the ivy looking for fruit, and then seized them.

"I don't like dral," Terith stated. "They aren't as loyal, or as intelligent as fruit dragons." His mind churned as he considered what had to be done. Kyet had not yet faced battle with the Outlanders. In only a few months, in high summer, he would ride by Terith's side to stop their invading bands. Terith had to know that Kyet would follow any order without hesitation.

More importantly, Kyet had to know that.

"How can you expect to win the challenge with Akara?" Kyet asked. "This year's race will be all about the climbs. You need one of the fishing dragons. You need a velra."

"All the trained velra in the Montas are already owned by riders," Terith said. "None of them will lend out their velra for the challenge. It's too dangerous. Besides, I have plans."

"Why not bargain for one of the crossbred racers?" Kyet insisted. "They haven't got quite the climbing strength of the velra, but better top speed. You could make up the difference on the long stretches."

"Kyet," Terith said plainly. "I've never lost a race, ever. And I've fought in seven summer campaigns against the Outlander horde. Why should I worry about this race?"

"Pert," Kyet mumbled under his breath.

"What's that?"

"Nothing . . . it's just, I overheard from the watch at Erden that Pert was riding in the challenge."

"Pert," Terith said in a low voice, flexing his hands into fists. "Very well. I'll keep that in mind." He leaned the spear casually toward the young rider. "Kyet, kill that dragon. *Now.*"

Kyet turned to Terith, eyes wide and horrified.

"Quickly. Do it."

Kyet seized the spear and hurled himself at the dragon, thrusting the long spear through the open door of the cage.

With reflexes unmatched by any other creature in the Montas, the dragon leapt backward.

But there was no escape in the small space between the open cage and the cave wall. Kyet's spear punctured a lung as it rammed through the young dragon's chest.

The wounded dragon reared its head back and gulped air, preparing to let fly a gust of furnace-intensity flame. Before it could, a second bladed shaft plunged into its scaly underside, straight through its heart. A wheeze escaped the dragon as its body shuddered and fell still.

Terith dropped the end of the spear he had thrust into the dragon and grabbed Kyet's shaking shoulders. "Well done."

"Why?" was the single word that escaped Kyet's lips.

"Now you know," Terith said. "You can kill. You can follow any order. You're a rider."

Kyet took a shaky breath and flexed his fists to suppress the trembling in his fingers.

Terith waited as the teen coped with the sudden death of a dragon he had raised from an egg.

"I murdered it."

"No," Terith said, "the opposite. A timid dragon endangers its rider in battle."

Kyet nodded and yanked his spear free, a last savage act that gave him a shudder of remorse.

"Worst of all it would have made weak breeding stock," Terith said, "undoing everything we've worked for."

Kyet knew it, but the task was tantamount to killing a friend.

"Sorry I missed," Kyet said, shaking his head in frustration and disbelief. "We almost lost it there. They're so fast."

"You trust me," Terith said. "Now I trust you." Terith looked Kyet in the eyes. "See for yourself."

Kyet's eyes flared with the white light of the awakening as the young truth seer searched Terith for any sign of doubt or deception. His countenance changed, as if Terith's own confidence had flowed into him. His young face hardened with a look of determination. "Yes, sir."

Terith turned to leave. "And you know," a smile crept onto his lips, "dragons aren't the fastest thing on this megalith."

"Yes, chief... er, champion—I suppose you aren't chief yet... that's still Ferrin. Anyway, good luck at the feast," Kyet called.

The glorious and ominous sound of the word *chief* rang in Terith's ears as he climbed back out of the keep and up the stone steps.

There was only one chief of the Montazi, but the time for change had nearly come. Terith could feel it. This time, this challenge, a new chief would be chosen.

"I'm ready," Terith whispered to himself.

The awakening chose the chief; he had no choice in the matter.

Whether the sign was given this year or not, Terith was proud of what he had accomplished in Neutat. His riders were disciplined and skilled. The Outlander invaders had never reached the village on his watch.

On top of that, Kyet had passed his improvised test. To Terith it was like his left arm suddenly having more strength.

Coming to the top of the stone stair and stepping into a clearing, the never-defeated rider found himself cornered by a small army.

He ran his hand through his short-cropped sandy hair and gritted his teeth, eyes darting from one side to the other, his posture losing none of its swagger.

"I see I'm outnumbered," he said to the gathered militia.

Mischievous grins broke out among the otherwise stone-faced assemblage.

"The Suma is nearly here, and I have to go to Ferrin-tat for the feast of the challenge. I'm afraid I can't tell you stories tonight."

The children of the village swarmed their champion. "You promised!"

"Tell us of the time you captured the Outlander chief!" cried a dirt-smudged boy.

"Tell us of Toran's conquest," begged another.

Terith folded his arms and looked at the impetuous child. "You've heard that one a dozen times already." His eyes scanned over the scrawny bunch of hardy survivors. "And besides, I wasn't even born until Toran's conquest was nearly over, so I can hardly know if I'm even telling it right. Get one of the elders or grand matrons to tell you."

"A legend!" one boy cried.

"A legend . . . let's see." Terith racked his brain. With so much on his mind, it was as much as he could manage to remember where he was. "All right. Here is the legend of all legends."

"Yay," a boy chirped. His tiny hands formed fists and his arms wiggled with anticipation like the branches of a bush in a windstorm.

"Sit."

The children dropped to the ground like overfull sacks of ivy fruit.

"Long ago," Terith began, "at the beginning of our age, before Toran, before the Montazi or even the Dervites, the Outlanders ruled the inland plains."

"That doesn't make sense," Mya interrupted. "You should call them inlanders if they lived in the inlands."

"I'll call them primitives. That's what they were—still are. Anyway, long ago when the primitives roamed the inlands of Erdal, our enlightened ancestors came to settle here. They arrived on the backs of the great dragons—dragons so large their wings stretched across the deep from one megalith to another."

"I want one."

"Where did they come from?"

"From far across the Outland wastes," Terith explained, "a place of magic and peace. The awakening comes down to us from them."

"Oh, I've heard this one before a hundred times," a young girl said. "I know it by heart. The ancestors settled the plains and then the Outlanders killed one of the dragons. The rest of the great dragons left and then the settlers drove the Outlanders out of the plains, and that started the whole thing with the Outlanders trying to get through the Montas to the plains of Erdal every summer. Supposedly only when all the settled realms are brought together will the great dragons return—the end."

"I guess you've done my job for me," Terith said smugly. "I'll just be on my way—"

"Hey, she cheated!"

"Tell us about the challenge!" cried another lad.

"Yes!" the other children echoed. "Tell us of the challenge."

Terith rolled his eyes and raised a finger. "One more story. But you won't get another after this one."

The children gazed expectantly, eyes riveted in perfect silence.

"The Montas is the most dangerous place you could ever hope to live," Terith began. He looked at each of the faces of the children. "The survival of the Montazi relies on good breeding. That is the reason for the challenge."

"Tell us about the race part," whispered a very young boy who was sitting on his older sister's lap.

"Yes, I was getting to that," Terith said, reaching out to tweak the toddler's nose. "Only the bravest of the riders are named champions and allowed to compete in the challenge. Each successful finisher may choose a mate from among the noble eligible."

"Oh, just tell us who you'll choose," Mya begged, clasping her hands together, eyes gleaming with expectation. "You must have decided by now. Is it Lilleth?"

"The race hasn't even been run yet," Terith hedged. "But I will tell you this. It is no easier to become one of the eligible than it is to become a champion. Eligible women must have a deep mastery of the awakening. It passes only from mother to child, so a rider must have a mate with skills equal to his own."

"Some of the riders die in the challenge," said one of the boys to his mop-haired friend.

"But not Terith," the friend added, his eyes alight with faith. "He's the greatest rider in the Montas—greater than Ferrin."

"Perhaps," Terith said, "But he's getting old anyway."

"Better than Pert, too!"

"Well, I must agree with that," Terith said.

The boys seated in the front smiled double wide, looking as though they would burst from pride.

"The race begins one week after the welcome feast," Terith continued. "And the feast will be tomorrow at Ferrin-tat, so you understand why I must be going."

"But what about the race?" the mop-haired boy urged.

Terith looked over his shoulder. Two more children had come in from the rear, shepherded by his friend Tanna. She laughed at his predicament as she settled the toddlers on the dirt next to Terith and retreated to the back of the group.

"In the race," Terith continued, excitement creeping into his voice, "the dragons must pass through all the obstacles. There are canyons, bridges and," Terith paused for emphasis, "a long, dark tunnel. But of course, the most dangerous thing about the race isn't an obstacle."

"It's the other riders' dragons," shouted a young boy, leaping to his feet and pumping his fists. "You have to fight them off!"

"Right. You've got to watch your back," Terith said, enjoying the boy's energy. *A rider in the making.*

"Why don't you ride with a companion to keep your wing, like the others?" another boy asked.

"Because nobody else can keep up, stupid," said the fired-up youngster.

Terith chuckled at his antics, before continuing. "The race starts at noon. The champions fly all day and all night and must return to the starting place before noon the next day to win a mate. The first to arrive back at the starting place is the champion of champions and gets the first choice from among the eligible. A bond is made if the match is right."

"What does it feel like to be bonded?" one of the girls asked.

"I imagine it is a lot like kissing," Terith said to a chorus of laughter.

"Yuck." Several boys' faces contorted with disgust.

"Terith," Tanna chided, "bonding is not like kissing and you know it."

"All right, so it isn't like kissing. It's about sharing your awakenings. You have to let go of everything and share yourself, mind and soul, with your mate."

"Still sounds gross," mumbled one of the boys.

"And then . . ." Tanna prompted, obviously enjoying seeing Terith have to talk about romantic things.

Terith swallowed and continued. "Then the bonded couples keep a summer of promise and are married in the fall when the dragons mate and leave for the sacred plain."

"Will you win?" asked Mya. She was slight in her physique, but indomitable in spirit, the likeliest of the Neutat children to become eligible, given a few more years.

Terith's words came with a confidence that surprised him. "Yes." He smiled. "I will win, because I have help that no other challenger can match." He looked over the young of Neutat. "I think that about covers it. Off to home now, all of you, before the scorpions come up from the canyons to feed."

The young scattered obediently out of the clearing, some stretching their arms out and running around like they were dragons and others firing imaginary arrows at them.

The last to stand was not a child, but a childhood friend.

"Tannatha."

The leather-working seamstress smiled weakly. She gathered her long skirt in the front with one hand. Her words came haltingly.

"Did you ever feel like . . . like your future lies somewhere else? I mean . . . outside the Montas?"

Terith narrowed his eyes thoughtfully. "Why?"

"No reason. I . . . well, I just came to wish you good luck."

Terith nodded and gave a smile. "You know, Tanna, I wouldn't have gotten this far if it wasn't for you."

His friend shrugged her shoulders. "Actually, I always hoped you would lose the challenge." She gave an unconvincing laugh and smiled sadly.

Terith avoided asking why she wanted him to lose, but it appeared the unbidden reason was going to come out anyway.

Tanna blushed. "It isn't that I want somebody else to win. I just thought if you lost you would . . . come back here and stay."

"You mean, settle down in Neutat and choose a mate?" Terith asked.

Tanna rocked on her ankles again looking like something inside her was trying to find a way out through her heels. "It sounds strange, but I always held out this needle of a hope that you might decide there was more to me than leatherwork and stitching. I . . . I guess it's just a silly girl's dream I never grew out of."

She's admitting to a secret lifelong crush on me? Now?

"I know I'm not like Ferrin's daughters," Tanna admitted. "I haven't got the breeding to have the awakening. The nearest I ever came to glowing was having an oil lamp blow up on me." She brushed a strand of matted brown hair away and locked eyes with him. "Still, I always felt this *something* about you." She waited for some acknowledgment, some resonance of shared feeling.

Terith scratched the back of his neck wondering what to say. He hadn't prepared for this kind of conversation. "Tanna, you're five years older than me. And besides, I thought Werm fancied you. You seem to like him well enough."

She shrugged. "I . . . I do. It's just . . ." She looked up into the milky early evening sky. Her pause grew into an awkward silence until she whispered softly, as if afraid of the words. "Sometimes you have to let your dreams die, so you can wake up and live your life." She looked away, blinking back tears.

Terith took a breath and waited. He certainly didn't need Tanna complicating the political situation. "Tanna, really—"

"Terith, your future is more important that you realize . . . I wish I could explain it." She turned away and wrapped her arms around her own waist.

I'd better say something nice or I'm going to regret it, he thought.

"Tanna, you know I really appreciate you making all my gear. If there is anything I could do to repay you, I would—I will," he said, realizing how empty the words sounded. "But you know how it goes. I ended up a rider, and then champion, and now I'm about to ride in the challenge. If I finish in time, I'll have to choose one of the eligible."

"If that's supposed to make me feel sympathy for you, it isn't working," Tanna said sourly. She flipped a lock of hair behind her shoulder. "How you get stuck in these terribly terrific situations . . ."

"Tanna, I didn't know all this would happen. We have to find a way to make the best of it. We're Montazi. We're survivors."

"I know," she said. She unfolded her arms and put one hand on her lower back while the other hand squeezed the bridge of her nose. There was some kind of internal battle going on. Terith had seen it when Tanna faced a barrel of strong mead with an empty mug.

"Tanna, you'll be all right," Terith said. It sounded pitifully hollow.

Her mouth opened to speak, but she choked back the words. She turned as if to leave, but paused. "So . . . who are you going to choose?"

"Tanna!" Terith exclaimed in exasperation. Of course it was Lilleth, but how could he just announce it? And what if he lost and Lilleth was chosen by another? Would he want Enala to know that he would have rather had her sister?

The pent-up angst came to a head as he blurted out, "How should I know who I'm going to choose?"

A woman stepped into view on the path a few yards from Tanna.

Her feet moved soundlessly over the smooth flagstones. She wore a white dress tinted with the unmistakable pale blue of the afala blossom. It curved gracefully around her figure to a beaded bodice. The long, loose sleeves swayed as she stopped on hearing Terith's voice. The branch of a broad fern shaded her face, but Terith had no doubt who it was. In that moment he knew he had made a desperate mistake.

Tanna's mouth dropped in a silent gasp. "I'll just . . . be on my way." She stepped onto the path, ignoring the newly arrived woman, either out of spite or embarrassment, and scuttled out of view.

Terith breathed, becoming vaguely aware of his heart pounding harder in his chest. "Lilleth?"

"Is that who you wanted me to be?" she said calmly, stepping from behind the broad fern.

Terith couldn't tell from her voice whether she was angry or smiling. He ran over and scooped her into his arms. "Are you trying to get bitten by scorpions?" he teased. "You know it isn't safe to be out this late alone."

Lilleth locked her hands behind his neck and swung her feet down giving him a good stare.

She saw things. Terith knew that. Even when she wasn't calling the awakening she still saw things.

"Stories for children . . . and a test for a dragon rider," she whispered, discerning his most recent memories. "You never rest, do you?"

"I . . . I wasn't expecting you. To come—I mean all the way down here."

Lilleth broke her gaze and let her hands slide down to his arms. "I didn't walk all the way," she said quietly. "There were ore carts. And I rode Werm's new pulley down from Hintertat—that was bumpy."

Terith laughed.

Where were the insects? he wondered. Terith couldn't tell whether all other sounds had stopped, or whether Lilleth had simply overwhelmed all his other senses. Like all Montazi, she had a light tan on smooth, hairless skin, and large eyes. Though some Montazi had streaks of blond or white in their hair, Lilleth's was all one color, a dark brown shade, the color of polished hardwood. Her deep brown eyes drew him away from gazing at her gently curved hips and generous lips.

"Did I ever tell you that you're gorgeous?"

"Yes," she said, holding his gaze. "And I do need an escort back."

"Of course," Terith said.

"Unless you have a date with some other eligible, perhaps?" Lilleth said.

"Uh, no. No. No. Definitely no."

She smiled. "So sure?"

Terith grimaced. "So you overheard that . . . me . . . yeah."

Lilleth laughed. She never giggled like Enala, whose bubbly laugh was as contagious as a fortnight plague.

Lilleth's eyes narrowed. "Can I make do with you?" she said, voicing more doubt than Terith wanted to hear.

She stepped away and looked east to the darkening sky. "Can I trust you, in everything?"

Again, Terith's heart pattered with anxiety. He didn't dare answer.

"I seek loyalty," she said, without looking at him.

"I know," Terith said. "And I—"

She held up her hand. "Mya? Is that you hiding in the moss vine? And your friends?"

Multiple sets of feet pattered away in panic.

"You too," Lilleth said, pointing to one Terith couldn't see.

The sounds of retreating eavesdroppers faded.

"So you came all the way down to Neutat just to see me?" Terith ventured.

Lilleth swished her skirt as a foot-sized buzzing scorpion moved past her and into the cover of the moss vine.

She had just saved the children from its paralyzing sting.

Terith would have hurled one of his knives at it, but Lilleth wouldn't have approved.

"Well . . . partially," she said. "I came to see Tanna. But at the moment she probably doesn't want to see me."

"Yeah." Terith wondered what Lilleth could have wanted the seamstress for. Then recognition dawned. *Her past.*

"You wouldn't have seen anything to make you doubt me," Terith said confidently. "I never kissed her or anything."

"She was too old for you anyway," Lilleth said knowingly.

"Why, then?"

Lilleth opened her mouth, and then closed it. She offered her hand. "The high road has fewer scorpions. Shall we?"

The journey to Ferrin-tat with Lilleth by his side was as pleasant as any he had ever taken. Terith spoke of dragons. Lilleth talked of the other eligible and their considerable talents. The easy tranquility was only marred by Lilleth's mention of Pert riding in the challenge.

Pert, the dangerous rider from the southern Montas, had left a trail of dead bodies in the deep on his way to becoming champion. There was no doubt he knew Ferrin's time as chief was short. He wanted to be chief, and it did not bode well for anyone that got in his way.

Lilleth's voice wavered as she spoke of Terith facing Pert in the challenge, belying a deeper dread.

She spoke with an unnerving certainty, a hope-starving fatalism. "There is something dark in him."

As she turned her eyes to look at Terith, they said unmistakably, *I fear for you.*

CHAPTER 4

Erdali Realm. Citadel of Toran.

Reann raced down the corridor of the castle clutching a bundle of documents to her chest.

"Act your age!" the head housekeeper Hamut barked at her.

"Trying!" Reann replied instantly, hurrying past. Then she stopped suddenly. She would officially come of age at the summer solstice, only a month away. She would no longer be a ward of the citadel.

She would have to leave the castle.

Reann shook off the worry and hurried again down the corridor and down two flights of a wide circular stair.

Although nobody knew precisely what her age was, Reann inwardly held that she still had another half year of being seventeen, hoping the few extra months would add more curves to her figure in the place of other features she would be glad to be rid of, like her hollow cheeks and a few freckles.

"Tromwen! Lord Tromwen!" she called as she hurried through the castle foyer and out the double doors into the courtyard. The early summer sun had just begun to light the sky.

By dawn, as promised, she thought in a moment of self-approval.

"Late, as usual," said the page on duty as she stopped beside the carriage he was attending. His name was Ret, or "Wretch" as Reann preferred to call him. He was lanky and older than her by a year at least. He had taken a permanent servant position at the castle, a hopeless end Reann desperately wanted to avoid.

Between heavy breaths she gave her reply to Ret. "Lateness . . .

attends greatness. Cercanis the Conqueror . . . *Essays on Efficiency, Volume Two.*"

"Ah, Reann," a voice called from the carriage, interrupting Ret's reply. "Is that you I hear citing etiquette?"

Reann pushed a lock of twisted brown hair away from her face as the Wretch opened the carriage door.

Reann stepped smartly up the step and past Ret who sniffed and crinkled his nose at her as she passed, as if to suggest she stank.

She hadn't taken the time to tie her shoulder-length hair back, as she usually did. But it wasn't as though she didn't wash—although she had been busy for the past few—well, she didn't want to think about that.

Ret would pay regardless.

Reann sat on the carriage bench across from Lord Tromwen.

The governor was tall and charismatic, though not handsome—he was older than the fortress itself. He ruled the Tandal province, several days' journey along the Erdal River's east fork.

"You haven't worked all night again!" Tromwen said, smiling broadly.

"It helps that you're the last of the governors to leave the annual conference," Reann said, reversing the compliment, as the rules suggested. "Your dedication to keeping our realm together is a virtue."

"I hope I don't abuse your kindness with my personal requests," Tromwen offered on a softer note. "Dealing with governors like me must be a burden."

Reann rolled her eyes at the thought. "The rest only care about their provinces. I don't see how the realm stays together without a sovereign."

"Twelve years," Tromwen noted in his always-pleasant voice. "We've lasted that long without Toran."

"Thirteen," Reann corrected. "With all the bickering and intrigue, if I didn't have chores to sneak off to I would be a permanent blackmail researcher."

"Speaking of . . ." Tromwen said, rubbing his hands together. "What do you have for me?"

Reann handed over the first bundle of documents. "The count's claims to the Olter vineyards are invalid due to a prior treaty with your late father's estate." She thumbed through the stack to a handwritten document and turned down the corner. "I've explained it all here."

"Very good," Tromwen said, his eyes twinkling with delight at the discovery that would keep the famous wine flowing into his markets.

"Also," Reann continued, "your cousin from Telith Province, who wants you to give up your water rights in the Verim Heights, had an illegitimate child, which I'm sure he wants kept a secret." She handed the last document, this one sealed. "I've taken the liberty of writing your response. You can break the seal and read it if you like."

"Too much bother," Tromwen said. "I'm sure you captured the gist of the accusation." He pressed his ring to the still-warm wax. "Done." He smiled gently. "You're a very special girl, Reann. You've got the genius of your mother. I knew her. Pity she was blind. She was a fine court translator—a natural."

"Hmm," Reann said awkwardly, not sure whether to tell Tromwen that translating really wasn't very hard or whether to just accept the compliment.

"None of us expected your mother—what was her name again?—to run off like that. But maybe it was a blessing after all, with you being here at the castle with the library to help folks like me."

"Well," Reann said, admitting a smile, "I do enjoy reading."

"But you know, Reann," Tromwen said seriously, "You can't stay here forever reading books. Have you found an employer? You could be a tutor, or—"

"Still looking," Reann said, though she hadn't started. She wasn't going to leave the castle. She was going to find her real employer—a person whom nobody knew. "I'm not of age yet. I'm still a ward of Toran's estate."

"Oh, so is that the legal term for castle servant?" Tromwen said with a smile. "I don't suppose I can argue the point with you. I haven't got half your wit."

Reann grinned at the compliment. She treasured every reminder that she was more than just a thankless maid. Whatever her future held, she could hold on to moments like that.

Tromwen gave a kind smile. "Well . . . until next time, you'll be well?"

She nodded and ducked out of the carriage.

"Dash it all," Tromwen said with a start. "Reann, one more thing!"

She turned back.

"The Benevolent Fraternity of Traders is having a ceremony in a few weeks to honor someone called the Lady of the North, and they want a noble to present the award."

Reann had overheard a Furendali governor say to his fellow who bet on a losing hand at cards that he "would have had better luck with the Lady of the North." Apparently, it was a nickname for a woman with a very cold heart.

She was getting an award?

"What sort of ceremony?" Reann said. Her interest was piqued to know that allies from the northern realm would be arriving.

"She led a rescue expedition in the dead of winter to save a stranded group bringing supplies overland from the frozen harbor at Zingat."

"Amazing," Reann said.

"Yes, it's all very inconvenient. But I'd rather—"

"You'd rather not come all the way back here just after you left, and you need a really good excuse and someone else to attend in your place?" Reann guessed.

He nodded with a smile that showed a look of relief.

"Consider it done," Reann said. The ceremony was two weeks away. There was plenty of time to make arrangements. Besides, Reann looked forward to having an excuse to inject herself into the event. It was a chance to gather otherwise unreachable information about a favorite mystery, if she worked things right.

"On then," Tromwen said. "A journey that starts ahead of the sun . . ."

. . . *stays ahead of trouble,* Reann thought wistfully. The roads were not as safe as they once were, especially for a wealthy man.

The driver clapped the reigns and the carriage rolled away on the cobblestones.

"He was about to tip me," Ret said indignantly. "You interrupted him. You owe me a half piece."

Reann rolled her earth-brown eyes. "What would you do with it, waste it on mandolin strings and rum?"

"Just mandolin strings," Ret corrected, as he parted the stringy hair that perpetually hung in front of his eyes. "And why didn't he tip you?"

Reann dipped her hand into her apron pocket and drew out a full piece. She opened her palm proudly, showing the copper coin bearing the compass mark of Toran. "He pays me in advance. I worked all night in the library for this."

"I worked all night in the stables."

"Oh, that's what I smell," Reann said, wrinkling her nose.

"I thought I smelled old maid just now," Ret said.

"Just sour grapes."

In a flash Ret snatched the small coin and swallowed it.

Reann gasped.

"Just borrowing it. I'll return it in your room in a few days." Ret's face took on an entirely new level of smugness.

For once, she was speechless. She turned and stomped back toward the castle.

"Reann," Ret called. "I'm just kidding. I have it right here. I palmed it."

Reann made a grimace and never gave a second thought to turning around and conceding defeat.

Let him feel guilty a while. He can return it with an apology.

"Sorry," he called as she returned through the kitchen entrance of the gray granite castle.

He'll have to do better than that, she thought, pushing the Wretch from her mind. The conference of governors was over. It was high time to get serious about finding her future employer.

The king.

There was no publicly acknowledged heir to Toran, but those closest to him believed he had fathered several heirs in secret. If one of those could be found, Reann would take her mother's place as court translator, a nonexistent position in a castle without a king. Yet despite years of studying Toran's past and the chronicles of his reign, Reann felt as though it would take a lifetime to find an heir.

She didn't have that long.

Walking swiftly behind the cook who was bent over a pot of broth, Reann plucked a roll from a kitchen basket and pocketed it for later. She moved quickly through the mostly deserted corridors on her nearly worn-through slippers, stepping soundlessly over the rugs and flagstones. She stopped in front of a large oak panel reinforced with rusted iron braces.

She had only been away for a few minutes and now the room was—

Locked!

Doubtless, the head butler had done it to spite her.

Reann looked over her shoulder, then quickly loosened a tie at the top of her blouse and reached into a pocket sewn on the inside, between her breasts—as secure a location as she could invent. She fished out her cast replica key and turned the key in the lock. The click of the latch gave her a tremble of pleasure.

Placing both hands against the great door, Reann pushed with all the force her teenage body could muster. The door gave way, swinging inward a crack with a woeful screech.

Reann crept in through the gap.

In the space beyond lay the treasure of Toran—endless shelves of books lining the walls of a grand room.

On the opposite wall, gaps in the window shutters streaked the dusty air with blades of light.

Reann hurried across the room and pushed the shutters open, flooding the shiny marble floor and the tall shelves with sunlight.

Summer, after the governors' annual meeting, was the off-season for diplomacy, and the fortress operated liked a high-end inn for traveling dignitaries. But paying visitors would be rare, at least until the midsummer gala, a festival in honor of the late king's birthday, which drew riffraff and nobles alike.

For now, the library was hers—no cleaning work to interfere, no tutoring lessons to give, and no dignitaries asking incessant questions.

Even the old Furendali wash lady Effel, whose life's purpose was keeping Reann out of the library with cleaning work, was gone on a pilgrimage to her home village in the frozen plain beyond the northern mountains.

"Pity. No one to give me extra chores," Reann chimed. She smiled at the thought and gazed around the familiar room stacked with long rows of leather-bound tomes.

Someday, and hopefully soon, she would discover the identity of a young heir in Erdal and the historians would write her name alongside those of Toran and his empire builders.

As it was, Reann had no regent and no future. All her daily slaving was in the hope that someday this castle might once again have a king. Reann wanted to feel needed, and not for washing and cleaning—anything but that. She was only a servant because her mother had left—or died, or both—leaving Reann the sole heir of her late grandfather's military pension. Rembra had been Toran's sergeant at arms.

Reann served as an orphan ward of Toran's estate. Day and night she slaved at laundry or dishes. It was a life, but one she had worked every spare moment to escape.

If there was no greater purpose than mindless work, she might as well run away.

But where would she go?

Nobody had a better chance at finding the heirs than she did. She had Toran's records. She had the library. And now she finally had the time.

Tying back her hair, she went to a long table to sort and file the documents she had copied for Tromwen. As she turned to replace the records, a piece of color caught her eye—a slice of brown paper amid a stack of glossy tan official documents.

It was on the seventh shelf and just out of her reach. Among the bound official records on treated parchments was a faded piece of scratch paper, a subtle difference revealed only in the direct morning sunlight.

Draft documents didn't belong in the library, which meant somebody had left it by mistake.

Reann felt a surge of excitement. "Interesting."

She climbed a stepladder and reached for the document, noting a creeping brown hue along the edge.

The misplaced note was at least a decade old.

Reann grabbed the bundle of documents and retreated to the table. Her anxious fingers pulled at the knotting of binding string ineffectually so she bit it with her teeth.

"Open, will you."

The tie snapped and the leather folder of loose papers burst open. Reann caught the stack of pages as they scattered and quickly recovered the delicate parchment. It was stuck to an official record by a red smear that looked suspiciously like—

"Raspberry jam."

Reann felt a pang of vicarious guilt, though it couldn't have been her weakness for raspberry jam and frequent sneaking of bits of forbidden food into the library that had stuck these records. The pages were far too old.

She detached it by tearing the corner from the old record and found that beneath it were another three pages.

The header on the handwritten manuscript read, "For translation only. Destroy upon completion."

There were two sets of writing occupying every other line. One had short letters, inconsistent spacing, and poorly shaped circles. It was unmistakably Toran's pen. Between those lines were markings Reann had never seen before. It was a new language—or an old one.

Reann nearly screamed with excitement. "Sacred place beyond," she whispered. "It's his diary!"

Apparently, he had ordered his words to be translated into some kind of secret language, perhaps so that if the journal was found it would be impossible to read. Except these pages had words from both languages, interweaved line by line.

She scanned the script.

"This is so simple. I . . . I can read this."

Reann read both lines together, looking from one word to the much neater script below it, puzzling out the beveled letters made of lines meeting at different angles with decorative curls on the edges. She read,

In my thirty-third year, the Serbani council of nobles banished Tira to Hersa, knowing that if they killed her, the deadly power she possessed would immediately flare up in another magician in their realm.

It was a terrible mistake. Tira has knowledge of the turning points. Her change magic would have been far less dangerous with anyone else. I did not find out about the matter until it was too late. This unfortunate turn strengthened my resolve to counter the danger she poses to all the realms.

After her banishment, peace reigned for a time in Serban, in my plains, and in the Furendal to the north. But my heart turned to the legends of the ancestors. I had no rest. The mystery of the Lyrium Compass weighed upon my mind heavily.

I delegated right of rule to the council of governors and took a sabbatical journey alone beyond the Montas, to the Outlands. My adventures were many in that desolate place. I witnessed their customs, their slavery, and their crafting of unbreakable iron. On I traveled, eastward, through heat and sand. I came to the edge of my life in that dreadful place.

Then she came to me.

Dariel was the first of the Rizertari that I ever laid eyes on. None

other I met ever compared to her. She felt my presence on the sands, like a distant moaning on the wind and came to my rescue. The Rizertari gifts are kin to the Montazi awakening and the Serbani change magic, but more in harmony with the millennial tide.

We traveled at night on skelter, a kind of small desert land dragon that feeds on the venomous insects of the desert that would kill any camel or human to enter the great wasteland. Coming to the edge of the desert, the Rizertas Range, the birthplace of the ancestors, rose gradually out of the sand, coming to a great—

"What's that?" blurted a voice from behind her.

Reann jumped out of her chair and clutched the papers to her chest. "Ninat, how many times have I told you not to sneak up behind me while I'm reading?"

The servant that had startled her was several years younger than Reann, pencil thin, and almost impossible to notice if you weren't looking.

"You don't have to get all worked up about it," Ninat said. "It's not like you're reading that book with all the naughty drawings."

"That was an anatomy book," Reann said. "It's for physicians."

"And curious girls who want a peep at—"

"Don't you have anything else to do?" Reann asked.

Ninat just giggled at Reann's guilt-ridden expression. She pointed to the documents Reann was protecting with both arms crossed in front of her chest and took a step toward them. "Are those for your special project?"

First guess! Is it that obvious? Reann moved casually behind a chair, trying to keep her distance from Ninat's quick fingers.

Her only consolation was that Ninat's tone was mostly indifferent. Reann's project meant little to Ninat, except that when Reann was reading there one less person to tag along with.

Reann decided the best thing to do was simply admit the truth—part of it anyway—and hope Ninat's curiosity moved on to something else.

"Yes," Reann said. "It's part of my research regarding the estate of Toran."

"The legend of the secret heirs, you mean," Ninat said. "Everybody else has given up on looking after so many frauds turned up. You're just obsessed with it."

"I am not obsessed," Reann said.

"Then let me see what you're reading."

"No," Reann said. "This record is not meant for . . . you."

Ninat raised her eyebrows. "Fine. Be that way. I'll send the head butler. I'm sure he would like to know what you're up to."

"Excellent," Reann said. "I've been meaning to tell him about the missing gem in the royal Dervite veil in the display nook on the third floor. You wouldn't, by chance, know who might have taken it to their keepsake box in the girl servants' quarters?" Reann's un-flinching expression took on a new level of confidence.

Ninat's pale skin blossomed in a ferocious red blush. "Me? No, never."

"The head butler might have ideas to the contrary," Reann added. "Given your past interest in gems."

"Reann . . . no," Ninat said, her voice pleading. She risked a whipping if she were caught stealing again.

"Well, if you see him, be sure to send him my way."

Ninat crossed her arms and stormed out of the library.

Few of the castle staff took any interest in Reann's hobby. But nosy Ninat was still a risk to manage.

Reann sat again at the table, this time facing the door. She read eagerly, enthralled with the discovery of another realm beyond the Outlands.

The Rizertari—the ancestors still exist!

But so much of the document made little sense. What were turning points? And what was the Lyrium Compass?

But more interesting than it all was the mention of Dariel's pregnancy.

My time in the Rizertas was short. My greatest regret is that I did not reach their dragon sanctuary. A turning point in the Montas approached. Crossing the desert by a northerly route in winter, we came to the stretch of bare rock called the Ceiling. Furendali spear throwers guided us back to Erdal. The millennial tide was on the rise. I gathered my cavalry in every village we passed through, promising new conquest for the empire and glory. Eager soldiers flocked to my banner.

I sent Dariel to Ferrin of the Montazi, their new chief, proposing an alliance against the horde. He was the first northern chief in memory and sought stronger ties with Erdal, but my greatest joy was that Dariel was expecting a child.

She gave birth in Neutat, on the day of my victory over the Outlander horde, at the predicted turning point. Great was my grief at her passing. The child was a son, my first, and half brother to my firstborn. With his life, the fate of the Montas will rise or fall.

What follows is the account of our journey through the megaliths of the Montas Realm and the battle with the Outlanders . . .

The script ended abruptly. Reann turned over the last fragile sheet but found no more writing.

In all her life, Reann had never discovered anything like this. *The second heir was born in Neutat on the day of Toran's victory.* If revealed, this single fact would allow Toran's heir to claim his throne. It mentioned a firstborn child as well—a girl.

That would have to be someone from Erdal or the northern realm.

Reann knew of Toran's rumored travel in the Outlands, and had heard of his travel guide, who was supposedly an Outlander. Dariel must have been in Toran's inner circle. She added the name to the short list of other names she considered likely trust keepers. Godrin, the mathematician—missing after the last battle with the Outlanders; Rembra, the captain at arms—her own grandfather who had perished in battle in the west deserts of Dervan; Ferrin, chief of the Montazi. But who from Dervan, the Furendal, and the Serban?

Had the Serbani insider been Tira? Reann shuddered at the thought of the witch queen.

The significance of this document was not lost on Reann. It

exposed the existence of not one, but two children of Toran. She would protect it the only way she knew to be perfectly secure: lock it away in a place only she could reach.

Rereading it, Reann memorized the text, as well as the strange characters of what now seemed to her to be the Rizertari language. Then she took a lit candle and touched it to edge of the pages, and watched the marvelous record turn to smoke and ash.

A sense of peace clashed with the stirrings of deeper emotions within Reann. What Toran's translator had failed to do, Reann had finished.

Lost in a world of desert dragons, compass-like letter symbols, and Rizertari magic, Reann retied what turned out to be a volume of customs duty exemptions and pushed it back onto the high shelf.

A clattering of hooves rang out in the courtyard. Reann turned quickly, thinking for a moment that it was a pile of books falling. Then she descended the ladder and rushed to the open window over-looking the courtyard.

The stable groom rushed out to meet the new arrival. Wretch was always first on the scene if there was money involved.

Reann squinted to make out the features of the newly arrived man on the horse. He wore a wide-brimmed business hat and the usual black traveling apparel of the finest quality. He dismounted and tossed a coin to Ret, who guided his horse toward the stables.

The horse looked fresh. Reann decided the outsider had probably bought it in the village after arriving by river ferry. His luggage would follow with the delivery coach.

The new arrival paused to gaze up at the citadel. He pulled off his hat and drummed on it anxiously, eyes moving over the exterior of the stone with interest. He was the perfect picture of gentility, rarely seen in these days. By Reann's reckoning, he was in his early twenties.

And he was devilishly handsome.

Reann leaned back to be sure he didn't see her spying on him from the window. She listened, heart beating anxiously, as his well-cobbled feet strode purposefully toward the castle.

"So it's back to your usual games again." The chief butler stood in the open doorway with his fists nestled in generous love handles.

"I'm cleaning," Reann said firmly. "You needn't attend me. Besides you don't have any work for me anyway."

"Cleaning, eh? It looks like you've been dusting the insides of a few books with your fingers."

"Cleaning . . . and such."

"That's what I thought." The bald and rotund man could only shake a warning finger at her. The washwoman normally tasked Reann, and the butler had no ideas what chores she was supposed to be doing.

"Shouldn't you be off to the tavern?" Reann asked. "It must be ten o'clock by now."

"Not quite ten," the man returned.

"And leaving so soon?"

He wagged his finger again.

"Oh, and you are most welcome for coming to thank me about the missing candlesticks," Reann said casually. "You'll find them in the gallery closet—that's three merits as I recall."

"Three more merits . . ." he grumbled as his perturbed expression turned for the door in retreat.

Reann held the record for merits, and not because she worked harder than the other servants did. She simply paid attention.

Except when she daydreamed.

As she walked back across the marble tiles swishing her skirts, she imagined the floor was a ballroom. Footsteps sounded alongside hers, and they waltzed: Toran and Dariel. Reann's feet turned in time, stepping expertly into spins and lifts.

When the library door let out another woeful screech, it nearly sent her into a panic. She quickly retied the top of her blouse and clasped her hands dutifully behind her back. But then another feeling filled her, a kind of confidence. It was like nothing she had ever felt before. Her heart stilled. She stood straighter, ready, and unafraid. She felt as if she were a cavalier, dressed in armor.

What is this? she wondered. Life suddenly seemed certain, despite all the uncertainty. The feeling swirled in her. It was as if she were once again with her mother or standing atop a hill riding a charging stallion. So many feelings at once crammed into her, Reann wondered that her heart didn't burst.

A black-booted leg moved into view, and then the full figure of the recently arrived stranger.

He was tall, and he was even more handsome up close, with sharp, keen features—handsome in a cold, untouchable way that made her want to do just the opposite.

"Here we are," he said, stepping into the room. He held his broad-brim hat between his hands and drummed his fingers along the edges of it eagerly, as if waiting for the first slice of a fine pie.

"Can I help you?" Reann asked, still wondering at the swelling emotion that continued with her. *Was it him?*

His eyes turned to Reann, noting her with a look of surprise, as if the furniture had talked. "Help me? Not likely."

Reann felt her ears warm as she smoothed the front of her apron unnecessarily. "I read six languages," she offered. *Perhaps seven,* she thought, recalling the strange language on Toran's diary.

"Can you read this?" He gestured with his thumb to the door.

Reann considered for a moment the idea of going to the door and shutting it rather than leaving. It put a flicker of a smirk on her face that she quickly banished.

Besides, it was a rhetorical question, she decided, and so she didn't move. Peasants were not to answer rhetorical questions—it was in the rules somewhere.

When Reann did not take the hint to leave, he asked, "Are you the keeper of the records here? A bit young for a salaried official, I think."

Reann let out a shy smile. "No, sir. I'm no person of employ. I was born in this castle. My mother attended the court, but she is gone. I serve in her stead, having no inheritance."

The young man's stoic expression changed. He lifted his head and made a thin-lipped conciliatory smile that faded. "I . . . I am sorry for it. It seems we share a commonality." He spoke with open cordiality now, as if her story had somehow changed his impression of her value.

"Nay, lord. I am a peasant."

"I mean we have both lost our parents." He sat upon a wooden chair at the long reading table. He removed a boot and shook out a small rock, put the boot back on, and ran a finger under his collar, loosening it on the side of his neck where his skin was a shade whiter, like a scar from a burn.

Not wanting to seem too anxious to know his business, Reann tried for a distraction. "You must have traveled far," she volunteered. "Are you sure you won't first take a rest? I shall be available at your later convenience if you wish."

"I've missed the conference, haven't I?" the man said resignedly, blowing a wisp of brown hair out of his eyes.

"I'm sorry. It only just ended the night before last."

The man shrugged and spun his hat on the table absently, gazing around the room.

"Are you a governor, sir?" asked Reann. He seemed quite young for that kind of position.

"I—well, sort of."

Reann carefully maneuvered into sitting range of a stool and slid onto it quietly, not wanting to appear rude by sitting in the presence of the lord, but daring herself to try.

"Less than two fortnights ago my father was the governor," the man started. "He has since passed on."

"Oh," Reann whispered.

"When I had buried his body and mourned seven days with my kin, I came in his stead to attend the conference of governors. But," he gestured to the empty room, "I'm rather late."

She didn't believe a word of it. "Which province does your family rule?"

"I call Treban home," he confessed after a moment's pause. He made wide, unconvincing gestures as he described the place. "The harbor was overrun by pirates not long ago. They burn here, plunder there, and sail for the next town. We have no peace, nor the strength to fight them by ourselves. Old allies betray us. Not even my father could reign in the rebel villages. Sympathizers and cowards outnumber the cockroaches."

"The other governors all speak of similar problems," Reann commented. "Not that I eavesdrop, it's just . . . "

"Of course."

Reann drifted closer to the young lord, taking a seat on a footstool beside the table. "May I ask what it is you need from the library?"

"No."

"Very well, then. Supper is served to the guests in the dining hall," Reann noted, "and breakfast in your quarters."

"You won't be joining us for supper?" he asked.

"Why no, sir. I must be in the kitchen washing the dishes."

"Ah."

Reann nodded and left the room. The feeling that had overcome her the moment the gentleman entered the room seemed to drain like the water in a tub, leaving her empty and ready. For two days, the experience tortured her. She asked every living soul in the castle about the man, but none knew any more than the rest. Most of all, she wanted to know what he was looking for in the library.

Could it have been her?

She laughed at the thought.

CHAPTER 5

Montazi realm. Ferrin-tat.

L ow hanging clouds over the Montazi capital of Ferrin-tat glowed with the reflected light of dozens of torches on posts.

Terith adjusted the red sash draped over his shoulder, feeling like an archery target. It was a gift from Enala and Lilleth's stepmother Tirisa, so he kept it on.

The other guests waiting for the feast to begin milled about the open-air courtyard in front of Ferrin's enclave, representatives from villages across the Montas realm, mostly the old, powerful, and rich.

For centuries, the Montazi chiefs had been riders from the wealthier regions in the south. The move of the capital north was Ferrin's doing. It gave the realm a stronger presence in the area where the Outlanders were a constant threat. The move had a noticeable impact on trade with the Serban.

Ferrin was the first northern chief in memory.

Some were determined to make him the last.

Thoughts of politics turned Terith's empty stomach, and the distant sounds of one of Enala's tantrums suddenly became much more interesting.

Terith followed a short path that ran past a porthole in a wooded ivy stem. In Ferrin's office, lit well by costly oil lanterns, Lilleth and Enala stood facing their father, their backs to the porthole.

They were the same height, though Lilleth always seemed taller because of the way she handled herself, and Enala seemed more like a grown-up child with legs that were the envy of all, and the occasional temper of an irate toddler.

"Father," Lilleth said calmly, "I think Terith is old enough to decide with whom he wishes to keep company." She turned to leave, but Enala snagged the side of Lilleth's dress with her hand.

"She spent all night with him!" Enala cried.

"You were welcome to come with me to Neutat," Lilleth said calmly, prying her dress out of Enala's hand. "It was such a pleasant walk."

Enala glared. "Oh, that's all you did—just 'walk'? You know I had to help in the kitchens. They're next to useless without me."

"Just because you want to show off your cooking, doesn't mean—"

"Girls," Ferrin said. His chest was round and stout and his hair feathered with gray. His beardless chin was laced with several battle scars. Few Montazi, Terith among those few, had enough facial hair to warrant a regular shave. "I don't have time for this bickering."

"If she sits with Terith at the feast," Enala said, her voice dropping to a low and deadly tone, "I'll spill my wine on her dress. Then she'll have to go change, and I'll have him the rest of the night."

"I'll lay you across my knee, child!" Ferrin roared.

Enala turned, bent over and lifted up the back of her skirt. "Just get it over with now."

"Enala!" Lilleth gasped.

Terith pulled his arm in front of his face and crouched below the window, trying desperately not to laugh.

A few minutes later, in the grand open-air courtyard, Terith leaned against a gold-embroidered floor pillow. Other riders in the challenge lounged about on similar reclining seats, mingling with the eligible women and elder nobles.

The women's eyes danced with delight at jests and trite poems, while the challengers' words of flattery spilled freely into the courtyard full of eligibles draped in luxurious silken clothing.

In momentary pauses, their eyes drifted toward the daughters of Ferrin—Lilleth, the wise, who was speaking politely with the elders, and Enala, the firecracker.

Enala, having won the battle, sat astride the back of the pillow that Terith leaned against. She ran her fingers through his short blond hair to spite the other eligible women, especially her sister.

Terith looked from the red sash draped across his chest to the nine other sash-bearing riders seated and leaning on the pillows among the gathered dignitaries. Only one kept his attention.

Pert.

That man, leaning against a column, stared back at Terith with unblinking eyes.

Terith held his gaze until Enala tugged on his hair, playfully and protectively. As he turned his head away, Pert moved to the corner of his vision, where the light of the awakening first flared in his mind. There, against a backdrop of flowering plants and other guests, Pert's entire body looked like a hole in his field of view, as dark and black as the volcanic rock of the megaliths. He recalled Lilleth's words, *There is darkness in him.* What Terith saw out of the corner of his eye was real.

The feeling of darkness seemed to crawl up inside Terith until he turned his attention to Ferrin, who was rising to give the invocation of the feast.

Despite his growing age, Ferrin was strong-shouldered, with only the slightest bend to his back. He had vivid blue eyes that burned like torches with the unquenchable confidence of a lifelong rider. His own victory in the challenge two and half decades earlier had ended with an exceptionally brilliant flash of the awakening that signaled his rightful place as chief of the riders and their realm.

According to Terith's sources, namely Mya, the children of Neutat had it two-to-one that whoever won this year's challenge would show the sign. As for who would win, the odds were evenly weighted on Pert and Terith.

Ferrin gave a nod to his wife Tirisa and then raised both of his hands over his head.

His court musicians, wind organ players, and flutists stood.

"The Suma has begun," the first lord of the Montazi announced, beginning the customary oblation. "The dragons are returning from the sacred plain."

A gong sounded.

"May we live to see them return year by year."

"May we live to see them return!" echoed the gathered nobles, challengers, and eligible.

The gong sounded again.

"And may the ragoon fire burn until the blessed hatchlings emerge."

"May the hatchlings emerge," sounded the gathered faithful.

"Let the feast of the challenge begin!"

The orchestra started at once, filling the open-ceilinged court with the eerie and entrancing sounds of the wind organ and double pipe bass flutes.

Ferrin took his place on the center rug and a chorus of conversation arose among the excited guests.

"Seven days until the race," Terith whispered to himself. "And then we see."

Enala rested her hand softly on Terith's shoulder.

Terith smiled vaguely, conscious of the eyes that weighed his every move, especially of Pert's. The leather-clad warrior from the southern Montas was in a class of his own, both for lethal skill and for treachery. Admirers and stooges hovered around his short, stout figure, even fellows with too much hair upon their faces and arms to be Montazi—likely foreign allies from the Serban coast.

His ambitions were no secret.

Pert had dared no mutiny yet. The people still followed the chosen ruler, but his influence spread like a plague, and no less deadly. More than a few rival riders had fallen under mysterious circumstances.

Like Terith, Pert commanded his own flight of riders. Terith recognized two of Pert's comrades skulking in the shadows.

"Who invited them?" Enala said. She leaned her head toward

Terith's to follow his gaze and surreptitiously looped her arm over his shoulder.

"Nobody. They aren't champions."

"Then why are they here?"

"Me." There was only one rider in the Montas who could stand up to Pert, and that made Terith a target.

As plates of food passed among the guests, Terith deliberately kept Pert's sour expression in view. But Pert's presence wasn't the only peril.

Another problem was on its way across the courtyard carrying a large tankard of honey mead. The portly man had a glossy look to his pallid skin and greedy eyes.

"Ah, Terith!" He shook Terith's hand vigorously, pulling him to his feet. "Tellim of Cafertat—good to see you again."

Terith had never met the man who managed to maneuver himself between Terith and Enala—no small accomplishment given Enala's tenacity. He steered Terith with an arm over his shoulder to a nook behind a tall shrub. "Not nervous, are you?"

Terith shook his head. The less he said the better. Tellim was a wealthy trader, judging from his gold tooth and gem-studded rings. Apparently he had come to bargain for a son-in-law.

Enala stared daggers at the man's back. She dangled an empty wine glass between two fingers, apparently contemplating the likely permanent effect of a bright red yaz wine on the man's expensive clothes.

Terith suppressed a smirk.

Sensing Terith's distraction the man looked back, but Enala was suddenly engaged in conversation between two old men.

"Looks like you're a busy man," he said with a knowing smile that doubled his chins. "So let's get to the point. I have a son in the race—Gomder. Interesting lad. But he's not a favorite to win."

"Best of luck to him," Terith offered.

"Keep your luck. You'll need it against Pert." Tellim crowded closer, pinning Terith against the shrub. "Now, we both know it could get messy out there. Anything could happen. Assuming Pert wins and grabs one of Ferrin's daughters . . ."

Terith started a rebuttal, but Tellim spoke smoothly over his words. "Of course you'll give it a go, and why not? Plenty of eligibles in the field this year." He marshaled an arm around Terith again and turned him to face the corner of the courtyard where several eligible girls were gathered around Pert and his cronies. "Onneth, the redhead over yonder, is my daughter. Gifted with sensing peril to anyone or anything she cares for—quite useful if I may say so. A fine young woman. I daresay I could make an introduction. Of course she's second heir to my fortune—we could change that to first heir if it tips the tables, eh?"

"Interesting idea," Terith said, spying Enala approaching with a glass full to the brim with bright red wine she must have taken from one of the elders. "If you'll excuse me, I'm sensing some danger myself."

Terith sidestepped the trader in the blink of an eye and collected the glass from Enala's fingertips as she raised it over his head.

"How thoughtful of you," Terith said, keeping the glass at arm's length. Tirisa, Enala's stepmother, was only a half step slower to the scene. She collected it from Terith with a relieved expression.

"That was too close," she breathed, returning to Ferrin's side.

Enala locked her arms around Terith's waist. "Well it worked. And now you're mine."

Out of the dragon's nest and into the deep, Terith thought.

For Terith, navigating the political mire of the feast and managing Enala's mischief was as bad as open battle. The difference was his dragon wouldn't do him any good here—especially against Enala's tactical maneuvers.

She casually blocked his path as he stepped toward the pillow where he had been eating a moment before.

"Oh my," Enala said. She placed her hands possessively on his chest. "That's intimate. I didn't know you were so forward."

"Forward?" he wondered.

"All right," Enala said. "Forward." She took another step closer, comfortably pressing against Terith, her blue eyes gleaming with pure delight.

Terith's eyes instinctively, guiltily flicked to Lilleth.

Of course she was watching. She quickly turned her back to Terith. It was worse than a slap to the face, which Terith would have gladly traded to just have Lilleth turn around and look at him with her soft sable eyes.

Great.

As generous amounts of food and drink dulled their appetites and senses, elders and matrons finished their conversations and meandered back to rented rooms deep in the gargantuan ivy roots that fed the curtains of oversized ivy hanging over the cliff walls of the Ferrin's megalith.

"Yaz?" Terith offered, raising a plate of candied fruits to Enala.

"Goodness, yes," giggled the precocious temptress, who never seemed to have grown out of her adolescence. She sat down and plucked two of the fruits from the tray Terith held. "I haven't had one in two seasons. Father sent our extras to Haventat." She ate one of the fruits, eyes twinkling with delight.

Enala's long, straight, yellow hair fell on Terith as she leaned over his shoulder. Meanwhile her hand surreptitiously lifted the platter out of his hand.

Terith laughed, but his eyes drifted to the woman standing across the courtyard, only a few yards away.

Lilleth was Enala's elder by two years, and infinitely more regal. She wore a loose, plain gown that rippled in the gentle evening breeze. A single tie secured it around her waist. A matching ribbon was woven through her long light-brown hair the color of almonds, glossy, and smooth as silk. She was solemn and gentle.

Terith thought back to Mya's passing comment on the trail.

"Will she be satisfied with a simpleminded man like you? My mom wants to know."

Of course, she had just been trying to goad him into saying something.

I'm not simpleminded.

Terith took a yaz fruit from the platter and chewed it. The buzz on his tongue gave warning too late. The fruit was steeped in distilled liquor, and Enala had just finished her third.

That's trouble.

"Shall I tell you something naughty?" Enala teased, fingering a fourth yaz ball, just out of Terith's protective reach. She wore a halter top that exposed her midriff, paired with a gossamer silk skirt, anticipating the imminent summer heat.

"Best if you didn't," Terith said uneasily. "But I expect you will anyway, just so that you can see me embarrassed—why don't you put that platter down? Those are rather potent."

Enala gave a laugh of delight and raised the platter out of his reach.

"My legs," Enala said, lifting her white skirt to show her sun-bronzed legs, "are longer than Lilleth's. What do you think about that?"

"I . . ."

"Well, what do you think about it?"

"I suppose it shouldn't matter so long as both sets are covered up," Terith said, swallowing and checking behind him to see who might be watching.

"But what if they *weren't* covered up?" Enala said, eyes daring Terith to come up with an answer. She leaned back and bent her legs, causing her skirt to slide up her thighs.

"Lord Ferrin!" Terith called, loud enough to startle Enala, but not loud enough for Ferrin to hear over the scattered conversations.

"Terith!" Enala squeaked, sitting up as if a blood hornet had just bit her. She even tinged a shade of pink in the face.

Terith gloried inwardly at actually getting Enala to show a touch of embarrassment, which made her all the more attractive.

Terith made a reach for the platter, but Enala swept it expertly away.

"You are as much trouble as I am," she chided, glancing around the diminishing crowd. Her eyes sparkled with new mischief. "Terith, why don't you invite me on a walk?"

"I suppose you've had enough yaz to warrant an escort," he admitted, as eager to leave the party as any. He cast a glance over his shoulder, meeting Lilleth's eyes for the first time as he stood to leave with Enala.

He tried to make an expression of apology, but Lilleth had already averted her eyes.

It stung. With everything happening so fast, the only sure thing about the challenge was getting hurt or hurting someone else.

Here he was at last, a champion. He was in control of his own fate. Yet he felt swept along, as if there were nothing he could do to change it and it was carrying him toward something he knew he could never return from. Change was coming.

Enala sidled alongside Terith as they passed through blossom-laden trestles. Her blond hair caught highlights of flickering lamps in the distance. Once outside the glow of the courtyard torches, she took his calloused hand in hers and threaded her fingers between his. "I love to walk. Don't you like walks . . . with me?"

"It's nice," Terith admitted, eyes flying about for watchers. With Enala by his side he was unassailable—except by accusation. Though he didn't mind Enala's attempts to interest him, he wasn't excited about explaining a midnight excursion with Enala to Lilleth.

Their path took them around the perimeter of the Ferrin's luxurious enclave, along boardwalks that overlooked the deep canyons surrounding the natural citadel. Giant ivy leaves draped from every corner like great green-veined tapestries.

Terith surveyed the shadowed cliffs. An irregularity in the leaves might be one of the merciless dragon predators hanging motionless waiting for prey to stray within their reach.

Enala likely had predatory intentions of her own.

Terith kept a cautious, comforting grip on Enala's hand. She was as coordinated as any of the Montazi, but a trip and fall into the blanket of constant fog that shrouded the canyon deep was instant death: death by broken bones, flesh eating flies, or sinkhole. Any way you like it, the deep was death.

"Perfect," Enala exclaimed as she saw her destination. She hurried forward, tugging Terith along the walkway that wound down several switchbacks of stairs to a wicker pagoda on a terrace.

"Get out, you," she snapped, stomping her foot angrily.

A brief buzz sounded before it was silenced in a satisfying crunch. Enala flipped the arachnid carcass off the cliff with her sandaled toe.

Stomping a scorpion half the size of her foot was not the sort of thing most girls did to endear their would-be lover. "Sorry," she sang to the falling scorpion carcass. "It's a private party."

"I could have gotten that for you," Terith offered, as a falcon snatched the scorpion's remains from midair.

Enala simply fastened her eyes on him, took both his hands, and led him into the clifftop pagoda outfitted with poufs.

Terith realized the pagoda's military value immediately—an archer's station.

Enala likely saw only its romantic isolation from the prying eyes of the feast.

"I'm so glad none of the dragons have tried to make a nest here," Enala said, "or I might have had to kick them out, too."

Terith laughed. "Give it a week. The mating pairs are still returning to the sacred plain."

"What do they do there all winter?" Enala asked as she fluffed a pillow.

"Gather as clans for protection, find their mate, and then just lie around and wait for the return of the rains," Terith said.

"Let's be dragons," Enala said, plopping on a cushion. "Now where is my mate?"

Terith gave a disconcerted cough.

"Only, if you were my mate," Enala continued, "I wouldn't let you eat any of that nasty ragoon weed. Dragon breath is unbearable. I don't see how you can even endure getting near them."

"They have to eat it," Terith said with a laugh. "The ragoon weed rots in their extra stomach until the fumes are flammable. That's how they make fire to heat the solid amber yolk of their egg and free the dragon within."

"Oh . . . the dragon within," Enala said playfully. "So, challenger Terith, will you stroke my hair if I sing for you?"

"If . . . if you insist," Terith said, his voice betraying real interest. He had experienced Enala's entrancing voice on enough occasions to have a shiver pass over him at the thought of it.

Enala sat in front of Terith with her back to him, while he ran his fingers through her straight blond locks that draped over her narrow shoulders.

As he touched her hair, unsure of quite what to do with it, she began to hum and then sang out a long, beautiful note, as if calling to eternity itself. The air seemed to draw in around them as her voice trilled and lifted it into harmonies with its own echoes. The haunting sound sent chills down Terith's spine. The melodies stirred the deepest part of his soul, as if he were waking from a kind of living sleep into a state beyond awareness wrapped in blissful oblivion where feelings swirled effortlessly, like colors on a painter's palate. The Montazi awakening gave her voice strange, entrancing spiritual power.

Terith passed out of time and space. His spirit left every pain and regret behind. All around him, peace and serenity lapped in a rhythmic ebb and flow. His fingers stopped moving through Enala's blond hair. A glow grew around him, lighting his eyes. His own awakening was hastening. Never had it been so close without his own life in peril. The horizon lightened as strength flowed into his arms, and the speed of his heartbeat and the wind slowed noticeably.

Terith hovered near the edge of a trance, until he felt Enala's hand slide up his thigh.

He jolted. "Hey! What are you—?"

"I was just about to say," Enala covered in a soft voice, "that Pert would rather see you fall into the deep than beat him in the race."

Terith roused his senses. It had been almost six months since he had heard Enala sing. The dry season hadn't improved his resistance—or Enala had been practicing. But the past few minutes had been as close as he had come to paradise, and as far as he had been from the constant duties of a champion.

Terith rubbed his eyes as the light faded like a closing flower blossom.

"It's not like Pert hasn't tried killing me before," he managed. "Remember when he sawed my saddle strap half through before that Outlander raid, hoping I'd not see it and fall off in the Outland desert somewhere? I'll be fine."

"Yes, but this time he has a *velra*."

"A fishing dragon?"

Enala nodded.

"You saw it? It's not a strythe? It wasn't one of those mountain goat hunters with the big fangs?"

Enala nodded overtly, as if begging for her hair to be stroked once again. "It was a velra. I saw it when it arrived at the keep this afternoon in a *big* cage. It has those spiny teeth and hook claws. And it has a blue belly. That's how I knew. I've seen them flying around the inner lakes."

With Pert's advantage on his mind, Terith could think of nothing else. "I thought all trained velra were already owned by wedded men. Pert must have . . ."

"The air is so cold all of the sudden," Enala whispered. "Why do you not put your arms around me?"

Terith unclasped his double-folded dragon-wing cloak and set it on her shoulders absently. He stood and paced the small pagoda. "I can still beat him. I can't keep with him on the ascent, but . . . I am going to have to bend the rules. I have no other choice."

"It's not worth it," Enala pleaded. "You don't have to win the race. You don't even have to enter! Pert wants my sister. You know that. He'll try to kill you if you get ahead."

"But I must enter."

Enala stamped her foot. "I won't have you die! Even if . . . I have to marry someone else. I could just run away after the wedding and come find you."

"I won't die, Enala. I promise," Terith said. "And thanks for the tip about Pert. I can still win. You'll see."

Terith turned and ran back over the walkway, leaving the younger daughter of Ferrin to pick her way back along the rope trestles by herself.

He might have run all the way back to Neutat that night, had not a ghostly figure blocked his path on the southeastern bridge.

"Hello, Terith."

"Who is it?" Terith's eyes strained out into the darkness, seeing through the misty air only the outline of a form ahead of him on the living ivy rope and slat bridge.

The gentle sway of the figure and the stillness of everything gave the answer.

"It's quiet here," she said with a voice that sounded as though she were smiling.

Terith said nothing for a moment, heart racing and adrenaline robbing his wit. "Have you been waiting for me on the bridge this whole time?"

She shrugged.

"You knew I was coming?"

"You always run away when things get political. Did my sister finally scare you off?"

Terith leaned against the ivy rope that ran along his side and relaxed.

Lilleth sauntered into view and leaned against the opposite guide rope stretching her arms outward along its length, gazing down into the haze drifting over the deep.

Terith felt the tension run out of him as her calmness seemed to pass effortlessly through the space between them.

"Apparently her legs are longer than yours. Did you know that?"

Terith said. "It must have been a very important piece of news because as soon as she'd had enough liquored yaz, she told me herself."

Lilleth laughed gently. "I don't blame her. She's burning up with spring fever. She's nearly as bad as the Furendali."

"Not you?"

Lilleth turned to face him, her long eyelashes and full lips no longer in silhouette. "I'm an autumn girl."

"Like the dragons."

She smiled knowingly. "Your sudden midnight excursion . . . it isn't about some new bit of information regarding the race, is it? The velra?"

Terith huffed a breath of frustration. "I can beat him. Why don't either of you trust me?"

Lilleth shook her head. "His mount is far superior. Your problem is the climb. You weigh too much for a fruit dragon, even a large one. A strythe might do if you had one."

"It's too late to change dragons now, and besides, even if I could manage to trade for one—and train it—we just haven't got the resources to support the mountain dragons in Neutat."

"You could come live with us up here in the clouds," Lilleth invited. She stepped forward, eyes gleaming, dress alight with cloud-filtered moonlight. "It would be enough to have you here with us . . . with me."

"Enough just to be here? And just what is that supposed to mean? I shouldn't enter the race, just let Pert win—and marry you? Am I not good enough for you or Enala?" Terith burst out defensively.

Lilleth looked for his eyes, but Terith avoided her gaze.

"I—I'm sorry. I know you care about me—want me to be safe, but . . ." Terith sighed anxiously.

Lilleth slid her hand down her thigh, gathered a bit of skirt and moved it gently from side to side. "Are you sure you belong in Neutat?" Lilleth said simply. She always spoke as though she knew better, and she always did. "Does a bird belong in the nest where it was born?"

"Ferrin needs me there," Terith replied. "The people of Neutat can't defend themselves against the Outlanders. Every summer the horde comes in greater numbers."

"They sense our loneliness," Lilleth whispered. Moonlight glistened off her bottom lip and the pale skin of her neck.

A chill ran down Terith's spine.

"The alliance crumbles all around us," Terith said. "None of the other realms send help."

Terith froze as Lilleth slid her fingers gently around his wrist, in a delicate grip that instantly drew his attention toward her.

"There is always something we can do," she said, as her eyes searched his face. "Destiny is a song we make, not a book we read."

"That is why I defend Neutat against the horde," Terith said. He mustered the resolve that Lilleth had so easily deflected. "And that's why I'm going to race."

"Terith." She hushed his lips with a soft finger. "I want to know something. Would you have me or my sister if you have your choice?"

Terith, unsettled, dodged the question, despite wanting to shout the answer that he wanted her. "I would have peace first, and then let Ferrin decide."

Lilleth dropped his hand. "That isn't how it works with the challenge, Terith. You choose."

The wind stirred the air around them, plucking leaves into small vortices.

"I have my own future to consider," Lilleth said. "It's the one future I cannot see. I have to make it myself. We all make it—together. It's our choices that weave it, not fate."

Terith winced at the truth of it. "I know. I just . . . feel like a stream headed for a gorge that's being pulled into two different falls. I can't tell which way I'm headed or see where it leads."

"May I?" Her offer was disarming. Her commanding voice pushed all other thoughts out of Terith's mind.

"What?" Terith said. But he knew exactly what she meant.

"Shall I look into your future?"

Terith's heart beat twice and stayed out of rhythm as the wind picked up again and began to sway the bridge. Terith tried to speak but stopped abruptly. The sound of his breathing and hers merged into a matching rhythm as if Lilleth were somehow part of him.

She was summoning her awakening. He'd never felt it, but he had seen it, and there wasn't anything he could do about it. It was like a whirlpool that pulled at the veil of eternity until it tore open and spilled its secrets before her. But it took time to summon. Perhaps he could distract her.

"Lilleth, why don't—"

Lilleth took both of Terith's wrists in her hands, her touch soft and disarming. He was powerless at the first brush of contact. Her skin, luminous, was full of rapturous, potent vitality. "Terith, you have never let me see your future. Are you afraid?"

A rider had no fear. Past and future were both open to the seer, but this time she would look forward. The wind whipped around them, licking their clothes and slapping hair into their faces.

"Terith, look at me. Let me see."

Raindrops began to splatter against the large ivy leaves dangling from the bottom of the bridge, driven by the sudden crosswind. Her awakening siphoned nature, like a whirlpool at a sinkhole, drawing in everything in an unstoppable rush.

"But what if I am maimed or I become a villain? I can't make you carry that burden."

"I want this, Terith."

Her face was close, her lips very close. The snapping of branches punctuated each gust of wind.

"How far can you see?"

"Days, weeks—I see only events. I can't choose what I see, and I only see those things I cannot change."

"What difference will it make? If I die, I die."

"Let me see your eyes." It was a regal command, but soft.

Terith lifted his gaze until he stared straight into the eyes of Lilleth. His world vanished in a moment of rapture.

Electricity sizzled through the air. A bolt of lightning avoided the bridge and slammed into the side of the megalith as a thousand points of light flickered around his body, gathering into streams that poured into Lilleth's white-rimmed eyes.

Terith felt time and space siphoning past him, as if his fate was unrolling from inside his own body.

Light eclipsed Lilleth. She was silhouetted, angel-like for a moment in time. Her face formed an expression of rapture that turned in an instant to a look of horror. Lilleth screamed and covered her face. She tipped and collapsed onto the slat floor of the bridge.

Terith knelt next to her but couldn't encourage any speech out of her. She only wept, shivered, and wept again. "The deep . . . not the deep . . ."

Terith shuddered involuntarily, but he reached out, almost automatically, and lifted Lilleth in his arms. Her strength was entirely gone as she hung limply against his body. He stood and carried her back toward the great house where the ivy taproot plunged into the core of the megalith.

Lilleth's voice rang in his head as he carried her. The blood-chilling scream and those ominous words: *The deep . . . not the deep . . .*

Terith did not have to wonder what the words meant.

She saw me fall.

Terith seemed unaware of anything as his mind wandered through the mist of his past and future in a daze. He made his way back to Ferrin's enclave, not feeling the burden in his arms. He let Lilleth down on a pillow under the braided reed canopy of the courtyard of Ferrin's lair. His heart filled with a sense of immediate anxiousness.

Now was the time for action. Pert had a velra. That was what mattered. Ferrin's race aimed to fatigue the dragons early with a series of punishing, rapid ascents, to spread out the challengers and reduce clashes later on. It made for a more exciting race since most of the spectators would be watching near the start. A fishing dragon was a born climber, with forearm wings that had bat-like proportions. With its smaller legs and narrow head and nothing to excess, the blue-bodied dragon had a supreme advantage. Pert's dragon would come out of the climbs with energy to spare.

Terith's fruit dragon was a grazer, as comfortable on the ground running and leaping as it was in the air. After the exhausting initial climbs, his dragon might never catch up to the larger velra.

Then I find another way.

For that, there were preparations to make. Visions of the future did not matter. Lilleth's dreams could not determine his destiny.

She whimpered as Terith stood to leave.

Then Enala was there, standing beside a stone pillar like another ghost, still wrapped in his dragon-wing cloak. Her shocked gaze shifted from her would-be lover to her tormented sister and back. Shock and fear, anger perhaps, showed in those eyes, feelings no one could sing away.

"She looked," Terith explained lamely. "I—I didn't want her to see. She's a bit shaken up. I think she'll be all right. I'm sorry. I'll be back in a few days. But I have to go."

As he left, Lilleth broke into a wail. Her sobs rang in his ears, like an echo that followed his paces.

CHAPTER 6

Erdali Realm. Citadel of Toran.

Reann's queries about the visitor turned up little information from the other servants. She had no choice but to take up researching the matter personally—spying, as Ret called it. She ought to have been researching her future employer. The logical side of her brain told her that she had only a few weeks to change her situation as a servant before it became permanent, and the other logical side made the excuse that only a few weeks of research wouldn't make enough difference. With those sides locked in argument, Reann followed her heart. She had felt something when the visitor arrived. She wanted to know why.

He got up early and did exercises of some sort in his chamber. Reann could tell from all of his heavy breathing and grunting.

The second morning as she listened at the keyhole, she detected the whistle of a sword blade.

He spent a lot of time walking the halls. He cornered folks at random and asked them questions, but only when he thought he was alone. And, of course, he always spent time in the library, usually in the historical section, pulling out books at random and flipping through pages.

Reann decided that whatever his business was, he had no idea what he was doing.

Reann's interest only grew from her hours of surreptitiously watching him as she mopped the already-gleaming floor and re-sorted stacks of books that she had already put in order.

When she came to the library on the fifth day, leaving the door ajar, the young man stood from his desk, pushed the door closed and walked over to the table Reann was needlessly dusting.

Her heart beat with expectation.

He fingered the brim of the hat in his hand and spoke in a low tone. "Interesting work."

Reann blushed slightly. She stopped dusting and looked up into his eyes.

Having her full attention, he continued. "I have something that may be of more interest to you. There is a mystery here . . . about which I have some clues."

Reann's eyes widened. She suppressed the grin that tried to sneak onto her face. It was happening at last.

"I ask for your help," the handsome young man said, "but only if I may have your solemn word to not speak of anything I may tell you."

"I cannot promise not to tell anything," Reann said. "For if telling is the lesser of two evils, it would be the better choice."

"You speak too much like an educated lady," he said delightedly.

"That is very kind of you," Reann replied, wary of the flattery—she did this sort of buttering-up all the time to Ret.

"I suggest a compromise," he offered. "I will tell you what I am looking for. If you deem it a worthy cause, you will promise to aid me without disclosing our findings, except by my permission. You are already the keeper of many trusts, no doubt?"

Reann likely kept more secrets than anyone else in the realm—all five realms if it came to that.

"Agreed," she said confidently. The rush was upon her. She was going to hear a secret.

The man gestured to the chair opposite him at the reading table. Reann seated herself with her legs together and to the side, as etiquette suggested.

"Are you loyal to the kingdom of Toran?" he asked, his earthy eyes gazing directly into hers. "Say either way, it doesn't matter to me."

"I am loyal, for my part."

"Good enough," the man replied quickly.

Reann breathed a sigh of relief.

"There is reason to believe," he said, whispering and leaning very low over the table, almost speaking into the hat in his hands, "that Toran did, in fact, leave heirs."

Reann's mouth opened as a feeling of joy and disbelief washed over her. The uncertainty churning in her stomach turned to excitement. Was it fate that had brought them together to find the heirs?

And the heirs were just the beginning of the mystery. There was the mark of Toran, his inner circle, his lost memoirs, and the Lyrium Compass. What was a Lyrium Compass? What did it mean? Was it a gathering, an organization, some ingenious invention?

Seated across from the handsome lord, who could only be five years older than her at most, Reann's spine tingled with interest. She shrugged casually. "I've heard that rumor."

"Five heirs, to be precise," he continued, emphasizing that he knew they existed—more than mere hope. "And I intend to find them. Will you help me?"

Reann wondered whether there was a catch, but it was all quite simple. She would help the man find the heirs. There was nothing else to it, except the secrecy. Reann could easily understand that. Toran had many enemies. Information in the wrong hands could betray the heirs.

Satisfied that she was not doing anything dishonest or rash, she replied, "Well . . . why not?"

"Will you swear?"

"I accept your offer," Reann said decisively. "What token will you have of my pledge, an oath on the Guardians' golden gate or the fires of the seventh hell? I've made plenty of both."

"Only the token of the honest heart," he said, apparently unsuperstitious. "But I suppose if we are to be engaged on the same cause, I ought to at least know your name."

Introductions between different classes were always awkward, and this belated one doubly so, but it meant she would be on par with him and she would be part of the mystery. Reann gave a measured smile. "I'm Reann."

"And you may call me Verick."

"Lord Verick," Reann mused, trying to place the origin of the name.

"Oh, it's a common enough name in Treban," the visitor said quickly.

Reann knew he had not used his real name, but proceeded amicably anyway. How she knew he lied, she couldn't tell, but she always knew. Always.

Despite his acting, this man claimed to possess clues to the greatest mystery of the age, one Reann had pursued since her childhood. This Verick was worth entertaining.

"Here is the trouble," Verick said. "Toran spent most of his life crusading. He could not defend an heir here in Erdal while he was off on a military campaign."

"Naturally," Reann said politely.

Verick continued quietly as if to avoid being overheard, though there was nobody else in the library. "That suggests his heirs were born on his campaigns."

Her mind already engaged on the puzzle, Reann stood and faced a large wall map of Toran's united realm at its zenith. She traced a finger along the route of Toran's conquests: north, east, south and west. "If the heir was born on a campaign, then the mother would have been someone close to Toran, someone with whom he traveled."

"Local nobility?" Verick suggested.

"Not likely," Reann replied.

"What do you mean? Surely Toran, a king, would never have joined with a common peasant."

"At war Toran fought and slept in the field beside his soldiers," Reann explained. "He would reap from sunup to sundown alongside his own farmers. The uniter of the five realms was no respecter of station. Noble or not, Toran judged by heart, not by inheritance."

Slouching, Verick made a grimace. "But the thought of such a union is rather . . . disconcerting."

"Not to a peasant," Reann said. "That is the key."

Verick sat up straight. "What is the key?"

"Toran's enemies were nobles themselves. They would be on the lookout for babies born to noblewomen out of wedlock or to ladies whose husbands were away during the month of conception. According to Toran's wisdom, his heir would appear to his enemies as a mere commoner."

"But that is the very point," Verick exclaimed, putting his fist into his hand. "It's infuriating. How is anyone to know who the heirs are? How are the heirs themselves to know?"

"That's why you're here. Isn't it?" Reann guessed. "You want a list."

"Well, I thought I might find something concrete."

"Such as a roster of names and birthplaces," Reann said.

"Er, yes."

She shook her head. "Why would he ever do such a careless thing as to record every piece of evidence regarding the heirs on a single parchment?"

Verick self-consciously tucked a leather folder jutting out of his waistcoat back into its pocket. "There are . . . indications—clues, as it were—about the heirs. All very cryptic, I'm afraid. Perhaps the two of us can piece all of the meanings together."

"Such as?" Reann replied in a level voice.

"Does this couplet mean anything to you? *The eyes of the blind see anew; They behold his fortress ever true.*"

Reann gave a considering nod. "Perhaps it refers to someone who doubted Toran—didn't see his potential—but then turned to his side once he became powerful. Perhaps a mother was a former enemy?"

"Speculation," Verick said, unimpressed by her improvisation. He sat forward and rubbed his thumb and forefinger as if holding a lucky charm. "Feels like I'm missing something obvious." He turned his shoulder in a moment of indecision. "Have you ever heard the name Dariel?"

Reann's breath caught in her throat. She had seen the name only in the secret document she had burned the day Verick had arrived.

Should she tell him?

She had agreed to help but hadn't volunteered to tell everything she knew, or even to answer all his questions—a useful caveat. If she started talking about it, where would she stop? Obviously Toran was hiding the information in the diary by having it scribed into an arcane language. Was it hers to reveal?

"I have heard," Reann said, "that she was Toran's travel guide in the Outlands." She added quickly, "But I have no documents on the matter." That part was true.

Verick nodded. "Hearsay is of value as well. There is often a nugget of truth in every rumor."

Reann let out the breath she had been holding. If that had been a test, she had just passed.

Verick stood up and tugged his waistcoat into place over his belt and scabbard. "I shall meet you here again in the morning."

Reann gave a short bow. "Do get some rest, sir. I shall attend to my duties this evening to give us sufficient time to research the problem on the morrow."

"Excellent."

"And . . . shall I cast a hint among the busybodies that you are investigating a land dispute?"

"Yes, that is as good an excuse as I could imagine. That will explain all our peering at maps and old documents."

When Reann had seen him to his rented quarters, she dropped into the laundry chute, and slid to the kitchen, where she finished the day's many remaining dishes. Then she returned to the library, her head awash with new thoughts and new hopes, but weighed by an equal measure of new fears. Chief among them was the fear that she might actually succeed. Her life would be utterly transformed, no longer a servant, but a courtier—a translator, like her mother had been.

No more worrying about the fate of the realm. She could imagine that, having a king and queen in the castle, and children—princes and princesses. She could be a royal tutor.

That kind of stability and stature would attract suitors—educated ones, travelers, traders, merchants, perhaps even nobles.

Perhaps not nobles. But still . . .

It all depended on whether she could trust Verick. One part of her wanted to believe him.

Her tabby cat, Ranger, appeared at her side. He rubbed his fur along her leg, begging for her attention.

"The pieces don't add up, Ranger," she said, picking up the overweight cat and scratching its head. "You saw that man Verick, didn't you? He wasn't wearing any jewels or rings or anything like that. I've seen nobles from Treban. They have mines. They always wear big gaudy jewelry to prop up their pride. You'd get along quite well with them, I think. You're always chasing after things that clink."

Ranger kneaded his claws into her arm.

"Well it's true. But you probably think this Verick fellow left off the jewels for safe travel," she said matter-of-factly as she drifted past geologic treatises and into the geography section.

"But his ears weren't even pierced—did you see that? And he kept his hands upon his hat, as if he weren't accustomed to fingering other things like rings or bracelets or necklaces. So he isn't Trebani. The southern accent was real, though. That's the mystery of it.

"He could be from a little farther south, Ruban perhaps. What do you think?"

Ranger hissed.

"That's what I was afraid of."

Reann's heart beat heavier in her chest as she clutched a volume labeled *Ruban.* There was a missing piece, she realized.

What's in it for him?

CHAPTER 7

24 years earlier. Serbani Coast.

Nestled in the fortress-like walls of the secluded harbor were more than a hundred ships. The assembled fleet of battle frigates, converted fishing boats, and merchant vessels slept in the morning calm, slack sails hanging like gray tapestries in the misty air.

An old seaman sat peeling potatoes on a stool on the deck of Toran's flagship, the *North Forest.*

Standing nearby, Toran noted the old man stopping to rub his knees.

An old man's aches were a sure sign of a storm. Even Toran, only a year shy of forty, could feel the dropping pressure in his bones as wisps of fog moved quickly through the harbor. A sail flapped as the breeze took up the slack.

"I told yer," said the man. "I said it was comin'—the big one. Better to weather it in the hollow than out on the open seas. Ay. Those waves will be heavin' to heaven and higher."

"And what of the enemy?" Toran asked. The unassuming opinion of an old sailor was worth a dozen midshipmen. "Won't they seek shelter? What if they come here?"

"Plenty of spots for shelter on the coast," said the old man. "No, they won't find us, never. There's three hundred and seven fjords on this stretch of the southern bend—the easier for smuggling."

"The witch queen's smugglers and pirates know these harbors almost as well as my Serbani captains," Toran noted. "Still, with the hurricane brewing, they'll have their own necks to worry about. I doubt they'll be hunting us."

"Quit yer worrying and start peeling." The sailor tossed a small kitchen knife to Toran, the supreme commander of the alliance.

Toran tucked it into his belt. "Weather permitting."

Two more sails flapped hard, then a third.

"It's begun." Toran whirled about and barked orders to the yeoman on the watch. "Sound quarters. I want every ship in the harbor secured tighter than a—" Toran cut off his colorful sea-speak as a cabin boy emerged from the pilot's map room.

Bells rang out one after another across the harbor. Decks filled with seamen who bolted up the webbing to tie down the sails.

"Are we going to shore for the storm?" the cabin boy asked Toran, with a touch of hope in his voice.

"No, Nehal. A captain does not leave his ship. Besides, we're still waiting for three more ships from Ruban to rendezvous. I can't go to shore when my men are at sea fighting that storm."

"The men say we'll be barfing sea biscuits all over the place when the waves get rolling. And we can't open the portholes either or it will let in too much water."

"I'll take it under consideration."

"Why are we in this harbor?" Nehal asked.

The lad was much too keen.

"I think this place holds some . . . promise," Toran replied.

"What makes you think this place is special, sir? I see no shadows of the future here—it is . . . just empty."

"The doings of a conqueror are not so easily explained to a cabin boy."

"I think you chose this harbor for a reason," said the boy. "I saw your markings on the map."

"I erased those markings."

"It's not my fault I see better than most."

"Don't you have studying to do?"

"No, sir. I've finished all three books you gave me to read. I've started reading the maps, but there isn't much to learn—just memorizing places." He leaned closer and whispered. "I can see them in my mind, like paintings—even places I've never been to."

Of course, Toran thought, *his mother is a witch.* Such odd abilities thrived in the Serban race. The power of change was so concentrated in the coastal clan, even more than the Montazi. Early in life, their gifts were ambiguous. But in the end, fate would give them only the power to change one thing: dreams or plants, moods or motion, winds and waves, or as Nehal's mother, healing wounds, the power to stop death. When they died, that power passed to a younger magician in the very same day. Each power was unique to one Serbani.

Though Nehal was Toran's ward, he had taught the boy nothing about the life cycle of Serbani magicians. He kept many things to himself.

Hard work, brotherhood, and loyalty were as powerful as any curse a witch could conjure.

Except Tira.

"Have you ever met any of your mother's relatives, Nehal?" Toran asked.

"No, sir."

"Don't."

"Yes, sir. Can I climb the mast? I want to watch for the Rubani ships."

"No, stay by me. I may need you."

"Yes, sir."

At least the boy had enough discipline not to complain about the admiral of the makeshift fleet being overprotective. The lanky six-year-old cabin boy already had a year at sea. He learned twice as fast as the junior officers and remembered twice as much.

"Have you turned seven yet?" Toran asked.

"No, sir."

"Well, you'd better hurry it up."

"Yes, sir. I'm working on it every day." Nehal cracked a rare smile.

A gust of wind rippled over the water, rocking boats like corks in a bucket. A second gust followed, blowing around the cove as if looking for an exit and not finding one.

It never stopped.

"Is this your first hurricane?" Toran asked over the noise of the rising wind.

"Yes, sir—look at that." Nehal suddenly pointed to the inlet at the gap in the cliffs. "Another ship has come."

Toran stared. The prow of the vessel was just discernible in the distance—a dragon's head.

"Guardians help us, Nehal. They found us."

"Hersians!" Nehal shouted. "Hersians in the cove!"

Toran flinched as the first broadside thundered. A barrage of cannon balls tore into decks and exploded into the hulls of the outermost Serbani ships. Each blast felt as though it were taking a piece of Toran's heart.

Thousands of Toran's loyal sailors turned their eyes to the sea. All at once they knew the horror of the predicament.

On the brisk inbound wind dozens of corsair ships rounded the point, blocking the only route out of the harbor, setting off their cannons in turn and obliterating the unlucky first line of Serbani fighting ships.

Trapped in the secluded harbor, Toran's ships were clustered densely with hatches latched, sails furled, and anchors dropped in anticipation of the incoming storm.

They were dead in the water, or soon would be.

Forsaking rank, Toran joined the sailors in hauling lines to set the sails. In moments, the pace on the deck of his flagship increased to utter chaos.

Commands to weigh anchor sounded belatedly across the decks of nearby ships. More took cannon fire as the enemy ships poured into the gap and emptied full broadsides into virtually helpless vessels.

Nehal kept by Toran's side, but fled behind a barrel when the sounds of the massacre became unbearable.

Toran turned from the boy, taking in the mass of pirate ships in the harbor. The enemy ships ran out in two lines, like claws reaching out on either side, surrounding the trapped Serbani armada.

Flames climbed the masts of five of his ships and in moments, twelve, and then twenty.

Serbani ships answered back with scattered fire, but the cannons were quickly silenced by crossing broadsides from enemy gun decks.

Toran stood mid-deck trying to see a way out the massacre—and this was just the beginning. The real massacre would start when the ships began raiding the unprotected Serbani ports.

"Captain!" Nehal shouted from where he cringed behind a barrel. "We have to get out of the harbor. It's a trap."

"Yes, and I led us into it," Toran roared angrily. He paused, wincing, as if trying to squeeze the grief of his body. "This is the end for us." He did not attempt to make polite denials, as if the facts were somehow avertable.

The boy's face twitched with emotion, fighting back a sudden urge to cry.

"Nehal, if you want to be by my side, you must be brave. I need someone brave by my side."

"Yes, sir."

"The honest brave children are made Guardians in heaven."

Nehal nodded and started from behind his hiding place.

"Hold fast!" Toran dove and tackled the boy.

A cannon shell exploded into the ship's stern, sending wooden splinters overhead and high into the air.

Both were on their feet again instantly. Nehal glanced at the point of impact then straightened and bit his trembling lip. He stood with his heels together and his arms tucked behind his back. "Are we . . . going to die, Captain?"

Toran put a hand on his shoulder without looking. The two stared straight at the incoming warship that had just blasted a hole in the ship's stern with its bow cannon. Nearby, sailors desperately hauled in the anchor.

"Nehal," Toran said. "I'm afraid the only men that will leave this harbor alive will be on Hersian ships."

The enemy dreadnought was closing fast, cutting directly through the center of his helpless fleet, chasing his admiral's flag.

"The only ships that get out of here are Hersian . . ." Nehal rehearsed. "Then you'd better get one!"

Toran exchanged a surprised expression with the boy. "I just might."

The approaching dreadnought was a wide-bodied vessel, built to ram. Oars raised, the ship listed slightly as its helmsman worked it against the gusting wind to keep Toran's flagship, the *North Forest*, in its sights.

The Hersians wouldn't ram the ship and risk sinking such a prize. Toran and his ship would both be taken back to the witch queen's island to net a hefty favor from the demon ruler of the corsairs.

The Hersians meant to board the *North Forest*.

The pirates were greedy. That would be their undoing.

"Nehal—quickly. Get the dragon skin bag from the chest in my cabin. Climb up the mast as high as you can and dump it out on the deck. Then wait there until you see me on the deck of that dreadnought, then swing across. Go!"

Nehal nodded and darted aft toward the captain's quarters, dodging sailors as he went.

The dreadnought closed quickly against a backdrop of explosions and flaming masts. The Hersian pirates had the wind at their backs, black sails hoisted and guns loaded. Dozens of the Hersian ships slashed through the helpless Serbani fleet. To Toran, it was like being in a collapsing house, trapped and watching one pillar at a time crumble and crush a loved one in a helpless, hopeless horror.

Toran had time to issue only one order. "Under and over!"

The command echoed across the deck and Toran's men dove overboard in droves as the dreadnought maneuvered alongside Toran's flagship. Hersian sailors packed the enemy ship's deck, waiting for the distance to close to grappling range.

Toran glanced at the mast of his ship. Nehal was climbing with difficulty. The bag was at least half his weight.

"Do it, Nehal!" Toran shouted, praying his voice would be heard over the roar of the battle.

Nehal looked to Toran then dumped from the bag a staggering amount of gold coins. Glittering, gleaming, gold circles bounced and rolled across the deck.

The pirates on the looming dreadnought leaned forward, pressing against the deck rail as their grappling lines shot out greedily toward the *North Forest*.

Toran gathered a great breath, bolted for the far deck and launched himself off. A terrifying fall later, he splashed into the water and surfaced among the able Serbani seamen, sturdy Erdali cavaliers, and enormous Furendali spear throwers who had already abandoned ship. Toran found only a few survivors bobbing. As if the chilly sea was taking its own toll, the men went down one by one.

The tactic was meant to look that way.

Toran dove. Deeper and deeper he swam, kicking and pulling with desperation. The pressure tortured his ears. His lungs throbbed and bucked, desperately trying to release the load of air they held. His fingers went numb at the ends. His whole body racked with convulsions as his desperate lungs fought with his mind to take in a breath.

The hulls of both ships drifted above, one wide dark shape alongside the sleek form of his abandoned flagship.

Toran could hold his breath no longer. His whole body screamed out, tempting him to gasp, to suck in, to swallow.

Toran kicked for the surface, struggling to get his water-soaked boots and trappings clothes toward the surface that now seemed to never get any closer. But he was not alone.

A stronger swimmer caught him under the arm and pulled him toward the rippled ceiling between air and death.

Quietly the two surfaced on the far side of the dreadnought, joining the silent company of his crew.

Rising and falling in the growing waves, Furendali spearmen, hulks of hair-covered men, threw grappling hooks trailing heavy, water-soaked lines that snagged the railing on the deck many yards overhead. Toran took the first line, climbing toward the deck of the enemy ship. As he scrambled up the slick outer hull, he passed the ship's painted title *"Devil's Tail."*

The noise of battle hid any sound of their sneak attack. Deafening explosions echoed off the steep cliff walls and the roaring wind carried every shouted word into oblivion.

When Toran reached the first row of openings in the ship, he gazed in where rows of slaves sat still, their oars retracted.

None so much as opened their mouth when they saw him.

They want the ship to be captured. They're betraying their masters. Betrayal!

Was it possible he had been betrayed?

Only the captains and commodores knew the rally point, and only three were yet to arrive. All of them were from Ruban.

Traitors.

Toran's heart bled empty at the thought that a cabal of well-to-do backstabbing doubters had ransomed the lives of thousands of his volunteers who had come to help the Serbani fight against the Hersian menace.

It was the Rubani who had sold his location to the Hersians.

The hollow, cold, unfeeling emptiness—he had felt it before, once, deep in a cavern.

Tira had stolen the crystal pendant that activated the Lyrium Compass. He had caught her using it—she would have siphoned the life out of him if her sister hadn't been there to prevent it. Tira had chosen power over his love.

He should have killed her then, when he had the chance.

Betrayal.

Disbelief at the brazen treachery burned into rage. The Rubani had sold him and their own Serbani blood kin to the Hersian menace.

A single thought drove out all others.

Never again. No more betrayals.

Anger fueled his formidable frame as hand-over-hand he hauled himself higher. He reached the deck and put his iron grip on the rail where ten grappling lines were already teaming with men climbing out of the sea. He gave a great pull and vaulted onto the deck of the *Devil's Tail.*

The pirate sailors were abandoning their posts, swinging from the masts onto the gold-speckled deck of the *North Forest.* Others dashed boldly across unsecured boarding ladders and even hung from the grappling lines, desperate for the spilled treasure. The Hersian pirate mercenaries already on the deck of the *North Forest* clobbered each other in a mad dash for the massive wealth that littered the deck—the entire annual tribute of the Montazi. Even the *Devil's Tail*'s captain appeared in the fray.

Toran charged at the pirates still left on the *Devil's Tail.* Behind him, massive Furendali spear throwers and his able Serbani mariners surged onto the deck. A bevy of tavern-clearing tackles sent dozens of the Hersian pirates overboard.

Toran drew the potato-peeling kitchen knife with his left hand and used it to draw a sailor's eyes before knocking out the hefty sea-faring Hersian islander with a skull-crunching punch that drew a roar of cheers from the warlike Furendali storming the deck.

Toran continued his berserker assault, driving toward the side nearest his own ship, chancing occasional glances into the masts for the cabin boy between backbreaking open arm tackles and shoulder-dislocating throws.

A sword came within his reach as a pirate tripped over a fallen comrade. Toran yanked the sword free of the pirate and wielded it with all the rage he could summon. Blade in his hand, the enraged attack took on a deadlier color. The steel cut down opponents like a scythe moving through yellow Erdali barley fields. Fueled by his near single-handed onslaught, the storming of the *Devil's Tail* quickly turned from a dangerous stunt to a miraculous heist.

The grappling lines snapped loose as his sailors cut them free.

The dreadnought's sails caught the fiercely whipping wind and the captured ship surged away from the *North Forest*.

A counterattack broke out from the galley and a bevy of pirates—the slave taskmasters—climbed onto the deck from below.

Toran drove his saber through two of the pirates with one stab, like game hens on a spit. He kicked his sword free and whirled to separate another man from his sword arm. Desperately he searched the masts of both ships for the cabin boy.

Nehal was nowhere to be seen.

Toran turned his eyes back to the thickest fighting in time to see Nehal drop out of a net, lock his arms around a pirate's neck and clamp his legs around the man's waist like a monkey. "Sock him, somebody! I've got him pinned."

Toran put a heavy fist into the unlucky pirate's gut, plied Nehal off, and tossed the heavier of the two over the side.

"What did I tell you about fighting with the men?" Toran roared.

"Don't start a fight you can't win. Or was it, 'don't surrender when you can still fight'?"

"Oh, I can't even remember now." Toran leapt onto a water barrel lashed to a mast and bellowed to a sailor near the helm. "Get this ship turned around!" He shouted down through the grate into the galley. "Oars out. Spear throwers get below deck—back up those slaves." Toran's crew leapt into action, readying their escape out of the hell they were trapped in.

"That's the only way out," Nehal said, pointing toward the gap in the cliffs where ships burning with black smoke and listing awkwardly jutted out of the water like tombstones. "We have to go against the wind," Nehal shouted as a broadside gust rocked the vessel.

"Furl the sails!" Toran ordered. "Tie them down!"

Sailors scampered up the rigging. As the heavy sails collapsed, the pressure against the ship slackened and the work of the oars sent the ship surging forward with each thrust.

The work of death was all but finished on the deck, but all around the harbor it continued in urgent, merciless horror. Explosions of gunpowder ripped through decks. Flaming pieces of ships littered the water where bloodied and dismembered bodies floated among the detritus of the massacre.

Ahead, a lone ship, the *Fair Acres,* captained by a young Serbani commodore named Eastwick as Toran recalled, had cut across the enemy and slowed the attack. The bold move was soon to become suicidal. The ship, which had just emptied its cannons on both sides, was about to be overtaken.

"Mark the *Fair Acres!*" Toran bellowed to the Serbani who had taken up the helm. The man gave him a confused look, so Toran leapt up the ladder, grabbed the wheel and turned it until the *Devil's Tail* was headed for the *Fair Acres.*

The Devil's Tail's oars stroked the water rhythmically from one deck below the guns, closing the distance to the *Fair Acres* and its attacker.

"Ramming speed!" Toran ordered.

Drums beat below decks, speeding the pace of the rowers.

"Ready guns to starboard."

"They don't know," Nehal said with a grin as he came up to the pilot deck. "The pirates think we're coming to help them fight the *Fair Acres.*"

Toran nodded, pleased at Nehal's intuition. The attacking frigate turned and came broadside to the *Fair Acres,* taking cannon fire in return. But its wind-filled sails carried it swiftly past the *Fair Acres*—a wise move, considering the *Devil's Tail* was coming up the opposite side, ready to deliver a brutal broadside before the men on the *Fair Acres*'s cannon deck could cross over to ready a volley on the port side—a nautical one-two punch.

However, Toran's cannons fired deliberately early, missing the stern of the *Fair Acres* and slamming into the enemy ship. In quick succession, three cannonballs broke into the Hersian frigate's hull near the waterline and a fourth cannon shell hit a powder keg. A series of deafening explosions blossomed in a storm of red and yellow flame.

Nehal gave a smart salute to the infuriated pirate captain whose vessel would soon be at the bottom of the cove. Meanwhile dozens of sailors from the sinking *Fair Acres* swung on lines across to Toran's dreadnought, adding to his crew.

"I say, I made it!" shrieked a long-limbed man as he fell from a swinging mast line and rolled across the dreadnought's deck.

"Not him again," Nehal said disappointedly.

"Ranville!" Toran bellowed. "Get below before I throw you overboard. To the oars—every man to the oars!"

Toran looked back. The enemy frigate that had seen Toran's treachery coughed thick, black smoke. No signal from that wounded ship could warn the Hersians that one of their own ships had been captured—he hoped.

Rain splashed down on the deck as the hurricane released a violent barrage on the harbor.

"Into the storm!" Toran shouted, pointing to the gap in the cove that led to ocean. "Take us out!"

The *Fair Acres* captain climbed to the pilot deck and joined Toran at the helm to brace the wheel as the ship pitched over a huge breaker and onto the other side of the huge ocean swell.

"Heading, sir?" the captain shouted over the wind.

"Due south, Eastwick. Take us south."

"South?"

Toran narrowed his eyes. "We row for the storm, for Hersa and her unguarded ports. We'll take the fight to their coasts and force them to turn back to defend their own."

"Yes, admiral." The subordinate captain turned and bellowed a bevy of orders that echoed across the deck as the *Fair Acres* seamen fought to tie down the last of the sails. "We aren't out of the fight yet."

Toran leaned into a second swell. As the ship rose, another Hersian frigate, triple-masted with double-gun decks, rounded the point and turned into the gap of the inlet, blocking the *Devil's Tail*'s path.

"Toran, we don't have enough men to man the guns and the oars," Eastwick shouted. "And we're too slow against the wind. We're sitting ducks."

Patience spent, Toran roared back at the young captain. "Haven't you got a magician or something? What are you Serbani good for anyway?"

"I have one," Eastwick replied.

"Well, where is he?" Toran shouted.

"How should I know?"

"Pellin!" Nehal cheered. He jumped up and down on the deck pointing to the center mast. "The weather mage!"

Toran looked to the crow's nest of the tallest mast. A lone man with a gray beard that whipped in the wind struggled to keep his balance in the pitching sea. As the ship crested a wave, he raised both hands over his head.

A tingle ran up Toran's spine and all the hair on Nehal's head stood up. A look of smug satisfaction crossed over Eastwick as a single, tiny flash of lightning danced down from the sky and flickered about the inlet until it made contact with the enemy frigate. Suddenly twelve bolts of lightning forked downward, joining into a torrent of electric fire. The sails glowed blue for one silent moment before the thunderclap reached the *Devil's Tail,* followed by an even more deafening blast as the gunpowder detonated. The combined firepower obliterated the ship, sending broken, flaming pieces of hull and deck spinning in to the storm.

"Is that good enough for you inlanders?!" Eastwick shouted triumphantly at Toran.

"Get Pellin!" Toran bellowed.

The exhausted magician rolled sideways and collapsed over the railing of the crow's nest, but his secure line held and he swayed loosely like a marionette while a fellow sailor climbed to his aid.

"Grace of the Guardians," Eastwick sighed as he wiped damp hair away from his face. "I never saw anything like that."

"He just blew up the ship!" Nehal cheered.

A huge wave swelled in front of the ship. Toran seized Nehal under one arm like a bushel basket and clamped the steely grip of his other arm around a belay pin. A wash of heavy seawater hit them like a slap of a giant's hand.

Eastwick held the wheel as the ship climbed the swell and pitched down again, in clear view of the open ocean.

"Who is rowing down there?" Eastwick hollered. "It's like a legion of monsters!"

"It's my Furendali—the northerners!" Toran called back over the roar of a wave that crashed over the ship's bow. "And I'm going to join them—Nehal, you too."

The boy, dangling in midair under Toran's arm, had no choice.

"We may actually survive this storm if they can keep that up for another twenty-four hours . . . maybe . . . then what? Dungeons, we just lost the fleet! The entire fleet."

Toran turned and set his stony blue eyes on the captain. "There is more to this world than battles and blood. It is something we can only do together and it cannot be stopped by traitors."

Sea spray eclipsed the captain and Toran hardened his grip on the ladder rail, squeezing Nehal hard enough to get a shriek out of him.

Eastwick's face appeared through the sheet of white water. "What are you talking about?"

"One point of the compass at a time, Eastwick. Go south."

Turning point indeed, Toran thought. His heart bled for the thousands dying in the harbor. His body shook with grief as he climbed down the ladder to the cannon deck, then descended another to the oar deck. Beneath the grief was rage, the righteous indignation of a betrayed king.

Those traitors of Ruban who sold out their own Serbani brothers and the pirates of Hersa who ceaselessly raided the coast—they would both pay. The peaceful Serbani had never dared to attack the Hersian homeland before. That was about to change.

Fate would recompense their due, and Toran would help it along. The war had reached the turning point. Tira had won the battle, but the fate of the Serbani nation would not be turned, not by her.

The fate of the Serban traveled with Toran.

Nehal, the third heir, had survived. So would the Serban realm.

On his feet again on the slave deck, the cabin boy looked up at Toran. "What are you going to do, sir? We can't fight their fleet. You only have one ship."

"Yes," Toran said as the ship pitched violently.

The sea-worthy cabin boy checked himself easily with his arm linked through the ladder by the crook of his elbow. "You aren't worried? You aren't afraid?"

Toran shook his head. "No." He smiled at Nehal. "I have everything I need. It's time to end this war. We sail for Hersa."

CHAPTER 8

Montazi Realm. Neutat.

L ess than a week before the challenge where he would go up against a backstabbing opponent with a superior dragon and paid henchman at every turn, Terith stood facing an even more challenging task.

"What's the worst thing that could happen?" he asked himself.

Terith raised his fist and rapped the oval workshop door. "Tanna? Hey Tanna, I need your help." The panel swung inward under the force of his hand, revealing the leather workshop in its usual disarray, tucked into the hollow of a fifteen-foot wide great ivy stem.

Tanna's voice called out from her back room, "Come back later. I can't help you right now."

"Can't help? The race is six days away!" Terith marched into the workshop and threw back the leather curtain that divided it from her bedroom.

He was met with a scream.

Terith had a brief glimpse of her short brown hair, stalky limbs, button nose, and eyes that sparkled with spunk and indignation. Instead of a blouse she was wearing a corset laced about her waist with ribbing that supported her chest.

"Terith—how dare you!"

He backed out of the room, stifling a giggle.

"Tanna, what are you doing?"

"I'm trying on a riding corset, not that it matters."

"A riding corset?" he laughed. "I've never heard of it."

Tanna's flaming face appeared in the curtain gap, "That's because I invented it—"

"—to intimidate a dragon?" Terith said with smile tugging at his lips. "Not sure that's going to work."

"For your information, it supports—oh, never mind." Her face vanished behind the curtain.

Terith raised an eyebrow in a bewildered expression. "Girls don't ride dragons."

Her face reappeared, her expression daring Terith to repeat it, and then disappeared again.

Touchy, Terith thought. *One minute they're heartsick and the next they'd roast you on a spit.*

Tanna emerged buttoning on her work vest with its various sharp implements for gouging and cutting leather protruding out of its many pouches. Her fiery expression only added to the potency of her arsenal, making the popping coals in the hearth seem pleasantly cool by comparison. "What business do you have barging into my bedroom?"

"It's about the race. I need your help."

"More help? I've sewn everything from your boots to your riding harness, even that dragon-wing cloak—where is that cloak?"

He wasn't going to admit having left it with Enala, so he pretended not to hear her question. "I just need one more thing, a sort of chest harness that has—" Terith cut short his explanation when she covered her ears.

Tanna lowered her hands, crossed her arms, and stared through him. "You know what I want."

Terith blew a strand of loose hair out of his face and rolled his eyes. Killing the runts was something Tanna abhorred, especially because she would willingly raise any one of them—though Terith would never trust her with a hazardous creature that breathed fire if threatened, didn't hesitate to use its razor talons, and harbored unpredictable mood swings. *Just like Tanna.*

"It is not the way of the Montazi to spare the weak," Terith said.

Tanna stomped the floor in disgust. "Then you can make your own harness. You haven't got anything to pay for it anyway and it will take me five days—plus a few nights, I'll wager, to put it together—what is it, by the way?"

Terith raised his hands to pantomime a harness strapped to his chest. "It has four straps, with buckles and a ring on a swivel here in the center. The straps are interwoven with ivy fibers for strength, and the lining—"

Tanna interrupted with a scream, "Dah! There you go again, trying to trick me into making you another contraption. And I almost fell for it. Is Werm involved with this scheme?" she demanded.

Terith didn't have a chance to answer.

Tanna made to move past Terith and out of the workshop, but he sidestepped into her path. "Tanna, please."

"So you can marry a rich girl and live on a fat plantation way back in the upper Montas while the rest of us paint the border in our blood."

"That's not—that's not why I'm riding in the challenge."

Tanna made to step around Terith on the other side. He interposed again. "Please, Tanna. It's my only chance. Werm already agreed to give me his biggest whistlers. All I need is a harness."

Tanna's eyes widened, her lips forming into a laugh that came out in a single, "Hah." She shook her head. "You're honestly going to strap yourself to a firecracker."

"Yes."

"Can I watch?" Tanna's face had a luxurious expression, like this was a once-in-a-lifetime chance to watch Terith finally make a mistake.

"If we get it ready in time."

"Deal." Tanna laughed to herself. "Riding a firecracker! What are you going to think of next?"

Terith looked down at her vest and blinked. "Are you still wearing that thing?"

"None of your business. Now out! I have a lot of work to do and your ogling isn't getting any of it done."

The door banged shut behind Terith. "Looks nice, anyway," he muttered under his breath.

Terith picked his way through lush greenery, moving over and under the enormous roots that spread out radially over the top of the megalith. He rounded the central summit of Neutat and descended the slope to the keep.

"Redif, report," Terith hollered.

The keeper hobbled out of the keep and waved to Terith.

"Fifteen dragons healthy and war ready. Eleven in training."

"Excellent," Terith said. "Remember, it's quality first, not quantity."

"I'm pretty sure I taught you that, Terith," Redif said with a knowing nod to his apprentice Endle.

"He taught the wind how to whistle, too," Endle added.

"Well if I didn't," Redif bragged, "at least I taught it how to fly—and I taught you how to muck out the dragon cages, which is what you'd better be doing before I feed you to one of them."

Terith clapped his hand heavily on Redif's shoulder. He was taller than the middle-aged man by a full head. "You know, I heard you were the one who broke the first wind—are you really that old, or is that just a rumor?"

"Young upstart!" Redif roared, his dreadlocks swinging as he shook his head at Terith.

Changing the subject, Terith lowered his voice, "Listen, Redif. Pert has a velra."

"A fishing dragon?" Redif said doubtfully. "But all the trained velra belong to rich folk in the upper megaliths . . . I suppose the owner suffered an unfortunate fall, courtesy of Pert."

"I don't know," Terith said. "But there's a chance he hasn't trained very long with it yet."

"Perhaps he won't need to," Redif said warily. "This changes everything. He has the advantage."

"Where is Akara?" Terith asked, avoiding his gaze and anxiously surveying the cavern. An idea was brewing in his mind, something reckless.

"Resting in the rear of the keep," Redif said. "I took her out last night for exercise."

"Good. Let her rest again tonight. Then take her out tomorrow and expel all her fire."

"But Terith, the race is one week away. The ragoon weed must seethe for fifteen to nineteen days—depending on the quality—before the rot will ignite."

"Expel all her fire, and gorge her on fruit, both stomachs. Rest one day, and repeat."

"Terith, you'll be helpless without fire. If Pert is in the race—"

"I intend to stay in front. And we won't have time to feed. Akara has to have enough energy to fly the entire route without stopping."

"If that's how you like it," Redif said, his tone doubtful.

Endle piped up. "I suppose if the other riders play rough, you can always get Akara to puke some seeds on them."

Nobody laughed.

In the next two days, Terith did what business he could: updating routes and schedules for border patrols and authorizing new excavations near the taproot for additional dugout homes. The weather was hot and muggy, more so than it had been in the higher Montas. Here the cliffs were still rising inch by inch with seismic thrusts as frequent as every week.

There was always plenty of work this time of year, besides the challenge of training the youth. Today he had a special task for Mya. He only had to find her, something her mother claimed was significantly harder ever since the young rider Kyet had taken an interest in her.

Terith knew all of Kyet's hiding places. He'd used them himself.

Terith carried a leather bag concealing a yard-long cylinder made from overlapping layers of pasted parchment—a whistler. The tip was pointed in a cone and a small wooden kitchen funnel made the base. He climbed over an ivy root and skipped over a piled-stone ford that crossed the taproot spring.

The stream water seemed unpleasantly tepid, much warmer than he remembered it to be.

Horned and fanged bugs scuttled into the shade of broad ferns and under boulders as he approached—stinging or biting were practically mandatory for bugs on the megaliths.

Terith moved quickly to avoid herds of bloodthirsty flies and gnats from congregating around him.

Thankfully, buzzing scorpions avoided the flat tops of the megaliths altogether, preferring the canyon walls where pecking falcons could only hunt scorpions at peril of becoming a snack for the predatory dral.

Terith raced along the edge of the megalith, each step of his quick feet landing perilously close to the precipice until he turned in at another steaming stream and found the pair sitting together in a clearing.

"Ah-hah."

Kyet jumped up with an astonished expression on his face.

Mya giggled.

Terith folded his arms. "Figured I might find you both here. I wonder if I should tell your parents where I found you."

"I was just showing her this dragon egg. It was abandoned last season," Kyet said quickly.

"Sure you were."

At fourteen and twelve, Kyet and Mya were Terith's best and brightest.

"Sorry, Kyet, but since you are the only truth seer around, I'll have to hedge my bets." It was a monstrously useful talent, but that didn't help when the teller in question was Kyet.

"He was trying to kiss me," Mya tattled, with a snort of a giggle.

Kyet's face plunged through varying shades of pink and rose before finally reaching a brilliant crimson blaze of embarrassment.

"If you kept at your riding as well as you did at chasing girls, you might someday outdo me," Terith said honestly.

"At chasing girls?"

"Off with you," Terith said with a laugh. "I need Mya."

"What for?"

Terith gave a determined stare and Kyet tucked the stony dragon egg under his arm, waved a limp goodbye to Mya and trotted back down the trail toward the village center.

Mya peered interestedly at Terith's package.

Once Kyet was safely out of earshot, Terith opened the leather bag.

"Wow, a whistler!"

"Shhh."

"Where did you get it?" she asked softly. "From Werm?"

"Yeah. Only this one is special. Would you like to help me test it?"

"Me?"

"Yes, you. Remember when I taught you how to sound distances?"

"Of course. I just make some rising and falling tones and listen for the beats of the echoes."

"If I send this straight up, can you tell me how high it goes?" Terith asked. "It's very important. I need it to be exact."

"I ... well, I think so. I've done it with dragons, though I stopped trying when one of them dived at me."

"This is much smaller than a dragon, so you'll really have to focus your voice on it."

"I can try."

"All right. I'm just going to—" Terith whirled around. "Come out, Kyet."

Kyet mumbled and grumbled as he stomped out from behind a bush.

"Thank you for coming back to volunteer. You just won yourself a special honor."

"I did?" Kyet said in a confused and cracking voice.

"Yes." Terith planted the whistler—Werm's foremost finned pyrotechnic creation—on a stone and handed a flint to Kyet. "You get to light it."

"But I'm not wearing any dragon leathers. It could fry me."

Terith smiled. "You'll have to risk it."

Mya chuckled as Kyet bent down to strike sparks against the fuse.

"Be ready," Terith said.

Mya nodded.

A crackle sounded from the whistler. Sparks raced up its fuse. Kyet watched in awe at the chemical wonder, too entranced to duck and cover. The rocket blasted skyward, throwing Kyet flat on his back.

An instant later, a rhythmic throb filled the air. Mya's voice gathered power as the rocket climbed a trail of smoke higher and higher. Finally, it turned over and Mya's supernaturally amplified call cut off abruptly. She knelt down and gasped for air.

Kyet, wide-eyed and black-faced, stood up and checked for remaining eyebrows. "Wow."

Terith tried not to laugh at Kyet's white eyes staring out from a soot-covered face and helped Mya to her feet. "How high?"

"One hundred sixty-seven paces."

"You sure?"

"Pretty sure."

"You'd better be. Somebody's life may depend on it," Terith admitted.

"Whose? Yours? Oh—I get it. This is your secret weapon for the race, isn't it?"

"All right, enough questions."

Whatever inquisition Mya was preparing fled the instant the ground lurched. Terith was thrown onto his back but was up in an instant.

"It's just a tremor," Kyet said, putting a hand under Mya's to help her up and hanging on in case the megalith rocked again. Or maybe he was just making an excuse for physical contact.

Terith grabbed them both by their shoulders, "All right, enough fun. You two get back to the—"

The second rumble sounded with a great crack that seemed to splinter straight though Terith's bones and right up to his teeth. As the tremor rolled away, a fine mist boiled up from the deep as if something from dungeons of black hell had just been unleashed. Moist, hot air swirled over Neutat.

Terith's mind raced. He'd heard about this kind of thing before. *Steam vent.*

"We have to get off the megalith. Now."

"What's wrong?" Mya asked.

"Hell just broke loose," Terith said, "Literally. Werm told me this might happen. If the ivy taproot breaks into the lava reservoir under the aquifer, all the water runs into the molten rock and turns to steam."

"What did he just say?" Kyet mumbled. "It turns into a stream?"

A screaming jet of superheated vapor sprayed into the sky making a roaring sound like the whistler, but infinitely louder.

"Oh, steam. Right."

"Mya," Terith ordered, "sound the evacuation."

The girl hesitated.

"Now, Mya!"

Mya took in a long breath and held it for a moment as light gathered around her. Terith and Kyet covered their ears. Mya made a piercing shriek that shattered the air. Birds scattered from trees and filled the air by the thousands.

Terith grabbed Kyet. "Get your dragon and get clear of the megalith."

"Where do I go?"

"Fly to Erdal if you like. Just get out of here!"

Kyet nodded and raced ahead down the path.

Terith followed, leading a winded Mya by her arm as she struggled to keep up with his bounding paces.

Farther down the megalith, stone-lined paths filled with curious children climbing down from their tree forts and workers leaving forges.

"Sound the alarm again," Terith urged. He stopped for a moment to let Mya catch her breath.

Mya closed her eyes and the air around her crackled with a burst of pure, awakened energy.

Terith clamped his hands over his ears and squeezed.

Mya's opened mouth gave a second deafening shriek.

That was when the villagers jumped into action. Villagers coursed onto the bridges, laden with backpacks of emergency supplies, some carrying toddlers in their arms. Dragons lifted out of the keep one by one as the keepers released their locks.

A second burst of steam shot into the air, this one soaring hundreds of feet overhead. Rocks crumbled from the sides of the megalith as a great hissing issued from the center near the taproot.

"Get on my back," Terith shouted.

Mya leaped onto his back and clung to his neck as he raced down the steep path, stopping only long enough to pry Tanna out of her workshop. "Run!" he cried, echoing the shouts of the villagers, but the bridges were already clogged with fleeing people.

"Werm!" Terith bellowed, turning toward the tinker's assembly yard. "Werm, I need another bridge!"

"I'm on it!" the overweight thirty-something hollered from nearby.

"Good man," Terith breathed, racing up a side path shaded by wide-leafed fruit trees to the complex stone-lobbing mechanism where Werm was already in action.

"Stand clear," Werm warned. The heavyset and prematurely bald scholar grabbed his skull with both hands, as if to keep his brains in place. Behind him, an intricately lashed trebuchet assembly groaned against the force of its raised counterweight stone. Werm stroked his handlebar mustache for luck and called, "Launch."

The release of the counterbalance heaved a massive anchor stone trailing guide ropes in a slow motion arc that ended with a crash in the trees on the other side of the canyon, a narrow span of only forty yards.

"Dead on," Werm bragged to one of Terith's foot soldiers. "I told you."

"Get the ropes taut," Terith shouted, as men joined up to haul in the lines. In seconds, pulleys were racing out along the new ropes towing a temporary bridge.

It filled almost immediately.

"Terith," Werm called from the engineer's seat of the wheeled catapult, "what about the southwest porch?"

"Seventh hell and a half," Terith swore in frustration.

Mya released her death grip on his shoulders to cover her own ears.

"I forgot about that," Terith said. "I don't know if anybody is down there today. But get some archers to the south corner just in case."

"What if it blows?"

"Just go!"

Terith turned back, heading for the keep. He lifted a whistle from under his tunic and blew twice.

No answer.

He redoubled his pace.

"Shall I make the call?" Mya volunteered.

Terith stopped, his lungs searing from the breakneck run. "Can you?"

Mya repeated the sound of the whistle exactly, but many times louder. Her cry was answered by a distant, "Reee-aaat!"

Terith smiled. "It looks like we're going to make it off this rock after all."

"How?"

"Have you ever ridden a dragon before?"

Mya eyes widened in terror.

Akara shot over the smaller clearing, pinwheeled like a kite on a string, and landed next to Terith. Proportioned for agility on air or land, Akara was the largest fruit dragon in the region, with a twenty-foot wingspan, weighing a solid seven hundred pounds. She was a flagrant yellow with veins of red and green streaking her sides. The scintillating gold scales of an emergent queen flecked her short snouted head and neck.

Head held high and wingtip claws picking anxiously at the ground, Akara knew it was time to go.

"I'm not getting on that—"

Before Mya could protest further, Terith pulled a spare tether from a sidesaddle, whipped it around Mya who was still on his back, and tied it in front. "Just in case."

"No!" she panicked, now tied to Terith's back.

Terith climbed onto Akara and felt the jolt of her powerful legs as she leapt thirty feet straight up, before catching the wind with her forearm wings. Head and paddle tail bobbing in counter rhythm, she beat her winged forearms down hard to keep the extra weight airborne.

"I'm going to die!" Mya cried. "No, don't go higher!"

Terith guided Akara in a wide loop around the megalith, inspecting for anyone left behind. From the air, he watched the three bridges drain. The megalith was nearly clear.

Terith urged Akara forward with cued whistles as the sounds of rocks cracking under pressure ripped the air, like Outlander cannon shots.

Akara spotted it first and picked up her stroke rhythm.

Ahead, on the southwest corner, Werm was in trouble. His generous mass was swayed on a second makeshift ropeway that the archers had set up on the south side. He and two of the bridge makers pulled their way along the loose, two-rope support. Just ahead of them on the ropes were a woman and two children.

"Move," Terith urged, squeezing the words out through Mya's persistent bear hug.

The hissing from the taproot stopped abruptly.

"It stopped," Mya noted. "Is that good?"

"No!" Terith said in a panic. "Not now."

"What's happening?"

Terith cursed again, but this time Mya didn't try to cover her ears. Her hands weren't going to let go of Terith for anything.

"The root must have swelled in the heat and sealed the crack," Terith said. "Now there's no way to relieve the pressure, until the whole thing blows up."

"The entire megalith?! But Terith, that's our village."

The muffled cries of the people still on the ropes intensified. The children were off first, reaching the safety of the far cliff, then the mother. Only Werm and the archers were remained on the ropes, hands on one rope, feet on the other. The swirling air from the steam venting had set both wires swinging so wildly that it was all they could do to hang on.

Terith snapped the reins to one side and bent low as Akara spiraled over into a breakneck dive, straight downward

Mya screamed into Terith's ear. "What are you doing?"

"They aren't going to make it. I have to cut the ropes."

The swinging ropes rushed into view. Akara pulled up as Terith shifted his weight. In moments, the ropes would pass directly beneath him.

"Terith," Mya said anxiously, "You can't cut a rope that thick by just swinging a knife at it. It's like trying to chop a small tree in half with a kitchen knife."

"That's why I'm going to cut it in the middle of a dive." Terith yanked his signature saber-like, long knives from the sheaths on his calves and locked his heel hooks into the riding harness.

"Are you crazy?" Mya shouted into his ear. "If you crash into one of those ropes we'll end up in the deep—I've never even heard of anyone trying this sort of crazy stunt. I don't think you've thought this thr—" The rest of her rebuke choked off in a scream of terror.

Terith opened himself fully to the awakening.

The world slowed as the falling dragon plummeted through the sky toward the ropes. His dragon dove for the narrow gap between the two ropes. Akara threaded the harrowing obstacle in the blink of an eye while Terith sliced at the upper cord twice, one knife diving into the cut made by the other knife a half a heartbeat before.

As Akara pulled out of the dive, Terith looked back. The upper rope strained and then snapped, sending Werm and the archers plummeting toward the opposite cliff face, dangling from the line for their lives like fish on a stringer.

The air around Terith seemed to fill with light. Akara's wings, soaked with the new strength, stroked twice as quickly, slowing their descent. Overhead, clinging to the rope like monkeys on a vine, Werm and the archers crashed into the foliage of the opposite cliff wall, disappearing under the cushion of the massive ivy leaves.

A moment later, the megalith detonated behind Terith in an inferno of steam and rock. The sound of the blast drowned out everything. The ropes, the cliff, and the sky disappeared in a cloud of dust. Akara was tossed into a spin by the force of the shock wave, darkness filled the air as steam and debris soared a thousand feet into the air, eclipsing the sun. Terith was helpless as the stunned dragon went limp and spiraled into a flat spin.

Seeing streaks of green shapes in the rain of rocks, Terith loosened his heel hooks and leapt for his life with Mya still tied to his back.

His hands ripped through ivy stems that rushed at him until his leg caught on a branch that held, flipping them both upside down.

Mya was unconscious as Terith struggled to right himself in the tangle of ivy that was rapidly turning gray as the dust of the explosion settled. The awakening waned. Pain returned and his unnatural strength finally ran out.

He was halfway or more into the deep, with no way up but climbing. Worse, he had no riding leathers to protect him from the buzzing scorpions.

Worst of all, his dragon was gone. It was as if he was suddenly missing half of his own body—exposed, undone, destroyed.

Terith's inner drive to survive screamed at him through horror and the shock, until one thought pushed out all others.

Move.

In the dim light filtering through the cloud of steam and falling rocks, Terith spied what he hoped was the cliff top.

It was a long way up.

Weighted down by Mya's still unconscious body and exhausted, he set his slim hopes on the longest climb of his life as his world rained down around him.

In the dark mist below, the deep opened its throat and waited.

Dizziness set in as Terith gripped the slippery vine and drew himself upward. The ivy was a hanging plant, so the vees where the stems branched all pointed downwards, giving no footholds. Forcing himself into motion, he drew his knife and notched the ivy cord twice for toeholds. He continued, notching the stem, stepping, and notching and stepping again. His hands and boots were quickly drenched in sticky sap. Sunlight made its way slowly into the swirling haze of darkness. As it did, the wildlife emerged. Here and there, the buzzing of scorpions grinding their legs and the anxious tapping of their stings against their carapaces sent chills into Terith's spine.

The painful memory of previous stings made his hands sweat worse.

Coming to the top of another bed-sized leaf, he spied one of the large cliff-dwelling scorpions.

Mya stirred.

"Quiet, Mya," Terith whispered.

She moaned. The scorpion angled toward the sound and leapt. Terith moved his arm to intercept the scorpion before it reached Mya. It struck him in the upper arm near his shoulder and drove its stinger deep. Terith swung his body against the cliff, smashing the scorpion against the rock and then flung the twisted exoskeleton of fist-sized beast into the deep.

The venom felt like a fire burning inside his arm.

Terith let out a sharp gasp of pain.

The poison spread quickly causing his muscles to tighten like a catapult winch. His arm bent and twisted abnormally as his breathing became quick and shallow. Leaning his head over the leaf, he struggled to keep from succumbing to shock.

Mya's cries of fright roused him. Realizing he could still use his fingers on his stiffened arm, Terith proceeded to climb once again, leaning awkwardly to place his hand on the ivy and then loosening his grip as he stepped upwards to allow the hand to slide.

His elbow was frozen, and then his forearm began to cramp. After the next step up, the buzzing sounded again, then another scorpion joined, and a third.

"Mya?" Terith whispered. "I can do no more to save us."

Mya screeched once with the voice of the pecking falcon and the looming scorpions scampered back into cracks in the rock.

A feeling of hope spread into Terith's heart.

Then an ivy rope tumbled past them.

"Hey there, lazy. What took you so long?" called a voice from high overhead.

Only one person was that obnoxious.

"Tanna?"

"Grab hold of the rope. I've got your archers up here and your fat chemist. We'll pull you up."

"Who's fat?" bellowed a familiar voice.

"Werm!" Terith shouted, as the chorus of buzzing sounded again.

"Move it, dragon boy," Tanna called.

Scorpions gathered in clusters, emerging from their hives, sensing movement on the vines.

Terith leapt off the cliff face and caught the rope with his legs and good hand. Mya got her hands around the rope, allowing Terith to twist the rope around the heel hooks in his riding boots. The rope lurched upwards as a skull-sized scorpion leapt past them into the deep. The horde of buzzing scorpions raced upward along the cliff face, trying to keep pace, but the archers had tremendous strength because the rope accelerated, moving upward as if being pulled by a—

A boulder flashed past them, moving the other direction, tied to the other end of the rope.

"Whoa!" Terith shouted, as the vine hauled them upwards at a rapidly increasing speed.

Werm had evidently come up with a clever way to get them up quickly by tying the rope to a stone and looping it over an ivy stump, but Terith immediately doubted whether Werm had thought about how to stop the rope once he got it going.

Terith, with Mya tied to his back, soared headlong upward toward the woody stump of ivy root jutting out from the edge of the cliff top. Terith had to slow down or he and Mya would be smashed to bloody pulps by the collision.

Hoping his momentum would carry them the rest of the way, Terith let go of the rope with his hands, but the ivy rope was still tangled in his heel hooks and spun him upside down before he got free.

Terith slammed feet first into the bottom of the stump. "Ow!"

Mya on his back, Terith hung like a bat from the bottom of the stump that stretched out over the canyon.

He wasn't falling. That was the interesting part.

The end of the rope lashed out over the stump and then snapped downward, disappearing into the mist.

"Heel hooks," Tanna mused proudly. "Who thought to put those on your boots? Hmmm?"

"Yeah. Thanks, Tanna. I owe you."

Werm leaned down, cut the tether and lifted Mya to safety.

The moment her feet were on the ground, she pointed to Terith. "He swore."

Tanna looked at Terith with her sternest expression and shook her head.

"No I didn't," Terith lied as his face reddened from being upside down.

"Yes, you did," Mya tattled. "You said 'seventh hell and a half.' My mother says if you speak of the dungeons then the devils there will bother you—and besides there's no such thing as a 'seventh-and-a-half dungeon.'"

Terith twisted, trying to find a way to get his heel hooks free of the stump and not fall back into the deep with one lame arm.

Werm reached out a hand and pulled Terith up by the back of his shirt.

Back on firm ground, Terith brushed himself off with his good arm. "Well, since it doesn't exist, the demons there can't bother me," Terith said defensively.

Mya, on the verge of tears, pointed at the ruined megalith that had been their village and cried, "What do you think that was?"

"It wasn't my fault," Terith said. Then the bitterness of Akara's fall struck him. She was gone.

Terith—feeling dizzy, nauseous, and shaking from the scorpion venom—put one knee down on the megalith. "It wasn't my fault," he said, his voice weighed down with grief.

"Is he doing penance?" Werm wondered aloud. "I've never seen him do that before."

"I suppose," Tanna admitted reluctantly. "Dungeons, what's wrong with his arm?"

✠

Hours later, Tanna leaned Terith's sleeping, fever-ridden body against the bowing two-foot-wide stem of a thick succulent plant.

Werm moved into view from behind a twisting yaz tree trunk, watching the unconscious rider.

"Did you drug his flask?" Werm asked.

"Azastra blossom," she confessed. "He wouldn't have slept otherwise."

Werm's shoulders drooped, even more than usual. "He's lost

everything. He won't stand a chance against Pert." He ran his hand over his balding forehead and then rested his fist on a roll of fat over his suspendered trousers. "Wish I could do something."

Tanna clutched her arms around her waist as if she were cold. She looked up at the cloud-covered sky as a light rain began to fall. The drops mingled with two large tears that welled in the corners of her eyes. "He hasn't lost everything," she said. "He still has us."

"Tanna, the race is only two days away," Werm argued in logical fashion. "It takes the better part of a day to get to Ferrin-tat. Meanwhile our villagers are still relocating to our place of resort. It's an organizational nightmare."

"It's no different than a drill for an Outlander raid," Tanna said dismissively. "We can't give up on Terith just because—"

"Our homes, tools, workshops, and everything we own got blown into the Outlands," Werm said bitterly.

"Yes, lovely, Werm. I couldn't have said it better myself."

"So what do you suggest we do then?"

Tanna bit her lip pensively and then said suddenly in a conspiratorial tone, "We just need to get him out of here—make sure he goes to Ferrin-tat. Once he's gone and can't fuss over any of us, we can get the whole village to join in. Redif can trap him another dragon. Besides, it's that firecracker of yours he needs to win."

"It's an incendiary projectile," Werm corrected with a hint of pride.

"Any idea why he wants to strap himself to it?"

"Haven't the foggiest."

"Oh well," Tanna said matter-of-factly. "We'd better get started. I'll head for the place of resort to scrounge up some materials. You stay with Terith and get him on the way to Ferrin's place as soon as he's up—tell him to ask Ferrin to send help or something. Then see what you can recover from Neutat. It looks like the northwest side is still intact."

"I still think you're crazy," said the chemist.

"Do it, Werm. Or face my wrath. We aren't giving up on him. He never gave up on us."

"Fine, I'll do it. Trouble you for a goodnight kiss?"

"Werm—"

"I'll just . . . get these ropes ready."

CHAPCER 9

R eann was dizzy when she finished putting away the last of the historical volumes Verick had torn down from the second tier shelves. But she wasn't dizzy from the ladders. She left the library and scampered down two flights of stairs to the basement. Her bare feet felt light as she almost skipped along a curving portal that ran around the outside of a circular ceremonial hall. It ended in a small room with heaps of laundered rags and linens. She sighed and collapsed onto the pile of laundry.

It had been a perfect day, perfect since the first moment.

Verick had invited her into his room while he had breakfast and they had shared tea together—like friends.

Reann had never before had tea with a noble.

They had talked about Toran. They had walked the grounds in the morning for exercise and Reann had taken his arm for surer footing on the castle wall steps—taken his arm. It was like holding an oaken bow.

Research had gone fantastically well. Verick had spared a clue that Reann had immediately unraveled. It was a reference to a book of clan law, where Reann discovered the legal requirement for a conqueror to produce an heir with a mother from the conquered clan. Toran had ruled five realms, so legally he had to produce a joint heir for each.

She had also discovered a caveat. The conqueror could choose the mother. And there was a time limit to produce a joint heir to consummate legitimacy of the union of the realms: five years from the date of the alliance. With bounds on the heirs' birthdates, she had vastly narrowed the search. It was real progress.

Encouraged, Verick had promised to reveal additional clues. Reann grinned at the thought.

Verick seemed to truly understand her. He obviously found her interesting—choosing to keep her company on his walk and at breakfast. From someone so reserved, even a little attention was intoxicating.

Reann blushed at the thought. But more than that, the possibility of actually finding an heir was suddenly becoming real. With Verick's help, there could be a new king on the throne, a new future not for her, but the entire alliance of the five realms. Anticipation bubbled up insider her as her mind churned through the details of the day. The expectation grew with every passing moment.

Verick had eaten dinner with the rest of the visiting nobles and then disappeared into the village to interrogate the locals about Toran.

At least that's what Reann supposed he did. She still had chores to finish and couldn't spy. Beneath his layer of calculated calm was a shadow of hidden intent that Reann couldn't place.

It made him all the more interesting—another mystery.

Ranger yawned from where he lay curled on a pile of still-warm, sun-dried sheets. He made pains to get as much of his fur on them as possible, if only to get Reann's attention.

"Go ahead," Reann said to her tabby cat. "I don't mind today."

"What are you doing down here talking to yourself?"

"Hello, Wretch." Reann's back was to Ret. She didn't bother turning around. Her thoughts were more interesting.

The pause from Ret was longer than she expected.

"Need some help?"

Reann shrugged. "Not really."

"You all right?" Ret asked.

"Of course I am. Why do you ask?" Reann answered.

"Well . . . no reason really, except . . . I saw that Serbani lord down in the village. He sent me to ask for you."

"Me? Just now?"

"Yep," Ret said.

Reann stood up quickly. "Where is he?"

"At the cobbler. He was getting his shoes mended."

"It's late for shoe mending," she noted. Then again, Verick was a very thorough man. He probably had an evening appointment. "When did he send you?" she said, flustered at the sudden summons, and not having time to get herself presentable.

"Just a few minutes ago. The castle gate is still open. It's market day. Don't know why they bother this time of year. Nobody's around."

"Here." Reann shoved the towel she had been folding at Ret and hurried out of the folding room.

"What am I supposed to do with this?" Ret called after her.

"It's a towel," Reann called back. "It's for bathing. You should try it sometime."

"Very funny, Reann."

Reann hurried up the stairs and out of the castle, slowing as she passed through the castle gates into the village. If Verick was calling for her at his shoe appointment, it probably meant he had run out of people to question and wanted company—her company.

Or he had made a discovery. Both options were interesting.

She turned east down a dark street toward the river docks. It was a short walk to the cobbler, and as Ret had said, the streets were quiet and empty.

"Ah, Reann," called Verick's familiar voice as she neared the shop. "I thought you might like to see this."

Verick sat on a bench, minus his boots. Candlelight filtering through the cobbler's window curtain spilled onto the street, lighting one half of Verick's face. The summer air was warm and comfortable.

Verick gestured Reann closer and she took the initiative, sitting next to him on the bench as close as she could.

Verick had a large book on his lap. He spoke as if in mid-thought. "In theory, Toran could have had an heir in Erdal whenever he wanted. But his longest stretch of time in Erdal was after the last campaign in the west desert. He came home for good. Shouldn't his heir have been born then?"

Reann nodded, unsure of where Verick was headed.

Verick hefted the book. "This is a register. I bought it from the cobbler's wife."

"What sort of register?" Reann asked.

Verick held up a large bound tome. "Midwifery. It documents all the births in this part of Erdal."

Reann's heart sank. "And you want me to read every single one and crosscheck the parentage?"

"I thought it was splendid—ah, here we are."

The cobbler, an old man named Jebsen, emerged with Verick's boots. "New soles only," he said. "Uppers are fine quality. Should last a good many season yet."

Verick took the boots, tugged them on and allowed the cobbler to bind the laces. Verick left a handful coins in the cobbler's empty hands and strode up the road toward the high street. Reann followed, carrying the large book. Verick didn't speak of their business again until they had passed through the open castle gates.

Market day was the only day the castle was open to all citizens. That custom of Toran had survived, though few of the villagers had a reason to visit the grounds, except the occasional young couple on a stroll or children playing chase in the open space of the courtyard. At this hour, it was all but empty.

Reann kept her feet shuffling at an extra half pace to match Verick's stride, and eventually tucked her arm under his to keep balance as they crossed the wagon ruts.

"The ledger," Verick said quietly, "should give us some information about—"

A hunched man sauntering past in the opposite direction swerved suddenly. His clumsy, uneven footsteps staggered between Reann and Verick. He turned to her and gripped the cuff of her blouse. His breath reeked of bad ale.

"Trouble you for a half piece? A quarter?"

Reann shook her head. "I have none."

"Leave off," Verick said. "Do your begging at the market."

The man, his grubby fingers writhing like the legs of a weaving spider, turned to Verick. "You are a gentleman. Mercy from your grace." The beggar stumbled forward and bumped into Verick. The two fell backward. Verick stopped his fall by putting an elbow against the corner of the aviary's doorpost. He swore angrily and shook his arm.

Reann laughed. "Funny bone."

"It's not funny."

The beggar stumbled away, grumbling about heartless rich folk.

"Wait—" Verick said suddenly. He put his hand to his coat pocket and patted it. "You there—Stop! On your life!"

The beggar dropped his cloak and raced forward.

It wasn't an old man at all, but a much younger thief. Nor was he drunk, Reann realized. He had probably soaked his scarf in ale.

Verick jumped forward, chasing after the lithe fellow, matching him stride for stride.

The expert thief had only a few more paces before he was through the unguarded gate and into the safety of the dark, twisting side streets of the outer village.

Verick lunged forward and the two men fell to the ground.

Reann hurried to the spot expecting to see Verick grappling with the pickpocket.

Verick stood and brushed his knee. He reached down and tore his notebook from the limp hands of the thief, re-pocketed it, and slid his saber back into its sheath.

The thief did not move.

Reann gasped. "He's not . . . you didn't . . ."

The thief lay in a crumpled heap on the ground, his arms and head twisted at awkward angles.

Reann looked around the empty courtyard, horror-struck. Her breathing caught in her throat as panic seized her. "No. No. No." She looked at Verick. "What have you done?"

"I have rid your castle of an unwelcome thief."

Reann knelt and touched the young man. She shook him gently. "He's dead," Verick said simply. "I told him to stop, on his life. I gave him fair warning."

Reann pulled her hand back as it touched the warm, wet blood near the base of the young man's skull where Verick's lunging stab had landed. She stood quickly, her own blood burning within her.

"You can't just take the law into your own hands," she said fiercely. "He has to stand trial before a magistrate and receive sentence." She stared at Verick, hatred welling up in her.

"What I hold dear is worth more to me than this entire castle. You would be good to remember that."

The notes, Reann realized. She was relieved for a moment that Verick had recovered them, but that thought only made her angrier. "I'm going to report this to the watch."

Verick moved with such speed and force that the next thing Reann knew she was pinned against the castle wall with Verick's hand clamped on her jaw.

"Stop it," she tried to say through the pressure of his fingers clamping her mouth. "You're hurting me."

Verick's face leaned close. He spoke with malice that stabbed at Reann's wounded heart. She shuddered as his words hissed in her ear. "Listen to me, servant girl. You'll do exactly as I say, when I say, how I say or you'll end up just like that fellow in the street. And don't think I don't mean it."

Reann closed her eyes as tears welled in them.

"At this moment, you are an accomplice. No? Try convincing a judge when it's your word, a peasant's, against mine. You'd be banished without a thought . . . or worse, whipped and executed."

You can't do this, she thought, but every ounce of logic in her told her that he could do exactly what he promised.

"We understand each other?" Verick asked, his tone grave and deadly.

Reann nodded.

"I came here for a purpose. We are engaged on that cause and nothing will dissuade me—least of all a common thief."

Verick released her jaw and Reann gasped.

"You had better get rid of that body," Verick added, picking up the register Reann had dropped when Verick assaulted her. "Dead bodies with sword wounds bring questions I don't have time for. Cart it away and throw it in the river."

Reann looked up. The castle guard, totaling seven men with mugs of ale in one hand and halberds in the other were coming up the high street on their patrol. The patrol route on market day conveniently passed several taverns where they received their usual bribes of libations into their empty mugs.

"It's too late," she said, her voice choked with emotion. "They're coming to close the gate."

"Then use that clever mind of yours and find a solution."

Verick turned and walked briskly toward the double doors of the castle.

Reann's heart raced. Her mind spun. She looked again. The portcullis was closing. The guards and their lanterns would pass in moments.

She glanced back at the aviary. The very thought turned her insides to lead.

"Please," Reann whispered. "Move." She grabbed the young man under his arms and jerked. To her surprise, the underfed body slid easily. She frantically tugged on the corpse until she reached the netted enclosure of the aviary. The door latch opened at her touch.

Reann hauled the body in, praying the famed hunting birds did not mistake her for their meal. The hunting falcons flexed their talons and clicked their beaks expectantly.

Reann folded the dead boy's arms over his chest, quickly whispering an urgent prayer at a speed no monk would dare. "Guardians of the sacred place beyond, guide his spirit, avenge this awful deed and absolve my sin." Reann turned and dashed out the aviary and closed the latch as tears began to stream down her face.

Two inquisitive hawks fluttered down, followed by another.

She turned to flee the scene of impending gore and then turned back in a panic.

The lock!

She had almost made a fatal mistake.

She unlatched the gate.

A drunk who wandered into a falcon's roost, thinking it to be an outhouse, could not lock himself in.

As the approaching guards' laughter floated on the evening air, Reann staggered toward the castle, clutching her stomach. Her foot squelched as she moved, leaving a residue of the thief's blood on the cobblestone.

Demons spare me, she pleaded. She yanked off her slippers and made for the shadows under the west wall. She couldn't bring herself to think of the noises coming from the aviary.

She washed at a well—her hands, her feet, her apron—but no matter how she scrubbed, she couldn't feel clean.

Not wanting to see the other girls, Reann returned to the basement laundry. She stayed there until dawn.

Reann jolted awake with a scream as something gripped her arm.

"Reann?"

She clutched her hand to her chest and sat up, blinking. "Oh, it's just you, Ret. Where am I?"

"Laundry sorting room," Ret said. "I've been looking all over for you." He stood up nervously, shut the door, and leaned against it for a moment, saying nothing.

"What are you doing here?" she asked.

"I just—" Ret began, "just wanted to check on you."

"Why?" Reann twisted around and cleared her drifting brunette bangs out of her eyes.

Ret's expression clouded, his face pale. "Someone died last night."

Reann grabbed a folded towel and squeezed it. Her heart nearly stopped beating for fright.

"The girls said you didn't come in."

"You think I killed him?" Reann said defensively. "How could you suggest—"

"No," Ret said. "Don't be ridiculous. It's just . . . I found this body in the aviary."

"Oh my," Reann said, burying her face in the towel.

"Head Butler had me clean up the bones," Ret said with a grimace.

"Is that . . . Is that why you came down here, for a rag to wash up with?"

"Yes . . . no. Look Reann, it's pretty obvious, isn't it?"

Reann said nothing. Ret had that overprotective look written all over his face.

"I didn't think it was you in there—I was pretty sure. I mean, somebody had to have killed that guy and tried to hide the body by putting it in the aviary."

"No!" Reann gasped.

"I'll bet it was that southerner who did it," Ret said, staring forward at the wall.

"Verick?"

"Was he with you last night?" Ret questioned. "Did he escort you back to the castle?"

"Well, no. I . . . I left him there, at the cobbler's shop. His shoes weren't ready yet." Reann's heart dropped into her stomach as she lied. "But you don't know for sure he killed someone."

"Isn't he in the middle of some kind of land dispute?" Ret, the lanky stable hand, said. "I wouldn't put it past him to end a fight with that sword of his."

"I made that rumor up," Reann said before she realized she had said it.

"You spread a lie . . . for *him*?" Ret said in a strained voice. "Why? What else are you doing for him? Is he taking advantage of you? Is that why you were out all night? Dungeons! Reann—"

Reann shook her head. "No, I'm fine." A chill crept over her. "He's just trying to—"

"Trying to what?" Ret asked.

"Trying to figure out a land dispute," Reann rehearsed. She was sick at herself for lying to Ret, sick at Verick for killing that poor thief and threatening her, and sick at the thought of what she had done to hide his crime. She wanted Ret to leave and stop reminding her of it. She wanted to scream.

"So he killed a man over a made-up land dispute," Ret said doubtfully. "What has he got you doing that's so important?"

Reann wanted to grab Ret and hold him and cry on his shoulder. She wanted to run away. But she had to keep it together or else he would be sure that something was wrong and keep pressing. She only had a few weeks and Verick was her best chance.

Reann focused on her laundry folding, pained by every forced motion of pretended indifference.

Ret reached for the door handle and turned it slowly. "It just hurts when you find out your friend's loyalties aren't what they used to be." He turned and left the room. He was running by the time he reached the stairs.

The pile of laundry had somehow doubled in size.

Ranger stared.

"I didn't mean to," Reann said.

The cat yowled.

"Fine, you can go if you want."

The orange-brown cat headed for the door.

Alone, Reann fell back on the pile of laundry. "It's impossible." Reann thought about dodging him, about never going back to the library again. He wasn't paying her, after all. She could even run away, but something inside her wouldn't even allow the thought of crossing him. He had killed without a second thought.

But he valued Reann—or at least he needed her.

And she needed his clues. They had made progress together.

Reann was closer than ever to finding an heir . . . to finding a future that wasn't folding other people's laundry.

I'm not a servant.

Reann's reason for finding an heir, be it the Furendali girl, the Montazi boy, or another was clear. And she had only three weeks before she could no longer pursue it.

What was Verick's?

"Perhaps no *good* reason," she whispered.

Verick wanted the heirs for a reason that was all his own, a reason he would kill for.

I have to find an heir first, before he kills me too.

CHAPTER 10

Montazi Realm. Neutat.

Terith squinted into the falling sun as he gazed out over the ruins from the steam vent. Huge boulders hurled by the explosion had left flattened corridors through the forest greenery. Remains from the megalith of Neutat littered the tops of trees. Broadleaf plants were riddled with holes. Sap oozed from mortally wounded fruit trees broken in half by debris from the blast.

He tried to wipe the sweat from his forehead, but the elbow below the scorpion sting refused to bend more than a few inches. He only managed to smudge dirt across the corner of his forehead.

He was leaving Neutat with no idea how his people would fare in his absence—and only Tanna and Werm to oversee the salvage operations. Nobody had heard from the last patrol. He had no idea when, if ever, the next patrol would go out. One thing was certain. He needed help.

He would ask Ferrin for help, they had all agreed. But the request to reassign riders to the border would come on the eve of the most important challenge in decades. He wasn't hopeful.

The brutal thought stabbed Terith. He couldn't compete, and someone else would win the challenge.

Lilleth was lost. His future was falling out of control.

Is this what Lilleth saw? Was this the end of our relationship?

Terith set into a beleaguered jog up the trail, heading to Ferrintat, the one place in the world he didn't want to be, the place where he would personally witness another rider choosing Lilleth.

Pert.

The very thought made him nauseous.

The night hike into the upper megaliths passed in the usual blur of waking dreams and near misses. Every time his foot slipped an inch on a rope bridge, Lilleth's words seared his mind.

Not the deep!

It was mid-morning with the sun shining over a blanket of fog in the deep when Terith approached the megalith of Ferrin's capital. He passed a sleeping guard and stepped onto the bridge, legs weary and wobbly. He had come fifteen miles in the night, with only a little water at a few shallow springs.

Terith moved hand-over-stubborn-hand across the bridge. It was decorated with streamers and flowers welcoming challengers and spectators for the race. He was so weary that only after his hands and feet moved did his brain realize he was still going ahead.

When at last he reached the courtyard of Ferrin's enclave, he collapsed. His vision swam ahead of him, until the thought that Pert might be watching struck him with enough force to push his body up. He stood shakily as Enala rushed up to him.

"Father, come quick! Something has happened to Terith." Her hand set on the taut muscles of his arm and flinched back in fright. "He's bleeding!"

"I'm not . . ." Terith protested weakly as the courtyard filled with curious guests and servants.

"What is all this about?" Ferrin's imperious voice brought immediate silence.

"Neutat is . . . destroyed," Terith said. His hand shaded his forehead as little lights sparkled in his vision.

Enala, who still had Terith's dragon-wing cloak tied over her shoulders, kept her arm wrapped around his waist like a mother dragon protecting her offspring. Only Terith gave no indication that he wanted to be coddled. "He's hurt, Father," Enala said. She gestured to his shirt and arm stained with the hawk's blood Tanna had used as a mild remedy for the scorpion venom.

"I'm not hurt."

"He's been stung."

"What happened?" Ferrin asked evenly. "Was there an attack? Where were the patrols?"

Seeing the mix of curious, pitying, and spiteful eyes all around, Terith answered, "No, steam vent."

Ferrin's face clouded at the mention of the accident that had claimed the life of Lilleth and Enala's mother. He looked at the gathering crowd. "We'll discuss this in private."

Behind the closed door of Ferrin's conference chamber, after recounting the explosion and the evacuation, Terith finally sat against one of the large decorated cushions surrounding the walls of the round bored-root chamber. He mumbled apologetically, "Forgive me, my Lord," as he buried his head in his hands to ease the dizziness. "We can no longer defend the border," he said directly. "The patrols are in disarray."

"Terith, I depend on you. This is no small matter."

"I know, sir. But my people have limits. The soldiers have families."

"We all have families!" Ferrin shouted. "Everyone in the Montas has a family."

"Then let them help the refugees from Neutat."

Ferrin stroked a mustache comprised of a few long hairs twisted together that curled around the corners of his mouth. "I shall send riders to shore up that section of the border as soon as the challenge is complete."

"But—"

Ferrin lifted a hand. "There is order to the things we do here, Terith. I must consider the spirit of the people. The challenge is as much a necessity as the food we eat and the air we breathe. I think you of all people would understand that."

Terith gave a small nod.

"Then what are you to do about your candidacy in the challenge?"

"I forfeit," Terith said at once. "My loyalty is to my people. They need my help."

"And what of your loyalty to *me* and my family?" Ferrin demanded, speaking of his unwed daughters, both eligible.

"My dragon fell," Terith confessed. "The others fled. I—I can't compete."

"How is this possible? Was there not time to rescue your dragon? Is it not as important as any of your people are? Surely villagers cannot defend the border as well as a dragon rider."

"I did save her. I rode Akara and used the awakening to rescue Werm, just before the explosion. He wouldn't be alive if not for Akara. But the explosion stunned Akara. She fell into the deep. I caught the ivy and was rescued."

"The dragon was stunned—and not you?" Ferrin said.

"I was in the light of the awakening."

"Indeed. That's a nasty scorpion sting. I can see you've been to the deep."

Apparently, he had heard something of Lilleth's vision.

"Nearly," Terith corrected. "Nearly to the deep."

Ferrin breathed a weary sigh. "You always find a way to make my life more complicated." He waved the back of his hand to Terith. "Get some rest—or at least pretend to be tired so my daughters will have an excuse to dote on you and I can get some work done."

"Yes, sir."

He stepped from the chamber and walked down the hollowed-out corridor, as he turned toward the exit, his chest collided with a rock-solid obstacle—Pert.

"You dropping out or not?" the beady-eyed thug said with a cruel curl of a grin on his lip.

"Yeah," Terith said, meeting his wild gaze defiantly.

"Too bad."

"Why should you care?" Terith said with a boldness his physical condition didn't back up.

"I'd rather beat you fair, so everyone knows it as well as me that you can't hold a candle to my power."

"You mean so everyone knows that you'll kill to get what you want?"

Pert blew air out his squat nose and looked around with his small, dark eyes as if gathering laughs from his nonexistent posse. "He talks tough."

"You bring shame on the Montazi," Terith said.

Pert put a finger in Terith's chest and pushed him off balance as he stepped past. "You're the son of a whore, Terith. And you'll die like the bleeding-heart runt you are."

The awakening flared near the edges of Terith's consciousness. He held his breath to keep it from coming.

Pert sneered. "Go ahead. Take a swing. It's your suicide." He gave another snort of a laugh as he turned his back on Terith.

Terith waited for a full minute in the tunnel. Anger raged like flames on troubled water, but the undercurrent was doubt and disappointment.

He climbed up out of the ivy stem tunnel and into the covered terrace in the courtyard. A volley of questions came at him from nobles, servants, and villagers—anyone who had kin in Neutat.

"How many died?"

"Did you see Mayat or Sherel? Are they safe?"

"What happened?"

"Was there a landslide?"

Terith raised his hand to call for silence. His blood-soaked arm stopped their mouths.

"It was a steam explosion."

Another barrage of questions erupted.

"Nobody died," Terith barked defensively. "I got everyone to safety."

Except my dragon.

He pushed his way out of the crowd. Turning the corner, he ran into the other two people he desperately didn't want to see.

Lilleth and Enala stood in the path, both in high-heeled sandals with white leather ties that wrapped around their ankles and calves. Equal in height, Lilleth's earth-tone hair complemented Enala's airy blonde. The two, with their dragon-hide skirts, made a formidably imposing barrier.

They had on their "business" looks, Lilleth with her arms crossed and Enala with a fist on her hip. Either girl he could have handled alone, but together, there was going to be trouble.

"Where are you running off to so fast?" Enala asked.

"I'm going back to Neutat," Terith said, trying to sound as congenial as possible to avoid provoking the riled girls. His clenched jaw and doubled fists told another story. "There's no help for my people here."

"You have only been here a half hour," Lilleth said with her usual calmness. "Help will come."

Terith shook his head. "This whole trip was a waste of time."

"What's wrong with you?" Enala demanded.

"He's seen Pert," Lilleth said. "You can see it in his eyes."

"Yes, well, *you* can see it in his eyes," Enala said. "All I see is somebody trying to run away."

"From what?" Terith said defensively.

"From us, for one thing," Lilleth said.

"From the race," Enala added, "and from Pert."

"I'm not trying to run away," Terith said, "I'm helping my village."

"Well you aren't any good to anyone dead. So you're going to get some rest," Enala stated.

"I'm not—"

"Terith," Lilleth said resolutely, "you're coming with us."

"Why—what are you—let go of my arms. Hey—you can't pull my trouser strings. That's cheating. What—seriously. I should get back to Neutat."

"Nuh-uh."

"Sorry. Can't let that happen."

The girls let go of his arms and crossed theirs. They stopped in a shaded clearing near the second guesthouse on the lower terrace. "Now that you're here, we can't let you leave," Enala explained. "Pert would win."

"Look, my people need me right now. And even if they didn't, I can't race. In case you didn't hear, my dragon is *dead.*"

Lilleth looked at him pleadingly. "Terith, any of the other riders would lend you their dragon and forfeit if they knew it meant you could beat Pert."

"Yeah, until he threatened them," Terith said. "Besides, my moves are dangerous. I can't do them without Akara."

"The race isn't until tomorrow," Lilleth spelled calmly. "You have time. Now put your head away and give your heart a chance. You have to believe you can do it."

Enala leaned closer. "What? Are you afraid? I thought fear was impossible for a rider."

"How about this?" Terith huffed. "Lilleth looks into my future. If Pert wins, I go home."

"It doesn't work like that," Lilleth said.

Enala turned a fiery expression on Terith. "If you aren't going to even try, even for our sakes, then maybe you aren't a worthy champion anyway." She glanced at her sister, who nodded.

An uneasy silence fell over the shade trees, reaching all the way down to where their roots embedded in the great ivy stems.

"Terith, you have a chance," Lilleth said. "Guardians as my witness, I want you to be the man to fix all the wrongs in this place. But the world doesn't revolve around you." She spoke with stinging intensity Terith had never heard before. "And you aren't that man . . . yet."

Her next words came on the gentlest whisper the air could carry. "If you want to convince me that you are everything that I hope you can be, you have to prove it."

"Likewise," Enala followed, brushing a strand of hair out of her face.

Terith swallowed. His heart beat heavily and echoed in his hollow chest, but his head nodded.

What did he have to lose?

His life? It was already gone.

"I . . . I'll get some rest. Then I'll go to the keep and see what I can find, but don't get your hopes up. I'm still a tall rider on a little dragon. I haven't much of a chance."

"You must not lose," Lilleth said, her voice ringing with a measure of raw, natural power, as if trying to hold back her awakening. "Everything depends on it."

"I don't get it," Terith said, turning away from the desperate look in her eye. "Last time I was here I wanted to race more than anything, but both of you wouldn't have me risk it. Now, when I haven't got a whisper of a chance, you won't leave me alone until I swear I'll do whatever it takes to win."

Enala took a watchful glance behind Terith and nodded. Lilleth looked over her shoulder as well and then moved closer. "Pert has the dark awakening."

"The dark—the what?"

Lilleth clapped a hand over his mouth and Enala squished his cheeks together between her thumb and fingers. "Quiet." She checked behind for anyone else on the trail and spoke barely above a whisper. "There is a different kind of awakening."

Terith tried to imagine what sort of nonsense Enala had invented and passed on to Lilleth to pull off with a straight face. "You mean bonding or something like that?"

"Of course we aren't talking about that," Enala said quickly.

"There is a *permanent* awakening," Lilleth explained, "but the knowledge of it was decreed to die. To even speak of it . . ." She put her hands over her mouth, as if she didn't dare utter the words.

Enala wrapped her arms around her as if suddenly chill. "We aren't supposed to know—no one is."

"Know about what?" Terith wondered.

"If you kill a Montazi," Lilleth said, forcing the words out of her mouth as if they were poison, "while he's in the awakening, it is possible to bind whatever forfeited life force they have to you—I don't know how it's done. I don't even want to know."

"So it's like having a double awakening?"

"More like being alive and dead at the same time," Lilleth said. "Since you're in both places, here and the place beyond, you can't be killed. The extra life force awakens you to danger. It strengthens you."

"It haunts you," Enala added, "drives you to darkness."

"It sees without eyes," Lilleth said.

"It can strike at a distance, like a phantom's hand," Enala said, "strangle you or . . ." Enala, looking suddenly ill, didn't finish the thought.

Terith shook his head. "Wait. You think Pert somehow—"

"Not think. We know," Enala said.

"How?"

Lilleth exchanged another anxious glance with her sister before speaking. "The night after you left, Father asked Enala to sing for Pert. She sang to free his spirit, as she does for honored guests—it's Father's tradition."

"I didn't want to," Enala huffed.

"Enala can see the spirits she frees," Lilleth said. "And she saw—"

"Don't speak of it," Enala pleaded. "I can't bear to think of it right now."

"I may as well say it," Lilleth said evenly, "She saw the face of the person Pert killed and bound to darkness, and . . . he looked right at her."

"That's enough," Enala said through gritted teeth.

Terith had never seen the lighthearted vixen so shaken.

"That's how we know Pert has the dark awakening," Lilleth whispered. "He has part of another soul bound to him."

Considering what the sisters were saying about Pert's power, Terith realized he had been lucky to escape his confrontation with

Pert. The question was how Pert had got the dark awakening, and whether there was any way to unmake it.

"There's a dragon involved, too," Enala added. "I sensed that."

"The velra," Terith guessed.

"Yes," said Lilleth. "The man and his velra had a strong bond. They shared his awakening. When Pert captured its master's soul, the dragon was bound as well."

"Pert can draw you in," Enala said, "and siphon your life just as easily."

That shook Terith. If he tried to use the awakening, he might end up just like the owner of the velra, trapped in Pert's devil mind, dead but imprisoned.

There was such a thing as seventh hell and a half.

Terith gripped the sides of his head, trying to make sense of it. All his life, he had prepared for mortal enemies and fought with his hands. Now it was as if he were suddenly a child again, helpless. "I don't know what to say. You want me to stand up to Pert, but if what you're saying is true, there is no way I can fight him."

Lilleth looked to Terith, her eyes pleading. "If anyone could do it, you could. We've all seen your awakening. It's almost like Serbani magic. You are changing time. Perhaps if he attacks with the dark awakening you can hold out longer, find a weakness . . ."

The words were heartfelt, but not convincing.

Enala put her hand on his forearm and slid it up to his bicep, her blue eyes and crystal necklace gleaming. "You are Pert's nemesis. You were meant for this. No one else can stop him. If he wins the challenge, he will marry Lilleth and take the rule of the Montas when my father dies."

"Which will be as soon as Pert kills him," Lilleth added solemnly.

Enala turned away and wrapped her arms tightly around her waist, her features panicked and pale, as if she were reliving that moment of vision when she had seen the stolen soul. Terith had seen that same look on Lilleth's strong features after she saw his future. But on Enala's porcelain face, it was terrifying.

"The Montas will fall into darkness," Lilleth said, with a tremble in her voice.

A shiver passed over Terith. Subconsciously, he took a step backward.

"Pert told us about the dark awakening," Enala said with a hint of regret. "He visited one summer, a long time ago. We were telling ghost stories. I think he was trying to impress us. I thought it was a lie, until—"

"If I know Pert," Terith said, "The first thing he would do is kill the person who told him the secret. Then he alone would hold the knowledge."

"Except for Enala and I," Lilleth reminded.

Terith's eyes shot open. "He wouldn't dream of killing you—would he?"

Lilleth shook her head. "Who knows what the dark awakening does to his thoughts?"

Terith ran his hands through his hair to ward off the fog of sleep that kept creeping in around him. "I—I don't know what to do."

"Just don't panic. I'll take you to a safe place," Enala offered. "You can rest in the loft above the looms. The weavers are on holiday for the challenge. Pert wouldn't look for you there."

Terith shared a fleeting glance with Lilleth, their eyes pleading each other to keep safe. Enala grabbed his hand and yanked him in the opposite direction.

CHAPTER 11

Erdali Realm. Citadel of Toran.

The day after the terrible night that ended with blood on her hands, Reann had avoided Verick. The second day she had returned to the library, fearful of what Verick might do if she did not. They had continued the research, but Reann could hardly focus. The images from that night were stuck fresh in her mind. For the rest of the week she looked in books and sorted through stacks of records whenever she didn't have chores. Though routine dulled the horror of her harrowing night, aching fear never left her side. Alone in her bed in the silent darkness there was nothing to drown out its screaming. It followed her every footstep in the castle, an unseen shadow, the face of the thief, a bloody sword.

For once, Reann was glad to be awakened early, even if it was to do pointless chores. She dragged her mop across the floor of the seldom-used Galant Hall ringed by suits of armor and portraits of once-important dead people that not even Reann had the time or inclination to learn about.

With every swipe of the mop she wished somehow that she could just erase everything that had happened like the dirty, dusty footprints on the floor. She was trapped. If she refused Verick, he might think she had betrayed his trust. He would do the same to her as he had to the thief. But working with him was the best chance to find an heir. Her only salvation was doing exactly as he said.

She had only two weeks left.

The girls talked about it, asking Reann what she would do, where she would go, whether she would apply to stay on the staff.

She wasn't popular with the head butler. She hated him and the feeling was mutual. Perhaps she didn't even have that option.

Where would she go? How far could she walk in search of a farm or estate in desperate need of a librarian or a translator?

Unbidden, thoughts of her bloody footprints outside the aviary rose into her mind. Her breathing quickened in a panic at the thought that someone might have seen her footprints and recognized them. Reann put her hand to her chest and tried to suppress a surge of panic. Her chest heaved nervous breaths despite her every attempt to calm herself. She glanced at the other girls.

Nobody seemed to have noticed her panic attack.

Carena dropped her duster and looked at her reflection in a mirror while she twisted her hair up and posed.

"Stuff it under a handkerchief," Katrice said. "You think you're some kind of noble?" She dipped her mop in a bucket and splashed gray water over the flagstones.

"You know what I think," Illa said, jostling Carena for a position in front of the mirror. "I think she's all steamed up about that Serbani lord."

"Am not!" Carena said, trying to stomp on her sister's foot.

"Reann is the one all steamed up for Verick," Katrice said. She dipped the mop and swung it at Reann's feet. "Maybe you need some water to cool off."

"You know nothing," Reann said, feeling anger rising. She grabbed the bucket and heaved the wash water toward Katrice's legs.

Katrice jumped out of the way and knocked Carena into Illa who screamed as she toppled into a nook and sent a lit candle stand crashing to the floor.

"Spilled wax," Katrice moaned as she picked herself up. She glared at Reann. "That's impossible to clean up. You did that on purpose."

"I was just trying to help spread the mop water," Reann said innocently. "Anyway, just let the wax cool. It's easier to scrape up."

"Did you read that tip in a book?" Katrice said. Her expression was crusted with early morning orneriness.

"Yes," Reann said. "At least I can read."

"If you're so smart, why don't you clean up that candle wax yourself?" Katrice snapped back.

"Let her be," Carena said as she turned to look in the mirror again. "She's obviously got her feathers all ruffled because we touched on her secret love obsession."

"What will Ret say?" Illa said, picking her twiggy self up. "You leaving him all alone for a sad-eyed southerner—"

"Maybe Ret will be so bored that he will actually pay attention to you," Reann said quickly, feeling hot.

"As if I cared," Illa said.

"Illa likes Trong, the butcher's son," Carena said. "He's the only boy her age that isn't shorter than her."

"Ew, ew, double ew," Illa said in her best impression of Ninat.

"Anyway, Reann," continued Carena, "I don't know what you see in that Serbani fellow—except his clothes. He dresses nice."

"And he's probably rich," Illa added.

"Definitely," Carena agreed, as if reconsidering the matter. She took a turn in front of the mirror, gazing at her flaming red hair.

"Which of you is going to scrape up the spilled wax?" Katrice interrupted. "Because it's not me. I don't even know why we're cleaning this hall. Nobody ever uses it."

"It's for a ceremony," Carena said. "The Benevolent Fraternity of—"

"Traders!" Reann gasped. Her mind shot back to Tromwen's parting request to find a replacement for him at the ceremony. "What day is it?" Her stomach clenched in a double knot.

"The fifth," Illa said. "I thought you were the walking almanac."

Blood drained out of Reann's face. "It's today," she whispered. Her throat was suddenly dry, her palms instantly damp. "I completely forgot!"

Katrice screwed up her expression, "Oh, no you don't. You're not making up some crazy excuse just to get out of—"

Reann didn't wait for the rest of Katrice's complaint. She raced down the corridor.

"Reann! I'll tell the head butler!"

She was well on her way to losing her only likely chance to get potential clues from a well-traveled Furendali woman about Toran's first heir. Fear spurred her as she turned down a flight of spiral stairs, burst through the kitchen and out the door. She slammed straight into somebody trying to come in and fell forward in a tangle of arms.

"Oh," she said, staring Ret in the eyes from an uncomfortably close distance. "There you are."

"Just noticed me?" Ret said. He put a finger to his mouth and wiped some blood from a lip that was starting to swell. "Or is this a really desperate hug?"

Horrified at Ret's casual reaction to a full-body horizontal embrace, Reann jerked away, trying to extricate herself from Ret. She stood up, still horrified at her predicament and now horrified at the idea that she was going to have to ask the boy whose face she had just bloodied with her head for yet another favor.

Recovering her composure, Reann smoothed her apron and held out her hand to help Ret to his feet.

He got up on his own.

"Ret," she said hopefully, "I just remembered there's a ceremony today and I really need . . ."

A sly grin showed on his face, turning to disbelief, then rapture. "You actually forgot?"

Reann was sure she was going to be sick. Her blanched face turned river clay red. "Please? Ret?"

"What do you want?" he said, touching his fat lip again. "Tell me it isn't—"

"Your lock picks."

Ret shoulders slumped. "I'm already late for breakfast. I'm not going to get any, am I?"

"Ret, I swear I'll make it up to you," Reann said.

"Fine," he droned.

Reann leaned toward him to embrace him, but he flinched away, so she just grabbed his forearm and gave a squeeze of thanks.

"I want food. Lots. I mean it," he said as he walked back to the boy servants' bunkhouse.

He returned from the bunkhouse—which Reann avoided at all nasal cost—with his precious tools, which he claimed, when asked, were for stringing his mandolin. Perhaps they were originally for that, but Reann needed then for something else entirely.

She took a breath, wiped her sweating palms on her apron, and with a newly composed look of placid denial she took the keys and darted back into the kitchen. Her hip collided with a basket of eggs the old cook Denit had set on the corner of the low shelf, and the chicken eggs took their first flight prematurely.

"Sorry!" Reann hurried ahead to avoid the splatter of yolks.

"Reann!" Denit roared. "The head butler will hear about this. You'll get the belt!"

Reann's already flushed face turned even brighter as she imagined getting swatted across the butt by a head butler who enjoyed that sort of thing way too much the older she got.

Out of breath, she paused on the stairs. Then she dragged herself up to the second floor, hurried down the hall past the Montazi armor, a stuffed snow bear, several tapestries, and a sharp corner, another turn and came finally to Verick's door.

Reann put her hand to her chest where her heart beat so fast she couldn't even tell one beat from the next. She opened the door and her heart nearly stopped at what she saw on the other side.

Verick, shirtless, lunged toward her with his drawn saber.

Reann choked a scream as the blade came to a halt inches from her chest, grateful, for once, that she wasn't as top-heavy as Carena.

Verick finished his maneuver with a swish and a flourish and dropped the sword into its scabbard.

Reann kept staring at his broad shoulders and the muscles on his torso and stomach, unable, or unwilling, to meet his eyes. The white scar on his neck ran down a few inches toward his shoulder, the only flaw is his toned figure.

Verick turned his back and took a hand towel from a hook on the wall near his washbasin.

"I . . . have . . . something," Reann said.

"About my land claim?" Verick said evenly.

Slowly Reann found her mind refocusing. "Yes—no, well it's a chance. There is a ceremony this evening. It's for a good cause. The Fraternal Order—I mean the Benevolent Traders Socie—no, I mean—" The name Tromwen had used suddenly escaped her in a way that was so uncharacteristic that the embarrassment sent her cheeks into even a deeper shade of burgundy, now rivaling the crimson drapes. "Yes, er, the Benevolent Order—er, Fraternity—of Traders."

Verick's lip twitched only slightly with the beginnings of possibly the first smile she had ever seen on his face.

"Don't laugh at me," Reann said suddenly. "I didn't ask to be sent here to . . . interrupt you like this." Again she involuntarily eyed the defined muscles of his stomach and then abruptly turned aside, deciding it to be indecent, despite the fact that Ret and half the castle boys went without shirts outside for most of the summer.

"You didn't?" Verick said. He paced a step behind her and out of view, something that pained Reann for more reason than one.

"There will be Furendali there," Reann added, inclining her head slightly to keep Verick's body in her peripheral view. "We don't know anything about their . . . land claims," she said, avoiding the word *heir*.

"I didn't come here for goodwill ceremonies," Verick said, recovering his usual sober mood.

"But you've been invited to preside," Reann explained. "I'm sorry I didn't have a chance to prepare you. The invitation was just passed from Lord Tromwen, who is . . . *indisposed* . . . to the senior noble at the castle. And that's you."

"Me?" Verick said. "What do you mean? I'm not even Erdali."

Reann clasped her hands together and squeezed them to keep from shaking. "Well, the other guests at the castle are merchants and there's a physician and his wife, and a land speculator who pays well for his room . . . when he can. There's a mistress of one of the—well, you get the idea. You won't get this chance again," Reann said, giving up restraint and turning full around to face Verick.

"What sort of ceremony is this?" Verick said.

"I . . . I don't know . . . much," Reann said, realizing how odd it sounded. "Just that it is for a Furendali lady."

"Curious. And you've made all the preparations?"

"This very morning we cleaned the Galant Hall."

"And that's why you're so out of breath?"

She blushed again and turned her eyes down, ashamed at herself for using Ret and Verick to cover for her mistake. But it was partially Verick's fault. He had occupied all her time searching for the heirs and cleaning up murders.

"I don't like to be lied to—misled, whatever you call it," Verick said.

"No, sir." Suddenly she had a mind to leave, to run away from him and forget Tromwen and her promise to cover for his absence and kill her chance at a position in his court and possibly a suitor and a comfortable life.

At least she would have her life.

But no library. No heirs. No position.

Nothing.

Her heart sunk into her feet where they gripped the floor with icy resolution. Her fingers closed on the skeleton keys, and the beginnings of an idea took shape.

"If you'll excuse me, I should like to finish dressing for breakfast." Verick lifted his shirt from where it lay folded on a top of a chest of drawers.

Reann turned out of the room and closed the door quickly behind her, catching it just before it latched as a strange compulsion overtook her. Her stomach whizzed with butterflies. With the door open just a crack, she said in an uncharacteristically playful voice, "If you must."

She closed the door very slowly, let the latch click and dissolved into a wreck of embarrassment, shame, and excitement.

She had *never* done anything saucy like that in her life. She loved and hated herself equally for the moment of inexplicable flirtation with a man older than her and a lord on top of it.

As she hurried away, Reann's logical side recovered control of her mind and she confronted the likely certainty that Verick could only ever see her as a servant with an aptitude for sorting papers.

She sank into agonized embarrassment.

If Verick spoke to the head butler about her moment of indiscretion—it wasn't flirting—she would get a double spanking, with the head butler enjoying himself like a cat with a caught mouse.

Reann was in over her head. She had to orchestrate the event with Verick to present the award and find a way to get the time to investigate possible identities of the Furendali heir.

She had theories, of course. The heir could be a relative of the Arch Hunter. Or perhaps the child of a woman who had traveled with Toran's armies as they ranged across the north while driving back the invading Nots clans. Perhaps a cook, a seamstress. Perhaps the mother had merely been a villager in a town through which he had passed between skirmishes, a passing fancy with a fateful consequence.

Reann had only to narrow the options until she had the answer.

Today was her best chance. The remote regions of the Furendal were the most vulnerable to attack from the Nots clans. That was where Toran had traveled, and that was precisely where this Furendali woman had traveled on her winter aid missions.

Reann would make it her business to help the Furendali woman get ready for the event, giving plenty of time for questions. For that, she needed the right sort of supplies—formal dresses, combs, flowers, fragrances—and she knew where to get them.

Reann felt for the skeleton keys in her apron pouch and then tiptoed up to the north stair toward the third floor. Midway, she noticed through an open window a camp of Furendali-style animal skin tents. They were pitched on the west side of the castle where Toran's annual summer solstice games were held and castle players reenacted battles in pageant style.

Reann thought about Toran as she gazed out over the long morning shadows cast by the castle battlements that reached to the graveyard beyond the field and the small, barely noticeable gravestone of the ruler of five realms.

She had seen him; she had even met him. Somehow, she was drawn to the enigmatic leader. The pages she had found stuck in the folio with raspberry jam had only fueled her interest in the mystery.

There are heirs of Toran. Somewhere.

A tent flapped open and a woman emerged into the misty early morning light.

She was imposingly tall—like all Furendali—with stern features. Her lower legs were wrapped in white fox fur laced with leather straps and her feet shod in fur-lined boots. Her leather tunic with grizzled fur lining spilling out from the edges was buckled with a metal-studded leather waistband more than a handspan wide. The upper portion of her tunic was covered by a contoured breastplate. Reann was stymied as to whether it had been roughly beaten into shape, or roughly beaten out of shape by other frequent collisions with swinging hammers.

Her arms, uncovered to her shoulders, looked impressively strong.

This was the woman who would receive the award. Everything about her matched: her strength, her confidence, even her age—old enough to survive winter expeditions and young enough to have the reckless unfettered courage to undertake them in the first place.

On the field below, the woman inspected the grass near her animal skin tent.

Checking for footprints, Reann decided.

A dog emerged from her tent. Reann's blood chilled as the feral features of the creature became more apparent—its long snout and rounded shoulders.

It was a wolf.

Did the woman know she had slept with a wolf in her tent?

Then Reann noticed its studded collar. *She keeps a pet wolf?*

It sniffed the air, and its toothy, salivating, long-snouted grin tilted up. The woman followed its gaze up to where Reann watched them both from three and a half stories up.

Reann beckoned urgently to the woman to join her in the castle.

The woman inclined her head, pondering the bizarre invitation from a servant girl to follow her.

Reann checked that no one was behind her and turned from the window, covering the remaining steps quickly and silently, hoping all the while that the woman didn't bring the wolf into the castle.

Reann passed the head butler's door. It was shut, although no dish tray was waiting outside his door. He was still eating his morning mush. *Another late night at the pub,* she concluded. *All the better.*

After turning into the south corridor, Reann hurried to the third to last door. She managed to get the hooked tool into the key hole and press a spring-loaded pin.

No luck.

A second try with yet another tool also failed. Then, using both tools at once to mimic a double-toothed key, she finally managed to free the bolt.

She ducked inside the room, leaving it open a crack.

It was a guest bedroom on the fourth and top floor of the castle, one reserved for high nobles, usually women. The fact that it was rarely used had suggested to Reann that valuables were kept there.

She had cleaned the room enough times to know all its secrets.

Reann moved past a mirror that she didn't dare look into yet, to a locked wardrobe. She borrowed a dressing stool, climbed on top, and was grabbing the hidden key from the top of the wardrobe when the door creaked.

Reann looked back, the stool tipped, and she fell hard.

The Furendali woman was quickly at her side helping her up. "Nothing broken?"

The woman's voice was achingly familiar, high strung, hard-edged, and bold but ringing with a genuine tone.

Reann walked off the pain in her hip and inspected her elbow. "I'm fine, thank you."

"What is so urgent that I should climb three flights of stairs before I've had my morning pee?"

Reann's faced blanched. She hoped it was a more ladylike saying in the north than it was in Erdal.

"There's a chamber pot here I'm sure," Reann offered as she moved to the door, closed it, then drew the secure bolt.

"Not to worry," the woman said as her eyes moved over the deep cherry lacquer of the furniture in the room. "There was a fountain in the courtyard."

Reann's jaw dropped.

The woman smiled. "A jest—you Erdali and your obsession with cleanliness."

"Hygiene," Reann corrected.

"I'll just be a moment." She stomped—that was the only way to describe how a woman like that moved—to the recessed corner of the room, divided by a dressing partition formed of tall, hinged wood panels.

"There's a basin of water there," Reann added. "It fills from the water collected on the roof."

"Your roof leaks?" the woman said from behind the partition.

"Not . . . exactly," Reann said. She put the key into the wardrobe and opened it with a loud squeak to reveal a collection of very expensive looking dresses.

"Now," said the woman as she rounded the partition and rebuckled her enormously wide belt. "What is this about—oh, no you don't!"

Reann rolled her eyes. "This is Erdal. And you are here for a ceremony, so you should look your best. Now, I'm prepared to help you get ready—"

"In exchange for . . .?" the woman asked warily.

"A few words—some questions. I'm terribly curious about everything and it doesn't do to be a know-it-all if there are things I don't know anything about."

"Such as?" said the woman.

"You, the Furendali—just anything."

"So you'll stuff me into one of those horrible dresses and interrogate me while you're at it—that's your deal?" She glared at the hanging dresses: pink, chartreuse, and lavender, velvet, lacey and buttressed, like so many foes waiting to be slain.

"It's just for the ceremony. You'll look ever so elegant. And there is a nobleman here to present the award. Look, I'll put one on, just to show you that they aren't dangerous," Reann said. She lifted a light blue silk dress. It was simple, but finer than anything she had ever worn. Reann slipped off her apron and dress and traded her under-slip for pantaloons from a drawer behind the left door of the wardrobe, then did a reasonable job of tying on a corset.

"How do you pronounce your Furendali name?" Reann asked, attempting to find out her name without looking like an idiot—she hadn't even seen the invitation and Tromwen hadn't mentioned it.

"It's Trinah. And it's pronounced the same in Erdali."

"Of course," Reann said as she pulled the blue dress over her head.

Trinah reluctantly cinched ties. "Like tying freight to my dogsled."

"You have your own dogsled?" Reann said.

"How do you think I rescue people, send Everhart into the woods with a map?"

"Who is Everhart?" Reann asked distractedly. She slid hangers perusing for a dress she could fit Trinah into.

Trinah laughed. "Everhart is my sled dog, the one guarding my tent."

"That wolf protects you?"

"He's only part wolf, and yes, he does protect me. He can hear my voice calling beyond four miles and be by my side before the hour turns a quarter. He has killed many wolves defending me, and I likewise defending him."

"All right, your turn," Reann said. She pulled a long gray dress from the wardrobe.

"Not on your life."

Reann paused, considering the situation. "Do you want breakfast, or not?"

Trinah's eyes widened at the threat.

Furs removed and dress installed behind the partition, the woman took a seat grudgingly on the dressing stool. Even seated, Trinah was imposing.

The comb in Reann's hand was ready for the battle of its life. Reann tugged the wide-tined comb down through her thick brown hair. "So this award ceremony is because you rescued some stranded traders from winter storms," Reann said conversationally.

"Well, dozens of folks, and not all of them traders," Trinah replied. "Some I wish I'd left behind." She seemed more open to conversation than other Furendali she had met. Reann intended to make the most of it.

"I've heard the traders talk about someone called the 'Lady of the North,'" Reann said. "Was she a friend of Toran? Is that why they call her a lady?"

"No. That's me," the woman said. "My clan folk call me the Lady of the North because they think I'm made of ice and snow, and that's why I'm not afraid to go out in the storms. The truth is, I'm afraid, just like them, but I go anyway. Lady of the North isn't a bad nickname, considering the alternative is my prissy birth name."

Reann sensed a reason deeper than mere courage, something reckless. "I prefer Trinah," Reann said, in her own and equally opinionated tone.

Without her metal-studded belt and fur, the Lady of the North exuded an entirely different impression. It was beauty, but not the frail look of a thin young maid like Reann. She exuded resilience and a distant, lonely elegance.

Trinah had squeezed into a wide-necked gray dress designed to droop folds of fabric elegantly in the front, but the fabric stretched tight to admit her broad shoulders. Her skin was snowy, but not as pale as most Furendali.

Reann noted the lack of hair on her chest. There were all sorts of epithets the Furendali hurled at each other having to do with lack of hair.

Trinah's lack likely meant she was only half Furendali. There was more to her past than she was giving out.

"You are very beautiful," Reann said, tugging down again with the comb to break through a snag.

"Am I?" Trinah said. "I thought Erdali didn't like the look of hairy northerners?"

Reann decided to press her luck. "Well you aren't full-blood Furendali, are you? You'd have more hair if you were."

Trinah didn't answer.

"Anyway, I wish I had long, thick hair like yours. Mine just curls and knots if I try to grow it out, so I tie it back. And it's dingy even when I wash it. Yours is so shiny—is it from eating fish from the North Sea?"

"My hair was my mother's gift," Trinah said. "But I haven't much use for it in the Furendal. I keep it under a fur hat most of the year."

"Is your mother still alive, then?" Reann asked. Trinah was in her mid-thirties as near as she could tell.

"Yes," she said. Trepidation weighed her voice uncharacteristically.

"And your father too?" Reann couldn't stop herself asking.

Trinah said nothing.

"Any siblings?"

No answer.

"I'm sorry—I didn't mean to pry. It's none of my business."

"Make it one or the other," Trinah spouted finally. "I'd rather have prying about my business than all this prying on my head with that brush."

Reann still knew very little about the woman or any of her clan who might also be part-Erdali. She wanted to ask Trinah if there were others, but the time was not right. She needed Trinah to trust her—to have a connection. She decided, uncharacteristically, to open the topic of her own past.

She took a breath to gather the courage. "I haven't seen my mother for so long that I can hardly even remember what she looks like. She left the year Toran died. Nobody knows where she went. Some of them say she ran away. I just don't know. It's rather a terrible situation."

"Was she married?" Trinah asked.

It was Reann's turn to feel the uncomfortable heat of a prying question. She decided she would handle it like every other fact.

"Not that I know of."

"Any inheritance?" Trinah asked.

Reann considered the question. She had a small plot of land in Fordal, or so she had heard. But any homestead there would have long since decayed or been turned into a stable. There was nothing for her in that place—no help, no food, no employment, no future.

"I'm a ward of the castle because Toran was my grandfather's commanding officer. My place is here, until I come of age," Reann said, feeling uncomfortable that Trinah seemed to know something of her heritage, rather than the other way around. "I suppose we're similar in a way," she said, feeling now much more contemplative rather than adventurous. "We both lack fathers."

"That is rather impossible," Trinah said in her terse voice that sounded perpetually peeved. "I can explain if you like. It's the same for birds and the bears. You see, when it's mating season—"

"No," Reann said shortly, blushing slightly. "I only meant—"

"I know what you meant. What I don't know is why my personal affairs are so important to you. I've been asked questions before—all the same. 'Who is your father?' 'Are you part Erdali?'"

"Well everybody has their own interests," Reann said, sidestepping the issue of her personal obsession with the heirs of Toran.

"And what are yours?" Trinah said. "Speak boldly, or don't speak at all."

Reann boiled. Her words came out in a burst of anger and emotion and hope and exasperation. "I want to find the heirs of Toran—is that so terrible?"

Trinah stood abruptly and turned about, becoming so instantly terrible that Reann shrank back.

Tall, regal, and defiant, Trinah stared at her with a piercing look that Reann had never experienced, not from any angry butler or lord.

It was imperial, and in that instant, she knew.

All her life she had imagined a moment like this and she was utterly unprepared.

Trinah spoke with an air of absolute authority. "And what if you found an heir? What would you do about it?"

Reann shook her head. "I—I didn't know. I . . ."

"Would you expose her? Would you open her to slander and intrigue? Would you force her to leave her country and sit on a throne—a throne she never wanted, never asked for? *What would you do?*" Trinah demanded.

Reann reached back to a short chest of drawers to steady herself. She bowed low and the words crossed her lips with a reverence that surprised her. "You are the unknown heir of the five kingdoms," Reann clasped her hands and drew them back to her chest, hands that had touched the rightful queen. She brought her fingertips to her forehead, the Erdali reverence she had once given to the great king himself.

"Enough of this. I want some food." Trinah huffed and stomped to the door, threw it open, and vanished down the corridor.

Reann fell to the floor, on her knees. She began to cry.

Through everything came the realization that in a few short hours, Verick would be handing a medallion of honor to the first heir of Toran.

All the searching, all the work, for nothing.

As Trinah had said, there was nothing Reann could do.

Verick, on the other hand, was a lord. He could summon the council of lords. He could present her to them as Toran's heir. Then, Reann would have a queen to serve and a place to belong forever. The realms would be united once more, the bickering lords put down, the traitors and fractious rebels dealt with, the armies restored to their border patrols. The five realms would stand as one, united in their strength. It would be a grand era of peace and cooperation. It would all be as it was meant to, as Toran intended it.

Wasn't that what he had wanted?

But what evidence could Verick give of her claim? Her own word? Some clue or couplet from his notebook?

Even if they did expose her, would Trinah just run away, or deny it? Would Verick try to force her to take throne as she feared?

Or, Reann wilted at the thought, what if Verick wanted to make Toran's princess his queen? Would he try to gain her trust, to get the crown for himself?

Trinah was too old for him, in her mid-thirties already.

Still, the very possibility unnerved her. Her decision was quick and final, even if it killed her.

I won't tell him.

CHAPTER 12

Montazi Realm. Ferrin-tat.

Terith's eyes popped open and the delicious dream he was having about Lilleth vanished.

"Are you ready, sir?" repeated the servant boy standing on the ladder to the loft where Terith was sleeping. "It's almost time for the challenge. Here, I brought some riding leathers for you." He held up a bundle of heavy leather riding gear with sturdy stitching.

"Who are you?" Terith said hoarsely.

"Aon," the boy replied smartly.

"Aon?" Terith repeated dimly, struggling to remember where he was.

"Yes, sir. The keeper sent me. He figured you'd want something to wear for the challenge. You've got a few hours before it starts, though."

"Dank dungeons of the seventh hell—I slept the whole afternoon *and* night?" Terith sat up quickly, hitting his head squarely on an overhead ceiling beam of the weaver's loft. He decided instantly that despite whatever Mya had said about swearing, it was not a demon's doing.

Checking under his blanket, he was relieved to see that the sisters had at least left his clothes on while he slept.

"Who did you say sent you up here?" Terith said, banishing the last lingering remnants of his bizarre, tantalizing dream.

"Bergulo sent me, sir. On orders from the lady, I think."

"Which lady?" Terith asked cautiously.

"One of Ferrin's daughters. I don't know which. I've left your breakfast on the cutting table down in the hall. Bergulo is expecting you at the keep. You still need a dragon."

Terith rolled his stiff shoulder. "We'll see."

"The lady also sent your cloak." Aon held out the pliable dragon-wing skin.

"Must have been Lilleth," Terith mused, "because I lent it to Enala."

Terith dropped down from the loft and suited up in the strangely well-fitted riding gear: leather liners, trousers, a coat, a vest, a wide harness belt, neck wrap, and hood, finally replacing his own boots with the custom hooks. The protective leather garment was a quarter of an inch thick in most places. He pulled the protective leather hood over his head, but left the mouth cover down, for now. Only his eyes would be unprotected from dragon flame when he secured it.

"The leathers are Ferrin's, sir," Aon added.

Terith nodded his thanks and squinted out the window slats at the mid-morning sun.

"Dungeons!"

The race was only a few hours away.

He lifted his dragon-wing cloak and tied it over his shoulders. It was folded lengthwise and top to bottom so that the four corners met at his shoulders where two ties gathered the four rings that held the corners of the lightweight, nearly impenetrable dragon-wing skin.

"What are those rings for?" Aon asked.

"Handles," Terith said tersely.

"What do you need to hang onto your cloak for?" Aon asked curiously.

"In case I'm falling and want to slow down. I can pull those slip knots and the whole thing unfolds."

"So it's for gliding?"

"More of a drag chute, unless there's an updraft," Terith explained.

"Does it work?"

Terith caught a bloodsucking wasp in his fist and crushed it. "Let's hope I don't need to find out."

"You mean you've never actually tested it?" Aon said as he sat on a stool in front of a large loom.

Terith sat down and began shoveling heaping spoonfuls of cold porridge into his mouth.

"Your arm looks well enough to ride," Aon said cheerfully. "I had heard you were injured."

"Scorpion sting," Terith said with his mouth full. "But I've got bigger problems."

"You need a dragon."

"Exactly. Let's go."

Terith stepped out of the weaver's cabin and ran down the trail toward Ferrin's keep. Aon scampered beside him, trying to keep pace.

As Terith neared the keep, his gut wormed with anxiety about what kind of mount could be scrounged up at such late notice for an extreme cross-country endurance race.

He emerged from the dense forest and he stepped onto the wide landing field. It was like sauntering into the devil's parlor. Even Terith, who had worked with the creatures his whole life, felt sweat slick his palms. Getting a group of dragons together for a race was an especially good way to arrange an unscheduled massacre.

Nine oversized cages were spread out in the landing field outside the cavern that kept Ferrin's dragons. They ranged from cubical wooden boxes with windows to nearly spherical enclosures of bent crisscrossing ivy limbs, all resting on wheeled carts or carriage poles. Like birds, dragons were built light for flight and could be carried to races. It kept them rested, but mostly it protected the public.

The nearest thing in nature to a dragon attack was a lightning strike—the only difference being that, on occasion, someone might actually survive a lightning strike.

Pent-up and angry dragons lashed about, turning, seething, screeching, and roaring at each other. Keepers with long poles and wands of burning pecan wood, a pacifant, worked to keep the creatures at bay. The potent reek of dragon dung hung in the air, along with the lingering fragrance of death.

A tethered dral in a coop nearest the cavernous opening of the keep caught Terith's eye. Its jaws were huge and muscular. Clawed fingers on its winged forearms gripped log-sized bars. Motionless, its eyes tracked Terith below its grotesque, leafy headdress of flat neck spines. The face looked like death had collided with a forest and spit out a dragon. Its chest was large and powerful. Of all the dragon species, the dral had the longest and strongest finger talons which it used to snare prey as it hung along the sides of the canyons. Its forearm wings were camouflaged like leaves of great ivy down to the scalloped edges and veins of the great ivy leaves. There was always something dripping from the corner of a dral's jaw, either saliva or blood. The predators were built and bred to kill.

The next two cages held dragons with muted green and yellow coloring that resembled fruit dragons, but their build balanced their weight more forward toward their larger wings. Their neck spines were the shortest of all the dragons, which only made the rippled muscles on their backs more evident. Terith recognized the crossbreed racers, bred for speed and strength. These were the most docile—until the race started. Muscle tone was evident in both dragons. They were in exquisite condition. Neither snarled or made shows of strength, conserving energy, waiting for their chance to take to the sky on their clean-edged kite wings.

At the far end of the clearing Pert's mossy green velra turned continuously in its enclosure. It had long, hooked claws on its hind legs and a pale blue-tinted underbelly. Its long, thin, barrel-like snout was loaded with spear-like teeth that interlaced on the outside of its red gums. The fishing dragon was sleek with powerful shoulders. It was built for diving and then climbing with its prey locked in its teeth or talons. In Ferrin's challenge that had both steep and long climbs, a velra was the ideal mount. Seeing the size and form of the dragon did nothing to ease Terith's anxiety about his own situation. The velra was magnificent.

Closer to Terith a lithe, long-fanged, gray strythe dropped the ram's head it had been gnawing on and let fly a burst of fire into the air—it was tired of waiting. The green wood of its enclosure didn't catch fire, but the smoldering rope lashings had to be doused with buckets of water. It reared back in its egg-shaped cage and barked loudly enough to pain Terith's ears. Birds scattered from nearby trees and likely every edible creature within a mile dove for its burrow—including several curious children unwisely wandering the landing area who quickly ducked behind anybody nearby that would pass for a larger target. Keepers cranked on chains about the strythe's wide neck, pulling its head to the floor of the cage, where its mouth could not open far enough to expel the flammable gas of fermenting ragoon weed from its pouch-like second stomach.

Nearby its rider was rubbing oil on the dragon's well-kept saddle.

Perhaps too well kept, Terith noted. Oil burns.

In all, there were nine dragons for ten riders.

At least Pert wasn't around to rub it in.

"There is the dragon rider of Neutat!" thundered Bergulo, the keeper of Ferrin's dragons. He gave a hearty slap on Terith's sore shoulder.

Bergulo was a distant cousin of Ferrin, a muscular beast of a man that Terith had seen more than one unbroken dragon submit to on sight.

"Where's your mount?" he asked. "It's almost time to ride."

"It's dead."

"Dead? You're joking."

Terith explained the steam explosion, sparing the still painful details of Akara's fall into the deep. "What have you got that I could rent for the challenge?"

"I won't take a single piece from you for using my dragons," Bergulo stated firmly. "But Ferrin's dragon Bander and all our largest war dragons I moved north to the keep at Breytat last week to make room for the challengers' and visitors' dragons. Still got a few, but they're trained for sky chariot work and rather timid."

Breytat was the better part of a day's ride away. Terith wished he'd thought to come see Bergulo the day before. But he realized that even if he had gotten there in time to find a dragon, that it would have been exhausted from an all-night ride back to Ferrin-tat and unable to complete the challenge.

"Have a look." Bergulo gestured to the gaping opening of the cavern keep. "You might find something," Bergulo said unconvincingly.

Terith walked into the keep alongside Bergulo, appraising the reptilian candidates.

The dregs were a sorry lot, either too old or too young.

"None of these could complete the circuit in a day," Terith said. Bergulo nodded regretfully. "What other options have you got?"

"None, I'm afraid."

"What about last year's crop from Neutat—any winners?" Bergulo asked hopefully.

"Hardly. And I haven't got time to go back anyway."

Just then, a page hurried into the keep, careful not to shout. "Sir, there's another cage waiting at the crossing."

"Another cage?" Bergulo wondered, exchanging looks with Terith. "But all the dragons for the challengers have already arrived."

"It came around from the southeast."

In the distance, the service horn blared out.

Bergulo yanked the runner around and shoved him forward so hard that he stumbled in to a run. "Get the strongmen to the bridge, lad. Ha-hah!" He clapped a beefy hand on Terith's shoulder again with a heavy thud. "Just you wait. Something's coming for you. I can feel it. You're not out yet. Ten times you should have been dead by my count. Fate has an appointment with you, Terith. Come on!"

With all of Bergulo's overbearing optimism Terith had a hard time keeping up a healthy skepticism.

From the southeast . . . Neutat.

He jogged with the keeper after the page and joined up with a group of four burly soldiers coming down from the guard shack.

Across the lattice and rope bridge, with its spider web of constraining tethers running out from along its underside, was a long lumpy figure leaning against a ramshackle cage.

"Werm!" Terith shouted across the chasm. "What are you doing?"

"I brought your dragon. She was getting lonely," he sounded back. His words echoed off the canyon walls over the sound of the distant waterfall.

Terith hurried across the lashed slats and embraced his oversized friend. Akara lay curled in the cramped crate, looking as though she could burst the thing to pieces by yawning.

Terith wondered at the sight, eyes wide and mouth agape in a split-face grin at his eminent luck.

"How?" He walked full around the cart as four of Neutat's border guards, who had dragged the cart fifteen miles in a day, fed long poles through rings on the sides.

Werm put his fists on his love handles proudly. "I took the archers around to the east side of Neutat to haul out another temporary bridge. The damage wasn't so bad on that corner. And there she was, snarling and doing like dragons do. I supposed she survived that blast—just stunned you know. She must have woken up before those flesh-eating flies down in the deep of the canyon got through her hide. Got a few nicks I can see. Other than that, she looks ready."

"So you got back on the ropes after your last trip across," Terith said, eyes aglow with excitement. "That's surprising."

"Tanna threatened me."

"I believe it."

"The keep was in good order when we came to it," Werm said. "The younger dragons had come back, waiting to be fed—lazy critters. Redif got things sorted out with the devils while we got the salvage operation going. Part of the great ivy stems were tossed over the half of Neutat that's still around. A whole bundle of homes is still there—just upside down."

The guards and strongmen from Ferrin-tat heaved the cage off its cart. With the long poles over their shoulders, they began the careful descent to the center of the footbridge, where the sway was largest.

Terith and Werm followed, taking places at the back of the poles.

"How is Tanna?" Terith asked. "Is she taking charge at the place of resort? Is she checking on the women and the elders?"

"Uh," said Werm lamely, "why don't you just ask her when she gets here?"

Terith nearly let go of the pole. "What?"

"She says she's got something you need and not to let them start the challenge until she gets here."

"Noon is noon; I can't delay the start—she isn't still working on the harness?"

"You said it, not me."

"But—"

"The big root her workshop was in was just hanging off the side of the megalith," Werm said merrily. "It didn't look like it was going anywhere so she climbed down and went back to work. I can't imagine it looked any messier in there. Sways a bit in the wind, though. She was puking her guts out after a while—I guess I wasn't supposed to say that."

Terith laughed as he reshouldered the pole for the ascent up the other side of the bridge. The weight of the dragon cage on his shoulder seemed to erase every other burden.

At the upper landing, the strongmen lowered the cage onto rough-hewn stone supports. "Mind that box attached to the side!" Werm cautioned. "You don't want to be banging that around."

As the strongmen filtered away, getting an earful from Bergulo about their disorganized descent, Terith pointed to the crated box. "What's in there?"

Werm grabbed his suspenders and nodded knowingly. "Emergency supplies."

"No it's not." Terith sniffed the crate and broke into a grin. "It smells of sulfur. These are fireworks."

"Well somebody must have thought they were emergency supplies because they showed up at the place of resort." Werm laughed heartily, slapping Terith on the back. "Those are my best whistlers. Congratulations, you've officially got yourself a chance."

CHAPTER 13

Erdali Realm. Citadel of Toran.

Members of the Benevolent Union of Traders had been trickling into the castle for several days. That should have triggered Reann to remember the ceremony. It was an inexplicable lapse in attention bordering on irresponsibility, a sin so abhorrent Reann felt as though she would never be rid of it.

To forget something made her feel like a normal person who wasn't at all clever and hadn't a clue or a plan and had to make things up on the spot.

It was excruciating, especially since Ret knew. He never forgot this sort of thing.

And ever-present in her anxious mind was the moment that had frozen into her memory: Trinah, her gray dress, and the morning light slanting through the room and cutting across her hair.

She was the Furendali heir, a future queen, the product of Toran's secret clan union between Erdal and the Furendal, but the only thing she could do about it do was try to learn more about Trinah.

Did she have a plan to reveal herself? Did she know the other heirs? Would she hide from her heritage forever? When Verick discovered her, what would he do?

Meanwhile, dozens of arriving traders called for bags to be carried and room arrangements to be made, demanding the dining schedule and tours. Yet despite all the work that needed doing by castle servants, Reann in her elegant dress never got a single request to lift a finger.

Reann couldn't help but smirk as she briskly walked past Carena and Illa, who stared with narrowed eyes and whispered behind their hands to each other.

Reann even caught a few of the younger traders turning their heads as she passed. It was an utterly new experience and she loved it.

She felt like she was floating.

Trinah, rather predictably, was at the aviary grilling Ret about the birds' hunting capabilities.

"Is everything to your liking, Trinah?" Reann asked politely.

Trinah didn't answer.

After a few minutes of conversation about the birds' peculiar eating habits, Reann added, "I think they're beautiful."

Trinah turned and looked at Reann. "Do you need something?"

"I ... no ... just came here to make sure everything is satisfactory."

"Quite," Trinah said and turned back to Ret who suppressed a chuckle. Then she added, "Until you arrived. Are you here to ask more questions or have I met my quota?"

Ret snickered. Reann gave him a crusty look and swished—not stomped—away.

Still hungry for information, Reann walked around the outer wall to the small Furendali encampment and quizzed some of the stoic spear throwers. The only information she gleaned from their mumbles—between chewing on some potent-smelling jerky and passing exorbitant amounts of gas—was that Trinah's mother had been the one who braved the ice caves to reach Erdal in mid-winter to ask Toran for help after the Nots clans had invaded their northern realm.

Beyond that, Reann was left to wonder—and worry. She went to the roof. It was the only place she could be alone, avoid work, and not run into Verick.

She stepped onto the flat roof with its short stone perimeter interspersed by battlements, feeling the hot sun on her back as the summer breeze tickled her legs. She took a deep breath and walked to the edge, looking out over the valley below.

"Not one for crowds?"

Reann whirled around, her hands pressed against the bulwark.

Verick had stepped from the shadows and now stood between her and the stairwell.

Reann shook her head.

Verick walked closer and leaned back against the same section of rock.

Reann desperately wanted to run. He could throw her over the edge. It wasn't safe.

Verick ignored the hot afternoon sun on his black trousers, hat, and waistcoat. The only bit of non-black fabric on him was the white of his shirtsleeves—gold cuff links and buttons ever in place.

Compared to an oppressive black suit, Reann was glad her silken dress offered some access to the breeze.

"You're wearing a dress," he said after a tortuous pause.

"Yes," Reann answered. She looked down and then up at Verick's distant eyes. "Do you like it?" she asked, relieved to no end that the conversation was not about what had happened a few days before at night by the aviary, or questions about her loyalty to him.

He glanced at her again and said, "It will do."

As far as compliments went, Reann had heard better from Ret, who generally compared things to the animals he worked with. Even a devil like Verick could recognize a gorgeous dress when he saw one.

That was the last straw.

Trying not to sound miffed, Reann said, "Have you practiced your speech for the ceremony?"

Verick just gave her a look he might have reserved for overcooked turnip greens and changed the topic. "You spent some time with the Furendali guest."

"Yes."

"Well?"

Reann shrugged. "Trinah is not very talkative. I must have gotten a whole ten words out of her in the first ten minutes."

"And?"

"Difficult," Reann said. Her feet tried to shift away, but she forced them to stay where they were. She couldn't afford to look like she was afraid and hiding something. "I . . . thought I might learn more. Honestly I couldn't get her to talk about matters of family and relations with Erdal, Toran's first war against the Nots, or anything interesting." She'd been practicing that lie in her head all day.

"What *did* she talk about?" Verick asked.

"Dogs . . . and food," Reann said.

Verick gave a half smile and a breath of a laugh, looking utterly dashing with one foot crossed in front of the other and an elbow leaning against the battlement. But the strange feeling that had swept over her when she first met him now only passed in glimpses before being swallowed in the fire of Reann's desperate anger. Verick had threatened her. He was using her. It only made her more determined to not tell him that Trinah was Toran's heir.

And he didn't even say I look beautiful in this dress.

Hours later at the ceremony, Reann sat between Trinah and Verick, feeling short, slight, and put off.

The ceremony began with a long round of introductions, which gave way to anecdotes and banter back and forth amid the well-to-do and generally overweight traders. There were representatives from all the realms: tanned, exotic Montazi traders in leather and linen; hardy fur-clad Furendali; well-dressed Serbani from the southern coast; charismatic Erdali; and the quiet, mysterious Dervani from the west deserts in their flowing robes. The ceremony location rotated each year, and the master of ceremonies noted that the last time it had been held in the citadel, Toran had presented the award.

After the formalities, the master of ceremonies, a very wide trader who probably needed his own barge to get around began his introduction of the recipient. "For services above and beyond the call of duty, for bravery and courage and fortitude, for actions of valor and generosity, and above all, for benevolence to traders and the several villages of the Furendal—"

"Oh, get on with it," Trinah mumbled under her breath.

"Seconded," Verick said.

They exchange a pleased glance.

Reann frowned.

"For missions of mercy—reminds me of that fellow we honored a few years back. What was his name?"

"Speaking of missions of mercy," Verick whispered.

"I'll need your sword," Trinah followed seamlessly, "quick and painless."

The two chuckled—they honestly chuckled in the middle of a solemn ceremony, with Reann between them, feeling increasingly like a little sister.

"To present the award, we have with us," the master of ceremonies looked to his agenda and read, "the distinguished Lord Verick of—well, he's Serbani, isn't he? How about a cheer from our southern traders?"

The five Serbani traders in the room beat their tables with their mugs. Verick stood, tugged his vest over his sword belt and stepped forward.

The change in the mood was palpable, like an executioner's arrival at a dinner party. Trinah enjoyed it best of all, the deadlier the better with her it seemed. She had worn her spiked wristbands despite Reann's verbatim quotations about etiquette from Bennion's Compendium itself. *A formal gown with spiked bracelets . . . honestly.*

Verick placed his hands behind his back. He did not smile.

"Rise, Trinah of Evernas, or shall we say, Lady of the North."

The usually boisterous crowd refrained from cheering at her pet name.

Trinah stood and stomped to Verick. She faced him, not the crowd—him.

Look away, Reann willed, still angry at Verick and not enjoying the way Trinah just gazed at him with her Furendali-style, closed-lip smile.

"I hereby present you with this award." He handed her the

medallion of honor with its red ribbon, which she draped over her own her neck.

Reann shook her head in dismay.

There was an awkward moment where they ought to have embraced or shook hands. They just looked at each other.

Reann began clapping. The traders joined in and soon the place was awash with mug thumping, boot stomping, and whistling.

Trinah and Verick exited immediately while Reann sat and fumed. Nobody had excused her. When the ceremony finally turned to the business of arranging the next meeting, Reann excused herself.

She had hoped Trinah would be an ally, someone to make plans with, her hope for the future, but she was rapidly becoming a royal nuisance. Verick's attentions were not on the table.

Reann honestly loathed him for threatening her, but that didn't mean anyone could waltz in and laugh with him in the middle of a speech and make eyes with him in a solemn ceremony. For one thing Verick had never apologized or shown any remorse, and for another, he hadn't even complimented her on her dress, which was drawing almost as much attention as Trinah's at the ceremony.

Verick had no right to receive fawning attention from someone like Trinah. He hadn't earned it and neither had Trinah.

Being a future queen had nothing to do with it.

Leaving the meeting unexcused was mildly embarrassing, but not as much as flirting, which she had decided she was willing to try in order to wrest Verick's attention from Trinah. She didn't want him finding anything more about her.

But how would she get his attention away?

Would she stoop to flirting?

Flirting with him?

She was horrified at the idea. How could she? He had threatened her, grabbed her, and totally ignored the fact that she looked beautiful—the first two being the most important and the third being there because women like Reann did not forget.

As she searched the castle library for the pair, she realized she wasn't quite sure she knew how to flirt. Reann imagined the way Carena wagged herself in front of the village boys, sticking out her chest and tossing her red hair when she laughed and doing blatantly immodest things like putting her *leg* up on a chair!

She felt ill. Perhaps she could stick out her chest a little, arch her back, run her hands down her dress . . . *Guardians save me.* Reann was already blushing when she reached the rooftop to look for the pair.

They weren't on the rooftop or at the armory—she thought for sure they would be looking at weapons. She called for Ret from outside the stables—she wouldn't set a foot in there in her dress— promising him her breakfast if he checked for them in Trinah's tent. He grudgingly ran out the castle and all the way around the outer wall and back.

From the look on Ret's face as he returned, Reann could tell it hadn't gone well.

"You didn't say anything about a wolf being in there. It almost bit my head off!" he bellowed.

So they weren't at Trinah's tent. They didn't know about the loose door in the dungeon. Not the stables. Not the aviary, the armory, or the library.

Reann drew a breath of shock. *The upstairs bedroom!* She hadn't relocked it. *No . . . not a bedroom . . .* They could be doing anything in there. Anything but talking, she argued to herself, would be fine. But all the other options perturbed her even more.

She raced up the stairs, a new and strange feeling of desperation fueling her as she turned around the corner into the corridor with the "mistress" room, as it was sometimes called.

Reann slowed.

There was a light inside and the door was slightly ajar. Reann opened it carefully, fear awash with a confusing blend of feelings.

Verick had his sword pointed at Trinah, who had broken the arms and legs off a hat rack and wielded it like a spear.

"Come at me once more—I've got your strategy all figured out," Trinah said in a devilishly playful voice.

"Excuse me," Reann said, sounding a little too much like a mother reminding children about table manners.

The two turned from what looked like some kind of sparring match.

"Is there anything you need, sir, lady?" Reann followed, in her most servile pleasant voice.

"Not presently," Verick offered, breaking the awkward pause. He sheathed his sword. "I thank you for your company, Trinah. I should retire and give you your rest."

"The sun sets altogether too early here in the summer," Trinah replied with a smile.

Reann had a burning desire to stick her tongue out at Trinah, a thought that horrified her.

Verick bowed and turned out of the room.

At least he didn't smile.

Reann followed him as he turned into the corridor that ran along the north castle wall. "Any luck?" she asked when they were alone.

Finally.

"Dogs . . . and food," he said. "What did you learn from the other traders?"

"They were all . . . busy," Reann said. It was true they were busy, but she probably could have cornered a sloshed trader and gotten everything he knew down to the details of his last will and testament had she not been so totally preoccupied with the Trinah problem.

As they descended the north stairwell to Verick's room, the lord offered his arm, slowing to accommodate her long dress. Reann took his arm, feeling like she was betraying herself. She took her hand off the moment they reached the bottom of the stairs.

Pausing outside his room, Verick said politely. "Thank you, Reann. It was . . . an agreeable evening."

Reann wanted to ask if being with Trinah was what made it agreeable, but not wanting to hear the answer, she said in her most matter-of-fact voice, "Do you like her?"

Verick smiled. "Why, I do believe you are jealous."

"I am *what?*" Reann said, horrified that Verick would accuse her of feeling anything for him other than spite. *Seventh hell.* She wished the wall would just fall on her. But this was her chance to draw him away from Trinah. She would have to take it. Everything in her body screamed out in protest as she stepped to block Verick's doorway.

She smiled, her hands clasped together, and doing her best to look charming in her light blue, floor-length silk gown. "If I admit I'm jealous," she said softly, "then you should admit that I was the most beautiful girl at the ceremony today." She smiled demurely, with her weight on one foot, shifting her hip to one side.

It was true. Only a liar could deny it.

Verick gently took her upper arms, lifted her off the ground, moved her aside, unlocked the door, and stepped into his room.

"That doesn't count," she said as she began to shut the door, intent on getting the last word.

"There is more to Trinah than dogs and food," Verick said, just before Reann finished closing the door. "It would do you well to notice such things and not just read books. She has an unhealthy degree of determination, as if she can't live with herself if she is not risking her life to rescue someone. Toran had a similar trait. Such subtle indications could reveal an heir where other clues fail."

"Indeed," Reann said, feeling like gravy had just been poured on her hair. Quickly she followed by saying, "I know many people whose personalities are quite the opposite of their parents."

"Indeed. And what would that make your parents?" Verick chuckled at his joke as he pushed the door shut and latched it.

Reann stood stunned. If she thought she were clever, then she had just called her parents imbiciles. If she thought of her parents as daring or dashing, she would be admitting that she was frightened and homely. She took a step, turned back, and spoke into the door crack. "They were lucky!"

She imagined a smile crossing Verick's lips. Leaning against the stone wall outside Verick's room, feeling the cool of it seep through her thin dress, Reann closed her eyes and logic resumed command of her senses.

What am I doing?

She was playing a dangerous game with a dangerous man and the fate of a kingdom.

She knew Trinah was Toran's first heir. She had what he wanted. He had clues she needed.

How far would she go?

CHAPTER 14

Ferrin-tat, Montazi Realm.

Clad head-to-toe in stifling thick leather, Terith opened the latch on Akara's makeshift cage. The gate crashed open as Akara shot out and barked a "chit-chit-chraaa!" that sounded off the cliff walls. The fanged face of the shrieking dragon was only a few feet from Terith, and it looked as though it meant to tear him apart or devour him.

"Hungry?" Terith asked.

Akara flung her wings outward, stretching them over twenty feet in length. She inspected the bat-like skin flaps under her arms and then gave two gale-force beats as she took to the air. A veteran of several summer campaigns against the Outlanders, Akara had twice the strength from training of any of her nest mates and was deadly fast in battle, the pinnacle of her species.

Terith watched as Akara winged out over the deep. She was a magnificent dragon, but she would not be enough against the larger velra. His mind raced, running over his options and willing Tanna to show up soon.

Akara slowed to poke her head under some leaves on the far side, only a hundred feet away. In other spots, the canyon was even narrower, though its depth could not be seen through the swirling mist of fog a hundred yards below that obscured the deep.

With a thrash, Akara emerged from under an ivy leaf that was almost as large as she was, her jaws dripping with red ivy fruit juice. The greens of her hatchling scales were all but gone now. The five-year-old was streaked with brilliant yellow, rapidly approaching the solid gold of a queen that would signal her virility. After that she would mate and leave to the sacred plain every dry season along with the other nesting pairs—unless she were kept captive by a rider.

After a few minutes, Akara stopped feeding and simply glided on thermal drafts.

"Time to see how well you remember."

Terith pulled down his mouthguard and whistled a sequence of notes: one to signal the target search, the second a dive, and the third a climb.

Akara's head bounced three times, heeding each instruction. A hundred yards below, a stone bridge crossed the chasm, barely visible through the fog. Akara folded her wings and dove. The speed of the descent was incredible. In only five seconds she was pulling up, leveling, and gliding under the fog-shrouded bridge and then—she didn't emerge. Terith spied a glint of green and the thrash of another pair of wings. "Dral!" Panic surged up. Without fire, she was helpless against the predator dragon that had ambushed her from under the bridge. Terith sprinted along the edge of the cliff, arms and legs pumping, heart and soul refusing to believe he would lose her now after surviving so much.

Twenty yards later he leapt. Without a second thought, he plummeted over the edge. Wind whipped his face. The ivy leaves draping the canyon walls blurred at the edges of his vision as he hurtled past. Free falling into the abyss, he pulled the two outer rings of his cloak and hooked them into his boots. Seizing the other two metal rings between his hands, he stretched his arms outward.

The cloak popped into an airfoil behind him. Terith arched his back, turning downward momentum into a diagonal dive.

The foggy deep rushed up with open jaws.

Beneath him, the dral emerged on the side of the bridge, trapping Akara against the stone between its strong green wings.

As the stonework rushed toward him, the awakening lit Terith's senses, slowing the world. With all the force he could muster, he bent his arms and legs forward, bending the chute into an air brake.

He snatched both daggers from his calf sheaths and sliced the dral's wings top to bottom as he rocketed past.

The daggers, with their special counter-curved, wrist-catching handles did not rip from his hands, but the force of the impact knocked him into a backward roll and the airfoil collapsed around him like a snare trap, plunging Terith into darkness.

The champion rider tucked, continuing the roll until the chute popped out behind him as he spread his limbs, face to face with the deep. Already surrounded by fog, Terith pulled his left arm and leg in, loosening the chute on that side. He sailed sideways until he collided with the slick rock wall of the canyon.

No ivy hung there, where the dense fog dimmed the sunlight.

Terith scraped along the rock, shredding leather, until the slope weakened and he ground to a halt at the edge of the bog. The foggy air was rich with the stench of decaying ivy and fallen rotted fruits that piled in the slime-ridden swamp.

Terith choked on a lungful of fumes and quickly loosed the rings from his heel hooks. He turned and ran back along the edge of the cliff in the direction of the stone bridge. The rock ended abruptly at a short drop overlooking the bubbling mire of the bog.

A buzzing hum sounded from that direction. A cloud of the thumb-sized white, translucent biting flies rose up out of the bog, like a horde of winged piranhas. Terith froze, hoping the flies could only sense motion, but the bulged, segmented eyes had already fixed on their target. The bloodthirsty flies ricocheted off each other in their frenzy to get the first taste of flesh.

The hell-born greeting party made a buzzing drone so loud Terith could hear nothing of the battle between the dragons on the bridge.

Hope for dragon salvation from the sky on hold, Terith pulled up his mouth cover and spun the cloak over him. Dropping to his knees, he tucked the dragon-wing cloak under himself. Moments later, he was pummeled from all sides by incessant flies. The cloak plucked outwards as the feeding frenzy commenced in vain.

Terith's mind swam as the awakening dimmed.

The lightweight dragon-wing skin wouldn't keep them out forever, and the longer he hid, the larger the horde of flies would grow.

A crash sounded nearby, a mean thump of flesh on stone.

Terith shot to his feet and whirled the cloak, flinging hundreds of flies outward. He ran in the direction of the fallen dragon.

The limp mass showed vaguely ahead of him through the fog as flies pummeled his arms, neck and legs, looking for the tears and weak spots in his leather coverings. Terith's heart leapt at the sight of the headless green neck oozing blood.

She tore off its head!

Terith dove under the carcass of the defeated dral as the flies diverted toward the source of the dragon blood. The useless tendon-severed wing flopped limply as he hid himself underneath it.

The diversion wouldn't last for long. They would find him eventually.

"Fire. I need dragon fire," Terith muttered, feeling along the dragon's broken ribs. He moved his hands lower to the abdomen. Scraping back a palm-sized scale, he plunged his knife under it, making a tear in its underbelly. He sheathed the knife and stuck his hand into the belly cavity, reaching as far as he could.

A rope-like shape met his fingers, its gullet. He gripped it. Sliding his hand down, he found the ragoon pouch, the dragon's second stomach. Terith widened the hole with the knife in his other hand and pulled the gallon-sized stomach out through the hole.

It was full. This was a mating dragon just back from the sacred plain.

He cut it free, wincing as the acrid odor seared his eyes and throat. Terith quickly tied a knot in the severed back end of the pouch. Tucking it under his arm like a bagpipe, he wrapped his hand around the throat section and kicked back the wing of the dral.

The storm of flies converged on him.

He squeezed the pouch and sprayed liquid fire into the air in a wide arc, lighting the deep in a firestorm of self-combusting fumes. Like living fireworks, hundreds of the grotesque translucent flies darted blindly for cover, burning as they went, their bodies screaming and popping in the searing blaze.

Terith ran up the slimy side slope, following a seam in the moss-laden rock. Rivulets of vile condensation ran down the stone where the slope steepened into a sheer cliff. The seam in the rock narrowed rapidly to a finger crack. Terith was at a dead end.

Buzzing sounded again, growing louder with each desperate breath that Terith pulled from the dank air in the deep. He whistled three times calling for his dragon.

Nine heart-wrenching seconds later, Akara soared silently downward through the mist, the severed head of the dral still clenched between her jaws. Turning her back to the cliff wall, she beat her wings in a two-beat hover, blasting a fleet of flies back into the shadowy darkness below.

Terith leapt from the rock onto her back. As her strong wings carried him out of the fog, Terith welcomed the sunlight like an old friend he thought he might never see again. His heart beat heavily with the rush of the fall, the fight, and the thrill of his escape from the deep.

Ferrin's soldiers had come out onto the bridge. They waved and cheered as Akara rose out of the deep and over the bridge.

Terith dismounted when she neared the base of a waterfall-powered supply lift to save her the extra weight and conserve energy for the race. For a dragon, climbing altitude with a rider on its back was no less difficult than a man carrying another person up a hill.

Terith climbed into the wicker basket elevator, and with Akara gliding on the thermals, they rose together.

A loud crowd had gathered at the top platform. Apparently somebody had seen him jump and word had spread quickly. Out of the rancor of shouts, a familiar voice caught his attention.

"Just what do you think you are doing?" Tanna bellowed, dragging him by his collar from the wicker basket at the top of the fall. "The race starts in twenty minutes."

"I was just warming up. And there's a bit of ceremony at first, we'll be fine."

"Not funny."

"The dragon-wing cloak works, by the way," Terith said, grinning from ear to ear.

"Shut up and put this on." She shoved the chest harness at him, turning up her nose. "You reek like second hell!"

Terith buckled the harness and then pulled the leather thread waistband off Tanna's dress.

"Terith!" she snapped angrily as Terith wrapped the leather cord around the end of the of dral stomach.

"Dragon fire," he explained. "Can't have it leaking on me."

Tanna scowled. "A lot of trouble you are."

"The blood on your knives makes for a nice bit of intimidation," Werm added, hurrying alongside them as the crowd, including a surprising number from Neutat, thronged Terith on the path to the clearing in front of the keep. "What's that Akara has in her mouth?" Werm asked, gesturing at the severed dral head.

"Breakfast. You hungry?"

"Er, no."

Werm loaded a pack onto Terith's back as they moved along the quarter-mile shortcut to the keep. "There are three whistlers in there: one sharp-tipped, two with tether lines, plus the torch for the cave. Only one problem—how are you going to light the things?"

Terith patted the dral stomach. "I've got it covered. Everything else ready?"

"Ready," Werm said. "Just finished setting up your start."

"One more thing," Tanna added, "the signal beacons on the south range were lit last night. The horde is on the move again. The southern patrol didn't get back before I left so we don't know how far north and west the Outlanders have come."

"This is early in the season for the Outlanders to bring trouble," Werm grumbled. "Doesn't bode well."

"I'll worry about the horde after the race," Terith said, adopting

Ferrin's "tradition before trouble" philosophy. His mind was focused on one thing.

Terith and his friends rolled out from the forest trail and dissolved into an even larger crowd. Montazi crowded the landing area outside the keep for the start of the challenge. By Terith's estimate, there were over three thousand spectators lodged up in trees and camped on the sloping hillside above the green. Some poorly supervised teens made a show of wandering dangerously close to the winged terrors.

The dragons were all free of their enclosures, held only by insignificant rope tethers.

With the ceremony on the verge of starting, Terith strode purposefully across the grassy space. Eyes turned as he marched past, the spectators whispering and pointing at the arms of his leathers that were stained to the elbows with glistening dragon blood.

"What's this nonsense?" Pert said.

"Just tidying up a bit."

"He's been down by the bridge," hissed one of Pert's henchmen, coming up behind the short, stout menace to whisper in his ear.

"Setting traps, are you?" Pert accused.

"Actually, I was saving your hide. There was a dral waiting underneath the first bridge. I took care of it for you."

"What a story, Terith. Did you kill a sheep and pour blood on your hands? Rather pathetic."

Terith ignored Pert, but took a spot at the far end of the row of nine other challengers that had lined up in front of the opening of the keep. The reek of dragon gore turned noses as he went. "Ah, here she comes," Terith said merrily.

Akara flew low over the crowd, sending children under their mothers' skirts. Gleaming golden in the noon sun, she landed with a thump and hurled the still-dripping dral head into the center of the clearing.

Flaring her wings, her face turned in a long arc screaming a loud, "Ree-at! Chit-chit-chit!" It was a posture of absolute dominance— a threat and a challenge. Terith blessed her for it. It was a charade since she had no fire.

Bergulo and Werm worked to subdue her as the other dragons shifted their weight uneasily from foot to foot. Three of the dragons tucked their wings in a display of submission, to their riders' embarrassment. The dral stared unblinkingly at Akara, flexing its claws. Pert's velra hissed and raised its head, stretching its neck out, begging a fight.

"She's looking prime, mate!" Werm shouted eagerly, as he worked his way back through of the crowd toward Terith and the other nine challengers. "And she's in a good mood, too."

Pert glared at Terith from the center of the group.

That was when Terith felt it, a black presence probing him, jabbing at his consciousness.

Terith resisted the feeling of doubt and pitiful lack of ability that seemed to drain out his confidence like a slashed water skin. He felt exposed, guilty, weak. *It's just a trick.*

"Not feeling well, runt?" Pert grunted from outside Terith's reach.

The horror felt as real as festering battle wounds or the poison of bad meat in his stomach. It was an incapacitating, indomitable feeling of total failure.

Terith struggled to call up the awakening. So soon after he had exhausted its strength, no light came to his mind. Darkness seemed to close in around him like a wall, even as Ferrin stood upon a platform to make his speech. His words echoed in Terith's mind, behind the dark curtain Pert had closed around him.

"Greetings, all." Ferrin proceeded to introduce each of the challengers one by one.

Terith struggled for breath. *Hurry up.* Shallow, gasping breaths and a sudden dizziness forced Terith to put his arm on the challenger at his side to keep from falling.

"Hands off," the man said angrily, knocking Terith's bloody hand from his shoulder and shoving him away.

That was the trigger. The light flooded the horizon of Terith's consciousness. He pushed back on the bands of darkness. Chest heaving a deep breath of fresh Montas air, Terith stood tall, defying Pert's dark attack on his mind.

I'll have to keep my distance.

"Gomder, champion of the fine southern city of Cafertat," Ferrin announced to a smattering of applause. The somewhat scrawny rider next to Terith raised his arm then glared at Terith. He was the son of the annoying businessman that had bothered Terith at the feast.

He decided to keep an eye on him. Pert would have paid or threatened riders to gain allies in the race, and the bitter young southern rider with the picked-on look was too easy a target for Pert's domination.

"And lastly, Terith, champion of Neutat."

Terith raised his crimson fist into the air as a roar louder than the dragons sounded from the crowd. Looking over the faces, he realized nearly the entire village of Neutat had come to watch.

Terith smiled as the crowd continued to cheer, heedless of Ferrin's inaudible calls for order.

"Silence!" Pert cried imperiously, with a voice that rocked the air like a cannon shot.

The crowd fell into a stunned quiet.

"The rules are simple," Ferrin stated. "There will be no other rules." He read from a leather scroll, "Each challenger's dragon must pass all the obstacles—under the first bridge, over the second, through the tunnel of Drimwood, over the summit of Candoor—and retrieve a token. The dragon must return and its rider must enter the keep alive before noon on the second day and present the token.

"Each successful champion will be given the right to choose their mates in order of their arrival from among the eligible," he gestured to the collection of alluring and, most importantly, powerfully talented women gathered on the opposite side of the clearing from the riders.

This year, at their father's behest, both Lilleth and Enala were among the eligible, a nominally wise move to placate someone like Pert who might otherwise make a bitter enemy if they lost. But unless Pert took an unlikely third place, one of his daughters was doomed to a union with the twisted demon. Ferrin's sacrifice to keep the realm together threatened to destroy his family.

Anger at Pert welled up inside Terith as Ferrin spoke about the consequences of killing another rider.

"If a rider is slain by direct action of another challenger, the challenger responsible must accept the burden of the slain's debt, dealings, and defense of their village until another champion is chosen."

"Spoils of war," Pert said matter-of-factly, face forward, in the hearing of all the challengers.

Terith clenched his jaw.

"Riders to your mounts!" Ferrin called.

Pert knocked a few riders aside to command the point position in the group as challengers raced across the clearing, fanning out to their dragons.

Terith leapt on Akara and caressed her jaw. "Got something left for the race? Hmmm?"

She licked blood off her teeth, eyes alight, stretching her wings.

"Ride with the light," Bergulo said. "May you live to see the dragons return."

"May the dragons return."

Terith looked across the clearing. Enala was already in tears. Lilleth held her against her chest. Other eligible women waved to their favored champions.

Ferrin cried out, "Begin!"

CHAPTER 15

Erdali Realm. Citadel of Toran.

Putting aside her fear, Reann forced herself to keep up her regimen of research with Verick. She was rapidly running out of time, and progress toward finding an heir that would take the throne was painfully slow.

It would have gone infinitely faster if Verick wasn't so tight-lipped about the clues in the notebook of his that he regularly perused. He only occasionally shared tidbits with Reann.

It was pure torture. Her life was ending. She needed those notes.

A week after Trinah's ceremony, Verick sat across from Reann in the library, his feet on the table, looking pleasant and pleased.

How could she get his trust?

Reann had even considered telling him about Trinah, if only to endear herself more to him. But she was locked up inside about that. She had been burnt by a fire she didn't know how to control and wasn't ready to throw in more fuel.

The mid-summer gala, the solstice festival in honor of Toran's birthday, approached. The head butler had already come to remind her that the debt Toran's estate owed for her grandfather's military service would be paid up when she officially became of age.

"One week," he had said, not giving the traditional offer for a permanent staff position. "Then you will pack your things."

Reann looked over to Verick and caught him stealing a glance at her, something that filled her with strange feelings she didn't want to process.

Should she allow herself to enjoy his attention? Should she hate him?

Should she hate herself for wanting something she shouldn't? Should she just stop worrying?

Reann lifted a small document folder and fanned her neck to cool herself, but it wasn't the overcast weather that was hot.

Verick looked up from studying the notes that he never let out of his grasp. It was torture not knowing what those notes held: clues to the heirs and possibly clues to Verick's intentions and his past.

"Reann, what do you know of the Witch of Essen?" he asked.

Reann stopped fanning. "On what topic?"

"Her relationship with Toran, if you please," Verick replied.

Reann considered it. "It's complicated." She stood and paced slowly into the center of the circle of comfortable reading chairs. "Of course you know she was the twin sister to Tira, the witch queen of Hersa."

"I do," Verick said.

"Then you must also know that Toran was once betrothed to Tira. Their fathers had promised an alliance: Toran and Tira would marry and produce a joint heir," Reann added.

"Yes, I had heard as much," Verick admitted. "Though I thought it might have been only a rumor."

"Toran and Tira had a falling out," Reann said. "Then Tira was exiled by the Serbani magicians for some sort of treachery or other—I think she killed her teacher."

"True," Verick agreed. He leaned forward.

"They had opposite powers from birth," Reann said. "Tira had the gift to take life, and Onel, her sister, could save it—she became the healer of Essen." Reann toyed with the string at the top of her blouse as she considered for the first time the literal wording in the contract.

Joint heir.

A flash of intuition sent Reann dashing toward the historical section where she kept documents of special interest tucked in the middle of an impenetrable stack of financial contracts.

Reann lifted the pile of miscellaneous records and hurried back to the table. She flipped through the pile until she spied a very old one written in cryptic Dervite hieroglyphics.

"I've got it," Reann cheered, laying the sheet of parchment in front of her.

The southern noble leaned over her shoulder. "This is in Dervish—looks like a bunch of scribbles and gibberish."

"Not to me," Reann said. "This marriage contract was written out in Dervish so that other Serbani wouldn't come across it and make accusations. For Essen to side with Erdal rather than the Serban was treacherous. It's a mountain region on the border. They have equal trade with the coast and the plains."

"Interesting," Verick said eagerly. "What does it say?" He drew his chair next to Reann and leaned over her shoulder.

Reann's breath stopped as his chest brushed the back of her shoulder. Then she focused on the pictograms, extracting the meaning like oil from an olive press. "*It is hereby sworn that the first son of Erdal*—that means Toran," Reann explained, "*and the heiress of Essen, shall produce a joint heir to unify the* . . . oh the next part is tricky," Reann admitted. "I'm not entirely sure how it ends, but the gist of it is there."

"Curious," Verick said. "Tira was the heiress, but she was exiled. That would mean—"

"Onel inherited the contract," Reann said with a smile that quickly fell. "But she married Lord Angot, a Hersian political émigré."

"Then the contract was broken," Verick said, not hiding his dismay. "There never was a joint heir."

Reann returned the contract to the pile. Her fingers froze. "Unless . . ." The idea was plausible. "Do you recall that after Lord Angot died and the Tower of Essen came under siege, Onel sent to Erdal for help?"

"Yes, and Toran came," Verick said. This time he stood and paced. "He went straight from the Outlands with the dragon riders and his cavalry. They broke the siege."

"They saved the coast," Reann said. "So Toran was there. And at the time Onel was *recently widowed.*" A thrill of excitement ran through her, raising goosebumps on her arms.

"You think Onel mothered an heir of Toran? The Serbani *witch?*" Reann beamed. "It has to be."

Verick leaned closer, peering at the whirls and wheel-like pictograms on the contract. "Supposing this guesswork is fact, it begs the question: where is the heir now?"

Reann's mind sputtered. "I ... I don't know exactly. It shouldn't be too hard to find out where. There might still be some survivors living here and there."

Verick rubbed his chin and frowned. "Another dead end. Essen is just a relic now. It was abandoned after the truce with the Dervites. They say the old tower is haunted. Nobody dares live within its shadow. What else do we have?"

"It's the best I can do," Reann said.

"Are you proposing I saddle my horse and ride two weeks to Essen and dig through the rubble for more clues?" he said, his voice rising. "There *has to be something.* Is there anything verifiable?"

If he would give her full access to his notes, she could certainly make quicker progress. She could keep some of the better clues for her personal research and pass Verick measured amounts to keep him satisfied until he lost interest. But how could she convince him to give her the clues? Apparently she still didn't have his full trust.

"If we have nothing else," Verick said, sounding decisively final, "then I will find someone else to assist me with my research."

Reann gave an uncomfortable laugh. "I don't think that—"

"Perhaps you are not telling me everything you know." He stepped closer. "Perhaps there is some nugget of information you have gleaned from your lifetime of study in this—" he gestured with a hand, "place. Surely you must have met people. Surely you must have been privy to private conversations."

Verick stood directly in front of Reann, looking down at her.

"If you mean spying—"

"You know what I mean," Verick said. "If you can't provide anything of actionable value then we are both wasting our time. I have no need of you. I'll take my effort and my notes and move on."

She wasn't prepared for that. Verick could just leave. He could leave her alone, the way she was, a mean castle servant with no future to speak of and no . . . him. Reann's gut twisted. Everything was slipping away so suddenly. She had found an heir, but Trinah had gone, apparently determined to do nothing about the empty throne. Now, without any convincing evidence to continue his search, Verick could just leave Reann.

She was on the verge of something. Something was happening. She could feel it, somehow. Finding Trinah was just the start. Things were beginning to come together. It was as if her ship were just a skeleton of timbers being put to sea unfinished, to sink. It was all slipping away.

"Speculation," Verick said, "unfounded rumors—if this is all we can muster I can't see any point in continuing."

"That's—that's not necessary," Reann said.

"You know something . . . something that would put an heir of Toran within our reach? Something about the Erdali heir, or the Furendali, perhaps?"

"Ah." Her gut twisting itself over in knots, Reann struggled to keep her posture and her gaze steady.

She wanted to run. But she wanted a life even more. She wanted the notes.

Reann looked down at her servant's smock and then back up at the vaulted ceiling. "There may be something."

It's worth it, she told herself. *Just this one piece.* She had to get him to trust her—just enough information to get access to the notes. Then she could misguide his investigation with false clues and continue the search for the other heirs herself.

Reann's conscience screamed momentarily as she temporarily shut it into the coat closet of her heart. She held her breath, feeling her heart beat anxiously against her chest. Needing space, she turned away from Verick and sat on the edge of an armchair, not even caring that it was bad manners.

Trinah doesn't want the throne anyway, she reasoned. It was a sour excuse and she knew it the moment it popped into her head. But it stuck. *I just need a little more time,* she thought. *I can find another heir. I can make this happen.*

Reann interlocked her fingers to keep them from shaking. If she balked now he would know she knew something and extract it from her by force, or if he thought her to be of no value he might discard her somewhere.

The aviary.

Reann nodded, plucking courage and clearing her throat. "When the Nots clans burned the northern forests as a prelude to invading the Furendal, the starving wolves invaded the Furendali villages, stealing children and raiding their food supplies. Erdali records say a small group tried to cross the southern pass in winter to seek help from Erdal, but only one survived the descent under the ice sheet into the plains of Toran's realm."

"It was a woman," Verick seized, "of course."

Reann continued the tale. A note of confidence gathered in her voice. "Toran was so moved by her courage and the plight of her people that he gathered volunteers to lead the rest of the Furendali refugees down into Erdal. The next summer he led his volunteers against the Nots. That was Toran's first expedition outside the plains of Erdal. He was only twenty-six."

"This woman, she must have been very important—perhaps even the mother," Verick twirled his hand. "But where is the heir?" Verick asked directly. He stepped toward her again. His ever-present saber dangled by his side. "I grow impatient of your meandering."

He still doubted her.

"Births among the Furendali are recorded for taxation purposes and military service orders," Reann blurted out. She continued speaking each word warily, softly now, as if he was a wild creature to coax back into its den. "And their colonies are too small for an unwed birth to go unnoticed."

"My sources say there is not a single record of the birth," Verick said. His eyes flicked to the notebook in his vest pocket. "What do you know that nobody else does?" His posture cried out for the information. His hands gripped his sword hilt as if it were a safety rope and he were about to be tossed overboard.

"Well," Reann said, choking past the tightness in her throat, "the *female* births are not written down in the official record."

"The heir was a *girl!*" Verick gasped, as the missing piece of the puzzle slammed into place. "How did you discover it? Did you know the mother? Was she here in Erdal?"

Uneasiness settled over Reann, but she was so determined to prove that she was right that she squelched the feeling and continued explaining.

"And what about the *heir?* Where is the child?" he pressed.

"Verick," Reann said sharply, almost angrily, "the heir is no longer a child. Now, I cannot say I know for sure," a disclaimer far too weak to take back what she had already revealed, "but . . . last week at the ceremony . . ." Reann hated every word, but it also thrilled her. Every word made the experience more real. It had happened! She was real. There was an heir. "The spear throwers mentioned the woman who found the way through ice caves. She had a child."

"The heroine," Verick said.

"Yes," Reann said. "Toran followed her back through the caves and saved the Furendali refugees."

"A peasant?"

"Yes."

"Unwed."

"Yes," Reann said again, her throat getting tighter.

"A single child?"

Reann nodded.

Verick was nearly trembling, but he didn't speak. It was as if he too were facing a crisis of conscience. The two faced each other and the truth of the legend, the greatest mystery in the empire as it unrolled into brilliant reality.

"Who was it?" he demanded.

"The Lady of the North."

The moment she said it, she felt wrong. It was a foolish, utterly selfish thing to do. She couldn't unspeak a word of what she had already betrayed. She felt condemned, as if shackles were clamped on her wrists. The first time she had done something terrible for Verick, she could claim it was his fault. This time, it was all hers. Was she becoming like him? Was this who she was?

She shook her head to ward off the barrage of self-incrimination.

Verick eyed her discerningly. "You knew?" He stood up, eyes gleaming. "You knew she was the child of Toran's first campaign, yet you didn't tell me."

Reann felt as if he were about to seize her. Her heart raced in her chest. She opened her mouth and breathed out slowly, carefully, measuring the time while her brain lunged for excuses. "Yes, well, I didn't suspect she was a child of Toran," she sputtered, "until now."

Verick's jaw wormed before he said brusquely, "Perhaps you have allies you are not revealing, associations . . . but I have enough information to ponder for one night. Be on your way."

Reann went for the exit as if it might suddenly close and lock her in this place with Verick. Sidestepping the reading table, she knocked a chair over, which she left on the floor. She scurried across the room, slipped through the small gap between the reinforced door and stone wall, and darted down the hall.

In two steps she had leapt into the laundry chute and slid halfway until, breaking with her hands, she pressed herself out of the chute and into the adjacent corridor on the next the level down. She ran the opposite direction and down a flight of circular stairs to the dungeon.

Reann curled up in the corner of a dark cell on the old moldy straw. Hand over her mouth, Reann cried silent tears as she realized what she had done.

I betrayed her. I betrayed Toran.

Her betrayal of Trinah's identity to Verick was like a wound that never healed. She had thought that sharing it would make Verick trust her. With that trust she could get his clues and find the others. It had been a sacrifice for a greater purpose.

Instead, it was the worst thing she had ever done, and it had only made Verick more suspicious. The moment he said the words *allies* and *associations*, Reann had realized that Verick likely had allies and associations of his own.

Ranger entered her cell and curled up on her lap, demanding attention. Reann absently stroked his mottled fur, trying to reason what she had just done. She had exposed Trinah's identity to Verick out of a greedy curiosity about the clues he held about the heirs. Reann began thinking of ways to rectify the situation. Reann could always turn a situation to her advantage, provided she had what she needed and played to her strengths.

A smile crept across her lips. "Time to steal that notebook of his and find out who I'm really dealing with—and maybe get some extra clues to the heirs. I can find them first and warn them."

Verick's true purpose on one hand and the identity of Toran's heirs on the other were like the two jaws of a bear trap. Finding the truth was no longer a matter of simple curiosity. It was life and death. But she no longer had the luxury of waiting to find out. The trap was already closing.

"I'm going to steal those notes."

CHAPTER 16

Montazi Realm. Ferrin-tat.

Wings beat the air heavily as the challengers' dragons rose at the start of the race—all but Akara.

The fruit dragon screeched a protest as Terith snapped the reins that pierced the neck spines behind Akara's head. She turned her head obediently away from the rising group and ran over the ground, wings folded tight against her sides.

Startled spectators scattered as she crashed through the brush onto an overland trail. Bushes and branches whipped at the armor-scaled and leather-clad pair in vain.

The fruit dragon had the most developed legs of any of the species. Terith used Akara's speed to his advantage, gaining ground as they neared the domed summit of Ferrin-tat.

Terith turned the dragon aside into a clearing. She climbed into the cup of a waiting catapult, a new long-range version Werm had demonstrated for Ferrin only weeks before. Terith slashed the tether with his knife. As the huge counterweight swung down, Akara catapulted into the air, wings tucked full.

Cheers erupted from the crowd in the clearing behind them as they effortlessly gained valuable altitude, coming level with the leaders who had gone around the center ridge of the megalith.

Pert wasn't in the lead, at least not at this stage, but the sprint dragons would fall out eventually in the long climb to the summit of Candoor. Terith hoped his plans would be enough to get Akara through. Her training was as thorough as any dragon in the realm, but she wasn't bred as a pure racer. The dragons of Neutat were bred for something else entirely. For now, clever tricks kept him in the competition. But by the end, it would be down to grit and luck.

The sun shone through scattered clouds as the dragons began the descent on the opposite side of the megalith. Terith relished the feel of the air in his face. Below him, the already familiar first bridge approached. The other dragons were diving toward the low bridge, taking their heavy riders with them, but Terith stayed high. When all the riders had nearly finished their descent, and only after settling into the strongest updraft, Terith repeated the three whistles. Akara bobbed her head three times.

Then he leapt.

Akara tucked her wings in a drop-rock dive as Terith stretched his dragon-wing chute. His descent slowed into a gentle glide as Akara plunged fearlessly.

"Do it," he urged.

Less than a half hour after the near death experience with the dral, Akara fearlessly dove for the bridge again, the product of centuries of Neutat breeding solely for loyalty and courage.

Terith cheered as she passed under and dashed unhindered, slashing effortlessly through the crowd of dragons circling to rise against the down draft on the other side of the bridge.

This, the steepest climb of the race, began to separate the challengers. Two fruit dragons, burdened by their riders, had already set down on ivy branches to rest mid-climb.

Pert's velra, its massive wings punishing the air with solid savage strokes, passed the resting challengers without a glance, and made rapid progress on the sprinters. The fishing dragon looked stronger with each down stroke.

Quickest on the descent, the mounted dral, though large, struggled to keep its rider out of the fog of the deep. The pair wisely avoided a taxing early ascent, conserving energy in a gradual climb up the canyon.

Riderless, Akara beat her wings quickly and easily. Avoiding the velra, she turned back, corkscrewing upwards in the same thermal that lofted Terith.

As she rose toward him, Terith tugged an arm and leg to angle against the breeze. Gliding astride his dragon, he tucked his legs and dropped into the harness. Terith folded his dragon-wing cape as spectators along the bridge and the ridge cried foul.

"Read the rules!" Terith shouted. Nothing in Ferrin's reading said the *rider* had to pass the obstacles.

The canyon walls loomed on both sides, rising up to the peak-top village of Hintat and the second obstacle. They had to go over a bridge, a punishing two-thousand-foot climb in less than four miles of flight.

Gaining speed as she leveled, Akara pressed her advantage.

Below them, but farther along, the velra had taken the lead, continuing the rapid climb toward the second bridge.

Pert's cursing was even louder than the spectators.

"Yeah, well, I'm not done yet," Terith said in a low voice, as he stroked Akara encouragingly, "So get used to it."

As he bent forward to caress his dragon, Terith saw a flash of metal beneath him.

Crossbow.

Terith pulled Akara sideways hard, trading valuable time for hopeful distance. Pert's crossbow bolt whistled past, missing Akara's torso by less than an armspan.

That was pure luck.

He looked back. Pert was reloading.

The lightweight saddle flexed as Akara's ribs expanded with heavy breathing, but he couldn't let her rest, instead he forced Akara into erratic feints to the left and right.

Another metal dart shot past his head.

"Hoo-ah," Terith breathed, "that was too close." He squeezed both his knees to signal Akara to pull in her wings. The pair dropped quickly, swiveling back toward the edge of the canyon, avoiding a third dart but forfeiting the powerful thermal.

Pert claimed the center of the slipstream and came level with them a hundred feet away.

"See you at the end," Pert bellowed as his velra rose in the sky like the sun. "I'll be sure to wait around for you so you can congratulate me on my marriage."

Terith gradually slipped into Pert's wake, aware of the widening gap to the new leader, while behind him the dral and two cross-bred racers rose. Already the last five dragons were nearly out of the running.

As the second bridge came into view high in the distance, Terith kept Akara level. To his left, the village of Hintat shimmered in the sun. Spectators pointed as he flew on, straight and level, closest to the crowd but well below the leader.

"Keep it level," Terith said easily. "Rest up." He hummed a chant he often made when he seasoned her wings with ivy fruit oil. Her anxious heart's rhythm slowed, though she kept her side-set eyes on the other dragons as they increased their height advantage.

When the second bridge was only a few hundred yards ahead and still high above them, Terith unshouldered his pack and drew out a three-finned whistler. He slipped the whistler's thin tether line through his chest harness and squeezed a drop of ragoon juice on the fuse. It smoldered into flames instantly.

Terith aimed the whistler and ducked his head. His heart pounded.

With a bang, it ripped from his hands, soaring overhead as it spewed fire from the back end. Spectators crowding the ridge along the race route cheered wildly as the rocket sailed over the bridge.

"Missed!" Pert cried as the whistler cleared his still-climbing dragon by more than a dragon's wingspan.

Pert didn't know that the fins of the rocket concealed a grappling hook and the thick plume of smoke hid the thin, ivy fiber-cord tied to Terith's harness.

Again, Terith leapt from Akara's back. The rope pulled taught as the empty rocket lodged in the support webbing of the bridge a hundred and fifty yards over his head.

Hand over hand, like a man climbing for his life, Terith scaled the cord. His heel hooks looped the rope and cinched the rope intermittently as he pushed with his legs, then pulled with his arms, like an insane inchworm. Fully rested and riderless, Akara kept pace with Terith's rapid sprint.

Terith summoned the light of awakening. The passage of time slowed as his body accelerated. His hands raced up the rope, drawing strength from the edge of eternity where soul and sinew merged with the light. Terith's muscles blazed against nature, fighting gravity with undying energy.

The crowd from Hintat watched, awestruck at the supernatural climb. Terith had already climbed a hundred and sixty vertical feet without slowing.

Terith's world consisted only of the cord and the bridge. His mind centered on the goal. He had to reach the bridge first. Otherwise any challenger could slash the rope, sending him into the deep. Terith continued his brutal pace for fifty more yards and then released the full power of the awakening, something he had only ever done in battle. Glowing, as if backlit by the sun, Terith moved upward as easily as if he were horizontal, scaling the last third of the rope in a desperate blitz.

Pert was closing on the bridge.

It would come down to seconds.

The winded velra made a desperate effort, climbing several feet with each beat of its wide wings. It came level with the bridge just as Terith clutched the wooden slats of the bridge with a gloved hand. He made a final pull and hauled himself onto the bridge. His muscles seized in spasms. The tissues of his arms ripped with agony.

A long blade was in Pert's hand as he passed over the bridge, but it was too late to slice the cord. He drove the velra ahead furiously, hoping to increase his lead, while Gomder, the rider on the dral, closed from behind.

Akara crossed over the bridge just ahead of the dral, with strength to spare from the easier climb without a rider. Terith ran and leapt on, using the last of his fading awakening to pull himself into the harness where he collapsed, his muscles shaking.

Akara surged forward as the dral loomed just behind her.

Terith snapped the reins at the unmistakable sound of a dragon gulping air. Akara dropped several feet instantly.

A gust of dragon fire from the dral dissipated only a few feet behind Terith, bathing him in a stifling blast of heat.

A roar rose up from the crowd of Hintat spectators, a mix of screams, cheers, and curses.

"Rough play, eh?" Terith said, rubbing his especially stiff right shoulder and tightening his grip on his reins. He looked back to check the distance. The dral was now gaining, its hunting instincts overpowering its fatigue.

Terith guided Akara aside to let the rider pass, but Gomder's dral kept Akara in her sights. Terith watched in some disbelief as he knocked a broadhead arrow into a short-bow. He only had to wound the dragon to keep Terith from finishing.

"Too tired to play fair?" Terith called. "Maybe you want to leave the race early."

As Gomder drew back the stout bow and sighted, Terith angled the reins. Akara twirled in tight spiral, ducking under the dral. Terith pulled the leather tie free and squeezed the stomach pouch full of dragon fire. A concentrated blast of red blaze from the pouch raked the dral's belly, curling up around the sides of the narrow-bodied serpent.

Black smoke fanned by the dragon's wingbeats rose around Terith's attacker as Akara completed a circle, falling in behind the dral.

The maneuver cost Terith another hundred feet on Pert, but his henchman Gomder was in trouble.

Terith cupped his hands and shouted to the panicking rider. "Never oil your saddle before a race!"

The rider banked for the ridge as his flaming harness lit the afternoon sky.

He won't make it, Terith thought as the fellow headed for the trees not far from Hintat. The fire-damaged harness leaned to one side and Gomder pulled the reins hard, desperate to get land underneath him before the harness broke free.

His seared dragon shrieked in anger at Terith's attack, but rather than heading for a landing spot, it jerked its head toward Akara and let fly another blast of flame.

The sudden twist sent Gomder to one side, and with the shift of weight, the belly strap snapped and the harness rolled.

With the volley of fire inbound, Terith had no time to make his decision as Gomder toppled backward.

Terith leaned forward and Akara dove, folding her wings and accelerating.

The rider, tangled in the stirrups of the harness, swung under the dragon. The neck strap of the harness held for a moment, then sheared away, sending Gomder spinning into the abyss.

Akara matched the speed of Gomder's descent, then pulled up and snagged him with her powerful hind legs. They had lost a hundred and fifty yards in altitude by the time she pulled level.

Akara's eyes turned to Pert's dragon still ascending and distancing itself. For five long minutes, she struggled to gain altitude with Gomder in her claws, before she finally reached the cliff edge.

Terith whistled to Akara and she dumped Gomder into a tree.

Terith hoped it was full of blood hornets.

By now, Pert's velra was a waning spot in the distance. With the strength-to-weight advantage of the larger dragon, Terith had no chance to catch him in a distance race.

Akara breathed heavily, her strength slack from the arduous ascent carrying the weight of two riders. Terith cursed his luck—only a fool would ride a dragon as disobedient as a dral. The dragon had nearly cost his rider his life. Instead, it had likely cost Terith the race. Terith's instant decision to save one man was a half-witted stunt that had just sealed his defeat. For several minutes, he wrestled to make his heart understand the magnitude of what he had just done.

If the Montas fall to Pert . . .

Terith tried to keep his distant nemesis in view as the dragons settled into their migratory rhythm. He looked back and spotted the crossbreed racers not far behind in a half-wing formation, conserving energy.

If I can convince them to join a formation, he thought, *we all might have a chance.*

Terith waved encouragingly and slowed Akara, letting the racers close, while Pert's velra gained even more time.

Terith's dragon took the lead position in the formation. Both the crossbreeds moved in close behind its wings, catching the updraft of every wing stroke. The sizes of the dragons were well matched for formation flying.

Terith recognized the riders. Remo and Tamm were northerners who trained with him for a season after their commissions as riders.

"Now this is a race!" Remo shouted excitedly. "Three against one. We'll rotate lead—this is just what we needed."

Tamm hollered at Terith. "Did I just see what I thought I saw back there?"

"You mean Gomder?"

"He tried to kill you! And you just threw away a shot at the lead to save his foul skin. You're a fool, Terith . . . always were."

"Maybe we all are. But we have to catch Pert before the tunnel. I don't want to be stuck behind his fat dragon in there. It's the only place a small dragon has the advantage."

With the advantage of the wing formation, they gained steadily on the velra. As Akara's head began to wag, Tamm, the rider to his left, rolled into the lead position, breaking the wind for the other two.

And now we see, Terith thought, *whether two full stomachs of fruit can keep up with centuries of breeding for endurance.*

"Lead hard, Tamm. We can catch Pert," Terith encouraged.

"He'll attack us if we do," Remo called. "I'm happy with second."

"We can't let him win," Terith said fiercely, "for the sake of the Montas."

"Risky business, Terith," Tamm warned. "You're talking about our lives here."

"All our lives," Terith called back, "our families, our people. It's down to us. We're the only ones who can stop him. Besides, it's three against one."

"We came unarmed to save weight," Remo explained. "Picking a fight isn't exactly on our to-do list."

"You have dragon fire."

"Short range—not good enough against his crossbow. He doesn't miss, Terith. We don't have your awakening. We can't dodge crossbow bolts."

Terith gritted his teeth. "All right. I'll make you a deal. Just get me within range of Pert. If I can't stop him . . . then I'll let both of you finish ahead of me."

Tamm exchanged looks with Remo. Either way, one of them was guaranteed a daughter of Ferrin.

"Will you swear it?" Remo asked.

"On my mother's blood." The awakening passed from mother to son. This was an unbreakable oath. If he did not keep it, he could lose the awakening forever.

Tamm nodded.

"Deal," Remo said.

Terith felt the weight of his oath settle on him, a burden only his vulnerable soul could bear. He looked ahead. Pert was nearing the final bend in the canyon before the cliff-side entrance to the tunnel.

"Tunnel is coming up," Terith called. "We're running out time."

"Not yet, we aren't!" Remo cried.

Remo's entire body flared with light that quickly surrounded his bonded dragon, risking everything to release his awakening so early in the race. Tamm joined, his bonded dragon soaring with fresh energy. Both dragons beat the air with a furious intensity, as if they had just taken off at the start.

"Yeah!" Terith cheered as Akara settled in between the two accelerating dragons in a reverse vee, catching updrafts on both wings.

"Be ready!" Tamm shouted.

Riding the current ahead, Akara's breathing eased. She would have to be well rested for the fight.

"Are you going to make a dive attack?" Tamm shouted from the second position, silhouetted against the lowering sun.

Terith shook his head. "I'll make a feint and then go for the tunnel. I'll ambush him when he comes in after me. You stay back and let your dragons feed a bit until they're ready for the second half. Just make sure nobody else goes in ahead of you."

"And then?"

"Don't stop for anything."

As the trio of dragons closed the remaining distance in a burst of awakened speed, Terith drew the hood of his riding leathers over his head and pulled up the mouth cover, leaving only his eyes uncovered. A clash with Pert could end in fire.

When the long-snouted face of Pert's barrel-chested velra was only a few hundred feet away, it suddenly turned as it spotted the motion in its peripheral vision. Pert snapped the reins to slow his dragon, drew his loaded crossbow and aimed it across his arm.

"Watch out!" Remo shouted as the light around him finally faded.

"Break!" Terith called.

The gray-green crossbreeds broke left and right. Terith feinted an escape to the right, banking just as Pert fired. But Terith had no intention of fleeing. Akara's wings folded and she dropped precipitously in a barrel roll, diving clear of Pert's crossbow shot and heading straight at Pert.

The velra pulled up hard, keeping Akara in its sights as it gulped air, readying a blast of blinding dragon fire.

Instead of leveling for the fight, Terith continued his dive, streaking past Pert and straight into the dark shadow of the cliff wall. Fog swarmed around him as the entrance to the tunnel loomed.

Soldiers posted on the ridge overhead waved a flag, noting his arrival. The guards posted on the opposite side of the megalith would send a smoke signal to the summit of Candoor indicating which challengers had passed the tunnel.

At a breakneck pace, Akara dove into the openmouthed cavern.

"Left, right, down, right, down." Terith counted off the practiced maneuvers as Akara took advantage of her narrow girth, plunging ahead into the darkness. Terith drew out the torch from his pack and squeezed out enough fumes to ignite it.

Light spilled into a wide hall as Terith shot into the largest of the caverns. He pulled back sharply on the reins. Akara instantly spread her wings full wide, stroking hard to brake. Her strong legs absorbed the last of their speed as they slammed into the wall.

Sensing Terith's motive for an ambush, she took a perch out of view of the entrance through which Pert would arrive in a few moments.

Terith readied the spear-tipped whistler and tossed his torch on the ledge near the exit. The flames lit the chamber with a pale flicker, throwing back long, deceptive shadows.

The spear-tipped rocket had one purpose: killing a dragon. If he critically wounded the velra, dark awakening or not, Pert couldn't win the race.

Flickers of light danced in the opening of the cave as Pert's velra illuminated its path through the cavern with dragon fire.

Terith lit the rocket.

A burst of dragon flame heralded the velra as it entered the cavern and spread its wings, somehow anticipating the ambush.

The rocket shot from Terith's hands and ripped a smoking tear straight through the wing of the velra, missing its vital torso. Terith quickly drew his knife and dove aside creating two targets.

Pert's dragon tracked Terith and angled a burst of fire directly at him. Instantly Akara pounced on the much larger velra. But it was too late to stop the velra's fire. Red-orange flame swallowed everything in Terith's sight.

Terith wrapped himself in his dragon-wing cloak as the flame superheated the air around him. Terith rolled out of the cloak and onto his feet as waves of residual flame roiled along the roof of the cavern.

Akara's attack on Pert's larger dragon knocked the second half of the flame burst askew, giving Terith a chance. He leapt from his elevated position as Pert jumped from his dragon, bent on a midair collision.

Terith never even reached Pert. He was knocked back and down as if he had collided with some invisible obstacle. Terith's back slammed into the ground under the force of Pert's dark awakening. Terith's skull crashed against the stone with a hollow thud.

Head spinning from the impact, Terith had no chance to summon a defense as Pert clamped his hand around Terith's jaw and rammed him against the wall of cavern. His stunned mind didn't even register that his knife had fallen from his hand.

Terith's whole body was being crushed by the invisible pressure.

"Lilleth said you'd die in the deep." Pert spat in Terith's face. "She was wrong."

Pert plunged his fist into Terith's stomach, dropping him limp to the floor.

Unable to draw a full breath, Terith look up to see Akara pinned down by the velra. The saber claws of its hind legs grappled with her wings. It held her neck between its rows of needle teeth.

"And you won't need your dragon, will you?" His dark beady eyes and sweat-covered face glinted in the torchlight, pale and wild like a living skull.

"I know what you did. I know about the dark awakening." Terith forced the words out, fighting for breath as though he were speaking with a massive stone on his chest. "I'm not the only one."

Pert turned, ravenous. He flung his arm out, knocking Terith backward with force summoned from his dark awakening.

Terith hit the ground, grabbed his fallen knife, and struggled to his feet, his right arm clutched defensively over his ribs, concealing the blade.

His muscles locked again as Pert loomed in front of him wielding a power over his own body that Terith couldn't fight.

"Who knows?" Pert demanded.

Terith tried to swing his left arm that held the knife. His halted motion went deliberately high. Pert parried with his own arm and swung his own fist underneath it. But Pert's blow connected with the dral stomach that Terith had pulled in front of his abdomen.

The ragoon fire burst from the nozzle, straight into Pert's face, blossoming behind him into a powerful fireball.

Pert screamed as his uncovered face and eyes burned to a black char. The velra lifted its head as its master's face flamed.

Akara's wingtip slipped free of the distracted velra's grip and it rammed a clawed finger right into one of its large eyes. As its jaws opened in a shriek of pain, Akara drew her powerful legs up and kicked the velra into the cavern wall.

Terith met Akara in the center of the cavern and leapt on her back. He had almost made it to the narrow exit into the next section of the tunnel when Pert's crossbow dart slashed through the shoulder of his leathers. The grazing shot shredded his skin and the pain was like a lit torch against his arm. Blood trickled down his arm as Terith swiveled his head to catch one last glimpse of Pert's black, eyeless face erupt in a demonic scream of rage. His velra rolled to its feet and dipped its head to one side, looking for its master with its remaining eye.

Akara ran for the exit and Terith snatched the torch from the ledge.

"Remo and Tamm won't have any trouble getting past him," Terith said to Akara. "He's blind."

The fruit dragon's breakneck pace through the collection of branching lava tubes kept Terith's mind off the horror of what had just happened.

When he finally emerged from the exit of the tunnel Terith looked back but saw no blaze of dragon fire signaling the emergence of another dragon in the cool air of the twilight sky. That nobody was behind him was as concerning as it was a relief and a worry.

Where were Remo and Tamm?

Night fell as Akara stroked evenly toward the tallest megalith in the barrier range—the summit of Candoor. The queen dragon kept her heading by starlight, the glow of the half-moon, and her internal compass.

If the brothers' dragons were following him under cover of darkness, Terith might not see them until they were a few hundred yards away.

"Pert should be out for good," Terith said aloud, speaking to hear his own voice, to shake off the terror. Somehow, despite the likelihood, he doubted Pert was gone.

Except for occasional drafts of mountain wind, the air was mostly still on the long climb to the summit of Candoor. Terith ate a few scraps of dried meat and fruit from his bag of rations, but mostly he wished for water, a heavy luxury he hadn't brought enough of. Along the high ridges of the craggy peaks that formed the remote backbone of the Montas region, mountain goats scaled the cliffs, prey for the carnivorous strythes, but no great ivy. Food for fruit dragons was all but nonexistent. Akara would have to rely on her extra abdominal store of ivy fruit.

In the cold silence, Terith allowed himself the luxury of contemplating victory. So early in the morning, high above the silent hills of the upper Montas, everything was clear. The path to his future was open. Pert could not catch him, blind as he was. The other riders had strong dragons, but the challenge was as much a test of the rider as his dragon. If they caught him, he could draft on their wingbeats until the finish. A sprint at the end would play to his skill in riding. Summoning his awakening and bonding with his dragon, Terith could out-fly them with every trick he knew: leading the wrong way, piggy backing dragon style, forced ejection. He'd already done that to Gomder, cinching a heavy stone to the dragon's tail or dropping a scorpion on their dragon's wing—paralysis never helped speed in a race.

Victory was not certain, but his gambit had paid off. Akara was regurgitating and digesting the food from her second stomach. She hadn't stopped to feed and wasn't showing signs of slowing.

Lilleth was his. They would be one. He could embrace her, releasing everything to her, sharing his awakening until she saw the world as he did, moving in slow motion, and his eyes opened to visions of the future and the past. They would be one, bonded and promised.

Terith felt like shouting in excitement. It was so close now, just a few hours of riding to the summit and the final downhill leg to the finish.

Terith imagined the moment he would face all the eligible after the finish. He would show up at Ferrin's keep and stand in front of a row of fifteen eligible women winking, with folks in the crowd cheering and yelling. He was going to have to handle the situation delicately or he would have the rest of his life to hear about it.

Enala was the problem. Terith considered whether the threat she had once levied was really a jest.

"If you choose Lilleth, I'll just have to stab myself with a knife—nothing personal. And yes, it will be your fault."

Of course, if Terith didn't choose Lilleth, somebody else would. Somebody else would have her. Somebody else would hold her in their arms and kiss her on her precious ruby lips and think to themselves what a terrible fool Terith of Neutat was not to choose her. It set Terith's heart pounding with panic to imagine anyone else even trying to kiss Lilleth. She was a gem beyond reckoning.

Enala was fun, whenever she wasn't trying to seduce him behind her father's back—and sometimes when she was. What would become of her flirtatious affection?

Lilleth was different altogether. She was the sunrise over the morning fog, the whispering wind in the trees, and the allure of the unknown.

I want Lilleth.

But am I only choosing her to keep her from somebody else?

If no sign from the awakening came to signal a new chief, and something happened to Ferrin, Lilleth's husband would inherit the chief position among the dragon lords by default.

Remo, the older of the two dragon racers in the running, would be no worse than Ferrin, though easily swayed. But Tamm? He was a firebrand, always in it for himself.

Pert would be a disaster.

Besides, how would Lilleth feel if I chose Enala?

It would be a brutal disappointment for Lilleth to see Terith choose her younger sister over her.

He couldn't hurt Lilleth like that.

Their faces drifted in front of Terith, dreams of what was, or what could be: Enala swinging her dress; Lilleth putting her hand on his, sending chills over him.

I choose Lilleth.

With mind and heart at peace with his decision, he focused on the other worry that tugged at him: Tanna's warning about the horde. They were massing very early in the summer, risking their success against their summer crops, which meant they were confident of their chances in finally breeching the Montas Barrier.

They would not cross the Montas on his watch, and he had to protect Lilleth. That was motivation.

Several hours past midnight the summit approached, lit by the torches of the few soldiers who staffed the lookout. It was the farthest western point in the Montas, overlooking the sacred plain and prairies of Erdal beyond.

The men stationed on the chilly perch cheered as Terith's dragon hovered above the stand.

"Here's your token, Terith," a sergeant called, throwing up a gold coin with a hole in the center.

"Anyone else yet?" Terith asked, tucking it away.

"You're the first. Thought we'd see Pert by now. Water?"

Terith shook his head, though his own water skin was all but empty. There was no way to guarantee the soldiers weren't in the pay of Pert. He turned Akara quickly and let her glide down the mountainside, the cool air rushing past him.

The race was all downhill.

Terith let Akara bleed the hard-earned altitude faster than simple wisdom would suggest. The pressure was dropping, a storm was brewing in the east and the winds would be perilous and contrary for the rest of the flight. Staying low, Terith hoped to catch a bit of tailwind with the cool morning air that descended the mountain canyons.

Dawn lit the horizon by the time he reached the foot of the mountains and sailed out over the first of the remote eastern Montas in a red sunrise.

Gusts of wind whipped around Terith, tipping Akara's wings. Terith clipped his heel hooks into the harness. "Steady, girl."

The monsoon had begun. Gray clouds rolled overhead. The light of morning had given way to false night as the clouds cased the sky in blackness.

"Almost there. Come on," he urged.

Checking behind him for the hundredth time, his heart stalled.

The velra was closing from his left, wings tucked, dropping like a falcon onto its prey.

Pert's arrival woke the survival instinct in Terith. The morning chill that burned his fingers, the wind in his face, and the aches in his stomach, head, arm, and saddle-sore legs all winked into irrelevance. With the heavier velra in a superior position on a downhill race and Akara close to exhaustion, the contest was all but lost. The outcome was inevitable. A side-by-side downhill race belonged to the heavier beast.

But how did he find me? I blinded him.

Terith shook the dral stomach. It was stiff with rigor mortis. Little remained, if any, of the liquid fire. It couldn't be sprayed—only poured. His pack of fireworks was lighter now, with only one whistler left, besides the two knives at his sides. It was no defense against a crossbow.

But Pert can't see, Terith thought. *How has he come this far? And on a one-eyed dragon with a hole in its wing.*

Sensing Terith's anxiousness, Akara looked back over her shoulder.

"Your turn, Akara," Terith said. "It's up to you."

Thoughts of victory and bonding with Lilleth vanished. Suddenly survival was his only desperate hope.

CHAPTER 17

Erdali Realm. Toran's fortress.

Reann lit a new candle and snuffed out the short remains of the old one, using only as much light as she dared at this hour. Verick's notes lay open before her on the library table. Ranger, who had nearly cost her everything by following her into Verick's room and meowing loudly as she stole the notes from his jacket pocket, was diligently napping on a rug.

Reann had no pocket watch, but the horizon visible through the library window was noticeably lighter. Dawn couldn't be less than an hour away and she had yet to come up with a way to get the notes back into Verick's vest pocket before he noticed they were gone.

Reann was used to sneaking out of bed when necessary and forging a permission note now and then, but not outright dishonest things like breaking and entering, lying, and stealing. Her conscience raised a continuous alarm as she scanned anxiously through the pages of well-penned notes.

The first thing she confirmed was that the script was not Verick's. *Where have I seen that writing?* Reann wracked her memory for it. She'd read those curling delicate strokes before, somewhere in the library, among the histories, legends, or records.

Perhaps a member of the court, someone close to Toran?

She perused the scattered messages, all of them cryptic in some degree. They seemed like fragmented pieces of poems or unrelated comments. But with the hindsight of a month's detective work, many of the clues now seemed obvious.

"Toran keeps no Furendali in court, but in the kitchen."

That's Trinah's mother, Reann reasoned instantly. *She must have been a cook or serving woman.* She browsed for more clues.

"The lord, like the falcon, keeps a fledgling under its wings, save when he hunts."

This means Toran kept a child with him until he went to battle.

"The echoes resound, where all around the fallen lie still on the hallowed ground. Not bound by blood they stake their claim and have it answered: a new name."

Echoes all around . . . hallowed ground . . . This means Essen! Reann nearly giggled with delight. She had been right. Essen, the tower fortress where the witch healer Onel once lived, stood in the center of a volcanic caldera surrounded by cliffs. That was where the echo resounds. That was where Toran showed that loyalty was more important than blood. If this clue was about a child of Toran, what did a "new name" have to do with it?

The answer was so simple Reann gasped at the obviousness of it. Simple, brilliant, and something only a follower of Toran's equality-for-all ideals would ever consider.

"He was adopted," Reann said, speaking to herself in a whisper. Toran had secretly adopted the witch's son. It was so perfect and clever. Nobody would suspect Toran would adopt an heir. The witch wouldn't ever have been pregnant when Toran was in Essen, yet she was the mother! Toran had adopted the child of the witch of Essen as his heir.

"Why did Verick keep these secrets from me?" she wondered.

A sudden memory flickered through Reann's mind, like a shadow of the dreams her wakeful night denied.

"Ah, Ranville, you've brought my cup—the elixir of apples. Good."

"Nobody knows you like I do, Lord Toran. Drink up."

"Did you turn the apple press yourself, old Ranville? Or did you make Effel do it for you?"

The memory faded with Toran's hearty laugh that Reann ached to hear once more.

She shook her head. Why had memories of Toran's old cupbearer taken her attention? What really mattered was on the pages in front of her.

Another faded scrawl noted, "Love is blind."

The clue was utterly meaningless. The only thought that crossed Reann's mind was the memory of her mother—her blind mother, Toran's personal translator.

A thought.

A wish.

A possibility.

Reann's heart froze.

Could it be?

No. Impossible.

Possible?

A shudder passed over Reann as she considered that Verick had browsed these notes a hundred times. He had seen this clue, but he hadn't shared it with her. He might already know what it meant— a terrifying thought. Or perhaps he thought it was irrelevant or merely a trite rambling. Maybe he didn't want to bring up a clue without a way to justify it being more than a hunch. Verick was cautious. He was deliberate.

He doesn't want me to know.

It was an odd thought, made stranger by the unholy hour and the looming shadows of the library. As much as she wanted to dwell on the strange possibility, there was more to read.

Another passage grabbed her eye. "The shining cave is a living tomb. Within it lives a giving womb."

The King's Cavern? she wondered. The cave, famous for its forbidden crystals, was in the west, in Dervan, where Toran had hidden from Raffani robbers during his fourth crusade. So this clue had to do with the fourth heir.

Living tomb . . . womb. Did the mother give birth to Toran's heir in the cave? Had she died in birth?

How is that a living tomb?

The message continued in a crudely poetic fashion that made it even more frustrating. "Hawkish eyes watch the land, a window to his open hand. Evening comes and dreams take flight, recalling visions of the bloody fight. His enemies are kept at bay, in darkened halls of crystal and clay. The desert keeps the secret still, a regent's sword and his iron will."

The author of the notes knew something of the western heir. The heir was obviously born in the midst of the conflict but would now be living in secret among the warlords of the Dervites. Reann had only time enough to gather cursory details. Infuriating urgency drove her on. There was no time to waste analyzing now. Verick was the most urgent mystery to solve. Her own life would doubtless depend on it.

Reann skipped several pages of notes until she found the glossier ink of the evening before. This was Verick's own southern-style lettering made of terse letters devoid of flourishes: precise and unimaginative.

The oath to my dying mother will not escape me. Her last words are my charge. I cannot live and see that oath unfulfilled.

The five heirs haunt me. I cannot escape them even in my sleep. The closer I come to finding them at last, the more real my illusions seem.

I dreamt of a weapon in my hand, an assassin's knife. I raised it to strike, but the head in front of me turned and it was the library girl. I fled. My resolve is a mix now of too many colors of feeling. I doubt myself, though I continue what I began."

Those I seek become more real the more I learn. More capable, more alive, even more of a threat. My course is set before me. My fate was written in the preamble.

If I should fail in my challenge, these words will show I knew my duty. These words will show I sought my father's revenge.

Reann shut the book.

"Verick wants revenge."

No night terror was more stark, more horrifying. She could read no more. Her curiosity vaporized like dew under the desert sun. Her insides knotted with anxiety. Her pulse throbbed in a crazed rhythm.

Whatever it all meant, if she did not get the notes back to Verick, she would soon be as dead as the young man who first tried to steal the book.

The phantom thought of Ret discovering hawks pecking at her dead body nearly caused her to faint.

I can do this. I have to do this.

The first rays of the morning sun broke through the windows of the library. Reann stirred herself with a mix of valor and desperation riding on the whispers of strange, strange imaginings.

Love is blind.

Reann tied the notebook closed and moved quickly to the library door, inventing a plan as she went.

I'll wake him early for breakfast, gather his clothes for washing and slip the notes inside his vest. He'll reach for the waistcoat, find the notes there, and think himself clever for keeping them from me.

What she had read of Verick's dream made the trip upstairs all the more terrible. Reann faced the bedroom door. If he knew, and she knocked, she was dead.

Could she run away?

Concealing the notebook behind her back with a shaking hand, she raised her other hand to knock.

If I am a daughter of Toran, I can face any enemy.

Reann took a deep breath as a feeling like steel and ice moved over her, pulling her hand back.

Taking another calming breath, she knocked.

The door swung smartly open.

Verick was in his trousers, his white shirt unbuttoned. He stared at her with a look she couldn't understand. She ducked past him quickly. "Good morning, sir. I'll just get your wash."

She considered telling Verick to hand over the shirt as well. Staying up all night had her in a strange mood.

Shrugging away the confusing thought, Reann spouted off a long list of reminders as she collected his clothes. "Tea and breakfast are at seven in the dining hall—the staff is too busy getting ready for the gala to serve breakfast in rooms this week. The post goes out this afternoon at three. Oh, did I mention the stables are closed for cleaning—goodness, your clothing is immaculate for a week's wear." She bent and scooped up a shirt and some stockings, palming the notebook with one hand and lifting his vest with her other hand. "And what about this?" she asked. "Shall I wash it?" The notebook slid into the long pocket on the inside and she breathed a breath sigh of salvation.

Verick pushed the door closed.

Reann's stomach clenched. She pretended not to notice. "Your candle has burnt down. I'll fetch another." Reann moved about the room tidying things.

Verick turned, keeping her in view, still watching.

Reann stopped, feeling his eyes on her back. Live or die, she could no longer pretend to be a servant in the presence of someone who would betray the heirs of Toran. She looked over her shoulder, waiting for whatever threat Verick was going to unleash.

"I owe you an apology," he said softly. "The other night, when I was robbed . . . I was wrong. I acted rashly."

"The man you killed . . ." Reann said softly.

Verick cracked his knuckles and breathed out. "I could have wounded him."

Reann nodded, unsure of what to make of Verick's apology. That event was the most horrible thing she had ever experienced. Now he was asking her forgiveness for it? How could she?

A man was dead. Her dreams were tormented by thoughts of hunting hawks pecking at the dead youth's pale flesh.

"I treated you poorly as well," Verick said. "Your kindness to me was undeserved on my part. I took it for granted and repaid it with rudeness. It is a shame to my honor."

"It does you honor to apologize," Reann managed.

His hand touched her shoulder lightly and she flinched, unsure of what exactly she was feeling. Strange murmurings struggled within her.

"I do not wish for you to fear me," he said.

Reann blinked back tears, turning to hide her weakness from him. *I fear what you will do.*

Verick withdrew his hand.

"I don't . . . want . . . to be afraid of you," Reann managed, as she choked back tears.

"Please," Verick said. When she turned, she saw his offer of a handkerchief.

How could she take it? He wasn't the seeker of Toran's heirs. He was their sworn enemy. He would kill her the moment he found out that she knew his true intentions.

Still, she could just reach for it, take it, pretend it was a token of true friendship, or maybe something more. What was the harm in that?

Reann sobbed again and grasped the handkerchief. A moment later, she was gathered into Verick's strong arms. He held her for a moment until all her fears swirled in the storm within her, until nothing she knew matched anything she felt, until only the pounding of her heart and the solid thump of Verick's own beat out the worries and the pain.

"Please, forgive me, if you can," he said.

"I shall try," Reann said, drawing a shaky breath. "For both our sakes." She looked up into his eyes and summoned every ounce of strength she had. She pulled back and poked her finger against his chest. "You used me—you threatened me. Do not ever do that to me again."

Verick, stunned, said nothing.

"Can you promise it?" she demanded. "Promise it, or I'll never trust you."

"I . . ." Verick's expression was one of pure agony.

Reann hurried out of the room before another sob escaped her. She ran the length of the hall and down three flights of stairs.

"Reann?" Ret said as she hurtled out of the castle and through the citadel's open front gate. "What's wrong?" he called after her.

She turned away from the market and ran north into the hills, with no thought other than her own life.

A mile past, three miles past, Reann trudged along the river, along a path she had never set foot upon.

It was the road to Fordal, her mother's birthplace, where she had an inheritance—perhaps only a cellar or a collapsed ruin.

She could beg for food. She could work the fields.

Tears streaked Reann's face as she stepped barefoot over rocks and weeds. She climbed out of a ravine and onto a low hill, unsure of how far she had come and certain that she was as likely to die alone as not.

Her suspicions were confirmed immediately.

She was being stalked. The animal was only twenty feet away when she spotted it, a shape that conjured primal fear.

Wolf.

Reann's muscles froze.

It gave a hollow, greedy-eyed stare—hungry and wild—straight into her heart where fear burned out the halls of sanity.

"Everhart!" snapped a sharp voice.

Reann gasped. "Trinah!" She raced forward.

Trinah, wrapped in a brown leather cloak, stomped out of the cover of the trees on the northern side of the hill. "Oh—it's you," she said, lowering a spear.

"Trinah!" Reann cried. She ran right into the tall, strong woman, wrapped her arms around Trinah's waist and buried her head against her chest.

Trinah's arm shielded her. "Don't take it personal, Everhart. Obviously she prefers humans."

Everhart barked his disapproval.

Trinah lifted Reann's chin with her finger. "Reann, what are you doing here?"

She shook her head. "I . . . I don't know."

"That doesn't sound very much like you. Aren't you supposed to be an insufferable know-it-all?"

"Yes," Reann admitted as she choked on a sob.

"Out with it."

"Well—wait a minute," Reann said. "What are you doing here? Shouldn't you be in the Furendal?"

"I came back," Trinah said. "Obviously."

"Why?"

"I just dropped someone off at the river ferry."

"Who?"

"My mother."

"Your—who?"

"Effel," Trinah said.

"The washwoman?" Reann wondered at why she hadn't seen the similarity before. "The old bother who gives me chores?"

Trinah took Reann by her shoulders and pulled her away. "But that was not the only reason I came."

"Let me guess," Reann said. Her tone dropped a level and she stepped back, staring up at Trinah and folding her arms. "Verick?"

"Oh you're such a jealous tot," Trinah said with a twinkle in her eye. "I only gave him attention to bother you."

"You what?" Reann said. "You mean you were . . . teasing me?"

Trinah smirked. "It's what sisters do. Or—half sisters."

Reann's jaw dropped. She tried to scream or shout for joy, but all that came out were two giant streams of tears. "It's true?!"

She turned about and looked back at the white-walled Citadel of Toran gleaming in the distance. "Hallowed halls of the sacred place beyond . . . I am a princess!"

"Yes," Trinah said.

"And you knew!" Reann gasped, smiling as wide as Everhart, "The whole time."

Trinah sighed. "Emra was a few years ahead of me in school—yes, I went to school in Erdal and I hated every moment of it. After Toran died, my mother told me Emra's child was also of Toran."

"But when did you find out I was Emra's daughter?" Reann asked, her head swimming at the certainty that she really was the heiress of Erdal.

"The moment I saw you in the castle window," Trinah said

dismissively. "I recognize an insufferable know-it-all when I see one—you are about the same age Emra was when I knew her."

"Tell me something about my mother," Reann begged. "Tell me everything. What happened? How did she meet Toran? Tell me, sister."

Trinah turned and walked away.

"Wait!" Reann cried following after her, looking back to make sure the wolf wasn't going to gnaw on her heels.

Trinah stopped at a nearby tree and lifted a large pack off a broken branch. She unrolled a snow bear fur and set it on the ground. "Sit."

Reann dropped onto the white fur blanket, pressing questions as fast as they rushed into her mind as Trinah took a seat next to her. "But how did she become my mother? I mean you don't just wake up one day and the king of the five realms wants to marry you."

A sober look came over Trinah's face. She sat on the fur near Reann. Everhart circled them slowly and then disappeared into the forest. "Near the end of the last crusade against the Raffani in the west," Trinah began, "Toran led a scout party that fell into an ambush. Your grandfather Rembra and both his sons died defending Toran. The war was only weeks from ending."

"How terrible," Reann said.

"Yes," Trinah said. "And if the war had gone on any longer, your mother might have died, too. She was ill, with no one to care for her."

Reann's heart burned with curiosity.

"Toran found her at Rembra's cottage near Fordal, lying helpless on her bed. But she didn't know who he was. The fever had left her blind."

Reann's eyes widened. She had always assumed that her mother had never been able to see. "She didn't know it was him," Reann whispered in a reverie.

Trinah nodded. "He said that he was a poor soldier saved at a great price and that he had a debt to repay. He cared for her for months, cleaning and washing, making meals for her, until the spark of life shone in her again."

Reann's eyes gleamed.

"Do you know what he told her?" Trinah said. "No one gave speeches like Toran. He could light a fire in your chest with a single word."

"What did he say?" Reann said expectantly.

"'My heart beats eternally with the last throb of agony,'" Trinah recited, "'when the best men fell, buried in swords. I cannot give back what they paid in loyal love, nor can I hold it back. I must share it, or that love itself must die in grief and shame.'"

"You memorized it?" Reann said, surprised.

"Every word," Trinah said, smiling at the recollection. "Emra told me herself. It was the most beautiful thing I had ever heard." She looked at Reann. "There wasn't much else worth remembering. Furendali men belch their poetry."

Reann put her hands in her lap and let her gaze drift out of focus. "He was in love with her."

"He must have been," Trinah agreed. "He certainly wasn't in a hurry to leave."

"What happened next?" Reann pressed eagerly. "Did he propose? Did he tell her who he was?"

"When it was time for him to return—" Trinah said.

"—to attend the Council of Nobles, of course," Reann interjected. "He could skip court for a few months, but not the—oh, sorry. Go on."

Trinah pretended she hadn't been interrupted. "Emra begged him to ask anything of her in repayment for saving her life. So he asked her, 'Will you bear me a child?'"

"I can only imagine how she must have felt," Reann sighed. "He would have been—let's see—forty-five. He was her father's friend after all. But she consented."

Trinah's hard-edged expression softened. "I think she was his true love. The way she spoke of him . . . the look in her eyes—my mother never pined over his memory like that. It was clan law—I don't think my mother had a choice."

Reann blushed slightly. "I always dreamed my mother and father were romantics, bound in a fated love and torn apart by circumstance. That is the way it always is in the books."

Trinah laughed and gave Reann an appraising look. "Emra asked my mother Effel to watch over you, before she vanished."

Reann's jaw dropped. "A great load of chores—that's 'watching over me?'"

"There was more," Trinah said. "Should anything happen to Effel, the duty of looking after you would fall to me. Of course, I never would have come to Erdal to babysit you."

"You wouldn't have?" Reann said, disappointment ringing in her voice.

"A child of Toran can take care of herself," Trinah said. She looked up at the sky. "It is time for me to go. I will camp many miles from here. I have to be back in Evernas when the frost breaks."

Reann grabbed Trinah's arm. "But we're just getting to know each other. We're sisters. This is wonderful."

"Another time," Trinah said.

"We should talk for hours and stay up all night telling stories," Reann said.

"There's a Furendali holiday just for that," Trinah said. "You're welcome to join me for the winter solstice."

"Go to Furendal, in the middle of winter? It's freezing up there. There's a thousand feet of ice in the pass. I couldn't—"

Trinah gave a sharp laugh as she pried Reann's fingers off her arm and mumbled something about a puppy, adding, "Then I'll just give you your present now and save my pack the weight."

Reann couldn't even remember the last time she had been given a gift. Speechless, she watched as Trinah lifted from under her collar a thin chain that held a small leather pouch.

"It was entrusted to your mother by Toran," Trinah said. "She gave it to me to keep for you until you were of age. You're probably not of age yet, but being a know-it-all is worth a few months. I don't suppose it will hurt anything to give you this now."

She passed it to Reann, who opened the drawstring with fingers trembling with excitement and poured out the solitary content into her hand.

It was a faceted crystal as long and wide as her finger. It shifted from transparent to deep purple and back again as she turned it in her palm.

"What is it?"

"A crystal from the king's cave in the western desert. The walls of the cavern are covered in gems and it is forbidden to remove any. From ancient times, robbers who tried to steal from it were cursed and became stony men who could not bear the sun."

"But—"

"But the king may do as he pleases," Trinah said with a twinkle in her eye. "He took only this small crystal. It is very special. Do not wear it where it could be seen and stolen."

Reann gazed at the stone and clasped it her hand, holding it as tightly as anything she ever held. It was her mother's; it was her father's. They had both touched this stone, shared it. Reann embraced Trinah again. "I can keep it?"

"Forever. Now look. You have touched the treasure but haven't turned to stone, so you must be a princess after all."

"I am," Reann said with glee, forgetting that she wasn't superstitious.

"Let it remind you who you are, and never forget."

"I never forget anything—well almost," Reann said. "And I'm sure I can find the other heirs. I am excellent at finding clues and putting them together. We can all—"

"When they are ready, they will come to Erdal," Trinah said. She added in a severe tone. "Do not go looking for them. Your place is in Erdal."

Reann gazed at the scenery lit by long evening shadows, thinking rebellious thoughts.

"You must become all that your people need you to be. Only then will you command the allegiance of your people."

"Is that what you are doing in the north, gathering followers?" Reann asked.

"No," Trinah said sharply, as if offended. "I am simply serving my people."

"But you have their respect already. You would be their leader in an instant if they knew who you were. You've saved so many of them."

Trinah smiled again with her lips closed, in the Furendali fashion. "That's nice of you to say. But here I must leave you."

Reann looked back toward the castle and gripped Trinah's shoulders anxiously. "Oh please don't leave me here."

"Why not?" Trinah said.

Reann paused, trying to think up an excuse. "Wolves."

Trinah laughed shallowly. "Off with you. I have business waiting for me in the Furendal."

Reann gripped Trinah's hands one last time. Her heart throbbed with joy and sadness. Then she let them go, clinging instead to the pouch that hung around her neck.

"Everhart will see you back to the castle. He does not abandon pups like you."

Reann looked nervously at the wolf that stared back at her with those black eyes and long jaws. She looked back at Trinah, who had already packed up her snow bear rug and started the hike north.

"So I'm a princess," she said. "And I'm about to be kicked out of my own castle."

She could tell them all who she was. Would they believe her?

It was only after a half mile of walking that she remembered Verick. She hadn't even thought to mention him to Trinah—the one person who could have helped her. She winced, realizing she was still on her own.

Everhart emerged from the cover of a bush, head high and ears up as if looking for the source of her fear.

"Everhart," Reann said in as strong a voice as she could muster. "I'm going to be all right." Tears tried to squeeze into her eyes again.

"I'm the daughter of Toran. I can take care of myself. This is my kingdom. *This is my kingdom.*"

CHAPTER 18

Montazi Realm.

With Pert's dragon descending like a falling hammer, Akara thrashed forward, twitching her head from side to side, trying to keep the velra out of her blind spot as both fought the headwind.

For Terith, the end of the race was no longer the finish, but the instant Akara fell in range of Pert's dragon fire.

He looked over his bleeding shoulder. With both height and weight advantage, the velra was gaining fast. The dragons would collide in seconds. He faced the morbid realization that a collision with the larger dragon would be a death sentence.

Terith could not afford the luxury of an early death. The fate of his realm depended not just on surviving, but winning the challenge. He couldn't win or escape unless he could somehow slow Pert down.

A fierce crosswind caught Akara's stretched wings and Akara was forced upward, closer to Pert—the one direction Terith couldn't afford to go.

Terith instinctively gave the reins a hard pull to the side and Akara rolled upside down, leaving both Terith and Akara with their backs to the ground. At least he had Akara between him and the velra's fire.

Falling quickly, in moments, he would be forced to turn over to stay out of the deep and Pert would have him.

That's it!

In a moment of crazed desperation, Terith seized on the first idea that entered his head.

He let go.

Mid-roll, he spun out of the harness and hurtled into the fog.

Akara, sensing Terith's fall, folded her wings instantly, dropping just out of reach of the velra's stretched claws. Together, rider and dragon plummeted backward into the rank air of the canyon abyss.

In four and a half seconds of free fall, the furious clouds overhead had become just a narrow gray stripe between the blurred deep-green rock walls, until all was hidden by the gray gloom of the deep.

Terith had fallen into the deep, just as Lilleth foresaw.

Immersed in the fog, Terith whistled. Akara instantly pulled up, colliding with her back against his. Terith frantically reached the harness strap as Akara spread her wings to brake.

The sheer force of the pull-up maneuver was more than Terith's tentative grip could handle. His arm bent back and wrenched his fingers loose from the harness strap. Terith twisted backward off Akara and saw only gray fog for a desperate instant. Adrenaline rushed though him as he fell face first toward a rocky crag jutting out of the deep.

Akara's hind claws snatched Terith's thigh, her skill making the rescue as easy as catching falling ivy fruit. Her sure grip punctured the leathers covering his leg and carved long gashes into his thigh. It felt as though his leg had been doused in flame. The two plummeted together as Akara fought to slow their fall.

Terith's flung-out fingertips came up dripping with slime from the bog as Akara bottomed out, barely a body-length above the bubbling hell-swamp of the deep. Terith got one hand on the harness and swung back up into the saddle, lungs choking with fumes.

After one luxurious second of relief, the shock faded into an eruption of complaints from his limbs. There wasn't a single place on his body that didn't hurt, from his twisted arm to the slashed skin on his shoulder from Pert's arrow and the torn flesh of his thigh that burned like a firebrand. But he was alive.

Terith slapped Akara encouragingly on her back. "Come on. We're not out yet. Go!"

He glanced up, unable to see the megalith tops through the dense fog.

If that didn't look like a realistic crash, nothing will.

Would it be enough to convince Pert that he was the only contender left?

Enlivened by the falling game and her masterful catch, Akara surged forward. With natural reflexes faster than a human, she led the insane charge through the underworld.

Jagged moss-covered rocks jumped out at Terith through the fog as Akara carved an upward arc along the canyon bottom. It was a winding path, but free of the tortuous headwind that Pert faced atop the megaliths.

The huge white swamp flies buzzed around Akara but couldn't latch on to her slick wings, damp from the plunge through the dense fog.

"Whoa!" Terith ducked an overhanging rock ledge as Akara cut under it in a short turn.

The canyons ran mostly east and west, in the direction of the capital, but the routes twisted and split, sometimes recombining on the other side of a megalith, sometimes leading farther away. Terith navigated solely from memory in a world he had never seen, except from the top. A wrong turn would cost him a second, minutes, or his life.

Rain fell in intermittent torrents, clues to the gale force winds shifting angrily overhead.

Hours passed in the deep. Terith began to feel that if he wasn't the first to arrive, he might not finish in time. The deadline for completing the challenge approached, but Terith had no way of gauging the exact hour.

The final turn, the decisive moment.

"This should be it." Terith banked right and pulled up on the reins. If he had missed turns, he would be miles from his goal.

Akara beat her tired wings in a broken, frantic rhythm, climbing out of the fog for the first time since the false crash.

"There's a bridge. That's it!"

The high bridge of Hintat, the second waypoint of the race, was just ahead, and beyond it, Ferrin-tat . . . *and Lilleth.*

Akara, fatigued to the point of delirium, didn't seem to have the strength to get their combined weight up out of the canyon. Her heavy breath wheezed with desperation, and Terith realized that if Akara had to carry his weight to the top of the cliffs, her heart might simply explode.

But he had help Pert couldn't match—friends like Werm and Tanna.

He drew out Werm's last grappling hook rocket, clipped the harpoon line to his new chest harness and drip-ignited the fuse with dragon fire. He squinted his eyes as the burning fuse vanished into the cylinder, and a spout of flame erupted from the great firework, rocketing the harpoon upward.

Terith looped the cord through Akara's harness as the rocket flamed out and the grappling hook snagged in the ropes of the bridge and snapped taut.

The sudden force pulled the rope through the knot in the harness and tore at Terith's chest harness, pinning him to the dragon. Snagged by the grappling line, Akara whiplashed upward, momentum transitioning to altitude. At the peak of the slingshot maneuver, Terith slashed the rope and the pair shot into the air. They were in the open again. Terith looked back, smiling at the trick that had saved him minutes of circling to gain height.

No longer sheltered by the canyon, Terith again faced the full gale of the monsoon wind. The race was now an all-out battle against the storm.

In minutes that passed like moments, the megalith of Ferrin-tat and the finish grew near. Below, people waved and cheers came broken on the wind, giving no indication of whether Pert was ahead or behind.

Slipping the headwind, Akara dove into the trees. She whipped left and right around tree trunks, avoiding the wind in a feat of agility only a fruit dragon could manage.

Ferrin's enclave passed in a blur.

"Almost there."

Akara shot over the landing field and barrel-rolled in a gut-wrenching spin. Terith dismounted in midair and rolled to his feet on the soaking turf. He raced for the keep where collected rain spouted through the overhanging rocks like blood dripping from jaws.

If Pert had already returned, his dragon might be waiting behind the watery veil.

Terith sprinted ahead, splashing through mud heedlessly as the strongmen and keepers coaxed Akara toward her cage with offerings of food.

Whether the spectators were cheering or jeering him, Terith couldn't tell.

A sturdy figure emerged from under the cascading water. For a moment Terith thought it was Pert. But then he glimpsed the slight limp that belonged to Ferrin.

"Where is Pert?" Terith called. His legs barely held him as a wave of dizziness passed over him.

"It's almost noon," Ferrin replied, sounding frantic. "But you're the first back. Do you have the token? Guardians be praised—how did you get here in this weather?"

Terith fumbled to remove the gold coin from a buttoned pocket. "Here it is."

"Give it to me—hurry."

Rather than turn in the token and claim victory, Terith clenched the coin in his fist. "You're sure I am the first?" Terith asked, heart pounding.

"Yes," Ferrin shouted. "For the love of everything sacred, give it to me! There are only a few minutes left. You'll have first choice of mate."

Terith looked at the cavern and then turned away and drew both his long knives to cries of panic from the crowd.

"He's going to kill the others!"

Ignoring the commotion, Terith spread his feet and raised the weapons defensively, pivoting continuously as he scanned the sky.

He steadied his breath and cleared his mind, preparing to draw the awakening one last time.

Terith's oath closed around him, pulling at his heartstrings, where his spirit was wide open to the awakening.

"Two minutes. *Terith!* Listen to me. Nobody else will make it."

"I made a blood oath!" Terith cried.

Ferrin choked on rain and wind. "What oath?"

Ferrin stepped closer to Terith and reached out his hand, as if to touch his shoulder, but didn't.

"Remo and Tamm helped me pass Pert," Terith said, "so long as I would stop him."

"Did you stop him?" Ferrin looked into his eyes with wild hope.

"I burned his face half to ashes in the tunnel. Then he showed up half a day later on my tail without a scar. He has the dark—"

"Do not speak of it," Ferrin spoke quickly. He closed his eyes and lowered his head. "I should have seen this coming. I should have stopped him sooner." Ferrin's face fell, lost in a wash of regret. "It was all for the competition, I thought. One rider's drive would lift the others, but he has gone too far and I cannot stop him. My reign is . . ." Ferrin didn't finish the sentence. He looked up at Terith. "What now?"

"If Pert comes and I cannot stop him, I have to let Remo and Tamm finish ahead of me."

"A withered fool's oath, that was."

"A flight vee was the only way we could catch up to him. We had to work together. They did their part. Now I'll do mine."

Ferrin took a step backward toward the cavern. "One minute left. Terith, if you don't give me your token in time, you'll lose as well. I'll have no redemption for all that has happened."

Terith counted seconds under his breath. He tore back his hood and searched the sky. Was it there? A lone dragon?

The paper-thin trace of light around Terith brightened into a visible corona. He put his arms together, blades forward, tracking the flighty image.

Flapping wing, or ivy leaf on the wind?

"Ten grains left!" Ferrin called eyeing his hourglass. "Pert is too late. Five, four . . ."

Terith tossed the coin to Ferrin and leapt through the veil of water eclipsing the cave entrance.

Inside, the eligible women gathered in huddles. Previously pearl white dresses were drenched with water and marred by mud. Several screamed when he came in with his knives still drawn.

He hastily tucked them away.

"You made it!" Enala shouted. "Look at the hourglass—Guardians' Gate, he made it by a few grains!"

A brilliant, soaring feeling rushed through his body and seemed to lift him off the ground. It filled him from the inside until Terith thought he might burst.

"Look at him," one of the eligible gasped. "Did you ever see anything like that?"

Terith looked down at his body bathed in a brilliant white glow. It wasn't just the faint shadow of his waning awakening. This light permeated his entire being, throwing back long shadows in the cavern.

He'd been chosen. The right of rule had passed to him.

He felt it deep inside.

From outside the cave, the crowd roared with a mix of surprise and excitement at the blaze of light shining from the cavern.

"I knew it," Lilleth said proudly, smiling at Terith. "You're the new chief."

"Yeah, well you already saw it, didn't you?" Enala said with a laugh. She squeezed her sister in an elated hug before pinching her on the arm with a bit of latent spite. "I'm just glad it's over."

Lilleth embraced her sister. "Me too. I'll never come to another challenge as long as I live."

Enala drew back with an expression of thoughtful concern. "That depends on who gets chosen, doesn't it?"

There was only one champion to arrive in time.

"Oh no," the girls said in unison, both clasping their hands to the sides of their heads in shock.

Several other eligible girls joined in a new round of sobs.

This is my kingdom, Terith thought. A thrill of realization rippled through him. He had passed out of the world he knew into an entirely new one where all he saw was his to command, his to protect.

The excited chatter of the eligible echoed in Terith's mind from far away. He had hardly considered what might happen if Ferrin's charge fell to him.

The concentrated rush of awakening waned, but the feeling in Terith's heart did not as the burden of protecting the realm settled on him.

Terith unleashed a champion's smile as the mass of even more anxious eligible women came into focus in front of him.

Only two mattered.

Another of the eligible girls approached him. She had a narrow-faced, picked-upon look and a slight build.

"Thank you, Terith," she said. She suddenly leapt at him and wrapped her arms around his neck desperately. "Thank you."

"I . . . I'm not sure what you're talking about," Terith said. "Who are you?"

"Onneth, of Cafertat. You saved my brother Gomder yesterday."

Terith blinked.

"When he fell. After he tried to kill you."

"Oh, yeah. That."

Well, everybody makes mistakes, Terith thought, as Onneth blinked away tears, or batted her eyes at him—he couldn't tell.

"Terith," Enala cried, prying him away from Onneth, "Thank the Guardians, you're safe. I knew you would be chief too—sorry, Father." She curtsied to Ferrin, who had just stepped into the cavern with a mix of surprise and relief on his fatigued features.

"Terith?" Lilleth questioned softly, stepping closer. "Was anyone behind you?"

He nodded. "Pert. But he didn't come in time."

Sensing his unease, she asked quietly, "What happened back there?"

Before Terith could answer, Lilleth peered into his eyes and saw for herself. "You fought."

Terith nodded. "There was fire—he should have died, but . . ." Terith didn't finish, unable to speak of the dark awakening with the others listening.

"Look at you," Lilleth said. "Oh, Terith. This needs bandaging. Can you take it off?"

"I'll help," Enala volunteered. She yanked the shoulder section of his leathers up and over his head to reveal a long wound on his shoulder that continued to drip blood onto his torso.

Terith winced not at the pain, but at how awful it looked.

"That blood," Enala said, grabbing her sister by the arm for support. The dark of her pupils seemed as dark as the deep. "Pert did that . . . he's coming back. He'll—"

"Hush," Lilleth said, cradling Enala's head against her chest. "We're safe. Terith is safe." She wrapped a wool blanket over his shoulders to cover his wound.

Terith closed his eyes, feeling the new freedom, the new self that enveloped him. He was the champion of champions. It was all worth it.

"Terith?" Enala asked meekly, her eyes hopeful and full of expectation. "What about your choice?"

The room became still. For a long moment, he felt out this new awakening. It didn't matter now who he chose. He would be the ruler by right, not inheritance.

Terith opened his eyes. "I've thought about it, and—"

"No." Ferrin said, from just inside the sheet of rain that blurred the landing field. "You have been chosen as chief, and that means a ceremony. Realms come before romances."

He was met with a chorus of protest from the eligible.

Ferrin led Terith out of the keep. "We all saw the sign, Terith. Dungeons, half the crowd thought there had been some kind of explosion. It felt like my heart had dropped right out of my chest. I'm a free man. From now on, you must shoulder the fate of this realm."

Terith nodded. "Glad to." The grin on his face couldn't have been any wider.

"Well, then, it stands for a man like me, with two eligible daughters to bring that fact to your attention. I should hope to be your father, if you should choose one of my daughters."

Ferrin led Terith onto the now-crowded landing field.

The rain slowed to a drizzle. Terith was sure it had something to do with Ferrin's daughters coming outside. The muted tones of a wide rainbow showed in the thinning cloud cover.

The spectators were packed so tightly in the landing area that not a single person had room to sit. Children were stacked atop fathers' shoulders. Teens clustered on the tops of the open cages—all except Akara's.

The exhausted dragon eyed the scene with one open eye.

The crowd from Neutat was the most obnoxious, chanting Terith's name and joining in audibly painful renditions of clan songs.

Ferrin stood by Terith on the upslope portion of the landing area, facing the crowd. The eligible clustered in the front of the mass, along with their escorts surrounded by hordes of bonneted and blanketed busybodies feisty enough to beat back the crowds of pressing boys straining for a look at Terith and his bloodstains.

As for the women who held the front-most ranks in the crowd, the fact that Terith was about to become their ruler was a triviality that bore nothing on the only truly important decision of the day: would he choose Lilleth or Enala?

Terith suppressed a shiver. There was no way out. He'd raced himself into the tightest corner he'd ever been in. He was either going to get the silent treatment or a very close encounter with one of Enala's more dangerous kitchen utensils. Neither thought was very appealing, but one glance at the two girls who, in a show of solidarity were holding hands, reminded him about the numerous advantages of his situation.

They were gorgeous, even more so now that they were suddenly available on a permanent basis, with no conceivable obstacle between him and whomever he chose.

Enala gazed at his eyes, Lilleth at his feet. Neither let go of the other's hand for fear of what might happen. Anxiety turned his empty stomach.

Ferrin made a short speech about the change in rule. Then he placed his woven, iridescent robe, the garment of the champion of champions, on Terith's shoulders. Terith smiled and waved, but his stomach tensed when he saw a dark speck in the distance.

Pert.

The crowd applauded politely at Ferrin's gesture but silenced quickly, waiting for Terith's decision.

"Terith," Ferrin said in a voice that sounded years younger. "You've stalled long enough. It's time you made your choice."

Terith's heart missed several beats at the word *choice*. He stepped forward three paces and locked eyes with Enala. There was loving expectation in her eyes, and for a moment he wavered in his decision. He was chief; he could choose either.

But this was more than gaining a title; it was the binding of two hearts. He had already made his choice. He tried to tell her in his expression, but she only looked more hopeful.

Terith turned his gaze a few degrees and his world shifted. Lilleth's face was calm and assuring.

There were times when the thought of disappointing her had kept him from taking the sort of path Pert had chosen. She was his closest friend and the caring confidant of his young heart's turmoil after summers of war. She had a guarded romantic side as well—not as frolicking as Enala, but the same Montazi fire and passion flowed in her.

Whose children would you rather have in your house all the time? Terith almost laughed at the odd thought and had to lower his eyes to keep from smiling awkwardly.

Catcalls sounded from the crowd, some rooting for one sister or the other. Wedged in between the skirts of two middle-aged women was Mya's awestruck face. If he didn't make his choosing romantic, he'd have her to reconcile with. The boys of the village were watching from farther back where they could pretend to be passively disinterested.

There was one way to know if he chose wrong. He wouldn't be able to bond awakenings. He had never heard of that happening.

Terith took another step forward. He gave a short bow to Lilleth and then Enala. He bent his knee.

Heart thudding in his chest, he reached out and took hold of Lilleth's hand. Her hazel eyes met his. Her eyes welled with tears as he clasped her hand in his gloved one.

I should have taken off my glove!

Terith quickly slipped his hand out of Lilleth's to a shocked expression from Enala and murmurs from the crowd. Terith fumbled to peel off his leather glove and took Lilleth's hand again. A cheer rose up from those in the crowd that could see the choice.

"Will you be my mate, Lilleth, daughter of Ferrin?"

Lilleth's face made an expression of surprise and relief that Terith had never seen before.

Enala put her hand to her mouth, frozen and unbreathing. She shifted slightly, but it seemed a hundred miles away.

As he stood, Lilleth threw her arms around his neck. Her commitment was a complete mirror of Terith's. Her hands cupped his face as she found his lips and kissed him. Then she laid her cheek against his again and tearfully smiled with unrelenting joy.

Terith let the emotion flow through him, as he did when sharing the power of his awakening with his dragon. But this was different. It was Lilleth's love flooding into him, an awesome feeling of complete surrender.

This was it. This was his future. He held her, feeling her body against his as if it were moving through the leather and becoming one. The bond was made.

A vision of Pert and his dragon flashed into Terith's mind—shadows of Lilleth's awakening showing in his own mind.

Terith drew Lilleth behind him protectively as heavy wingbeats sounded overhead. His hands itched for the razor-sharp knives tucked at his calves.

Sounds from the spectators were a mixed rancor of belated cheers and jeers.

"Sorry, Pert. The time is gone," Ferrin said resolutely, looking up at Pert.

"Then *no one* succeeded?" Pert's voice ripped the air with intensity as his dragon's wing strokes beat the air only a few feet over the cowering spectators as his dragon landed in front of Terith and Ferrin.

"Only one," Ferrin said, "the champion of Neutat. The sign of the light came when he arrived. Terith is the chief."

"Impossible! Terith fell. He went into the deep."

Terith stepped forward from the crowd that pressed around him on three sides. Lilleth clung to his arm.

Atop his dragon, Pert turned from Ferrin and locked his eyes with Terith.

Pert's riding leathers were charred and blackened as if he had walked through the flame of a furnace, but his face was whole and new. *Healed! How?*

Pert looked at Terith, rage and disbelief showing in his unscathed black eyes. "I saw you fall!"

"I came back . . . as did you."

"Hear this, runt," Pert said menacingly. He glanced at Lilleth and then back at Terith as a cruel smile stretched across his bitter expression. "There is nothing that I can't take away from you. You'll lose it all, Terith." It was virtually a promise to kill them both when they were alone and unprotected.

"You made oaths to the Montazi," Terith stated, feeling his jaw stiffen with the resolve of a regent. "Do not break them on my watch."

The cursed rider yanked the reins, forcing his beleaguered dragon into the air. Pert turned to share his livid, seething expression with the gathered crowd. "Enjoy your time at the top." He gave a sick laugh. "The higher you climb, the farther you'll fall."

The velra lifted skyward, its chest heaving air.

"Get down!" Terith shouted as the dragon released a belly full of fire over the crowd, turning rain to scalding steam as dozens of spectators dropped to the ground in terror, saved by damp earth and a slim margin.

"He'll get over it," Ferrin said, a hollow phrase for an awkward moment. He turned to the business of dispersing the crowd.

Not until I'm dead, Terith thought.

By his side, Lilleth shook slightly.

"What is it?" Terith asked, sweeping a lock of hair away from her face.

"He killed Remo and Tamm," Lilleth said in a hollow voice. "I saw it when he looked it at me. He did it in the cave . . . Pert cried out for help to Remo and Tamm. He tricked them into stopping. And . . . now they're dead."

He took their strength too, Terith realized. *So that's how he healed.*

Terith lifted Lilleth in his arms and held her head against his chest.

Behind his chosen bride, Enala clasped her arms around her waist, a look of disappointment, hurt, and confusion on her face, while the other eligibles returned to the crowd.

Lilleth shuddered again.

"What is it?" Terith asked.

"Pert will try to kill you now—I didn't mean for this to happen. I didn't want to make him threaten you. I'm so sorry. I—"

"Lilleth," Terith said.

She looked up with desperation showing in her soft brown eyes.

"We have bonded. Our spirits forever united. No matter what

happens, I will never let my love for you die. No foe has the right to take that from us."

Aon crowded up against Terith as familiar faces gathered around them, calling congratulations. "Here's water, Lord. There's food in the keep if you need it." Terith took the skin with a grunt of thanks and downed half of it in a single gulp.

Ferrin drew in front of Terith and waved off the rest of the well-wishers, but the greeters refused to disperse until the better half of the thousands of spectators had embraced them both, many of his friends and many of hers. For Terith, the time passed in a moment, with Lilleth's warm hand in his.

Soon Ferrin, Terith, and Lilleth were alone, save the strongmen and keepers who waited to attend to the few returning competitors. Enala's absence was an unspoken void.

Terith drew Lilleth closer as his mind took a moment to weigh on his nagging worries about Pert and the gathering Outlander horde in the plain beyond the Montas.

Memories of a fight—flame and swords—passed into his sight. The scene was so encompassing Terith felt as though he were falling forward into it.

"I see battle raging," Terith whispered. "Is this real?"

"You have bonded with my daughter," Ferrin said with a note of reluctance. "Those are the visions of her awakening."

Terith sought Lilleth's eyes, replacing the scene with something imminent and peaceful. "Did you see this when you saw my future?"

Lilleth gave a tremulous nod. "Yes . . . and more."

"Are you sure it couldn't have been something from my past?"

Bergulo trudged over and put a meaty hand on Terith's shoulder, nodding to Lilleth. "Apologies, lady." He spoke to Terith. "Chief— used to saying that to Ferrin. The rally signal went out this morning from Erden while the challenge was still on. The horde is nearing the shallows."

"How long before they strike—weeks?" Terith asked.

"It's possible. I don't mean to worry you. This is your summer of promise and all." He nodded to Lilleth. "It's just, the men were all wondering . . . are you to going ride out with us against the horde this summer?"

"I am a rider with an oath. I keep that oath."

Lilleth dropped her head slowly against Terith's shoulder. "Terith . . ."

The dragon rider caressed Lilleth's hair and then whispered into her ear, "Go with Ferrin. I'll be with you soon. I need to finish with my dragon."

Lilleth summoned her strength and left the field guided by Ferrin.

"What of Akara?" Bergulo asked as he and Terith walked together toward the champion golden dragon. "If you ride with us, you'll want a sturdier mount. Ferrin rides a strythe. If you prefer that, it's yours."

"Akara has done enough," Terith said. "If I ride her until she dies, her strength will never be passed to a second generation. The strong must live to reproduce."

"She's an incredible dragon," Bergulo agreed. "Sure you won't just keep her through the summer?"

"And then another winter, and so on. I have to free her eventually. She's proven herself. Sooner the better. More offspring." Terith said the words, but it would take all his will to make himself do it.

Akara lay with one eye open, tethered by a chain in her cage.

Terith opened the cage, drew out his knife, and slashed the lashing joint.

The chain dropped.

Akara's head rose.

Terith stroked her face and then broke open the metal ring on her spine piercings. He tossed the reins into the tall grass.

"You have earned your freedom, Akara. You never need carry a rider again."

Akara stood, lifted her head cautiously and shook it, feeling the new freedom of tetherless neck spines.

"Go!" Terith called, his shaking voice betraying emotion. "You are a champion."

She hopped once, gave a shrill cry, and took to the air, disappearing over the ridge and down into the canyon.

"But for me, one summer more," he said quietly. "One last campaign."

Bergulo clapped his heavy hand on Terith's shoulder. "I'm with you, Terith. To the end."

CHAPTER 19

Toran's fortress at Erdal.

Reann had managed to pull off her risky scheme for getting Verick's notes back in his coat, made up excuses for her daylong absence with Trinah, and began to cope with the reality that she was the fifth heir of Toran.

Washing dishes, she nearly dropped a plate when she realized that she was working as an unpaid servant in her very own castle. She set down the dish with a slight tremble—her dish—then picked it back up and washed it a little better.

What if they knew?

What if Verick knew?

Within the day, her curiosity had grown into tangle of inquisitive intentions.

More had to be known. If Verick was a villain who intended to kill the heirs—including her—as she thought he was, she needed more proof than a diary entry. If he wasn't, as she desperately wished, she needed a reason to believe that he could be trusted.

She had to know more. The gala was only a few days away. Her time at the castle was coming to an end. But she couldn't reveal herself as Toran's heir not knowing if Verick would kill her.

Her plans took her back to the kitchens, where help was often skulking around looking for scraps.

"Wretch."

"Ret," he corrected, hands balling into fists.

"Whichever," Reann said. "I need your clothes. Lend them to me."

Ret narrowed his eyebrows. "And what am I supposed to wear—that skirt?"

"Wear whatever you like. You'll have the evening off. I need to do some work."

"You mean snooping."

"It's none of your business anyway."

"And it's yours?"

"Yes. And it's important."

Ret gave Reann a crusty look. "You'd better finish all my chores and not leave them half done like last time. I got demerits from the head butler."

"That was a rare circumstance," Reann said softly. "I'm sure I can get them all done this time."

"You'd better."

"Good. Take off that tunic."

Reann held up a blanket from the wash. Ret pulled off his tunic and trousers and wrapped himself in the blanket with a confused look that said, *How am I supposed to explain this one to the guys back at the dorm?*

Reann grabbed the clothes and called thanks over her shoulder, rushing off to the nearby armor room, avoiding the women servants' bunkhouse where there would doubtless be awkward questions about why she was changing into Ret's clothing.

The armor room was empty of people, as it usually was, since any servant caught in a room they didn't belong in either got demerits or got assigned to clean it—polishing armor was simply the worst.

Light from a window high on the exterior wall slanted into a mostly vacant alcove where odd weaponry hung on the wall. Reann stepped into the nook that was sheltered from the door, should anyone walk in. She hung Ret's attire on a dull spear point and quickly removed her skirt and blouse. Then she turned to reach for Ret's tunic.

She stopped when she saw her reflection in a shiny shield. The flaxen slip she wore—inadvertently left by a visitor last summer—followed her features nicely. It was a bit on the small side, but not too small, she thought, noting that at least it covered the essentials. What caught her eye the most was her face. She looked older since the last time she had taken stock of herself, and not so frail. It was more of a woman's face, but young. The thought brought a smile to her lips. Even her hair had grown—

Hair!

Reann clamped her hands over head but her tied-back locks spilled out incriminatingly from under her hands. She couldn't hope to impersonate a boy with her wavy locks of brown hair tied back in ribbon. The boy servants didn't wear tall collars that could hide long hair either.

Reann's hair was naturally curly. Her frayed ponytail reached to her shoulders. It was a comely fashion at best, and undeniably modest.

Now it was the problem.

Ret's hair was straight and dangled past his eyes, usually obscuring at least one, if not both. He didn't wear a hat either.

There was only one solution.

Cut it.

Reann considered the massacre. She gazed into the polished bronze, trying to imagine what she would look like with hair draping only just past her chin.

She loosed the ribbon that held her hair back, parted her hair down the middle, and let it in fall waves past her cheeks. Her eyes widened and then twinkled with interest.

She was going to look fantastic.

To seventh hell with modesty, she thought.

Reann reached into Ret's trouser pocket and found his pen knife. Boys were so useful for that sort of thing. It almost made them worth having around.

The first cut hurt. She could almost feel the hundred severed hairs crying out in pain. But she kept sawing at her locks with a blade that turned out to be dangerously sharp.

"A little less knife sharpening and little more attention to me," she said as she hacked another painfully long section of hair. Moments into the act, the reality of it struck her.

"Guardians of the realm beyond," she swore. "I can't believe I'm doing this—I can't believe I just swore and I'm doing this."

There was nothing to do but continue. She kept at it, working feverishly, if only to make the horror pass more quickly.

Unable to stop herself with the job half done, the murder of her hair was over in minutes.

The freshly hewn bangs had unkempt ends that played a few inches past her chin. She hadn't intended it to be *that* short, though it had to be if she meant to impersonate Ret, which was the only way to get near Verick without him noticing.

"Guardians forgive me," she whispered as her fingers traced her face, framed by waving lengths of brown hair. Her face seemed to have changed. Hair traced her hollow cheeks and curled under her narrow chin, like falling water dissipating into a mist above her breast. She no longer looked underweight, but capable and intelligent.

She imitated the queenly stare Trinah had given her, arching her shoulders back and lifting her chin.

"Looks good to me," said a voice from behind her.

Reann's heart jumped into her throat, realizing she was wearing only a thin slip. She clasped both hands over her chest and whirled around, crashing against the shield. "Wretch! What in the name of—"

"The dress looks all right, too," Ret said. He had replaced the blanket she had given him with another set of clothes, probably stolen from Kalen or Regimon or another of the stinky servants in the boy's bunkhouse. "But . . . probably a little too short," he added. His lips drew to one side as if he were trying not to laugh, leaving him with a distinctly impious smirk.

"Demons, Wretch," Reann cried. "Look away. This is my under clothing."

"Oh . . . yeah. Imagine that," he said, barely containing a chuckle.

"Ret, what do you want?" Reann said. Her eyes flicked left and right for cover but found none. She was now keenly aware of just how much of her legs were showing.

"I . . . uh, need my knife."

Reann gave him a fiery glare, as if trying to burn some modesty into him.

"Or you can turn back around and keep working on your hair and . . . I'll just wait here until you're done."

"I am not turning back around so you can gawk at my backside."

"What are you so worked up about? I can gawk at your backside whenever I want."

"Like when?"

"Like when you're mopping, you know, kneeling down on the tile and bent over with your arms stretched out like this while you wipe the floor." Ret bent at his waist mimicking the action.

Reann's jaw dropped as her face and neck turned as red as a poker right out of the fire. "You don't."

She hastily pulled on Ret's tunic and trousers, cinching it with a bit of rope Ret used for a belt.

"Are you going to keep your hair like that?" Ret said as she stomped over and shoved the folded knife back at him.

Reann stopped.

"Why would you care?"

Ret shrugged. "Maybe give me something to look at besides your—"

Reann swatted at him, but Ret easily leapt clear. She pointed a warning finger as she turned away slowly, making sure his eyes didn't wander downward.

"What about this mess, Reann?" Ret said. "Are you just going to leave all that hair on the floor like that?"

Reann's eyes narrowed. "Why don't you clean it up? You can collect every last hair and weave it into a cute little braid for a shrine next to your bed so you can lay there and stare at it and think about me and my . . . hair."

"Maybe I will."

"Don't you dare!"

Reann burst out of the armor room.

"Wretch!" a voice called.

Oh, that's me.

She rolled her head around the way Ret did whenever he was called by one of the kitchen staff.

"Get back in the dining room. Dinner is served . . . by you."

"Yes, ma'am." Reann said lowly, in an easy replication of the boy's occasionally cracking voice.

She was lucky the staff hadn't noticed the height difference. Ret had grown recently. It helped that Reann didn't slouch, and perhaps the staff was still used to imaging him as an impish twit.

Reann certainly was.

Look disinterested, she reminded herself. *And don't do things too politely.*

With the freshly cut bangs hanging in front of her face, Reann was scarcely recognizable.

Seven guests milled about the dining hall, drinking from glasses filled with wine from the famous vineyards that crawled over the gentle hills outside the castle walls. Four were nobles passing through on a summer holiday: three boisterous gents and a large lady who clung to her husband as if he were a handbag. Another guest was a surgeon in residence at Erdal. One was a well-to-do merchant in the fur trade. The last was Verick.

"Dinner is served," Reann stated disinterestedly in an expert imitation of Wretch's droning voice.

The nobles ignored her announcement, but after a few moments they paused their conversations and invited each other to the set tables. The practice of not providing large tables was general in high society, to avoid the appearance of a head position. Reann seated the four traveling nobles at one round service. The surgeon sat at a small table meant for two and laid the book he had been reading on the opposite chair. Verick and the merchant were left at the third setting.

Reann shuttled bread and poured drinks for the next few minutes. As soon as the gentlemen were eating their main courses, she "spilled" the wine on the floorboards, letting slip a filthy word under her breath that only a boy would use to cinch the ruse.

Returning with a towel, she set to cleaning the floor near Verick and the merchant, her ear inclined to their private conversation.

"Slow business, as usual," the merchant said. "Nobody wants furs in the summer when I actually have them. And what of your land dispute?"

"The evidence is mounting," Verick replied politely, "not all in my favor, unfortunately."

"Come all the way from Treban, have you?" the merchant asked.

"Thereabouts. It's a small holding," Verick answered.

"You look about the age to have been in the great navy," said the merchant.

"Missed that, actually," Verick said. "I might have been a cabin boy had I sea legs."

"Great war, it was—epic," the merchant said, eyes twinkling with reflected glory. "I saw the port of Ruban burn with my own eyes—demons as my witness. It was an awesome sight."

Reann watched Verick carefully for some telltale reaction that might prove her theories about his identity.

Verick answered in an unamused voice, "Indeed."

"Here's the funny part, though," said the merchant.

Verick's expression became confused. "How do you mean *funny?*"

"I heard all about it from a crazy old man down on the coast in Yerban—same name as you, in fact. Verick or Ranville, something like that."

Verick inclined his head, disclosing nothing.

"This old man was with Toran during the third crusade, after he settled with the Dervites and went off to fight the Hersians down on the Serbani coasts. The old fella was some kind of valet—cupbearer, he called it. Anyway, he survived the ambush at Toran's harbor since he was on Toran's own ship—the only vessel that made it out."

"I'm aware of that incident," Verick said.

"So you follow me on what happened next. Toran set off and burnt the unprotected Hersian shipyards and then spent a season capturing the very pirate ships that were out looking for him. That was when he intercepted a merchant ship filled with folks from Ruban—all woman and children refugees from well-to-do households. See, folks in Ruban knew revenge was coming. They were fleeing to Hersa."

"Yes, of course. This is all well known."

"But get a whiff of this." The merchant stuck his fork in a piece of overdone meat and shoved it in his mouth, speaking as he chewed. "Everyone thinks Toran found out that there were stowaways down in the ship's stores, the very men Toran was after—filthy traitors all."

"To the point, man."

"And then Toran done them in, all wicked and horrible."

"That is the story," Verick echoed.

"But where's the proof of it?" the merchant said, poking his fork forward at Verick as he wiped his hand on his shirt.

Verick stammered, "Well, none of the ship's passengers ever returned to Ruban, so obviously—"

"There's a reason for that," the merchant said with a knowing chuckle. "This old guy told me that Toran didn't know nothing about the traitors. In fact, all he did when he captured the ship was put the old crew and his own cabin boy on it and send it to Hersa with the Rubani. See, apparently, he was headed for Ruban and didn't want the cabin boy ruined by seeing so much violence so he put them on the first merchant ship to go ashore."

"An admirable sentiment," Verick said in a level tone.

"But the Rubani refugees on the boat were double crossed and sold out as slaves when they arrived at Hersa. Only the old codger escaped to tell the tale."

"The traitors and the innocents weren't murdered by Toran?" Verick whispered. He gave a moment's pause and wiped his lips with his cloth. "They were all sold as slaves?" Verick's voice was perceptibly anxious.

"That was just the women folk. For them traitors, it was a fate worse than death," the merchant said heavily, turning his chewing lips into a disgusted frown. "Don't want to spoil your dinner by saying."

"Tell me," Verick ordered, "if you please."

"Knew you was gonna say that." The merchant grinned with the look of a peddler who had his buyer hooked. "The refugees on that boat blackmailed that cabin boy into stealing extra food for their stowaways hiding in the smuggler's cabin, the traitors that led the conspiracy against Toran—you know, Dorgan the Traitor and his folk."

"Do proceed," Verick urged. His fist closed tightly on his fork.

"What them Rubani didn't count on was this cabin boy being all blood-loyal for Toran. The ship was just about twelve days sailing from Hersa—contrary wind that time of year—when a fella on the boat died of flesh-eating fever. So then the cabin boy took a piece of the dead man's clothes and made sop of it for mixing with the stowaways' food. It was a catching fever, by my beard. Those traitors rotted away with the same disease," the merchant said matter-of-factly, "before the ship set anchor in Hersian waters. The Hersians figured he put a curse on those traitors and sent their rotted skeletons as a warning, but Toran didn't put a curse on nobody. He had nothing to do with it!" The merchant roared with laughter.

A vein on Verick's temple rose and his nostrils flared as he cut vigorously into his meat.

"That cabin boy is the greatest danged hero in the entire war—except Toran, of course. And nobody knows where the kid is. That's what the old cupbearer told me. Ain't that about the funniest thing you ever heard?"

"I don't—" Verick began curtly. "Would you care to explain what is so humorous?"

The merchant downed his wine in a gulp and slapped Verick's knee in jest. "Don't you see, my friend? The whole legend of the Ruban Payment is a myth. Toran didn't turn nobody to skeletons. A cabin boy did in all the criminals—the very one Toran was trying to keep from seeing flesh slaughtered. Toran never had no power to curse nobody. He was a fool! But a lucky one, by my beard."

"Hardly amusing," Verick noted.

"The craziest part is, Toran got his revenge by showing mercy to the families of the very folks who betrayed him. It's the greatest twisted irony in the history of the realm. And it's a fact!" The beefy merchant smacked his fist into the table triumphantly and gave a ceremonious belch.

Verick set his fork against his plate, his face wormed into a look of revulsion.

"Told you it'd ruin your supper. Don't worry, that appetite will be back once you see some dessert. You, servant boy. Stop your gawking and bring my pie."

Reann scurried out of the dining hall so quickly she tripped on the peeling floorboard as she came into the serving kitchen. She fell headlong and threw out her hand to catch herself on a shelf. Her fingers landed on the lip of an ornate porcelain plate displayed on the shelf, saving her a faceful of floor.

The dish wasn't so lucky. It somersaulted through the air, landing with a crash just past Reann's outstretched hands.

The voice of the merchant boomed out, "That had better not have been my pie!" The nobles all gave amused laughs, audible through the tapestry curtain separating the rooms.

Reann looked at the cracked remains of the decorated plate spread across the floor. As she picked the pieces up, she thought of the cabin boy. He had spent more time as a child with Toran—her own father—than she had. It wasn't fair. Moreover, in true Toran fashion, he had abandoned the boy to fend for himself just as soon as he had the upper hand on his enemies.

Reann sucked in a breath of surprise. Then her face spread into a platter-sized grin.

"That's *him* . . . the witch's son." All the pieces fit together: found on the coast, kept by Toran's side during the war, fiercely loyal to Toran. He wasn't an infant—*the adopted heir!*

It was so like Toran that Reann could scarcely believe she hadn't thought of it before. What was blood to Toran?

"'Loyalty makes sons and brothers, not blood.'" Reann had heard him say it himself.

She relished the realization as she sorted into her apron the salvageable pieces of the broken platter—a one-of-a-kind plate, in fact.

The washwoman had emphasized that point many times, "Toran himself ate from it." The best Reann could do would be to hide the pieces in her bunk and hope that Effel didn't find them when she got back.

What Reann relished most of all was the piece of the puzzle the merchant had accidentally put into place. The third heir, her adopted brother, the witch's son, was born in the Serbani mountains and raised by his adopted father on the coast as a cabin boy.

Reann swelled with pride at her own genius. But even that was swallowed by a burgeoning feeling of love for her still-unknown sibling, one of the chosen heirs with responsibilities and a heritage as grand and as fragile as the exquisitely decorated plate that lay in pieces in front of her.

The platter had been a kind of compass design typical of the five realms, with a symbol at each compass point for each of the four border realms, with Toran's castle in the center and smaller compass points on the diagonals. Rather than simple symbols, this plate was rich with detail. Painted scenes had decorated the space surrounding the now-shattered compass: A castle—*the old one up on the hill that Toran moved to make his new citadel;* a ship—*Hersian;* five wolves in a full moon—*the third lying down;* a dragon with a tiny rider set between two pointed mountains—*not flat-topped like the megaliths of Montas;* and a desert hawk with sword in its claws—*its eyes are crystals.*

Reann's expression stretched into a look of triumph. This was the platter Toran ate from. It was part of the regular tour for visitors, in fact.

These are clues!

The tapestry flew open behind her and Reann jerked in front of the pieces, shielding them from view.

"Where's the pie, already?"

Washing the dishes Reann's head spun from the late revelations: the merchant's tale, Verick's strange reaction, and the clues on the broken plate.

Verick's demeanor hadn't hid his surprise at the merchant's tale. Somehow, he was connected to those events. It was time to confirm her suspicion that Verick was Rubani or, at a minimum, dangerously sympathetic.

She recovered her clothing from Ret, who had taken it with him to his bunkhouse as collateral—or perhaps he had intended to keep it for his shrine. Then she returned to the library, her newly cut hair bouncing along unfettered.

As she perused the books in the history section, a dark thought chilled her. The scattered pieces in her mind arranged themselves into a new portrait of horror. Breathless at the thought, Reann carried her candle soundlessly across the shadowy floor toward the biographies and censuses. The urge to turn and flee grew more uncomfortable in her chest.

She lifted her candle, checking again to be sure that no one else was in the library, yet felt no less endangered.

Reann moved past a movable partition designed to keep guests from disturbing the cache of noble records: lineages, seals, rights, charters, and relics.

Under the light of her candle, Reann ruffled through piles of documents until her fingers brushed a leather-bound book and spied the words *Genealogy of Ruban*.

Reann opened the volume detailing the ruling families of the Serban's most remote province. The record was one of the most complete in the pile, except for one recent name which had been deliberately burnt from the final sheet in the book. Reann knew that name—everybody did.

The name Dorgan was infamous in the five realms for treachery.

Reann leaned forward. On the official family tree, near the bottom was a charred mark, a place that once held the name Dorgan. And below that, a thin line led down to one name: Dorian.

I knew it. Dorgan had a son!

A subtle draft in the room gave her a powerful shiver. Reann quickly replaced the book of pedigrees and turned to a wall full of sectioned cubbies stuffed with rolls of canvas, reading titles and pushing them back as if she were sorting vegetables for market. Finally, she found her quarry.

The old leather tie came apart in her hands as she unrolled the stack of canvas sheets. She peeked around the partition to look back at the partly open library door.

She had left it open out of habit, perhaps. Nobody was awake this time of night, and the guards didn't patrol inside the castle after the gates were shut. She needn't worry about being discovered.

Reann dropped the pile of painted portraits facedown on the table. On the backside of each painting, the names labeled the pictured nobles. The wax seal of the noble, to certify the authenticity of the portrait, also emblazoned many. The names were largely unfamiliar until—

Dorgan. Her stomach turned. It was the first time she had seen the name written without the usual postscript title: *the traitor.*

Dorgan of Ruban, one of a cabal of Rubani nobles who profited from illicit trade with Hersa, had led Tira's corsairs to where Toran's fleet was sheltered in a cove. Dorgan's act had lived in the histories as the ultimate act of treason, disloyalty, and dishonor. Tens of thousands across all five realms cursed that name for the loss of their brothers, fathers, husbands, and sons.

She separated the canvas from the rest and turned it over to view the portrait. By light of the single candlestick, a gaunt face stared back at her. Reann's grip slipped on the candle, spilling wax onto the corner of the painting. The likeness to Verick was unmistakable.

She pulled her fingers back as if it were tainted by a plague, clasped her hands to her chest, and turned away from the wall of records, scarcely breathing.

Verick was really Dorian of Ruban, son of the greatest traitor since the dragon-slaying Outlanders of legend.

There could be only one reason for his seeking Toran's heirs.

As hated as Dorgan's name was in the five realms, Toran's name was equally infamous in its southernmost province for the burning of their port—their only source of livelihood.

The Ruban Payment.

By Reann's reckoning, Dorian would have been a young child at the time, left behind in Ruban when his father fled to Hersa. The burning of the port and the ensuing poverty and starvation had made an example to all the realms. No one had ever dared betray Toran again.

"He wants to find the heirs," she whispered, "to kill them."

Heart and head had a tug-of-war inside her. She knew two men. One a gentleman and friend; the other a fraud and a killer. One a foolish girl's wish; the other her doom. She almost wished she hadn't discovered Verick's real identity.

A creak sounded through the library and Reann's heart seized in her chest. Light from the hall cast a tall shadow into the library. The legs of the shadow crossed into a solid shape as the figure moved swiftly into the room. Reann spied the shadow of the scabbard.

It's him!

The evidence of her discovery lay scattered on the table. She would have no chance to make excuses. Curiosity would finally kill her.

Soft steps sounded swiftly and the shadow merged with the dark floor and walls.

He's coming to the library alone? Why? Whatever the reason, Reann did not feel safe. *He could kill me here, now,* she realized.

From the recessed corner of the library, Reann's eyes darted for a safe haven, finding only unscalable walls of shelves.

Even if Reann could have turned herself into a mouse, she wouldn't have found an escape. Behind her, the library ended in a walled corner.

Reann put out the flickering candle with her fingers, dousing herself in instant darkness. She shrunk back against the outer wall of shelves until her body pressed against the shutters of a window.

In answer, the shutters spilled open on their well-oiled hinges, revealing a starless, moonless night broken only by distant torches on the fortress wall. The courtyard was a twenty-foot drop.

In desperation, Reann climbed onto the sill, gripped the wooden shutters with her fingertips and swung outward. Her feet dangled free as the shutters patted against a cover of ivy. Reann's fingers turned white trying to keep her grip on the wooden slats.

She listened as footsteps moved in a deliberate pace toward her. Her lungs burned for air but she refused to breathe. More footsteps. Then silence.

The dull thump of something being set on the reading table reached her, followed by a scrape as it slid forward.

A book—what could he be reading in the military records section?

Paper rustled intermittently, signaling the hasty turning of pages. Then silence.

"Ah," Verick said with a note of pleasure at his discovery. "Here we are. At last. Wait, no."

The book closed.

At last, Reann thought. She clung to the window shutters with cold fingers. The strength of her grip began to fade. *He's leaving.*

"Dungeons of the seventh . . ." Dorian suddenly whispered. His voice trailed off.

His footsteps came quickly toward the window.

Reann attempted to move farther out on the shutter, but her hand slipped. Hanging by one arm, her unbalanced body swung outward, twisting her arm and leaving her facing away from the fortress. Her loose hand gripped a few leaves of ivy clinging to the stone wall, while her grip on the shutter frame slipped in tiny, deadly increments, like a clock counting down to death.

Verick's face flashed into view briefly—the man she had known, and almost trusted, and now feared, as Dorian. He glanced down into the courtyard. Across the courtyard torches wavered. Two guards headed for a night patrol on the castle wall approached from the gate house.

Dorian ducked back into the library. The candle went out. Then silence.

Reann waited three perilous seconds more before letting go of the ivy and swinging back toward the open window. She lifted her leg to catch the sill and grasped the curtains.

The thick cloth of the curtains held.

Reann crawled over the sill and slid to her knees on the library floor, shaking from head to toe. She gulped air and whimpered.

Then she noticed the empty reading table.

Dorgan's portrait!

It was gone.

Verick—or rather Dorian, son of Dorgan—would have to assume that somebody had found out his secret. It would only make him more dangerous, more desperate.

Reann waited, knees curled to her chest, her body shaking and unsure of whether it was safe to leave the library. Her doubts screamed that Verick might be waiting for her outside in the hall with another threat or to fulfill his earlier one.

Thoughts of the slain thief, his pale face, the blood on her fingers flickered through her mind amid images of Dorian in his room, his hand on her shoulder, his arms embracing her.

"No," she whispered, trying to make herself believe. "He's not going to kill me. Anybody could have found that portrait. He doesn't know."

Reann calmed herself. She breathed slowly until her thoughts became measured and sure.

He came to read something, she decided, *something about one of the heirs—something he doesn't want to share.*

Reann looked at the row of records, barely illuminated in the light from the distant lanterns on the fortress wall. The sheer number of books was staggering. He could have read any of them.

Reann tapped her finger on her chin and then gave a wry smile. *Nobody ever reads these books.*

Reann paced a step back and looked more closely. She used an old parlor trick, sniffing along the row of military records to see if any smelled less stale. One of the books had a distinctly less mustiness about it, and the faint smell of a candle scented with maple—like the one Reann had placed in Dorian's room a day before.

She pulled the book from the shelf, her fingers tingling with anticipation. It was a ledger recording payments made to war widows and their survivors. Reann carefully opened the cover and began pressing the pages sideways, feeling how they opened easily to pages where the oil from Dorian's perusing fingers eased the cling of the thin sheets. The book slipped open to a page in the last third of the book.

A gap in the late night clouds let a glow of hazy moonlight in through the window. Reann moved to the window and turned the book toward the light.

Names of slain soldiers occupied the first column. The second column was their rank, then their commanding officer, the date and cause of death, and the pension due. The last column contained details of the payment recorded by the commanding officer.

It was the law that each officer, a noble, was to pay the pension of his slain cavalry to the man's widow and kin.

The horror of it was that Reann knew exactly why Dorian had come for this book.

The birth of a child to Emra, the blind translator, was written in the midwife's record book.

An unwed courtier . . . and blind.

"The eyes of blind see anew. They behold his fortress ever true," Reann whispered, recalling how Dorian had mentioned the couplet from his notebook.

Reann's eyes stared at the text. She recognized Toran's handwriting as tears welled in her eyes.

Name of Deceased: Rembra of Fordal
Rank: Captain at Arms

Circumstances of Death: Perished defending Toran at the ambush of Devil's Canyon, South Dervan Lowlands, 7th day of the 40th week, 23rd year of the reign of Toran. Awarded the Order of the Diamond Star for loyalty.

Next of kin: Emra of Fordal, daughter

The name Emra was crossed out with a notation *presumed deceased* in newer, finer letters, followed by the words *Sole heir: Reann of the Citadel of Toran.*

The column for remunerations included Reann's granted status as a ward of the estate.

"He knows," Reann said. Her heart ached.

Dorian, her first crush, was her mortal enemy. Then she recalled his reaction as he read the words. It wasn't a snappy "gotcha" or a sinister, hissing "finally!"

He had whispered *no* as if he hadn't wanted it to be true. A sliver of hope pierced the darkness.

He cares for me.

Ranger sauntered into view and hacked on a fur ball.

"Stop being so light-minded," Reann chided. But the absurdity of it cracked on her like a falling piece of lumber. "No, you're absolutely right. Get it out. It's all just a matter of getting the bad out. Toran always said you can't win a war, you can only win friends. That's what I have to do."

"I can get the bad out of him, Ranger," Reann whispered. "I have to."

Dorian was the son of a traitor. Verick was her friend. She couldn't even bring herself to call him Dorian.

He was Verick.

Dorian had to die for Verick.

CHAPCER 20

Montazi Realm.

The business of preparing for war continued as it had for every summer in Terith's memory. Except in Neutat, where the preparations doubled. The villagers had split, half of them returning to Neutat and half remaining at the place of resort.

Ore from the upper Montas arrived daily, dropped in heaps at temporary forges set up in courtyards, transformed by the heavy blows of hammers into piles of arrowheads and swords. Werm and the engineers continued to repair the bridges, hoist root dwellings back onto the fractured megalith, and build paths to homes displaced by the blast. The ivy was sustained by the incessant rain as new roots plunged into the cracks made by the steam blast, webbing the broken rock back together. Creaks and groans were a constant nighttime serenade as the broken mass settled.

Terith sent two of his best yearling dragons to Tertat, Tamm and Remo's home village. It was an insufficient gesture of thanks to the men who had helped him beat Pert in the challenge, though the animals would certainly strengthen their strythe-fruit dragon crossbreeding program.

Terith took time when he could to be with his promised wife Lilleth, always traveling to Ferrin-tat by night to save a day's work. When the sun rose in the morning, the canyons echoed with the scattered cries of dragon hatchlings, the hope of the future.

It was solstice, and it was hot, so muggy it seemed the air itself was sweating.

The women of Ferrin-tat, especially the unwed, traipsed about in summer clothes. Terith wore no top, his shirt and cloak stuffed in a woven bag slung from his shoulder as he crossed the megalith toward Ferrin's keep, passing armed guards and bowmen and gathering as many friendly greetings as salutes.

When Terith arrived at the circle court, Lilleth waved to him. She wore a scant leather top. Her long legs peeked from between the folds of a side-split skirt. Seated on a cushion sewing, she was damp with perspiration in the heat of the early afternoon. It was the first time Terith had seen her wearing that kind of summer clothing.

"Wow, Lilleth, you look—"

"Like an Outlander slave," she said with a laugh and a conspicuous, yet very attractive, blush. "I know."

"Any particular reason?"

"You."

"Me?"

Lilleth leaned back into the retreating shade of an overhanging broad fern. She patted the pillow next to her. Terith dropped his travel bag but, instead of sitting, scooped Lilleth up into his arms, cradling her with the ease of something much smaller and lighter, but no less precious.

"I would think you were Enala, dressed like that, but for your eyes. I know those."

Lilleth took Terith's face between her hands and pressed a kiss against his lips.

The cherry red of her lips clung to his as she wrapped her arms around his neck and slowly put her feet down on tiptoes, almost floating.

At the touch of her lips, a flicker of awakening rose unbidden. Light from beyond the horizon flared in the corners of his vision, painting the world in an electric hue. A fresh breeze swirled around them. Whether it was in his head or real, Terith couldn't tell. It was paradise in her arms either way.

"Wow," he said, taking a breath. "Did you do that?"

"Do what? I thought that was you."

"It's hot enough around here as it is," croaked an old cook, leaning her head out of the kitchen door, "without you two steaming up the place!"

Terith laughed and took Lilleth's hand. They walked together, laughing as they went, taking the high road to the summit past the hot spring. No thought of climbing into the steaming water crossed his mind. The muggy air alone was as good as a sauna. He peered up into the late morning sunlight that shone in streaks through the low clouds.

As they walked, Lilleth lifted a bird from a limb and held it in her hands. "Look. These are northern birds come south for the summer rains, a backward migrant."

"Why don't they try to fly away when you grab at them?" Terith wondered. "I've never caught a bird without scratching my knees to pieces."

"It's because I don't try to eat them."

"Shall I pluck it and cook it for you?" Terith volunteered.

"No!" Lilleth let the bird fly away and looked at him with narrowed eyes. "Don't touch my little birdies."

"Your birdies?" His eyes strayed down.

Lilleth quickly put a finger under his chin and pushed his head up to meet her coy gaze. "Yes. They're pretty."

"I'll give you that one," Terith said. He cupped her hand in his and kissed her fingertip. "But how do they taste?"

"Oh, don't be so terrible. You're a man, not a beast."

"What makes you so sure?" Terith laughed. He kissed her hand and then her wrist, moving gradually up her arm.

"Oh, I'm sure," Lilleth said, putting her free hand on his bare chest where Terith's heart beat much too quickly for a casual stroll. "But are you?"

"When is the wedding again?" Terith stammered. "Not today?"

"Not for two and a half months," Lilleth sighed, taking his hand in hers, interlocking her fingers as the two meandered along the trail.

"And I have a war to win in the meantime," Terith said.

Lilleth slid her rolled fan from under her skirt tie, spread it, and fanned it over her chest, looking even more attractive. "Is it time yet to go to battle? How long can you stay?"

"The horde will strike before the week is out."

"How many are there?"

"Too many," Terith said, as a shiver passed over him. "I'm afraid a lot of—never mind that, Lilleth. Our time is our time. Let's enjoy it."

"You'd better," she said with a smile. "Because I'm not wearing this every day."

"You mean you want to take it off?" Terith said delightedly.

Lilleth gasped and smacked him playfully on the head with her fan. "Don't press your luck."

"Thanks, by the way," Terith said walking with her, their joined hands swinging gently.

"For what?" she asked, picking a yaz fruit and biting into it.

"For convincing me to ride in the challenge."

"You're thanking me?" Lilleth shook her head. "I'm not the one who got shot at, flamed at—"

"Punched in the gut."

"Punched?"

"Long story—it was in the tunnel."

Seeing the look in Terith's eye, Lilleth didn't ask. Thoughts of Pert dropped the tune of the conversation a shade.

After a minute of quiet walking in the dark wood, Lilleth spoke again. "About the war," she said. "I . . . I've been thinking."

"You can't change what will happen," Terith said softly. "Don't let it trouble you. Can't you just believe that things will work out?"

"I know, I should . . . But should we . . . I mean, what if you die? You will fall, I know. If I saw it, it happened, or will, I mean. I've spent a month learning to accept it. It's better than denying it, anyway. That's your job."

"Fair enough," Terith said. His heart ached for Lilleth. He didn't believe that what she saw would happen. It wasn't part of his story. His story was with her.

"This may be our only time together," she said softly. "Should we . . ." Her voice trailed off as she squeezed his hand more tightly. She faced him and looked him in the eyes. "Should we have a child now?"

"Now?" Terith choked.

"Is it the best thing to do?" she asked. "There's no other man for me in this realm. I know that. Without you, I would die a maid and have no heir and your line would perish as well. It defeats the Montazi way."

"But the oath," Terith said, voice a bit shaky. "We must keep the summer of promise."

"And what if you cannot?" Lilleth said kindly. "By not returning, is it any different than ending the promise before you go to war? Our marriage is forfeit in either case."

"You would join now," Terith said nervously, "and be a mother?"

Lilleth looked away in frustration. "I didn't say . . . I only meant to ask whether it was the best thing to do, given the circumstances."

"Hence the Outlandish outfit?"

A smile of embarrassment crossed Lilleth's lips. "Was it working?"

"Yeah. I can hardly get a sentence out straight—did Enala put you up to seducing me or something?"

Lilleth drew a shaky breath. "She'll be your sister before long, you know."

"Well?"

"We did talk about what ought to be done. I won't say what she said about it."

"Was she tipsy?" Terith laughed.

"Possibly."

"Were you?"

"Definitely."

Terith took Lilleth in his arms and held her against his chest. He whispered in her ear, "It is enough that you would give yourself for me and forfeit your reputation and honor. I will treasure it and give it two months more grace, and a lifetime if it comes to that. I will return. In the meantime, our awakenings will go undimmed and with a clear mind we'll face whatever comes."

"Chief!" a voice called from behind them on the trail. The sound was unmistakably urgent.

Terith turned his head and spotted the young man who had delivered his dragon riding gear on the day of the race. "Aon?"

"Sir, we've just got word from the border. Erden is overrun."

Terith's heart sank through his stomach. "The watchtower at Erden? How?"

"The horde crossed the Erden shallows by night and scaled the cliffs," Aon said. "They're moving across the megaliths, using our bridges—thousands of them are on the megaliths already."

"Attacking at night, crossing the deep with cannons," Terith said. "But . . ." It was a death sentence. "The Outlanders never sacrifice their own clansmen," Terith said in a confused shock.

Then he realized to his horror that only the first waves of soldiers would have died. In large numbers, it was possible to overwhelm the predators of the deep. His narrow escape had been because the flies had chosen the dragon carcass over him. But only someone who had been to the deep would know that secret.

Something has changed. He shook his head. "Dungeons of hell—thousands on the Montas!" Not even Toran had faced an army moving in the cover of the forested megaliths.

"Terith?" Lilleth said, holding back a sob.

He put his arms on Lilleth's narrow shoulders. "I must go, love. Now."

She looked up at him, eyes welling with tears.

"I *will* come back. That is a promise."

Lilleth bit her lip as a tear slipped down her face.

Terith embraced her once more and then released her, feeling her spirit separate from his as he moved away.

She collapsed to her knees.

"Aon, watch over her," Terith commanded. "Do not leave her alone until I return, not ever. Here is the token of my charge."

Terith unstrapped one of the two ever-present blades tied to his legs and passed it to the boy.

"I commission you, Aon of Ferrin-tat," he said, "as a rider of the Montazi. Swear you will keep this oath and protect my wife-to-be."

"I will," Aon said, through stammering lips, just a boy, but rising to manhood with his oath.

Terith leaned forward and whispered in his ear, "I can spare no men to aid you. You will have no strength besides your own. Every rider is needed at the front. May you live to see the dragons return."

"May the dragons return," Aon said, eyes staring at the knife in his hands, its leather handle stained in a dark red hue.

"May you return also, chief!" Aon called.

As Terith hurried away from his bride-to-be, his heart felt as though it had crumbled away within him.

He kindled a fire in its place.

Pages, keepers, riders, and champions all crowded the main hall of the keep. All that remained was the chief's call to battle, an ancient ritual, and the highest tribute to those who would leave and the last rite for those who never would return.

"You who are too young to ride, mark this well," Terith said, his voice defiant and ringing with force off the walls of the keep. He was clad in Ferrin's battle-tried armor, shin plates, gauntlets, and breastplate with the helmet tucked under his arm. "There is no birth into nobility. There is only one trait that earns you the right to ride: courage. Behold, your riders!" Terith held out his gauntleted hand, gesturing to the armored men. "Long ago we made the choice that brings us to battle. We chose the path of light."

"The awakening is nothing more and nothing less than the power of faith. It is honor-bound. We keep our oaths, and the awakening lives within us."

It was partly true, Terith realized with a shiver of regret. The awakening knew only a rider's deepest conviction. He must be true to the principles of his heart.

For Terith, honor. For Pert, treachery.

Both had access to the awakening for their own purposes.

Terith eyed the riders one by one, walking down the line. "Come, riders of the Montazi!" Terith raised his remaining dagger into the air, his tone soaring. "Ride with me. Ride into battle!"

The warriors began the rider's song. Others in the keep joined in. The notes rang around the cavern. The words told of honor and sacrifice, of motherland and kin.

As the last notes of the hero's chorus trailed into silence, Terith came to the end of the line. He clasped wrists with each rider in the ceremonial call to battle. Gauntlets clanked together. Eyes met. Wordless vows of loyalty exchanged in the sacred space between rider and chief.

To battle.

The riders numbered twenty-five in all. Seven from Neutat had arrived only minutes before, answering the rally call. Others would ride from Tertat in the high country and from the southern megaliths.

It was a force large enough to slay legions of soldiers in an open battlefield.

But the horde had the cloud forest for protection. They were using the Montas' own defense.

Some riders would not return.

Terith turned to the foot soldiers and pages. "Those who do not ride must not fail us: the scouts, the supply lines, the archers. You are our vital breath. Fight well." Terith gave a salute, his arms crossed in front of his chest, and turned to leave, as he had every summer for many years.

This time, he felt deep in his bones, was different.

Bergulo, Ferrin's dragon keeper, was the last in the line and joined Terith as they walked briskly from the keep into the wide green where the war dragons rested saddled and waiting. Bergulo was Terith's sergeant-at-arms, a man so impressively strong that Terith would take no other by his side.

Bergulo saluted Terith's lieutenant, a respected man named Rindl.

"Orders, chief?" Bergulo asked.

"Destroy the bridges at Erden," Terith said. He glanced at Rindl.

The lieutenant nodded his agreement. "We have to prevent any more Outlanders from getting on the Montas—make them cross the deep a dozen times."

"Give the order," Terith said.

Bergulo turned and roared to the riders, "Mount up! We ride for Erden. The bridges must fall."

The riders hurried onto the field where keepers and volunteers kept the dragons' reins. Sweethearts and mothers wept and waved as the young men climbed into the harnesses and closed up their faceplates.

Terith climbed onto the harness of Ferrin's strythe, a long-fanged creature named Bander. The flawless dragon offered strength, speed, and most importantly, a stomach full of hellfire. Riders checked harnesses and armor buckles and tied down weapons. Most had a small shield strapped across their back and carried either a short bow with arrows or a clutch of javelins, as well as rider's sword, the last defense if their dragon died.

Werm came up beside Terith, his lurching steps betraying his belly full of butterflies. "Terith, what of those in Neutat?"

Terith paused. The horde was crossing into the Montas at the Erden shallows, east of the crossroads that led to Ferrin-tat. Neutat was halfway between, but a half day's journey south. There was no way to position enough riders to protect both Neutat and the crossroads.

"It should be possible to get some of the villagers farther inland before the Outlanders reach the crossroads," Terith decided. "I'll send a rider. My remaining riders and I will take out as many of the bridges near Erden as we can to prevent more of the horde from moving inland. But Werm," he reached down and gripped the engineer's shoulder, "you *must* get to the crossroads with your catapult before the horde arrives. All roads inland pass through the crossroads—all the roads the horde knows about anyway."

"My stone bridges," Werm muttered, his eyes distant.

"If they capture the crossroads," Terith warned, "no place in the Montas will be safe. Can you break them—all of them? The horde could be there by midday tomorrow."

"I'll . . . get started," Werm grumbled. He stumbled backward and hurried off the field with his lumpy jog. Destroying bridges he had designed to last more than a century hurt him to the core.

"Kyet," Terith called. The dragon of the youngest rider of Neutat came in swift bounds until Kyet's smaller fruit dragon stood alongside Terith's. "Ride to the place of resort. If the path is open to the highlands have Mya signal the retreat. If not, warn Redif to prepare against the siege and cut down all the bridges through Neutat."

"But, sir?" Kyet complained, slicking his long jet-black hair away from his eyes and looking away in frustration. He knew it was a dismissal from battle. "I was halfway there with the patrol orders when the rally flares went off. I've only just returned!"

Terith fixed his eyes on Kyet. "The horde is upon us and you *must* bring Mya back with you."

"Yes, Terith—chief!" Kyet answered smartly. He was a good match for Mya, if he could keep their future alive.

"I didn't take a fall into the deep with her on my back so I could see her captured by the horde. Ride hard. We rendezvous at the crossroads. Before sunrise, I must have Mya at the crossroads."

Kyet saluted and blew his whistle. His sleek fruit dragon, a third year, kicked off and beat its wings into the air.

"Riders!" Terith called.

His sergeant and lieutenant formed up beyond his wingtips as the riders flew their dragons into a fearsomely tight group.

Terith scanned the army of fire-breathing war dragons, knowing every moment was critical. "Keep a wary eye out for those cannons and nets—one shot, one dragon down. Stay out of range or out of sight."

"What about their archers?" Rindl asked. "They'll have scout patrols at all the bridges."

"Stay low and tight. If we get past their front line, the soldiers in the rear won't be prepared to fight and their archers will hesitate to fire back over their own ranks. Our task is to cut off their supply lines at the first bridges and prevent more Outlanders from crossing into the upper Montas."

"But what about the Outlanders already on the megaliths?" Bergulo, the bulky dragon keeper asked. "Who will stop them?"

Terith knew Bergulo knew the answer. He only asked the question to bring up the topic nobody else would.

The battle plans were clear enough. Wherever the horde attacked, all riders within a half-day ride went to the front, no questions asked, no hesitation. The reinforcements would take the rear positions to defend the villages.

With the attack focused at Erden, the reinforcements would come from the southern Montas, from Entat the old capital, Cafertat, and the villages near Pert's fortress at Montasen.

"It takes a day to get here from Entat," Terith said. "When Pert's riders arrive, the southern riders will help us defend the bridges between the crossroads and the capital, or destroy them if they have to."

"So it's down to Pert in the end," the spindly Rindl said dryly. He was lanky, forty-something, and bald, but deadly with a spear and tactics.

"Let's focus on our job first," Terith said. "The front end of the column will be spread out—very dangerous. We can't be worrying about other things."

Rindl agreed. "At dusk, we meet at the watchtower."

"At dusk." Terith blew his whistle and snapped the reins. "Up Bander." The strythe, powerful, war-hardened, and long fanged, lifted into the air. Terith relished its strength as he gained altitude much more quickly than Akara could have borne him up. The riders launched in the air behind him, falling into a vee formation. The pace was aggressive. Every minute, more savage Outlanders poured into their realm.

A mile into the ride, Bergulo rotated into the lead position. "How are we going to take the bridges, high or low?" he asked as Terith moved into Rindl's position.

"Both," Terith said quickly. He turned to Rindl who was riding a brown strythe with enormous fangs that overhung its jaw. "Take Ferrin's troop east of the Erden shallows. Bergulo will bring the other volunteers around the other side. Both formations will cross behind the watchtower. That will turn their cannons backward, away from the front of the column. My Neutat riders will start some fires to keep the Outlanders busy while you attack the bridges."

Rindl nodded. "Circle around, attack from the rear. Got it."

"We'll look for the fires," Bergulo said.

"Rendezvous at the crossroads," Terith said. "May your dragons return."

"Dragons' return or no," Bergulo said through clenched teeth. "I'll personally escort a company of Outlanders to the seventh dungeon of hell if I have to. Break formation!" he called.

He gave a hand signal to his riders and the assembly broke seamlessly into three tight vees. Those who remained with Terith, all Neutat riders, descended into the canyon following Bander's silent wingbeats. The other two groups climbed and separated.

When the others were well out of earshot, Terith made a gesture and the vee inverted. Terith was at the back so his voice would carry to the men in front. "The deep is a fire bomb. Last time I was down there the air in the swamp was so rotten with fermentation it nearly exploded when I sprayed out a little ragoon juice. The air of the deep is hot, and the evening air of the Montas is cool. We only need to turn the air."

"A cyclone," said Trip, the liveliest of the Neutat with a clever smile. "If we draw up the swamp air, a spark will start a firestorm."

"The fire cyclones will keep the Outlanders busy while we cut down the bridges," Jand said, impassioned excitement showing in his only remaining eye. "I like it."

Terith looked to the right, where Nema flew, trying to judge what he thought of the plan. He was a gifted rider, nearly Terith's equal, a habitually impulsive type who managed to luck himself out of almost as much trouble as he landed himself in. After a few seconds, he nodded and whispered to Terith, "Guardians keep us. That fire will burn out of control."

Hours later, the group let down a half mile beyond the crossroads. The horde was just ahead. Behind them, the sun was setting in an orange sky. Ahead, the megaliths ended abruptly. The last canyon dividing the volcanic mesas from the unbroken plain was shallowest at this point—the Erden shallows.

The familiar watchtower atop the last megalith poured smoke into the twilight sky.

The horde, rather than attempting to bridge the shallows, had braved the deep and scaled the cliff walls on the opposite side. The flesh-eating maggots, vampire leeches, and scorpions could not stop so many at once. Never before had the clans made a cooperated sacrifice, using their sheer numbers to overwhelm the predators of the deep. And it had worked. The horde was closer to crossing the Montas than any time in memory—and on Terith's watch.

Terith led his team down into a hidden clearing.

"Cut that ivy," he ordered. "I want two lengths of fifty yards."

He dismounted and joined the riders as they ripped vegetation from long sections of ground-running ivy with cloak-sized leaves branching at intervals.

Terith secured the front of one ivy rope around the horn on Bander's saddle. "Just like the parades," Terith explained. "Everybody support a section of the ivy. We'll use the big leaves like the vanes of a windmill to stir the air in the deep. Nema, get the other length of ivy and take your patrol down the canyon on the south side."

"Parade ribbons are a lot lighter than ivy," Nema complained. He motioned to a couple of riders who hauled out another section of ivy.

Nema's twin Kema watched the other group of dragons with an anxious, pensive look. By nature he was not the warring type. He was a poet.

"How much longer?" Trip asked. "I can't wait to see the looks on their faces when we light up these firestorms—special Montazi welcome."

Ahead, in the distance, the other two teams would be circling behind the enemy, out over the Outlands.

"I can see their scales shining now, chief," Kema reported. "Both groups have begun the crossing maneuver. And I can see cannon smoke."

"Time to go," Terith called.

Nema's patrol of four riders ran along the ground dragging stems of ivy with massive leaves between them almost as large as the dragon wings. The dragons took to the air, the ivy leaves dragging on the tips of tree branches below.

"Up!" Terith called. "Haul up!"

Terith turned to his group and gave the go-ahead. Bander heaved mightily, leading the charge, any height hard won. All the dragons beat the air with four times their usual stroke rhythm. "Ride hard!" Terith called.

All the riders, in two groups of four, now bore the heavy drag of a dozen yards of broad-leaf ivy strung between each of them, the fans of their improvised aerial windmill. Nema's patrol banked right, flying over a canyon about twice as wide as the length of their giant ivy rope.

Terith's patrol angled toward the north canyon.

An uproar sounded from the mass of savages moving through the trees beneath them and westward over the bridges. They were moving inland, and fast.

He could only hope to stem the flow by taking out the first bridges and trapping the remainder of the horde on the first megalith and denying those yet to cross an easy entry point.

The first volley of arrows flew at their formation from the trees to their right.

Terith opened his channel to the awakening, ready to unleash his awakened speed.

As his patrol flew out over the fog-clouded canyon, cannons boomed in the distance, firing in vain at the high-flying patrols of Bergulo and Rindl.

The cannons took time to reload. After this volley, the dragons would commence their strafing runs, burning up bridges, starting at the Outland edge and moving inland, charging the Outlanders from their rear.

Terith had to keep their attention.

"Dive!" Terith cried as a second storm of arrows sailed toward his patrol.

He banked left, and a quarter mile away, Nema mirrored his action, turning right. In unison, the eight dragons turned in two wide counter-moving circles, accelerating downward, through the storm of arrows and into the canyon fog. Terith guided Bander in a wide spiral arc, spiraling downward into the canyon. The ivy leaves pulled backward against the increasing air resistance, braving a hail of arrows that rained down from the canyon edges above.

Two arrows pierced his strythe, though not deeply. Skin wounds could not stop a war dragon. The saber-fanged beast banked strongly into the turn despite the onslaught. A heavy arrow struck the center of Terith's chest plate and knocked him backward, but his heel hooks held and Bander stayed his course. He unleashed his gathered awakening and in the slowed motion dodged three arrows and blocked another two with his arm gauntlets.

As the circling riders plunged into the fog, the mist began to swirl. Terith drove their windmill headlong into the darkness.

"How much longer?" cried one of the riders, voice twisted by the wind and choked by rank air.

Suddenly the force of the drag lessened. The air was moving itself.

"Release!" Terith cried, hacking the tethered ivy loose from his harness with his remaining knife.

In the fog-deepened twilight, eight dragon wings flapped against the surging cyclone.

Terith turned Bander into the rising interior of the whirlwind. The air was choked with swamp gas as dragon and rider spiraled upwards as if shot from a cannon.

Terith called for a burst of fire as the dragons emerged at the top of the cyclone, just below the rim of the megalith. Tongues of flame spread out in pinwheel fashion, licking the outstretched fingers of the ivy stems. The firestorm, fed by the continual upthrust of swamp air climbing the cyclone, left a trail of smoke and burning ivy on both sides of the canyon as it moved upstream toward the shallows, gathering strength.

The swamp fire turned in the sky in waves of flame, broiling the walls of the canyons and then breaking out over the cloud forest.

That ought to get their attention, he thought as he rode the rising current of hot air higher, taking in the whole battlefield.

Terith's ears filled with the buzzing of tens of thousands of scorpions, all rushing up onto the megaliths, fleeing the fire. The screams of men joined the chorus. Savages fell by the hundreds as angry buzzing scorpions flooded the Erden watchtower's megalith. The watch post was overrun with a new and deadlier horde.

"Attack the Montas and it will fight back," Terith said. He directed Bander out of the billowing clouds of smoke. Across the megalith, Nema's fire was moving down the opposite canyon, scorching ivy as it went.

"Yes!"

Nema had done it. It was an awesome spectacle, as if the Guardians had summoned up a demonic curse to send back the horde. Several of the lower bridges were already burning by the time the Bergulo and Rindl's teams of armored dragons stormed the canyons in blazing dives like falling meteors.

No hail of arrows greeted them, only the symphony of chirping and the screams of the bare-chested, tattooed warriors as they fell to the droves of the hand-sized scorpions pouring onto the megalith.

Dragon fire from Rindl and Bergulo's diving dragons raked the high bridges. The structures flaked into cinders in the furnace-like heat. Two of the flaming ivy rope and slat structures collapsed into the deep, stirring more fires below.

Six bridges fell. The megalith of Erden was nearly an island.

Bergulo's dragon attacked an anchor post with a torrent of flame.

Guy ropes snapped back and the bridge full of warriors swung down into the smoke and fog of the canyon.

"One more," Terith said.

Rindl's patrol pulled high as Outlanders converged on the remaining bridge, concentrating their arrows in a deadly cross fire.

Kema turned out of his patrol, coming at the assembly from the west, high and fast.

Terith saw the rash move and had only moments to react.

He dove for the canyon hoping to draw their fire, while Kema's fruit dragon made a desperate dive, wings tucked full, toward the last remaining bridge. Arrows caught Kema in a cross fire and the falling dragon crumpled mid-dive. Kema's dragon's momentum carried it straight through the bridge, snapping the suspension ropes as its rider leapt free.

Dodging debris from the demolished bridge, Bander moved into a world of slow motion as Terith opened his awakening in full. The dragon stretched back his wings, extended his powerful hind talons and snagged Kema out of his death dive.

Terith blew his whistle as he pulled up level with the megalith.

"To the crossroads!"

Three war horns answered.

Echoes of "Fall back!" sounded around him as the dragons regrouped, flying low and fast over the megaliths, passing the isolated lead groups of Outlander strongmen.

Bander rose quickly on the far side of the canyon, rejoining his Neutat patrol as it merged with Nema and Bergulo's formations. Bander dropped Kema onto Nema's saddle and resumed his lead position in their retreating formation.

For once, the two brothers held off their bickering as Kema, still shaken from his near-death fall, clung to Nema's shoulders.

"Call in," Terith shouted. "Bergulo, Nema—how many returned?"

But even as the teams of dragons converged in the gathering dark, it was clear that some were missing.

"All accounted for," Bergulo said, "except Erim."

"We lost Trip in the fire cyclone," Nema reported. "Just couldn't—" His voice trailed off, choked by emotion. Nema would have a hard time forgiving himself for the loss of a brother from Neutat. Trip's body forever claimed by the deep. His witty jokes and cheerful courage would never lighten hearts again in Neutat.

As they beat their wings in the migratory rhythm toward the crossroads, Rindl's group closed from the south. "All returned," he called out, though no cheer echoed back from his men.

Terith couldn't help but notice that Rindl rode uneasily.

When they had outpaced the last of the fleet-footed Outlander scout patrols, Rindl brought his own fang-toothed strythe close to Bander.

"The horde at Erden is mostly trapped. As for the braves already on the megaliths, once we get the stone bridges down at the crossroads first, they'll be trapped as well. The Outlanders will have to cut lumber to put in temporary bridges. That could take up to a week if we're lucky, enough time to rally support. We could even call on the Furendali for help."

The immediate question went unanswered. Would their northern allies even come?

As their dragons sailed on the prevailing wind, Bergulo's gruff voice carried his thoughts. "It's the Outlanders that got through before the bridges came down that I'm worried about. The best warriors always lead out."

"How many crossed over?" Terith wondered aloud. "Not more than a few thousand. Could be more."

"And you think Pert will ride to stop them?" Rindl asked doubtfully. "Because if he doesn't, the crossroads is our last chance to slow them."

"And those bridges are stone," Bergulo reminded. "A catapult is the only way to take them out. But without dead accurate ranging—"

"He'll have ranging," Terith said, "if Kyet comes through."

"Speak of the devil," Rindl said pointing to the south, staring into the darkness with eyes lit by the awakening. "That could be him."

Terith banked Bander in the direction Rindl pointed. All was a shadow to him.

"Give us some light," Terith called.

Two riders on the wings of the formation let off bursts of fire.

"There are two people on its back," Rindl said. "One is a girl."

"That's them," Terith said. "Rindl, ride down and pick up Mya. I'll wager that Kyet's dragon is flying on prayers."

Rindl veered downward.

Terith turned to his sergeant-at-arms. "Bergulo, take two riders up the road to Ferrin-tat. Make sure Werm and his catapult make it safely. You have until sunrise. We can't hold them back for long in the daylight. Go!"

Bergulo saluted, whistled his riders into formation, and burst ahead in a heavy-sounding beat of giant wings.

"Nema!" Terith called.

"Chief."

"Go back to Erden. We need information. Hear out as much as you can from the enemy commanders. Be back by dawn."

"I'm already there." Nema's dragon lifted and banked to let Kema jump onto another dragon. He waved farewell to his brother, then broke from the pattern and dropped low. Terith prayed those weren't the last words he heard Nema say. Nema's awakened ears could hear what no others could. He was a valuable warrior.

"Be safe," Terith called. "May your dragon return!"

As Rindl came back into formation with Mya seated behind him on his saddle, Terith left the group to come wingtip to wingtip with Kyet.

"What news?"

"The place of resort was empty, except the sick and the old ones who couldn't move on their own. They said two dragon riders came and ordered everybody out to shore up the bridges. Nobody seemed to know anything about the invasion."

"Put the bridges back up!" Terith said. "But we've all been out risking our lives to cut them down!"

Kyet's young voice shook with anxiety. "I flew on to Neutat to spy out the riders they were talking about. I put down outside the village and watched. They were crazed, stomping about on their dragons, barking orders, threatening the villagers."

"Who were they?"

"Southerners by accent. I got close enough once to hear them shouting. But he saw me. I had to retreat into the forest. Once I lost him, I doubled back and found Mya at the water lift. We only just escaped."

"Good man," Terith said. *He's only fourteen—incredible, really.*

"Chief, those riders," Kyet began, "they weren't on orders from Ferrin—I mean you—were they?"

Terith shook his head. "No."

"But I can't imagine what they were trying to accomplish. Neutat is so far out of the way."

Terith sighed heavily. "There is another way onto the megaliths besides Erden."

"There is?"

"Toran's trail. It leads from the Outlands down into the Montas. The trail cut into the cliffside, hidden by overhanging ivy. The bridges are below the fog. Only champions know its course."

Kyet's exhausted expression grew confused. "But the Outlanders can't know about the trail. No champion would—" his voice broke off. He turned to Terith with a look that matched Terith's own horror. "Pert!"

"It looks like we'll be on our own at the crossroads," Terith said warily. "Save your strength. This battle is just the beginning."

CHAPTER 21

Erdali Realm. Citadel of Toran.

Following her late night, near-death experience, Reann saw nothing of Verick for most of the day, which only made things worse. Did he know about her? Was he laying a trap?

Not knowing what Verick was doing was the worst possible situation for Reann. Two discoveries had cut him in twenty-four hours. The first came in the dinner conversation with the fur trader who claimed Toran was innocent in the death of the Rubani traitors, making Verick's vendetta baseless. The second was finding his father's portrait in the library. Somebody knew his identity.

Like a wounded animal, cornered and confused, Verick could be dangerous, unpredictable.

By evening Reann was desperate to know what he was up to and, more than that, how he felt. Was he alone, angry, in denial, enraged? Did he blame her? Reann's heart ached for Verick as much as for her own plight—living in fear, his life's purpose a flickering flame of uncertainty. She ignored reminders from her conscience that her growing desire to find him was not merely self-preservation. She had other feelings, feelings that could undo her at the worst moment.

Verick wasn't in the castle. She'd verified that a half dozen times, and she knew all the best hiding places.

Where do people go when they can't swallow their problems?

The answer was in the question.

The pub.

If Verick was at the tavern in the village, he'd be inebriated and loose lipped. He might say something indiscreet. Or else he might be hiring thugs to kidnap her. Whatever he was up to, she had to know about it—for her own safety, and possibly that of her half siblings.

She only lacked an excuse to leave the castle and a disguise.

After some snooping, Reann found Ret in the courtyard aviary. She watched him feeding the hawks from outside the enclosure. Knotted cords formed a net that draped over a trio of large oaks with a small hut on one side for shade. Its roof was streaked with white trails of bird bombings. Several of Toran's hunting falcons were perched on the tree branches.

The raptors lived for twenty years or more, Reann recalled. With regret, she considered that some of them might have spent more time with Toran than she had.

Reann looked on, trying to keep as dignified an expression as she could manage. The aviary still terrified her.

Ret dumped a bucket of dead mice on the floor. The hawks did not jump on the lifeless prey immediately. They had some pride. Perhaps when Ret wasn't around they would excuse themselves to dispose of the unworthy offering.

"Where did you get all those dead mice?" Reann asked.

Ret nearly jumped out of his boots. "Where did you come from?"

"I asked first."

"Your cat leaves them at my front door," Ret said as he emerged from the hut. "He thinks it's funny. I get a half dozen every night."

"Gross," Reann said.

"Out with it," Ret said, picking up his mandolin near the door. "What do you want?"

"Did you play at cards all night again?" Reann accused. "You're awful ornery."

"I was finishing my chores you said you would do."

"I'll make it up to you," Reann answered swiftly. "Are you running errands in the village tonight?"

"Yeah. Food doesn't appear magically."

"Let me make your rounds for you. Go play cards or wrestle or whatever the boys are doing tonight."

Ret looked sidelong at Reann and plucked a strange note on the mandolin. He cocked an eyebrow and waited for her explanation.

"Just tell me your route, and I'll do the pickup." She did her best to sound matter-of-fact.

Ret laughed. "Well, you're lucky. There's an order at the bakery. Bread is light enough for you haul."

"That's it?"

Ret shrugged. "Too bad it's not the mill; you would have had loads of fun with the cart."

"Why?"

"Flour isn't as light as looks," he said, flexing his lanky arms. "Where do you think I get these?"

"Are you sure you're flexing?" Reann teased.

"The baker closes shop at seven," Ret reminded as he turned and walked back toward the castle, "so he won't sell you any old bread until then. And the gate closes at eight. Don't be slow or you'll get to sleep with the rats outside of it."

Frankly, that's the least of my worries.

Going outside the castle gates after dark wasn't exactly on the smart side. Her self-preservation alarms were sounding again, like when she had snuck into Verick's room. But either the alarms were getting quieter or she was growing deaf to the almost constant nagging.

I'm not a little girl anymore.

At seven o'clock Reann pushed the handle of Ret's two-wheeled cart out the castle gate. She wore a hooded cloak that she had transformed from a furniture cover. The sky would be dark soon and then nobody would recognize her anyway.

"What's the occasion, Reann?" the guard at the gate jested, blocking her exit. "You going to a funeral?"

"The almanac says rain tonight," Reann said. "If it rains, I have to cover the bread."

The guard looked up at the gray sky and shrugged. "You know you make an excellent hag dressed like that."

"Thank you."

The guard stepped out of her way but dropped his halberd down, blocking her cart. "Just don't be late—I'll lock you out, I swear. I won't waste my evening waiting around for you. Besides, you should leave the hauling to the boys. Why don't you let Ret do it and stay here and keep me company?"

"I owe Ret a favor," Reann explained. "Now let me go before I call for your sergeant."

The guard lifted his halberd slowly. "Get on."

She leaned against the cart and got the heavy wooden wheels rolling again.

"If you bring me back something, I might consider waiting an extra five minutes."

Reann stopped and looked back. "The brewer is on the way," she offered. "Make it thirty minutes and I'll bring you his stale ale."

"You're a sweetie, aren't ya?" the guard said with a gap-toothed grin. "I'll give you an extra twenty minutes. Take it or leave it."

"Done." She was headed for the tavern anyway. And it would make a nice alibi if she were accused—a win all around.

With her extra time secured, Reann shoved against the cart and got it rolling again. It would've been a lot easier if the wheels hadn't been closer to square than round.

Ret probably made it by himself.

Reann wondered how a kid so deft with his fingers when it came to making music could be so clumsy when it came to handiwork. She walked the cart down to the bakery and picked up a load of bread from the baker after a long, bothersome argument with his nosy wife about the fact that Reann was the castle servant sent to pick it up. Then she pulled the cart quickly back through the deserted market toward the castle. As she neared the side street leading to the tavern, she stowed her cart among some empty barrels, wrapped herself in the makeshift cloak, and walked briskly down the narrow alley.

It was already half past seven.

Reann stepped carefully past a few huddled figures on the ground, either dead or drunk. She wasn't going to stop to ask which.

The brewery was built against the side of a sloping hillock. Its pub was a low-ceilinged shack cobbled onto the front of the brewer's burrow. The narrow street wound around the obtrusion and continued into shadow.

An oil lamp lit the pub's entrance. Below it, a wooden sign creaked in the evening breeze. Reann could smell the freshness of the air coming from the river. It mingled with aromas of a ranker sort coming from the mire along the side street.

Reann approached carefully, wondering if this were not the best idea. Dull voices and throaty laughter spilled out through the open door of the pub.

Reann put a bare foot onto the weathered floorboards, expecting someone to shut her out immediately.

None of the regulars at the pub gave her any attention, but that could change if she didn't look the part. Reann huddled forward under the cloak and took in the scene, turning slowly as an old woman might do as she searched for her drunkard husband.

Large men sat on bowed birch-bough chairs around tables. Some played at dice and others arm wrestled while they listened to travelers' tales at the bar.

Sitting by himself along the side of the pub was a tall, gaunt fellow. White sleeves and a tan waistcoat stood out against the smoke-darkened black wood of a pub bench. He sat staring. His posture was rigid, hands gripping the edge of the table. A mug sat alone on the table before him, like an offering.

Verick.

Reann edged closer.

He wasn't meeting with thugs—or at least if he was, they hadn't showed up yet. But he wasn't talking either. And unless somebody got chatty with the morose foreigner, she wouldn't learn anything.

That didn't seem very likely. Reann cursed her luck. It had been a dumb idea to come here in the first place—a big waste of time. Paranoia or curiosity, whatever it was, she was no better off for it.

I'll just get some ale for the guard and get out of here.

Reann slipped between swaggering drunks. Men seemed to close in around her as she neared the bar.

"Excuse me. Could I trouble you for an old half bottle?" She pipped.

The brewer looked down at her over his large belly. His rotund red face shined out from under his beard.

"If you've got troubles, little girl, ale isn't the answer."

"I promised the gate guard. I've got a loaf to trade for it." She drew a round of bread from under her cloak.

The brewer made the exchange and set a browned glass bottle in front of her. He closed it with a stopper and gave a wink. "Now don't be sipping that stuff. It's not made for—"

"What have we here?" bellowed a voice. A viselike hand seized her arm and spun her around. "Drink and entertainment tonight!"

"Let me go," Reann said crisply and all too politely to faze the sloshed brigand.

The man yanked her cloak free of her clasping hands. "You can't dance with that cloak on."

She reached for the bottle, but the stubble-faced fellow grabbed her other wrist and wrapped a sweaty, hairy arm around her waist. He heaved her into an awkward turn and started into an off-color sea shanty.

A bargeman. Oh no.

More men joined in the song. Reann was torn from the first and passed into the groping hands of a second man. She tried to slap him but he dodged backward.

The crowd only grew more raucous.

"Let me go," she ordered.

"But the fun's just getting started," a man said from behind her as he squeezed her rear with both hands.

Reann tried to run, but a man caught her arms and pulled them over her head.

Men formed up like wolves in front of her.

Reann struggled frantically. She thrashed with her feet but a man seized her legs. The two tipped her backward lowering her toward the floor, prepared to take every advantage of her that their strength allowed.

"Don't," Reann cried. "I'm just a child. I'm innocent."

"Stand aside." The sharp order cracked like a whip over the noise of the brutes.

"She's just a serving wench," said a thick-bearded man holding Reann's legs said. "What do you care? Shove off."

The sound of a chair sliding back answered him.

"Unhand the girl," the voice commanded.

Several men drew back.

The man let go of Reann's legs and doubled his fists. "Want some fun of your own? I'll be glad to oblige."

The crowd parted enough for Reann to see Verick standing resolutely, hands placidly by his sides, his weight on his front leg—he wasn't backing down.

The crowd chuckled as the meaty pub brawler squared off against the leaner, but taller Verick.

The bearded ruffian struck outwards with his massive right fist, a power punch that would knock a heavy man through a door.

Verick disappeared beneath the blow, thrusted the man's punching arm upward and gave a sharp jab to his ribs.

Verick tossed the breathless man to the side as two more converged on him.

"Stop it!" Reann cried.

Both swung at Verick.

This time he stepped backward, lifting his foot off the ground as the attacker to his right charged at him. Verick's boot heel struck the man's weight-bearing knee, stopping him with the snap of a ligament. He crumpled with a scream.

Verick sent the second man backward with an openhanded strike to the middle of the chest. The drunk stumbled backward.

Another brute converged from behind. Reann had no time to shout out a warning. The hefty man clenched Verick's neck in the crook of his elbow and bore down with the barrel-sized forearm of a hammer-swinging smith.

Verick's free hand drove a thumb into the attacker's eye. The half-blinded man roared as Verick rolled him over his shoulder and spun to face the first ruffian who was red-faced and ravenous.

The angry man had a knife. A circle widened around Verick and Reann's attacker.

Reann struggled to free herself, but two men held back her arms, preventing her escape, laughing at both spectacles.

The angry drunk slashed at Verick with the knife.

The Rubani's hands were too quick as his arm counter-swirled across the arc of the knife. One of his hands seized the attacker's wrist while the thumb of his other hand jabbed into his attacker's upper arm, throttling the nerve. The knife fell free from his limp hand. A brutal sidekick from Verick sent the stout man sliding across the floor.

The room froze, then converged forward all at once in a frenzy of misguided loyalty.

Their answer was a flash of steel as Verick drew his shining saber in the blink of an eye. Without hesitation he slashed at the nearest of the attackers.

Reann closed her eyes. There would be blood now.

When she opened them Verick had his saber tip under the chin of the man who started the fight. Everybody else was back as far as the furniture would allow.

Verick backed his quarry against the counter of the bar.

"I'm unarmed!" the man pleaded.

"So is that girl."

"Mercy."

Verick sneered at the man. "Helpless? Scared?" He whipped the saber down, slicing the man's thigh.

He fell to the floor, face racked with pain.

"How does it feel being helpless?" Verick turned quickly and sent back the converging rabble with a swipe of his blade. "Who is next? Just a little fun. It can't hurt that bad." He took a fencer's step forward and lunged, putting the tip of his blade into the calf of another knife-wielding brute. In an instant, he had the saber turned the other direction, slashing forward angrily.

Men dove backward over tables but Verick was too fast. Red gashes appeared on hands and arms. The next moment the sword was pointing in the direction of the men that held Reann.

They loosed their vulture grips on her wrists.

Her skin burned from the chafing as she had struggled to free herself.

"I should kill you all," Verick roared, "you damned cowards!"

Again he whirled the sword viciously.

Men scrambled out the door. Others stood frozen against walls.

"You would shame a maiden—I'll teach you shame!"

Verick leveled his sword at one of the men closest to Reann. "Give her that bottle she purchased."

The man took the corked glass flask and handed it to Reann, then moved backward as if she had the plague.

He turned to the other man, the bargeman who had first grabbed her. "Had enough fun?"

He stammered something of a drunken apology.

Verick stepped forward. He whipped his sword through the air like a madman. "I asked a question!"

"Yes, sir. Enough, sir."

"It seems you've forgotten to pay for your pleasure."

The man blustered an excuse.

Verick pressed the point of his blade against the man's chest and spoke through clenched teeth. "Give her your purse. All of it, or I'll take payment in blood."

The man reached into his trouser pocket and drew out a sack of pennies.

Reann took the money without looking him in the eye.

She gripped the flask and the money and hurried toward Verick.

He picked up her discarded cloak and swirled it over her shoulders with one hand.

Ret's face appeared in the doorway. "Reann?" He shoved a much larger man aside and stepped into the dark pub. "Reann!"

"She didn't come back in time," Ret explained breathlessly to Verick. "Had to throttle the guard . . . saw my cart back there." He gestured at the rumble and remnants of the mayhem. "Missed all the fun, have I?"

Reann whimpered, tears welling in her eyes. She stumbled forward and fell against Ret's shoulder.

Verick retrieved his coat and stepped past them without a word. He disappeared into the alleyway, driving fleeing brawlers ahead of him through the alley like a haunt.

Ret led Reann quickly out of the alley. The long-fingered hands of the musician pushed her forward as she stumbled ahead, blinded by the tears falling freely down her face. Ret guided her gently to the cart and tucked her between the loaves of day-old bread. He pulled her the rest of the way back to the castle.

Reann continued to cry as they neared the gate.

"I should break this over your head," Ret hissed at the guard. He uncorked the flask with his teeth and poured the contents out on the ground. "Next time you send a girl to a pub to get your grog, it'll be your blood on the ground."

Reann had never heard Ret talk like that. Her shock at his tone lessened her tears.

"You can't threaten me," the guard said unwisely.

Ret looked straight at the guard.

The guard chanced a glance sideways. But there was no help in the street.

Ret was only eighteen. But he already had a reputation for settling disputes with his fists. Quicker that way, he claimed.

Reann tugged the tail of Ret's shirt. "Please."

Ret raised a warning finger to the guard. "I'll break your nose. And I'll do it twice just to be sure."

The guard raised his hands. He stepped backward and yanked a lever that released the gate. The winding wheel spun as the portcullis fell, lifting its iron counterweight.

Somehow the jaws of those iron teeth closing behind her seemed closer than ever. But the rising counterweight captured the other feeling in her heart.

Verick saved me.

I can save him.

"Enjoy your first tavern brawl?" Ret said in an unamused voice. "I honestly thought you had more sense."

Reann sniffled and climbed out of the cart.

"Street rats stole most of the bread," he muttered. "You shouldn't have left it alone."

Reann raised the pouch. "We can buy more."

"Is that gambling money?" Ret said incredulously. He led Reann by her wrist through the kitchen door of the castle.

"In a sense," Reann managed. Her throat was sore from sobbing and her hands still shook from the terror.

"Sense?" Ret replied. "A little more sense would do. I guess I misjudged you again. That's twice in one week—are you going to make a habit of this?"

"I had to know," Reann said defensively, shaking her arm loose.

"Know what?" Ret said, raising his voice and throwing his hands up. "What it's like to be a fool?"

"I had to know about *him*," she explained. "Verick is not from Treban, you know. He's got some kind of vendetta against Toran's secret heirs."

Ret opened his mouth, but fell silent. He stepped closer, checked over his shoulder and whispered. "He told you this?"

"I figured it out."

"How?"

"Research, Ret, how else? He hates Toran. He was just a child when the Ruban Payment happened. There was nothing he could do when Serbani marines burned the port." Reann clutched the front of her dress as the realization struck her. *Powerless . . . like me at the tavern.*

Ret raised his hands defensively. "Well, sorry to ruin your sleuthing. I guess you've got important business to take care of. In case you forgot again, the Summer Gala is less than a week away, and some of us have work to do." He turned for the dining room.

Reann followed him into the room where the dirty dinner dishes lay untouched.

"You didn't ruin anything," Reann said quietly. She began picking up dishes.

"Just leave it," Ret said. He shook his head and carried an armload of dishes back to the kitchen.

Reann hurried after him. "Ret, stop."

He began unstacking plates into a trough for washing, then spun around and pointed his finger at her. "You scared me. You know that?"

"I didn't . . . mean to."

Ret walked out in the dining room to get more dishes.

Reann followed. "I'm sorry."

"I don't have any family, Reann." Ret said. He stared at the far wall where a tapestry hung, his eyes distant.

"Neither do I—not here."

Ret turned around. A tear ran down the side of his cheek. Embarrassed, he wiped it away and lugged two half-empty pitchers back into the serving kitchen.

Reann chased him into the kitchen, grabbed him by the elbow. She leaned up on her tiptoes and kissed him on the cheek. Then she bolted out of the kitchen and hid in the dungeon.

Ranger meowed his disapproval from the shadows.

"You butt out of this," Reann said. "He's not that bad."

Ranger clawed the wall and whipped his tail from side to side.

"Go eat some rats or something."

Reann collapsed on the dank floor as tears came again to her eyes. "I wish my mother was still alive, Ranger."

The cat rubbed its fur along her skirt.

She scooped him up and held him against her chest. "Nothing is ever as easy as you make it seem."

Reann's nosing had almost cost her dearly. On top of that, she'd complicated her relationship with Ret in a most unsatisfactory way, and rather than learning some odd bit of information that might somehow help her, Reann felt like she understood even less about Verick that she had before.

Verick was not just the son of the great traitor with a tortured soul and blood vendetta on Toran's children. He also had a monstrous temper and gift for swordsmanship the likes of which the castle hadn't seen since the days of her father.

Beyond that, there was his vindictive sense of justice. He had protected her at the pub, something only a man of moral principles would have dared. But in doing so, he had showed that he was a man of lethal capability and that his dangerous wrath was unpredictable.

The more she meddled the worse the situation got. It was like quicksand. It was her own doing, but it was her life, after all, and she had to live it. She had to take responsibility for it. Nobody else would, or could.

I am the daughter of Toran. It's time I start acting like it.

Reann wiped her face on her sleeve and shivered.

"Listen Ranger, it's up to me to stop him. But I can't fight him. I can't even try to turn him in. Nobody would believe me, first of all. Besides, betrayal is exactly what started this whole thing in the first place. You can't win a war, Ranger. You can only win friends. I learned that much from my father. The point is, Verick isn't all bad. He just risked his life to protect me. What does that tell you?"

Ranger stared blankly and twitched an ear.

"Well, maybe it isn't so obvious to you. But all I need to do is get him in a situation where he realizes his best choice is to give up on his vendetta."

Ranger turned tail and trotted out of the vacant cell.

"Thanks for all the support!" she said sarcastically.

Reann mustered a few schemes, which on second thought all seemed ridiculously trite. Dealing with Verick wasn't at all like getting Wretch in trouble with the head butler.

And on top of that the Summer Gala, the annual celebration of Toran's birthday, was coming up and she would hardly have time to—

That's it—the gala! Dozens of nobles, Toran's strongest allies, would be arriving at the castle. She had one chance.

The gala would be the turning point. She knew it, deep in her bones, she felt it, like the feeling she had when Verick had arrived. Something was happening. Something was rising—chance? Fate? She had to seize it, make it her own, or Verick would.

Only one thing was certain. Only one of them would survive that night. Her best weapon was the one she was terrified to touch.

Love.

✠

Sunlight blazed through the open windows. Dust danced among bright beams that lanced through the library.

Reann paced the floor. Ranger listened dutifully from his seat next to the long table.

"What if he accuses me of being an heir of Toran? How am I going to hide the fact that I saw his notes? How am I supposed to do my own research without telling him anything more about what I know? How can I—"

The door creaked and Verick walked in with shadows under his eyes, hinting that he had a fight with his pillow and lost.

Gauging his crestfallen expression, Reann guessed the merchant's tale about his family's bitter demise had haunted the Rubani during the night—or perhaps even the part about Toran showing mercy to his family.

Or perhaps saving her life?

Ranger swaggered out of the room without acknowledging Verick.

"Are you quite all right, sir?" Reann asked, sympathy spreading through her body for the broken-looking man. "Shall I get you some tea?"

"Yes, thank you," he said, collapsing in the armchair.

Reann left to get a pot and the tea service.

It was strange to see Verick subdued as he was. Wasn't anger the first reaction to disappointment? How could Verick discover that his life's quest was in vain and then keep the heat of that emotional inferno inside?

Was it a ruse to lull her into a false sense of security?

Reann worked without noticing what her hands were doing. She tried to imagine the heart of a man twice broken. But the closest she had ever come to understanding a man was the Wretch. And he seemed about as familiar as a mysterious fungus most of the time. The one man she should have known, loved, cherished, and understood was Toran who was an endless mystery.

Verick might be a volcano about to erupt.

Dare she dance on the lip of a volcano?

That thought was the first in a series. Reann's pace quickened. Her posture straightened and, in moments, she returned to the library with swagger aplenty.

She poured his tea and handed him a cup on a platter. "You didn't sleep a wink last night."

Verick sighed deeply and gulped the tea.

He waited several minutes before speaking. Reann put a hand on top of his, like Ranger did with his paw when she was feeling low.

"You're a kind spirit to have pity on me over lost sleep," he spoke, almost in a whisper.

"You went out of your way on my behalf. I hope nothing of the bad business last night has troubled you, sir." Reann could no longer bring her mouth to use the name Verick. And she had to bite her tongue to keep it from calling him by his true name—Dorian.

He said nothing.

Reann waited. She squeezed his hand for comfort, like a daughter or a niece might. Verick was much too young to be a father of a teenager, but perhaps a toddler if he had married young, which Reann doubted. His spirit was so tormented he would find no solace in love until his inner wounds healed. It was all because he had believed Toran had killed his father and his co-conspirators on the ship.

Toran had unwittingly let them go. Rather his cabin boy—her adopted brother—had killed them.

Toran had no part in their gruesome deaths.

Minutes passed by in silence. Reann waited as patiently as Ranger would.

"Have you ever known something," Verick asked suddenly, "have you ever believed something for so long, as long as you've had the wit to remember . . . felt it deep down and then found out it wasn't true at all?"

Reann's heart began to beat anxiously. "Don't we all?" she said mildly, wishing for a better phrase than the dull one that escaped her.

"I mean, how is one to go on as he did before, after discovering such a thing?"

"You can't," Reann said. "You can't reason any of it into your heart. You can't squeeze emotions out like lime juice when the only thing in your stomach is a peach pit."

Verick's lips turned weakly upward for a moment in a chance smile that faded.

"Isn't that how you feel?" Reann asked.

Verick shrugged. "Truthfully, I don't feel quite up to doing more research today." Without finishing his tea, he stood and walked back toward the library door, shoulders lowered, face fallen . . . *like a man without a friend in the world.*

"Perhaps a bit of fresh air?" she said hesitantly as he disappeared into the corridor without reply.

Reann went to do chores but returned to the library after lunch.

Verick was there, facing an open window with his hands behind his back.

"Are you here to finish your research?" Reann asked. She hoped beyond hope that his reason for being in the library was something else, something more desperate. Yet she couldn't hold out any hope if the research continued. It would be her end.

"I'm afraid events of late have rather put me out of the mood for reading," Verick said quietly.

Reann reached the table next to him and closed an open volume. She stood near him and held out her hand. "There is only one thing to do in times like this."

Verick held to her fingers limply as she led him into the open floor in the center of the library. "What do you mean?"

Reann set his hand around her waist and put the fingers of her other hand between his.

"Dance."

"Dance?" Verick sputtered. "I . . . you . . . me . . . now?"

"The Summer Gala is only four days away. We all need practice."

"I don't believe I intend to attend any festivals," Verick said. "That was not my purpose in coming to—"

"Yes, but anyway, I've seen the invitation list to the gala ball, and your name is on it already. You're the only representative of note from the Serban. I'm afraid bowing out would put you in a very awkward place."

"You saw my name on the list?"

"Yes, and I took the liberty of adding myself as your attendant. It's a political strait, that gala. You wouldn't want to have to traverse it without a guide. Besides, I dance well enough."

"Are you always this presumptuous?" he asked with a wary expression of pleasure.

"Yes."

"You leave me little choice in the matter."

"By design. Do you waltz?" Reann turned in the three-beat step. Verick's well-trained heels followed her around the long table, avoiding chairs deftly.

"Or shall we do a peasant dance?"

Reann started into a quick off-rhythm folk twirl.

Verick laughed as the twirl lifted her up off her toes and then him.

"You're very good yourself. I should think you would take the lead," Reann reminded.

Verick did. He danced out his emotions in a slow minuet and then another waltz.

"Would you wait here for a moment?" Reann asked. "If you mean to dance, we should do it properly."

Verick turned his hands up. "I am at your leisure."

Reann rushed out of the library and down to the servants' quarters. She turned Ret out of his bunk, where he was plucking his mandolin and skipping duty. "Come on, Wretch," she urged. "Our patron needs music."

"What . . . where?" he blustered. "But it's my day off."

"Just follow me."

Ret, as curious as any boy of his age, kept pace. "What in the name of the great river do you need music for?"

"Now look professional," Reann urged as they neared the library. "Fix up those ties."

Impatient, Reann did them up for him while he blubbered about being perfectly capable of tying his own shirt.

Reann followed him into the library.

"Ah," Verick said enthusiastically, "a mandolin."

"Would you like some music, my lord?" Ret asked, as anxious to show off his prodigious skill as Reann was to turn up her dancing heels.

"The peasant dance again, I think," Verick said.

Ret nodded and set into a dizzying jig on the mandolin.

Reann and Verick joined hands and turned about the library between and over chairs, dancing many tunes and styles.

Onlookers gathered in the doorway as they danced, and then more, until they spilled one by one into the room. A chambermaid brought up her flute and joined the music making, and two old ladies led each other in an awkward waltz.

"A moment, dear," Verick said, stepping away to cut in between the elderly pair. "May it be my pleasure," he said, taking one of the old women into a slow dance of turns about the long table and returning to trade for the other. The old women clapped and the young girls laughed. When a harpist and a drummer filed in, Ret took a turn dancing with Reann. It took all her skill to avoid his stomping feet.

"Are you doing that on purpose?" she asked.

Ret let go and stomped himself back to his mandolin. "Well, if you're not going to be grateful…" He plucked up a classic tune and led the merrymakers into another round.

The wine found its way up from the cellar after the gardeners came in for their lunch break and brought the menders and cooks in for a few turns.

Reann led Verick out into the corridor while the rest of the castle kept on with the merrymaking, then onto the quiet balcony where the wind whistled over the plain and tossed her hair playfully.

"Isn't that better?" she asked.

"Are you a witch," he returned, "that you do such magic with people's hearts?"

"There is good in most places," Reann said softly. "Where you least expect it, even, and always when you need it. Lose the bad in finding the good, and you will have your peace."

Verick's face was puzzled.

"But now I think you need some rest," Reann said softly. "I expect you'll be up and about tomorrow—a new man, I hope."

His expression darkened a shade. "But I never even told you about my trouble, and you seem to think it has gone away."

"It will never go until you let it," Reann said. "And peace will never come until it goes."

"I am a tortured soul until then," he said, staring into the distance, the wide expanse of the great Erdali plain with its golden fields stretched out before him.

"But a happy one, I think," Reann said, offering her hand like a lady requesting her leave.

Verick took it and kissed the back of it almost without noticing he had just graced a servant. It was the way he put her hand down slowly that interested Reann most. Interested and terrified.

She covered her breast modestly, where her heart sounded drum-beats. She curtsied deeply, face filling with red.

But something about the way Verick had looked at her gave the feeling of ice creeping over her.

He knows.

CHAPTER 22

Montazi Realm. Ferrin-tat.

"No. I haven't got anything," Enala repeated. "Search the kitchen if you like. The last group took my kitchen utensils too—a lot of good a paring knife will do against an Outlander sword!"

The lad turned away from the kitchen door and padded toward the armory.

Enala felt sorry for a moment. It wasn't the boy's fault supplies were short. Ferrin's foot soldiers and archers were told to bring a week's rations. With no time to prepare, most had grabbed barely enough to last a day. Still, inquirers came to her kitchen, never seeming to believe that a rich man like Ferrin could run out of anything.

Desperate for something useful to do, desperate to get out of the kitchen, and most desperate of all for some word about how the dragon riders fared, Enala stole across the courtyard toward the back road to the keep. The light of the setting sun set an orange fire in the sky.

She passed Ferrin's office in the ivy root and looked in at the porthole. Her father was gone to the armory, she supposed. There were maps scattered on the table. Her stepmother Tirisa opened the door to the office, followed by two of the soldiers. "Listen to me. You are to begin the evacuation the moment the alarm is raised—no." She lowered her head in resignation. "We can't risk the village if the horde reaches the crossroads. Just begin the evacuation now."

"But only the chief can order evacuation," one of the soldiers said as he was handed a route map and shoved out of the room.

Enala couldn't help overhearing the other soldier's reply as they jogged down the corridor toward the tap-root hub. "There may not be a chief tomorrow."

Enala's mind froze at hearing the words, her decision made in a moment. "Yes, there will."

Enala sank down outside the window wondering just how she would go about it. There was a chance she could find Terith in battle. She could protect him.

"Tirisa," sounded Lilleth's voice from the window hole, calling their stepmother.

"For the thousandth time, just call me 'Mother.' What is it, dear?"

Enala listened but Lilleth didn't answer right away.

"You've got a cloud on your heart," Tirisa said. "You must let the rain out."

"I've run out of tears for one night," Lilleth said quietly. Her voice was broken in a way that pained Enala, despite all her jealousy.

"Come," Tirisa said. "I'll hug the tears out of you."

Enala turned and stood up to peer through the window.

Lilleth was wrapped in a shawl, still wearing the breezy skirt from her ruined date with Terith.

Enala had suggested Lilleth try to have a child before the wedding only because Enala couldn't stand the waiting any more than she could bear Lilleth's haunting descriptions of Terith's imminent death. One way or another it had to end. For Enala, each day Terith was engaged to Lilleth was like seeing him die over and over.

The worst of it was the fact that she couldn't give up. She kept thinking of ways to get him alone, get him to change his mind, seduce him and void the engagement.

The last idea seemed the best option. If Terith was going to die anyway, what would it matter if he spent his last moments with her?

It mattered to her. For eternity, it mattered.

Enala's soaring machinations ran aground as Lilleth spoke. Her older sister stared past the stepmom's shoulder as if watching a scene playing out before eyes. "I know," she said.

Tirisa pulled back and looked Lilleth in the eye. Her voice became serious. "Lilleth, what do you know?"

"I saw both," she explained.

"Both?"

Lilleth nodded. "I asked Terith to see into his future, but I saw both: his future . . . and his past."

"Astonishing," Tirisa said. "How did you manage that?"

Lilleth shook her head. "I don't know." She smiled as the vision came into her mind. "He was born on a rainy day. It was the day of the victory. I saw his mother—beautiful—but I don't think she was Montazi. I've never seen someone quite like her. Perhaps an Outlander, but different."

"Lilleth," Tirisa said. "You saw Terith's birth? Is that possible—seeing that far back?"

Lilleth nodded. "The awakening chooses. The mother, she died after giving birth. She died just before . . ." Lilleth's mouth opened as if to speak, but refused to form the words.

Tirisa listened intently. "Lilleth? Just before what?"

"Before the father arrived."

Enala's heart skipped a beat waiting on Lilleth's words.

"I saw his face. Blue eyes like diamond. Battered armor—he was strong . . . I know who it was."

"Lilleth, you mustn't—"

"It was *Toran.*"

A shock ran through Enala like a scorpion sting to her heart. She almost lost the strength in her legs.

"Mother, I don't know what to do. I can't let him die."

Enala clutched her pounding heart. *Neither can I.*

She ran through shaded paths, under roots and over ravines, around boulders and past heavy broad leaves that thrashed at her. The archery range was near the top of the megalith. She leapt the gate and opened a chest in the range master's closet with a key from her satchel. Enala lifted a prize bow, worth more than most Montazi could ever dream of paying. It was ornately decorated with metal inlays that covered its stout, wooden curves.

It was beautiful, but its thick wood was not weighted for a woman's draw.

With practiced speed, Enala placed the bow in a levered stand, pulled the lever to bend the bow and hooked the bowstring. She slung the quiver over her shoulder, lifted the strung bow, knocked an arrow, and drew until the string was even with her cheek.

"If they even touch him . . ." she whispered in a cool voice.

She loosed the arrow, completely missing the target twenty yards away and obliterating a scorpion moving across a tree ten yards past the target.

The prize bow and its quiver of ten arrows that had been in the locked case were the only weapons left at the range. Enala took the bow and the remaining nine arrows, all of which were tipped with red venom, and turned her thoughts to how she was going to get to the front lines.

The roads were packed with foot soldiers racing for the cross-roads. Would she just run along with them and say she was just out for morning exercise with a quiver of venom-tipped arrows?

A summer dress wasn't going to work either. If going to war was optional, looking perfect was not.

The armory was crammed with soldiers, but there were other ways to equip for battle.

Enala ran back past the weaver's shop where she had regrettably resisted the temptation to snuggle in with Terith when he was help-lessly exhausted after the steam explosion.

She was still bitter about that, especially after he had gone and chosen Lilleth—and he didn't even have to! He was the only winner. He could have chosen her.

Enala knew she was more fun—and better looking. Hundred-to-one, she was a better kisser. Lilleth didn't have the necessary creativity.

The fight wasn't over, as far as Enala was concerned. So they had bonded—men bonded with their dragons to share their awakening. Big deal.

That thought suddenly caught Enala like a foot snare. *Bonding* . . . She started ahead again, quickly reaching her interim destination: the alcove, a theater depression with log seats facing a small stage. Under the backside of the stage was a crawl space used for storing props and ceremonial clothing.

Enala kicked the bolt free and stabbed the scorpion waiting behind the door with the end of her bow, and then hauled out a wooden box.

Tossing robes and ceremonial masks aside, Enala gathered whatever pieces of metal she could find. She exchanged her lavender dress that she had stolen from Lilleth for the kind of chain mail skirt men wore to cover the gap between their thigh plates. She wrapped the belt double round her slender waist to secure it and then donned a ceremonial bronze breastplate formed of two ornate crossing metal leaves. An ornate metal headband and shin braces finished her warrior queen ensemble.

The breastplate, except for its leather buckle, left her back bare, but she was an archer and didn't need armor there anyway.

Now, for my ride.

Enala raced down to the keep. With the riders already gone to the front, it was virtually empty. Only a page kept watch on the few remaining dragons: yearlings, hatchlings, and dragons trained for pulling the sky chariot.

The sky chariot, of course, was too large for her to get in the air on her own. Besides, it took four trained dragons.

Enala spied Terith's dragon-wing cloak hung on a peg near the entrance and made it a last minute addition to her outfit, besides its more practical value for keeping her warm on a night flight.

"First watch, supper! Food at Ferrin's kitchens," Enala called from her hiding place behind a stand of saddles.

At the sound of the voice, the page looked up, confused and hopeful.

"Get moving or you'll get nothing," she called again from the shadows.

The lad fell for it.

The page dashed out of the keep, his empty stomach leading the way.

Enala stepped out from behind the saddles and was greeted by a savage hiss. She nearly peed her chain mail skirt. Two young dral stared at her with their leafy, frilly faces loaded with teeth. On the opposite side of the cave, a clutch of yearling fruit dragons snapped their jaws and reared back in their cage, stretching their necks in a show of force to the intruder.

Enala shoved her face up against the bars of the nearest dral cage and hissed back at the dragon. The dragon snapped at her face, but she swatted its nose with the point of her bow and grabbed its neck spine when it flinched and then yanked its face against the bars.

Its great unblinking eye stared at her. She smiled and said in voice that left no room for doubt, "You're coming with me."

Enala breathed in, taking light and life and energy from everything in sight. The awakening closed on her as she unraveled the barriers in her mind. The dragons began to change color to her eyes. In the light of her awakening, their souls began to shine through their scales in brilliant yellows, greens, and oranges.

Enala called to her chosen dragon in song as she slid open the three locking pins on its cage. The other dragons curled up, slumbering as her song lifted them into ethereal bliss.

The stirrings it caused within Enala were a fortunate or unfortunate side effect. Every time she opened herself to the awakening, the desire to bond became stronger.

Open to her every thought and suggestion, the dral stepped out of the cave. As she closed the gate behind it, she sang a verse of submission and it knelt. She climbed on its unsaddled back, wrapped her arms around its neck, and closed her eyes.

Her last thought channeled through the awakening was *Find the others*. Exhausted and drained, she closed her eyes as the dral spread its wings and took to the air in three quick beats. She relished the connection to the dragon, the bond, but she had no control of its reins.

Montazi Realm. The Crossroads.

Arrows rained down around Terith, black darts streaking through the pre-dawn glow.

"Return volley," Terith called. "Red arrows."

The choice to use venom-tipped weapons this early in a fight was a desperate one. The arrows could be sent back by their foes and kill as many Montazi.

"Aim!" he ordered.

The squad of archers tucked in behind him drew their bowstrings.

"Loose!"

The deadly volley felled a group of barbarians headed for the bridge.

Voices across the narrow chasm shouted in the Outlander tongue. A veteran of ten summer campaigns, Terith recognized many of the deadlier phrases.

"Move!" Terith shouted. "They've marked us."

From across the canyon a resounding boom shattered the air. The space Terith and the dozen archers had just vacated exploded in a tangle of torn branches and shredded leaves.

"Where is Werm with that catapult?" Terith muttered under his breath. The canyons at the crossroads were narrow, which was why the bridges were made of mortared stone rather than lighter rope and slat suspension. He couldn't destroy them without the catapult.

To his left a dragon landed on an arched stone bridge only thirty yards long, taking a defensive position. It was one of the two dragons that had gone with Bergulo to guard Werm's catapult on its hurried overnight trek down from Ferrin-tat.

He must be close.

The newly arrived dragon, topped by a rider in armor, lowered its head and breathed a gust of fire at the vanguard of warriors who surged at the beast, swords and pikes drawn.

Terith watched in horror as a thrown spear sank into the rider's abdomen. His dark silhouette fell back, disappearing into the deep.

Undeterred, the strythe charged the remaining men, trampling two, leveling a handful with its tail, and upending one with its mounted head spike. The last of the warriors met its fangs.

A second boom sounded and the dragon disappeared in the smoke of the explosion, claimed by the deep.

So quickly they fall with none to replace them.

Terith rallied the archers. "Mark that bridge! Nobody gets across!"

The men dropped to one knee, nocked their arrows, and aimed at the warriors who braved the open bridge. Arrows sang out with twangs from the bowstrings as Terith searched the dim edge of the opposite canyon for the location of the Outlander's cannon. A flurry of activity between two broadferns betrayed the location. But Terith was helpless to attack it. His dragons were all down. Many fell defending the approach to the crossroads, fighting to slow the raiders' advance. The rest met with disaster as the surprisingly organized force thrust upon them all at once in the early morning. Bander had been one of the first to fall, caught in the deadly hail of arrows.

Terith kept his hope out for his unaccounted riders: Nema and Kyet. If one dragon could still get airborne . . .

In the gray morning light, a shadow moved overhead, coming from the west, behind him.

Terith looked skyward hopefully.

A lone dragon hovered high over the raiders. A heavy black stone dropped from its claws, accelerating to the ground. The crash of wood and the shatter of stone on iron sounded from the broad fern clutch where the cannon hid. It was an expert stone drop, handily disabling the cannon.

Terith couldn't tell who had done it. He could scarcely make out the shape of the dragon in the dim light, let alone the rider.

It was large, and its wingbeat was typical of a fruit dragon. As arrows sailed upward to meet it, the dragon spiraled downward, taking cover in the canyon.

Expert, Terith noted. Only Nema could make that kind of maneuver.

Spared the onslaught of the cannon, Terith risked a jog along the canyon edge to the southeastern bridge.

"How goes it, Rindl?" he asked the lieutenant.

"We can hold until sunrise, I think," he said. "My last three riders attacked the exposed flank and tipped their cannons into the deep.

"Excellent."

"Before they fell," Rindl added. "The volunteers are keeping the bridge clear with short spears and arrows." He pointed to the dark edge of the megalith diagonal from their position. "Ferrin's archers assault the flank. But they've sustained heavy damage. Guardians help us—this is all we have."

"Can they hold the southern megalith?"

"They'll need reinforcements before the morning is out," Rindl stated. "How's your fare?"

"The northeastern bridge is nearly taken," Terith confessed. "I will make my last stand there if necessary. Keep your archers trained on your bridge. Flee if the megalith is taken. Get back to Ferrin-tat and lead the retreat into the highlands."

"Yes, chief." Rindl looked the champion in the eye and nodded a quiet acceptance of Terith's veritable consignment of his own life.

Returning quickly toward the vulnerable bridge, Terith searched the skies again for the dragon he had seen. Then, at last, the sound of creaking wheels broke in Terith's ears like angel song.

"Werm!" he cried, dashing ahead through the trees into a clearing as the catapult rolled to a stop and a gaggle of engineers and soldiers rushed to chock its wheels.

Mya was ready with the range-to-target information. "One

hundred eighty-two point five," she said, pointing to the southwest bridge. She turned and pointed south. "Two hundred ninety-six."

Werm mumbled calculations from atop his rolling contraption. "The north bridge," Mya continued, "one ninety-four."

"One ninety-four," Werm repeated. "Load that second stone," he ordered, gesturing the strongmen from Ferrin-tat to the pile of heavy rocks Terith's men had gathered in the night.

"What about the northeast?" Werm asked.

"It's blocked by trees," Mya said nervously. "I can't sound through to it."

"I've paced it," Terith volunteered. "It's one-twenty or so."

"It'll have to do."

"Loaded," called the strongmen, checking the sway of the catapult while Werm bent to read the weight gauge. "Seven and two nocks—at one eight two." He sat in the aiming chair and rolled a great wheel until the bridge was centered in his bore sight.

"Crank to eighteen notches, plus one mark," Werm ordered as the men set to turning the winch.

"Wind speed?" Werm asked.

"Northerly, one mark," answered a skinny soldier standing in front of a small wind flag.

Werm adjusted the great wheel back a degree.

"Eighteen mark one," the solder reported.

Werm released the lever and the catapult heaved the massive boulder in a giant arc.

The three-hundred-pound stone traced a perfect parabola and smashed through the center of the south bridge, obliterating the keystones. The whole assembly vanished into shadow as the stones in the bridge peeled away from the foundations.

Werm heaved a visible sigh of relief as Montazi warriors nearby cheered.

"Keep it up," Terith encouraged. "I'll give you as much time as I can."

A thin hope wavered on the horizon.

Terith drew his sword and prepared to summon his awakening. Bergulo joined him moments later, drawing his heavy sword and matching pace. He brimmed with light as well.

"Where's your dragon?" Terith asked.

"I exhausted it avoiding archers on the return," Bergulo said between breaths. "I'm not as light as I used to be. My mount fainted on the ascent and broke a wing a mile and half back. I raised that poor dragon and had to kill it myself."

"I'm glad you made it," Terith said as honestly as any phrase that ever crossed his lips.

The two warriors plunged headlong through the jungle-like forest toward the vulnerable northwest bridge.

"Yours?" Bergulo asked.

"Dead."

"Well," Bergulo said, catching the only glimmer of hope, "with the catapult we've got a chance to stop them. The pinch point is the bridge."

Terith focused his courage, banishing all doubt. "We will have to hold them off."

"What about the other riders?" Bergulo asked.

Terith shook his head. "Kyet had to land. He carried too much weight too far. He's behind enemy lines. And Nema—he's not back yet either." Terith swallowed. "We don't have any more dragons. I saw one, but . . ."

The keeper nodded grimly as they came to a stop behind the last cover brush. Around them, bodies of the archers lay riddled with arrows.

"Ready swords," Terith ordered, as if speaking to a company of riders.

Bergulo hefted his enormous blade and raised his shield.

Terith drew his own saber, the short weapon of a rider. He lowered his visor and clutched his remaining knife with his shield arm. It was a poor replacement for the shield that went down with Bander, but a welcome one.

Ahead, Outlander warriors, hulking masses of tattooed flesh, charged onto the bridge following a giant of a man with a double-headed battle ax.

"Charge," Terith ordered.

"Wait." Mya burst out of the ferns nearby, pointing to the sky. "There's another dragon."

Terith paused on the verge of charging into the Outlander horde at odds of two against hundreds. Overhead a dragon came from the north—a bit off course to come from Ferrin-tat.

By the wing cadence, it seemed to be a dral.

"That's not a rider," he said instantly. "Look, it's coming in directly over the front line—that's suicide."

"I recognize that dragon-wing cloak," Bergulo said. "Who would have brought that into a fight? A load of trouble."

Terith wondered if Tanna had managed to get on a dragon. Then he realized he had left his cloak in the keep at Ferrin-tat. Tanna was in Neutat, to the south.

"She did not!"

Mya cheered. "It's Enala!"

A bevy of arrows greeted the young dral as it labored over the treetops. It took a shot through its wing and screeched in protest. The dral pivoted and began to retreat west.

"Oh good, it's leaving," Bergulo said. Then the cloak fell.

"She jumped!" Terith gasped. He raced toward the falling wind sail cloak, praying Enala made it to the megalith, rather than the deep.

The bowed cloak filled with wind and sailed toward his position at a dangerous speed.

Terith sped ahead of the others, crashing ahead, chopping branches out of his path. He looked up and caught of a glimpse of armor and skin glinting in the sunlight before he was bowled over.

"Thank the Earth, you're all right," Enala said, from her position on top of Terith.

"Ow," Terith said. "Enala, what are you doing?"

"Saving your life," Enala said. She stood up. "Come on, get up."

Terith, flattened, took another moment to get his breath.

Enala stood over him. She refolded the cape and tied it around her bare shoulders.

Terith's eyes followed her toned legs in gleaming shin plates, past her chain mail skirt, to her shapely ceremonial bronze breastplate that seemed to offer both in equal measure. She had a strung bow over her shoulder. It was a magnificent weapon. But he could tell from the construction it would take more strength than Enala had to draw it.

He was wrong.

Enala hurried to pick up her scattered arrows.

"You call that battle armor?" Terith asked.

"What do you call it?" she said, smiling.

Trouble, Terith thought, pleased despite himself. He climbed to his feet as Bergulo and Mya reached them.

"Terith, they're coming across!" Mya called.

"Enala, Mya stay out of this," Terith said.

"Terith, wait!" Enala called out as he crashed ahead through the trees. "I have to talk to you."

But Terith's attention was elsewhere.

Outlanders had come onto the bridge and were already two-thirds of the way across, led by a man twice the size of Terith.

Again, he primed his awakening, feeling the world come into a slowness of motion. Beside him, Bergulo flared, summoning bear-like strength.

Terith sidestepped the giant and knocked him askew with a swipe of his sword. Then he plunged into the mass of attackers whose faces were still half hidden by the dawn shadows. His knife drew blood as quickly as his sword in a mass of felled limbs and punctured guts.

Terith was large for a Montazi, but not for an Outlander. His advantage came down to his armor, his courage, and *speed,* terrifying speed. Blood sprayed the air from the edges of his of whirling blades. Impact after impact landed in a blazing battery of foot, fist, and steel.

Beside him, Bergulo's heavy sword crashed down and across with unstoppable fury. The man laid down a dozen or more warriors, his awakening rolling back the age of his body. With primal strength, his legs kicked warriors onto their backs. His sword cleaved bones; his awakened power was matched only by animals the size of dragons.

Sunlight spilled onto the megalith ahead of them as they reached the far side of the bridge. A second band of warriors charged.

Terith hurled his knife, cutting down the leader, and then charged forward. Bergulo summoned a bloodcurdling war cry and knocked a warrior into the abyss. Terith felled another with his sword, in time to recover his thrown knife.

A blow to his shoulder plate forced Terith to one knee. He dodged the second blow and thrust his sword into his attacker. He kicked the Outlander's corpse back and whirled to parry a sword strike with his knife. The short blade of the knife shattered from the impact, but Terith's sword was already hilt-deep in the Outlander's abdomen.

The impaled warrior, screaming in warrish devilment, grasped Terith's blade by the cross handle in a death grip, as another massive warrior with a tattooed face and blood-painted arms rushed to attack Terith before he could free his sword.

Terith snapped the man's head back with a jaw-crushing uppercut and turned to block the deathblow with his armored forearms, but the strike never came.

The fletching of a Montazi arrow sprouted in the surprised Outlander's neck as he collapsed.

Terith had no time to wonder where the arrow had come from. He seized the slain warrior's curved sword and freed his own, whirling both blades to cut a warrior down, desperate to close the distance that had come between him and Bergulo.

He was three paces away when a pike thrust between two of the warriors attacking Bergulo. It caught the great man in the stomach. In the light of his awakening Terith saw it all happen in terrifyingly slow action.

Bergulo fell. Warriors raced past him onto the bridge.

As Terith fought toward Bergulo's body, the passing light of his awakening caught on Terith.

With new vigor, the chief of champions pursued the warriors with vengeance and downed two. He ducked two arrows and turned a pike back on its bearer, sweeping several savages into the deep with the long pole, but a handful of warriors had escaped over the bridge, heading for the catapult.

Another red-tipped arrow dropped an attacker, whose upraised sword fell harmlessly against Terith's armor. The lone Montazi chief knocked him aside, ducked a heavy ax, and threw his shoulder into the back of the man. He toppled into his fellows. The three clung to each other as their feet left the bridge.

Standing on the bridge, Terith whirled again and again, his two swords lashed out, marking foes as quickly as they came, unaware that his arm was red with his own blood, the stain deepening in spurts.

An arrow ripped into his thigh and lodged against the bone.

Terith snapped the shaft as pain surged through his body and his leg collapsed. His awakening had passed.

A voice from the crossroads megalith drove him to his feet, a female voice.

"Get off the bridge!"

Enala?

But his enemies had closed the way. He was trapped on the bridge.

"No!"

Terith gave a mighty cry and charged desperately at the four warriors blocking his path back across the bridge. Attacking with his two swords, the two wooden shields splintered before the curved Outlander blade shattered against an ax.

Terith left the sharp stump of it in a warrior as he leapt onto the falling man's back and sailed over two more, landing at the corner of the stone bridge. A great stone ripped down through the air, denting the earth just beyond Terith where it bounced and crushed a pair of Outlander braves.

The foundation on the east side was cracked, but Werm had missed the critical keystone. He would have to reload. That meant Terith had to hold the bridge for another two minutes.

Seizing the lapse, fresh warriors rushed at the intact bridge, with Terith as their only obstacle.

As Terith lifted his lone sword to defend himself from an Outlander who beat at him with heavy blows, a whistle sounded from back across the bridge.

Terith knew the sound well. It was his dragon call.

Mya was calling for Akara. But Akara was gone. He had freed her.

The perfect imitation of his dragon whistle came again. He parried another swipe and knocked the Outlander's jaw askew with his gauntlet, only to catch a return hook in his ribs.

Terith head-butted the warrior as their hands locked on each other's swords. He drove a knee forward and then dropped in a sweeping turn, trading swords with the foe and taking out his knees with his own blade. Terith took back his own sword as again the whistle sound came from behind him.

Mya hadn't left.

"Get back!" Terith shouted. "Run!"

Terith whirled his swords desperately and to his surprise the clutch of warriors attacking him retreated backward.

A golden dragon soared over Terith's head and charred a dozen warriors with a gust of blue and yellow flame.

Landing beside Terith on the defended side of the bridge, Akara beat her wings forward heavily. The force of the gust threw charging Outlanders on their back. Akara wheeled about, leveling foes with her tail, spouting more fire and then leveling three warriors with a crushing swipe of her clawed wing. The men were simply too slow to match the speed and power of a dragon attack.

Beyond her reach, an Outlander archer on the bridge pulled a red-tipped poison arrow from his downed compatriot and raised his bow.

But the warrior was shaken as a second catapult stone crashed into the side of the bridge. His arrow went harmlessly high.

Stones crumbled and dropped into the deep, but the keystone held.

"Akara!" Terith shouted. He whistled the call to knock down

the stone battlements the Outlanders often built for cover against archer assaults.

The queen dragon turned her back, ducked a thrown spear, and hopped through the air toward the only stone object in the area—the bridge. The dragon thrashed the remaining Outlanders off the structure with her clawed wing-arms.

Her weight shifted the bridge and a stone separated from the edge and fell, exposing a keystone. Akara bent her head over the edge of the bridge grappling weak stones loose, widening the gap as she clawed with her strong hind legs, making frantic cries.

She'd destroyed a stone bridge once before near Erden, three summers previous, but this was a much larger bridge, manufactured by the greatest engineer the Montas had ever seen.

She needs more time. Terith dropped one of his swords and picked up a spear. He charged onto the center span of the bridge and heaved it at another archer. The spear, hurled by his wounded right arm, missed. But it set the archer off-balance and his arrow slipped off the bowstring.

Akara ripped the loose broken stones off the bridge with her feet and jaws until her hind claws closed around a keystone. Arrows flew and pierced her twice. Terith raced to Akara. He dropped an ax handle into a crack and levered weight off the keystone.

The mortar cracked once and then again. Akara beat furiously and at last, the granite keystone broke free and twisted downward out of her grasp and into the deep. Terith turned and ran back over the ruined bridge as the stones crumbled behind him into the abyss.

He leapt to safety on the Montazi side. Diving into the cover of the trees, Terith rolled and looked back.

Akara beat her wings once, turning in the air toward Terith. Blood gushed where the shaft of an arrow was buried deep in her chest. Her strokes stopped abruptly and she dropped into the deep, her golden scales glinting one last time in the dawn light.

"Akara!"

Terith rolled onto his back, heart and body torn. He struggled to remove the gauntlet on his wounded arm, but couldn't grip the slick leather straps. He seemed to be swimming in blood he hadn't felt moments before.

Ropes and grappling hooks sailed overhead.

Shouts of "Cut the ropes!" rang out as the few remaining foot soldiers rallied to defend the point of attack.

There were crashing sounds through the underbrush.

Someone was coming.

A moment later a familiar set of legs stood beside him.

Enala knocked an arrow, yanked hard on the string to pull it flush with her cheek, sighted without blinking and loosed the arrow with cool precision.

Satisfied by a scream from the opposite megalith, Enala ducked down and leaned over Terith protectively. "Mya," she called quietly. "Come quickly."

Mya stepped around a tree trunk, ducking behind a borrowed shield that two of her could have hid behind and wearing an oversized helmet.

"Guardians!" Mya gasped at the sight of the blood.

"What are you doing—" Terith started, before Enala interrupted.

"Saving your life." Her voice determined.

Terith began to think beyond the hopeless moment of his last stand.

"So don't get any ideas about dying on me now," she said firmly.

Terith couldn't see the extent of his injuries, but his waning strength promised a good deal of lost blood. An instant and terrible thirst came over him as he descended into shock. "Water."

"Here," Mya said. "Use my headband to tie that off." She handed over a lacy headband and then scurried off. "I'll get some water."

Something cinched hard on Terith's forearm. Then he was dragged face-first under a broad fern and rolled onto his back in the bottom half of a wide hollow log.

"Enala, why did you come?" Terith grunted.

"Must you talk?" Enala said desperately. She opened a small purse she had tied around her waist and pulled out a needle and thread. "Or would you rather I sew your lips shut?"

"A battlefield is no place for a woman. People get killed."

"You were doing a pretty good job of that on your own," Enala interrupted, "until I showed up."

A needle dug into his arm, tugged, and then dug in again repeatedly, sewing the gaping wound shut.

Terith considered the incredible accuracy required to hit a moving warrior in the neck with an arrow. "Probably . . . just . . . got lucky," he managed as a shot of pain caused him to clench his teeth.

"I could teach you a thing or two about getting lucky," Enala offered, her tone becoming playful, "if you're interested."

Blackness gathered around the edges of his vision.

"Busy not dying just now," Terith said, through clenched teeth. Crazed pangs of thirst seized him. "I just need . . . water," he said, hearing the echo of his petition, wondering if he had said it. Terith felt as though the world were rolling over on top of him. He rolled his head from side to side, unable to shake off the vertigo.

Then it seemed like nothing mattered. There was nothing to worry about. The pain would soon be gone.

Breathing was a bother. The scene dissolved into bits of dream and lost words.

"Oh, no you don't," Enala said. She leaned forward and whispered. "I've been waiting for this." She hovered with her lips an inch from Terith's. "Haven't you?"

She planted her lips on Terith's in a deep kiss.

Terith's waning awareness jolted in mix of pain and passion.

"Stop." Terith fought for a breath, but the kissing continued.

His pulse beat with a new tempo as Enala's lips pulled slowly away from his. He could feel her breath on his face, the smell of the orange blossom oil on her skin. "Enala, I'm engaged!" he protested as she moved to kiss his ear and neck.

"But you love it," she said tantalizingly. "I know you do."

Of course he did. He loved every second of it—which is precisely why he hated it. Terith tried to move but Enala had his arm pinned.

"Sit still. I don't want these stitches pulling. Or maybe if I lay on top of you . . ." Enala said.

"Ribs cracked," Terith protested.

"Oh, you just made that up," she dismissed. "Now let's get out of here." She reached back and unclasped the dragon-wing cloak, letting it fall to the forest floor.

She was beautiful against the morning sky. But Terith's vision went blurry. He shook his head as the effects of lost blood mounted.

"We have to go," Enala asked.

"They have ropes. And I'm out of arrows. Everyone else seems to have evacuated."

"You shouldn't have come," Terith said.

"But I did," Enala said. Her voice was tight with emotion, as if she would cry. "Terith, I saved your life. I won't let you die. I don't care if you're engaged or running into battle. I want you. I want you forever."

Terith had much he wanted to say, and yet he couldn't speak. She was wrong to take advantage of him, wrong to follow him into battle.

But she was right to love him. Terith was guilty of that friendship that had played with affection.

But it was innocent. Wasn't it?

Clouds of doubt mixed with lingering feelings of pleasure at her touch.

Was it any different with Lilleth? He couldn't imagine her face anymore. Enala's blue eyes blocked out all else.

Enala's foot shifted as she leaned closer and Terith's eyes nearly bulged out of his head. His mouth formed a gaping "Ow."

Enala moved back. "What did I do?" She looked at his thigh and gasped. "Good granite, you've broken an arrow off inside your leg!" She opened a pouch tied around her waist that and drew out a pair of small scissors. She cut the ties to his thigh plate.

"You brought scissors?"

"You didn't? Hmm. I'm going to have to take off your trousers."

"No!" Terith gasped. "Just cut them."

"Or . . . that," Enala admitted with audible disappointment. She cut back the leather of his breaches. "There's a fragment still in there—I can't reach it."

Mya returned with a familiar patter of feet. "They're coming across on ropes. We have to leave."

"Mya, quickly. Reach here. Your fingers are smaller. Can you get that piece?" Enala said hopefully.

"That wasn't one of your arrows was it?" Terith grunted.

"If it was, you'd be dead like all the rest I shot," Enala said indignantly.

Mya leaned over his thigh and grimaced. "Oh, this is really gross. I'm going to be sick."

"Can you reach it?" Enala asked as she plied back Terith's muscles.

"I can see it . . ." She reached into the wound, searching out the arrowhead.

Terith grunted, wishing a scorpion had bitten his leg so that it wouldn't shake from the pain. His muscles hammered in protest as waves of pain raked up his body.

"It's stuck—too slippery."

"Wiggle it," Terith groaned, eyes streaming with uncontrolled tears.

"All right, it's loose. That's it. It's out. Thank the Guardians."

Warmth and wetness spilled over his leg with fresh bouts of blood, followed by stinging as Enala poured cleansing water over the wound. Her sewing needle stabbed his skin again, stitching up the wound, a scarcely noticeable pain by comparison.

Mya opened the tie of a second water skin and poured it into his mouth slowly, patiently.

Terith tried to swallow, then lost awareness. He drifted.

CHAPTER 23

Montazi Realm. The Crossroads.

The ethereal tones of a soft song stirred in Terith's ears, pulling him back. Returning to his senses, he saw Enala leaning over him, just as she had been. It had only been a momentary lapse of consciousness as far as he could tell, but it was still terrifying.

"Mya?" Terith asked weakly.

"Gone, with Werm. She said he was going to launch a rope pulley across to evacuate the last soldiers."

That meant there were no dragons left to carry them across.

Dazed memories flashed images of the horror of Akara's last fight. She was the only dragon he had ever known to return after being set free. It had been Akara's four summers of battle experience that had led her to destroy the cannon with a stone, save Terith, and pull the keystone from the bridge. The loyal dragon had found the crux of the battle on her own, somehow knowing that Terith would be at the heart of it.

Akara was the last of the fighting dragons, and that meant Terith was the last dragon rider.

The chant of warriors heaving to a rhythm filtered through the trees. Outlanders must have already gotten across on a grappling line and were drawing a rope bridge across the narrow chasm.

"We have to get away from—" Terith began, but he closed his eyes as another wave of nausea rolled through him. His stomach tightened and his broken ribs burned anew. The anxiety of being on a soon-to-be occupied megalith was eclipsed by the jolt of pain.

"Terith, I have to tell you something," Enala said. "It's important. We only have a few moments."

Terith opened his eyes and looked into hers. They shimmered with tears of emotion.

"Your mother is not from the Montas," Enala said. "She was an Outlander."

Startled by the accusation, Terith sputtered, "That's impossible. I have the awakening. It only passes from Montazi mothers."

"I don't know about that," Enala said. "But when Lilleth looked into your future, she also saw your birth. It was like she was right there when you were born. She saw your mother. She was sure of it."

An arrow slammed into the tree behind Enala and splintered.

Terith shook his head. "Enala, please. We have to go—now."

"And then she saw your father," Enala said. "And he wasn't a dragon rider. He was . . . Erdali."

"What?" Terith said incredulously. "That's impossible."

"It explains your chest hair," Enala said.

"But how did she know he was Erdali?"

Enala leaned closer. She brushed his cheek, searching for words, not looking him in the eye. "Your father was Toran."

"Toran the Uniter?" Terith said, surprise and pain turning his words into a gasp.

Enala smiled. She looked into his eyes. "Terith, you are the heir to the unclaimed throne."

Deep within Terith, where his weak pulse fought to keep his eyes open, fought to keep the blood he had left moving, a shell shattered. "She knew. Lilleth knew all along."

"So," Enala breathed, "I just saved the heir of the five realms—and you didn't even thank me!"

Terith grappled with the enormity of the revelation. So little of it made sense, but when Enala had said the name Toran, it was as though a key had fit into a lock in his heart so perfectly, so securely, it was undeniable. It was who he was.

He wondered for a moment at the strangeness of his life, how he had been born into poverty, the ward of an outer village, and became a rider and champion.

The awakening had chosen him as chief.

None of it was a mistake. It all made sense. The odds of it were staggering, and the implications of it more so.

Then he remembered Tanna's question before he left for the feast of the challenge: *Did you ever feel like your future is outside the Montas?*

Tanna had been there at his birth.

A voice sounded from nearby in a harsh Outlander accent.

"Where are you going? Orders were to secure the bridge."

"There's still one rider left. He said to kill all of them. I want this one. I'll drink his blood."

Enala's eyes widened in panic, and suddenly Terith was afraid—not for himself, but for her.

Enala looked from Terith to the trees and back as desperation seized her. "I can't fight them. I've got no arrows. You're too broken to fight—they'll kill us." Enala winced at the thought of facing Outlander braves unarmed. "If I had your speed, I could—" She looked at Terith, hope suddenly filling her expression. "Terith, bond with me."

The idea struck Terith as tempting and treacherous in the same moment.

"With your awakening, I can fight them."

Reason returning, Terith replied, "But I bonded with Lilleth. I can't break the promise or I'll lose the awakening."

"But I won't," Enala said. "I made no oath. I need your awakening—more than Lilleth. They'll kill us both."

Footsteps crashed through the brush, likely following Terith's blood trail—Outlanders out for revenge on their fallen brothers.

"Bond with me. If you don't, we'll die," Enala said. "Please, let me save you."

She leaned forward, her lips hovering an inch above Terith's. "Please."

Terith knew he had to do it, despite the high cost. Enala would keep her awakening—she hadn't vowed. Terith would lose it forever.

He could no longer be a rider, no longer be the chief, and no longer marry Lilleth.

At least he could save a life.

Terith lifted his head and kissed her lips. They were soft. He felt only her lips as suddenly he felt her spirit meshing with his, wrestling for control of his heart. Terith opened himself to it. He knew he had to give himself completely or there could be no bond.

Release Akara.

Release Lilleth.

Release the Montas.

Release the awakening.

Keep Enala. Suddenly, having her was the only thing he wanted, a trick of magic or failure of conscience. Images of her playful laugh and her teasing eyes captured him.

It came. It came from all sides. The awakening drew up around the horizon enveloping them both, tying them in a torrent of light as powerful as the light that had streamed into Terith when Lilleth had read his past and future. Enala leapt back.

A warrior snarled close by. Enala, moving with the speed of Terith's awakening, dodged out of the path of an arrow and caught it in her hand as it passed.

She was even faster than he was.

Terith turned his head as Enala charged at the warrior. She ducked under his arm and ripped the corner of the razor-sharp arrow across his neck, then plunged it into the heart of a second attacker, stole his knife, and dashed through the trees a short distance.

Moments later, she was back and the awakening faded to black. Deep black.

The sky was bright. Enala was bright.

Terith was lost.

"I did it," she beamed. "The bridge is down. Guardians' golden gate, that was amazing—it was like they were standing still."

"Thanks, Enala," Terith managed, feeling unsettled and empty.

"Come on, we have a few more minutes now. I think there might be another way out of here. I saw something on my way in." She grabbed his upper arms and dragged him into the woods, away from the battle near the fallen bridge. Every step and breath pained him as the muscles near his broken ribs inflamed and cramped.

"Where are we going?" he asked.

"Here," Enala said. She leaned him against a tree trunk in a clearing.

Terith's heart leapt. *Another dragon!*

In the center of the clearing was Cymr, a fruit dragon with one of Tanna's custom saddles.

"That's Nema's dragon," Terith said with a note of hope. "I sent him back to spy on the horde. But where did he—"

A suppressed scream sounded from Enala from around the other side of the dragon. "Oh my, is he . . . ?"

Terith forced himself to his knees. "Nema?"

Terith dragged his bandaged leg behind him on one knee until he could see the body.

Nema lay face down. Cymr, one of the loyal Neutat breed, had stayed by its fallen rider, bound only by a small tether it could have easily snapped.

An arrow stuck out between Nema's ribs. It had pierced his liver or lungs. Somehow, Nema had had enough time to find a clearing and land.

Strange.

"He must have been in pain," Terith said. "It looks like he tried to slit his wrist."

Enala covered her mouth and looked away.

Terith's eyes took in the two-inch pocket blade sticking out of the ground and then his arm where the skin was crudely carved, its edges painted in rivulets of dried blood.

"Why would he do that?" Enala said.

Never, Terith thought, pulling himself alongside Nema's body. *Nema would never hide in the open, unless . . .*

"Could those be letters?" Enala pointed to the scratches on his arm. "I don't recognize them."

"And why would he tie his dragon to his body?" Enala asked.

"Because he wanted to be found," Terith said at last. "Besides, Nema can't write." He pointed to the red gash on Nema's arm. "I think that's a circle with a cross over it, like a compass—the symbol of Toran's kingdom."

"So what is that squiggle supposed to mean?" Enala asked. "A snake?"

"No, I'm guessing that means a road or a path," Terith's head reeled. "No . . . No. No! Toran's trail! Enala, he cut himself because he's trying to tell us we've been betrayed by our own."

Terith put his dizzy head in his hands. "This attack was all just a distraction. There must be a traitor leading a second Outlander force up Toran's trail." Terith's eyes met Enala's. "Pert."

Enala sank to her knees next to Nema's body. "But the horde is attacking here. And they're still coming."

Terith shook his head. Too few Outlanders had crossed onto the crossroads megalith. Too few arrows were flying. Too few cannons were booming. "There could be a hundred warriors across the canyon by now if they were trying."

"But they're not pulling back," Enala said.

"They're baiting us," Terith said, wiping blood from his chin with his good arm. "Keeping us engaged so we don't suspect they split their forces."

"We've got to tell my father," Enala said, her eyes fixing on Terith's.

"Of course. But I have a promise to keep," Terith said aloud. "I made an oath to protect the Montas realm when I became a rider. As long as I breathe, I must do what I can to stop them. We have a clear warning. The Outlanders will go across at the falls and up the secret stairs onto Toran's trail. There's still a chance I can stop them."

"What?" Enala said. "In your state? You can't turn back an angry swamp fly without hurting for it."

Enala wrapped her arms around Terith's helmet, holding his head against her neck for a moment.

"Enala, I need you to go to Ferrin."

"I know. I must go to Father and warn him," she said softly, without any urgency.

"Tell him I am taking Nema's dragon east to Toran's trail. I'll take out as many of the hidden bridges as I can. If I survive, I expect to meet his reinforcements at Neutat."

"But you'll fall," Enala said, biting the words as she said them.

"I won't."

"You will." Her voice shook. "Look what happened when you tried to take on the whole horde yourself."

"Enala, you know what Nema found out. The Outlanders are planning to cross into the Montas on Toran's trail and somebody we know is helping them—Pert, probably. I can't just sit here and do nothing."

Enala stood, entrancingly beautiful, a reminder of all that Terith could not have.

"We're alone," she said quietly. "This may be the last time."

Terith winced for more than one reason.

"We've bonded," Enala whispered. "Doesn't that mean anything to you? Because it does to me. It means everything. You mean everything."

"What are you going to tell Lilleth?" Terith said. "That we had no choice?"

Enala's eyes, bright and bold, found his. "We've bonded," she said. "That's all that matters to me."

He had bonded with Enala, a promise to her that had undone his oath to Lilleth. But what did such a promise mean now? He was not a rider anymore. What awakening he had would fade before the dragons left in the autumn. He had no right to marry an eligible.

The only way to keep the promise was exile, for both of them. And what of Lilleth? Just leave her? The thought was terrifying.

"I can't rule the Montas," Terith said. "I broke my oath. Enala . . ."

Terith's chest tightened. His breathing quickened. Something was taking hold of him, something disabling.

"I'm afraid," Terith whispered. His lip quivered. "Enala, I'm afraid."

"You can't be afraid," she whispered, a tear forming in her eye.

"It's gone," Terith said. He turned his head to see Enala out of the corner of his vision where the light of the awakening had shown him things as they truly were in a fleeting glance.

Darkness.

Terith's breaths gave way to a rush of panic. His breathing came in anxious gasps. "I'm dying."

"No," Enala said. "You've just lost the awakening. It's my fault." She put a hand on his chest. "Relax."

When his breathing at last returned to normal, Terith found his voice. "I don't belong here."

"You weren't even conceived in the Montas, Terith," said Enala coolly, desperately. "Your mother was an Outlander. But you made something of your life—don't throw it away."

"I don't understand," Terith breathed as pain in his ribs flared. "I had the awakening. I must have Montazi blood."

Enala's eyes looked into the distance as she spoke. "Maybe she had Montazi in her lineage. They keep slaves, you know."

His mind spun. Morning light danced off leaves in the canopy overhead playing tricks with his eyes. Vague memories flooded to him: the night walk from Neutat to the feast, the meeting with Lilleth on the bridge. "Lilleth knew," Terith whispered. "She knew and she never told me."

"She never dared!" Enala said, looking to Terith in desperation, voice filled with enough power and anguish to make Terith wish he had only his flesh wounds and not the knife-sharp feelings that rent his heart. "She would have lost you to another kingdom." Enala stifled a shiver as the beginning of a flood of tears brimmed in her blue eyes.

Terith lowered his head as her words assailed him.

Enala spoke as if she had to force her mouth to make the words. "You are more important than one battle, than one bridge. I came here for all our sakes, not just yours."

"So that's the reason?" Terith asked, cradling his throbbing ribs with his good arm. "You wanted me to break my promise to Lilleth . . . to give the alliance a leader."

"I came because . . ." Enala laid her hands over her collar, where mud mingled with blood clung, "because . . . I love you."

"I . . . I," Terith stammered, "I'm following my path, Enala. I'm doing what is set before me. I can't be turned any more than I can stop the seasons."

"You are more than you know, Terith."

"I know only my duty."

"You are the heir to the unclaimed throne. What will become of the alliance? Who will help us beat the horde? We can't do it alone."

"Does it matter?"

Enala wrung her red-stained hands into little fists. "Of course it matters. For the sake of the kingdom you must live! Look, I know what you want to do. You want to go out to meet them. You know where the Outlander army is. You think you know. And you think you can stop them, and maybe you can—but maybe you can't! Maybe you can't, Terith. Did you ever think of that?"

Terith turned his head slowly from Nema's motionless form and looked Enala in her azure eyes. "Is my blood any better than my men who died burning the bridges? Am I any better than the ones who stayed to slow the Outlanders while we fled across the bridges?" Terith shook his head. "They lived and saw their oaths fulfilled. They stood when I said stand. They fought when I said fight. They asked no questions. No tears. No pleading. They died with their oaths unbroken.

"Now my enemies gather. My time for sacrifice comes. Am I supposed to let these murderers walk over the bloodstained earth untouched? I can no more change my duty than I can go back and undo all the choices of ten years that made me champion." Terith put his hand to his forehead to steady his dizzy head. "Or the ones that left all my riders slain."

Enala's eyes begged. "Don't go."

"Enala, don't you understand?"

Her eyes showed no sign of change. "I understand that I love you. I understand we need you—I need you. Terith. Please." Enala's fingers found his hand and squeezed it.

"You can make it to Ferrin-tat," Terith said emptily. "Take the low path under the west bridge on foot. There is a way across and a trail up the other side. Werm used it during construction. The flies will be feasting on the fallen Outlanders at the east end of the megalith, so you'll be safe if you go quickly. I'll fly south to see how far the horde has come up Toran's trail. I'm the only one who can reach the bridges in time."

"Yes, I'm sure that will be excellent," Enala said coolly, "but not right now. You need a rest as bad as the dragon. There's water here, and your wounds need better cleansing."

"I know what you want," Terith said, eyes fixed on Enala's only a few inches away. "You want to keep me here. You want me to flee and break my last unbroken oath to defend the Montazi."

Enala knelt in front of Terith. She stroked his earlobe and traced his jaw. "The important thing is to keep alive what we have."

Terith nodded. "And what about Lilleth? I owe her my loyalty— I love her."

Enala dropped her head onto his shoulder, hopelessly. "Will I never have you?"

Terith could scarcely speak. "You'll have another champion." He felt her strange song leave him as she stood to retrieve his armor.

"Oh," she laughed bitterly, wiping tears, "you always say that."

"This isn't about you, Enala," Terith said. Visions of what was, what he should be, filled his imagination. "This is about doing what my father would do, any father."

"Toran wasn't a fool, Terith. And he would want grandchildren."

"I'm not even sure he wanted children," Terith said distantly. "He didn't seem too keen on making them a part of his life."

"Terith—"

"If he were my father, he would be proud to see me fulfill my oaths, whether or not I live. He would be proud to see me spill my blood alongside that of the loyal."

"Is that what this is?" Enala spouted. "A big guilt trip? Your men died and you didn't, so now you have to go out and commit suicide?"

"It's about duty."

"It's madness."

"It's the only thing I can do."

"No, it's not. You can do more. You can lead our retreat. You can regather our strength, stop Pert and—"

"I will. First, I must slow the horde. I have to give you time to warn the others."

"But you won't." Enala choked up, unable to argue any longer. There was nothing she could do to change his mind. Terith saw her resignation and her grief.

"You saved my life," Terith said after a pause. "I know . . . I don't know how it must feel to see me leave you again, to go back into peril."

Enala sobbed.

"Thank you. I wish you well. I wish you someone worthy . . . I was not."

"You know that's not true," Enala cried, tears streaking her too pale cheeks. "You bonded with me."

"I made an oath with Lilleth."

Enala turned away, eyes closed tight.

"Enala, I walk the path laid before my feet. It will bring me home."

"In pieces!" she wailed. "You'll fall!"

"Enala—"

Now she was beyond convincing as well. Neither could touch the other.

"Will you be safe to Ferrin-tat?" Terith asked.

Enala nodded.

"Tell Lilleth . . . tell her to look for the light at the edge of the horizon when there is no more hope. Draw upon that light. It can save her as it has me."

Enala's mouth opened as though she wanted to cry out in a mock laugh, but her throat kept silent.

"The light of the awakening will bring me home," Terith said. "And I will see you all again."

He stood, swung his leg that screamed in pain over the bowed dragon.

"May you return," Enala whispered almost soundlessly as the wings of Nema's dragon beat twice. The dragon prince took flight going southwest, to the canyon of the blood river, to Toran's trail, traversing the slender space between Neutat and the Outlands.

Into treachery or destiny, he flew. He didn't look back.

CHAPTER 24

Erdali Realm. Citadel of Toran.

Reann knew Verick's identity.
He, a sworn enemy, knew hers.

She wished for an instant that she could just melt away.

Her well-thought-out plan was hardly consolation for the kind of risk she was about to take.

You could call it brilliant or cavalier or brash all in the same breath.

Reann was no longer safe if Verick knew her identity. The power of her secret was lost.

Two can play at that game.

The thought struck her as awful and sadistic.

Had her father felt that way before going into battle, before springing a trap on unsuspecting enemies?

Dressed in her least ceremonious serving dress and apron, Reann busied herself tidying flower arrangements in the hall that ran around the outside of the ballroom. It was a squat ballroom, in truth, more of a basement crypt. But this was a stone castle built to withstand assaults, not to host parties. The room was a rotunda with two circles of pillars. The center ring of supports held up a ceiling that was all of ten feet high. There was just a double step-down between the inner and outer rings to a depressed floor section in the center that tended to fill with water after a storm.

The supports made dancing a chore, and there were inevitably collisions in which the pillars came out better than the dancers. But the ballroom had more floor space than the upstairs throne room and so it was used for such events as the Summer Gala. Toran said it had the feel of the cozy half-underground great halls of Furendal, so it was similarly decorated with furs and hunting trophies, rather than tapestries.

Tables had been arranged around the perimeter, while the center section, which looked more like a pit for dogfighting than a dance hall, was bare except for a few compass-themed flag runners along the pillars, the symbol of the five realms.

Near the back of the ballroom, on a rostrum next to the head table, was a guest list for announcing the official title of each the attendees at the evening gala. It was a tedious, ceremonious, and bothersome affair. But it was custom, just like the festival going on outside.

Cheers and hurrahs from ongoing games outside drifted in through the stairwells leading down to the basement hall. Folk from the nearby villages up and down both the east and north forks of the Erdal river were competing in the annual contests her father had begun early in his reign.

Reann was sure Ret would be winning a good share of the matches in the wrestling and boxing for his age class. But she was just as sure he would bring back more bruises than trophies.

Academic studies, on the other hand, provided a great number of generally useful skills, such as penmanship, or in Reann's case, forgery—something she'd been working at in earnest every spare moment of the previous two days. Reann's hand gripped the waist-band of her skirt. Her fingers held a precious sheet of parchment beneath the fabric.

She knew two things. One was that Verick was a man of honor, or so he seemed. The other, that he was extremely dangerous.

But the thing that made his danger real was secrecy—that was her real enemy.

And so the secrets would come out.

The success of her venture, her attempt to save her own life and convince Verick to abandon his vendetta against Toran's heirs, came down to a matter of wit and timing.

And Reann's time window was closing fast.

There was no way she could get to the rostrum with the servants and guards scattered through the ballroom. But she had a plan.

Cue the trays.

A clatter of noise signaled the arrival of trays of serving dishes. A handful of young men who had either taken early losses in the competitions or who had simply strayed within reach of the head butler and been conscripted into kitchen duty emerged from a stairway and turned into the outer hall.

"Use the side door," Reann insisted. "It will save you time."

"Where is it?" the first boy asked from behind a pile of stacked bowls.

"Right here," Reann said, hurrying to the narrow side entrance to the ballroom. "I'll hold the door for you."

"Just clear out," the boy hissed. "You're practically blocking the whole doorway."

Reann scurried into the ballroom ahead of the trays and led the young men toward the back of the room.

"Do the head table first," she instructed.

"We know what we're doing, you big know-it-all," a tall skinny boy hollered. "Who made you the boss around here anyway?"

Reann stepped out of the way of the boys, who would have started at the first tables near the main entrance, if not for her suggesting otherwise, even if they claimed to know what they were doing.

Reann mingled among the boys and centered bowls and redistributed silverware, a chore the boys would just as well leave to her.

Reann finished one table and moved toward another on the opposite side of the rostrum. She reached out and brushed the guest list with her finger and it slid off the podium.

Reann knelt and drew her own version of the guest list from under her skirt. She made a show of blowing off any dust and then replaced it on the rostrum. She tucked the old version under an empty tray that she kept clutched to her chest as she walked to a table near the side exit.

She left the tray on the table and stuffed the original guest list up under her blouse and tucked her shirt in. Then she scurried around the outer hall to the opposite side of the castle and walked up a spiral stair to the first floor.

Part one, success, she thought, her heart beating double time with all the anxiety of being caught in her mischief. "Now for part two," she whispered.

She had to get to the third floor on a day when castle servants and guards marked every exit and entrance to ensure the nobles preparing on the upper levels were not bothered.

The three dumbwaiters on the first floor were being loaded with food from the kitchens on carts. One of those shafts would be her shortcut to the guarded upper floors. But there were four people in the corridor, only one of which was working for her. The other three would have to be dealt with if she were to get past their food-guarding eyes.

As soon as Reann appeared in the stairwell and waved, a well-compensated friend of Ret's on the far side of the corridor dropped a porcelain dish.

The dish shattered with the sound of somebody about to get a beating. The three other servants in the hall turned to look.

Reann lowered the first dumbwaiter a few feet, tied the elevating rope off on a wall hook, squished into the elevator shaft, and wriggled upwards. Using the lead rope to pull herself upward, Reann wormed her way up the narrow space.

Getting to the third floor took all the athleticism she could muster.

Head pressed against the top of the chute, Reann waited in front of the closed dumbwaiter shutters.

Just a few more seconds . . .

"Hey, what are you doing up here?" a voice demanded.

"Just looking," answered a squeaky voiced teen—another of Ret's friends, compensated for a week's worth of chores, an amount Reann might never actually finish paying off.

"Hey, what's in this room?" the boy asked.

"None of your business. Get away from there."

Reann pushed open the shutter and stepped into the hall. She quickly closed the shutters and ducked into the recess of the doorframe opposite. Reann grimaced at the sound of Ret's friend being physically driven off the floor with encouraging slaps from the flat of a short sword on his behind.

Reann quickly opened the unlocked door to the room being used for dressing the gala attendees and closed it behind her.

A myriad of ladies and attendants were arrayed across the room in varying degrees of preparation. Some were being corseted. Others were having their hair set.

Reann quickly undressed to her slip, eager to be rid of her servant's clothing, and moved to a space in the dressing area where two young women about her age were waiting.

They were obviously Furendali. One was tall and large. The second was even taller and larger.

Reann needed foreign attendants for various reasons. Being attended to, as a noble should, was key. Second, being attended to by foreigners meant she was less likely to be recognized. The Furendali didn't have nobles, officially, but wealthy land owners were entitled to a similar level of respect and privilege. So Reann had contrived a plan to pose as the daughter of a wealthy Furendali land owner and borrow from Trinah's goodwill to get the help she needed.

"So sorry to have kept you," Reann said, stepping up onto a footstool in her plain slip and making a perfect imitation of a Furendali accent, a gift of tongue she had inherited from her mother. "You are the attendants Trinah recommended?"

"I'm Lina," said the elder, "and this is Toreen, my friend. Of course we came as soon as we received your message. But it was somewhat unexpected."

"Thank you for being available on short notice," Reann said.

"We really ought to thank you," Toreen said with a blush. "It gave us an excuse to leave school to come see the festival."

"I had so hoped that Trinah herself might come," Reann said with a sigh. "But she couldn't make it and asked that I attend in her stead. Only, I had just let my servants off for vacation—what was I to do? Trinah suggested I forward a request from her to ask you for help getting ready for the gala."

"You know the Lady of the North?" Lina asked.

"Very well, in fact. We are related."

The girls' faces exposed natural excitement.

"She saved my brother," Lina volunteered. "He actually doesn't remember any of it, since he was nearly frozen at the time. But it was she that found him. It always is."

"And she got us both accepted into the school in Redal," Toreen explained.

"Thank you very much for being here on the Lady's request," Reann said. "I'm a bit behind getting ready. Would you help me?"

"Certainly."

Reann did her best to imitate the other nobles being dressed by attendants, trying to do as little as possible on her own. Reann resisted the urge to push her hair out of her face.

Reann's dress, borrowed from the mistress room, hung on a post nearby where Reann had placed it earlier. The cream dress strung with pearl beadwork on the bodice was substantially more sophisticated than the one she had worn for Trinah's ceremony. Intricate lace formed the upper sleeves, while the lower sleeves and gown trail were loose and flowing. The girls lowered it over Reann's outstretch arms. "Where did you get this?" Toreen said with a gasp of amazement. "It must have cost a fortune."

"Where is your land holding?" Lina asked, as she began to cinch the lace ties on the bodice of the dress until it hugged her waist and hips, following her form. "Is it near Erdal?"

Obviously Reann didn't look Furendali. It was a fair question.

"Oh, it's not worth mentioning," Reann said. "I would rather hear about your homes in the north. I haven't spent nearly enough time there to know a half a wit about the Furendal, my father being a diplomat to Erdal and my mother Erdali. I even have an Erdali accent."

"You have a lovely voice," said the attendant dutifully. "You sound like the traders' daughters. They always get the best men."

Reann blushed. "But what about your homes?"

The girls gladly provided plenty of details, describing everything from the mind-numbing boredom of winter to the hormone-charged spring fever that universally infected all Furendali when the frost broke early each year.

As they finished cinching the dress, thanks to recent late-night adjustments Reann had made to the seams, it fit perfectly.

"Are you being escorted to the gala?" Toreen, the larger and taller of the two, asked.

"Trinah was to be escorted by a gentleman from Serban of some reputation. He shall have to make do with me, unfortunately. I suppose it would be best to keep to myself and not make disturbances."

"Never mind that," Lina said cheerily. "Make the most of it and you'll never regret it."

Of course, that was what scared Reann more than anything. "I only hope I shall look decent," she said. "I've been traveling and hardly had a moment to wash up."

"We'll take care of everything," said Toreen. "But it will help us if you don't fuss while we set your hair. It's so short—is that the fashion here in Erdal?" She combed Reann's hair with a bit of oil from an expensive-looking flask. It smelled like spring in a bottle. The frizzy edges transformed with each stroke of the brush into gentle waves that curled around her face with a soft sheen.

"I think your hair is lovely," Lina said. "Better for the summer—it's so terribly stuffy here. A headband would look serene. Yes, this jeweled one."

Reann's internal pendulum swung incessantly. Unrecoverable seconds marched away. The girls were moving too slowly. She would need a way to excuse herself, but not immediately.

Other ladies in the dressing room were gathering to go down to the dinner banquet and ball. Reann was late, just as she wanted—to avoid unnecessary, prying conversations.

Sensing her impatience, Lina said, "I wish you hadn't been so long in coming. I'm afraid you'll be late."

"I must look my best tonight," Reann said. "Much depends on it." She took a deep breath and tried to relax. Everything was set in motion. The guest list was placed, with the last entry running onto the backside of the paper—a very important modification from the original.

"Will you wear that leather pouch about your neck rather than jewels?" Lina asked. Her voice hinted that the leather pouch looked rather out of place.

"I'll tuck it into my dress—it was a gift from Trinah," she explained. Reann had no use for the crystal her sister had given her, but she also had nowhere safe to hide it.

The two Furendali girls conceded the point without argument.

"Can we gather up your other things?"

"Yes, thank—"

Oh—the list is still in my old shirt!

"No," Reann recovered quickly. "We can worry about that afterward. Now you both get along and enjoy the competitions. I should like to see you best a few of the Erdali boys in the sports."

The girls laughed politely, but then exchanged intrigued glances.

"Now off with you. Enjoy the festival. I'll be fine, thanks to your help."

The girls left the room.

"What is this?"

Reann froze.

It was Katrice's voice, directly behind her.

"Do you think this is this supposed to be a costume ball?"

Reann's chest constricted suddenly, as if her tightly laced dress had suddenly become a python. She couldn't breathe.

"That's you, isn't it, Reann?"

Carena moved into view to one side of Reann.

Reann stood facing the door. She could feel the heads of the remaining gossiping servants turning.

For two crucifying seconds she paused, unable to speak.

She was about to be outed by her own kind.

Reann suddenly turned around. She screamed and pointed at the floor near Katrice. "Is that a rat?"

A dozen other screams issued instantly, and Reann turned and dashed for the door.

She shut it behind herself quickly and sped down the hallway, acknowledging the head guard at the stairwell with only a slight nod of her head.

"May I offer you a hand with the stairs?"

"Not this evening," Reann said, making up an excuse on the fly. "The man waiting for me downstairs is a jealous fellow."

The two other guards with him laughed.

The stairs came at Reann in a blur as she hurried toward an end she could only hope for. Her heart beat triple time as she raced down the spiral. And suddenly she was face-to-face with him.

"So you decided to come after all?" Verick said, clipping a pocket watch shut and tucking it into his waistcoat.

"My apologies," Reann said, swallowing a gasp of breath. "I had some chores to finish."

"Understood."

"But I've saved you the trouble of a solid half hour of unrestrained socializing," Reann noted.

"You seem to be keen on making the introductions yourself," Verick said, "or else avoiding them."

He had pointed out exactly what Reann was up to. And the fact that he had pointed it out meant he had been thinking about it. And that was not good.

"Well, let's get a seat at our table. Have they already begun the introductions?" Reann asked.

"Just," Verick noted. "But I think we can make our way in the side entrance."

"Ah," Reann agreed. "The serving door—good idea."

Verick knew about the side door. If Verick should flee, if he should take her with him by force, he might even manage it without drawing attention.

He opened the door and Reann stepped through, finding only two open seats waiting in the spot nearest the exit.

"How convenient," Reann said with a forced smile, as Verick seated her on one of the two adjacent seats at one of the round tables arranged along the perimeter of great hall.

"Yes," Verick agreed, sweeping the scabbard of his ever-present saber aside as he seated himself.

Other couples filtered in the doors on the opposite side.

Reann looked to the head table. This year's announcer was none other than Lord Tromwen. She sucked in a breath of surprise and put her hand to the side of her face.

Tromwen stood at the rostrum, read a name then indicated the person when the man or lady stood to polite applause. He continued making introductions, commenting on each noble's heritage or the scenic beauty of their land holding, or mentioning a relative he had known. He was making the most of the attention.

The nobles, men and women, totaled more than seventy-five guests. At this rate, the introductions would last at least long enough to put her life in double jeopardy.

"I should start by saying that I have learned a few things of late," Verick said quietly.

Here we go.

Reann pressed her hands into her lap. "Things of interest?"

Verick nodded.

"Regarding your land holding?" she said cautiously, avoiding mention of the heirs for now.

"As it were," Verick said tersely.

He was on edge now, standoffish.

"And a few things about my attendant."

Reann looked at Tromwen but heard not a word he said. Servers mingled through the tables pouring drinks. One looked at Reann but did not recognize her.

Verick leaned closer and spoke into Reann's ear. "You were born not long after the end of the western conflict. Your mother was a single woman—blind. You'd be surprised what you can find about somebody when you talk to the right people. And it bears out in the records."

He knows.

"You might say . . . the eyes of the blind see too much," he whispered softly.

Reann became more conscious of the saber by his side.

"This being a celebration of Toran's legacy," Verick said ominously, "I thought I should find out a little more about the fellow. Interesting that you should neglect to mention that Toran reputedly vacationed one winter very near Erdal, just after the end of the western conflict."

"Yes," Reann said carefully. "Perhaps with some additional clues—"

Verick gripped her arm. "You have been in my room. Your cat's fur was on my bedspread. I can only assume you have had access to my private things, including my diary."

Reann said nothing as her stomach twisted into a knot.

Hurry up, Tromwen—you're talking me to death, literally.

"I have," Reann admitted. "But nothing I have learned about you changes what I feel. I think you are an honest person on a fool's errand."

"You don't know what to make of me," Verick said.

"Then tell me," Reann said, steeling herself. "What do you make of me?"

Verick placed a black-gloved hand on the table. It lay still when it usually would have fingered the edge of his hat. "As near as I can tell, you read and write six languages. There was only one person in Toran's court with that kind of skill, and even then only in speaking tongues."

"Emra," Reann said.

Verick looked at her, as if surprised.

Reann gave voice to the unspoken question. "Do you think I was born a peasant?"

Their conversation was buried in a roar of laughter as Tromwen made a jest comparing his cousin's swollen shape to the borders of his land holding.

Verick sipped his glass before answering. "Perhaps not."

Reann stared at him headlong. "I was, in fact, born to a peasant—an illegitimate birth. What with all the comings and goings of ambassadors, I might even be your cousin." Reann inclined her head considering the alternative. "Or I might be related to the stable boy. How am I to know? How is anyone to know?"

Verick lowered his voice. "We both know who your father is."

Reann listened as Tromwen read the next name on the list. There were still ten left to go.

"These people are as loyal to Toran's memory as anyone, anywhere. This is his birthplace," Reann said smoothly.

"I see," Verick said, looking down his nose as if looking at peasantry on display.

"So if I was, for instance, to stand up and say I were against Toran and his legacy, I would be in the wrong place—quite wrong," Reann added.

The power of Reann's advantage seemed to suddenly loom heavily over her companion. She paused, letting the words sink in, then continued in a very level, businesslike tone.

Verick's face remained impressively calm. "You insinuate. Speak to it. What do you mean by this supposed entrapment, this charade?"

Reann swallowed. "There are some things that you don't know, that I haven't told you yet. You also have many things which you have not yet told to me. And I think that this is the right place to do it."

A lady on their table looking at Reann nudged her husband and whispered.

"We can speak anywhere else with more privacy," Verick said

quickly, wary of the new eyes which exchanged looks with others on their table.

Reann spoke deliberately and slowly, so as not to appear nervous. "I know who you are."

Verick said nothing to that.

"I also know that the reason you seek my help is not to aid the heirs, but to get vengeance."

Verick opened his mouth, but Reann spoke quickly over his words. "But you learned the truth about what really happened to your family. Toran didn't kill them. And you are on a crusade without a cause."

"I have nothing to say to that," Verick replied. It was all he could say. Reann had said enough, loud enough, to put all sorts of questions in the minds of several eavesdropping nobles.

A growing number were giving attention to their tempered exchange of words. This was the breaking point. She had to win a friend before it came to fight or neither would come out alive. Either they both lived or they both died.

Reann turned in her chair to face him, drawing even more attention. She spoke very quietly, so that only Verick could make out every word she said. "Shall I speak the name of your father, then? I saw his portrait in the library. His face was very much like your own."

"Keep your peace," Verick urged plaintively, eyes darting.

"All right," she said. "I have a proposition for you."

Verick's face scrunched indignantly. "What proposition?"

"I think you are neither the villain nor the hero you imagine yourself to be. You're neither wicked nor brave enough."

"Aren't we all?"

Reann put her hand on his. "When we danced, you were a decent man. You were full of life."

Verick, again, said nothing.

"What you would do does not become you. It is a vile garment you wear and refuse to take off."

"I am what I am," he whispered quickly. "There is nothing you or I can do about it."

Reann placed both her hands upon his leg and leaned toward him earnestly. "Don't say that. You have a chance now. You have a chance to clear your name and put right what was done wrong. Killing the heirs won't make you whole. Two wrongs don't make a right—even a child knows that."

Reann waited as the storm raged inside the heart of the innocent son of a bloody traitor.

"What," his lips stammered, "are you suggesting?"

"I'm suggesting that you care about me. I'm suggesting that I'm your friend. And . . . that perhaps fate brought us together, to help each other." She looked to Verick with tears brimming in the corners of her eyes. "I know what you feel."

"You cannot know."

"Let me," Reann said desperately.

Verick's eyes flicked anxiously to the door.

"Find the heirs," Reann urged. "Return them to the throne. Swear it now, on your father's sword, and purge the sin of it forever. You would have glory in the histories—the great restorer, the bringer of peace."

"You mean to suggest that I—wasn't I already—how do you mean to—"

"Dorian of Ruban, son of Dorgan," Reann whispered into his ear. The very sound of the words coming from her mouth blanched his face. "I will give you this one chance. Make your choice. If you mean to be a villain, I will call you out as such in front of all these people." She swallowed. "But I care about you. And I need you. This day is my chance. And here I am, with you, trying to save you."

"I don't get that impression," Verick said. "More like blackmail. 'Do as I say or else.'"

"I've heard that before, from you," Reann said. "Don't you remember? But I've put that all behind me. To me you *are* Verick. You are new man, free of your father's guilt. And if you care for me at all, then give up your vendetta. Join me. Help me. We can find the heirs; we can reunite the kingdom, the way it was meant to be."

Reann took Verick's hand as it went to his sword hilt. His fingers trembled. She held them tightly between hers.

"I can forgive the son of Toran's betrayer as well as his son can leave his vengeance unclaimed. You know I am Toran's heir," Reann said quietly, admitting for the first time to anyone else besides Trinah that she was indeed the daughter of Toran.

The word *heir* was heard by at least three in the crowd. And the word passed quickly from mouth to ear through the guests like the wind moving over tall grass.

"Let us be friends," she urged.

Verick closed his eyes.

"Let us undo what was done while there is still time."

Verick squeezed his hand into a fist.

"Let your anger die. Let the vendetta perish in our new friendship. Say the word and I shall trust you with any secret to your dying day. You cannot turn from the path you choose. Now is the moment of destiny, for you, for me, for your people, and for the five realms."

He was shaking visibly. His face contorted into an expression of agony. "How can I do this?"

Reann put her arm around his shoulder and lay her face against his cheek. "Just be brave. There is nothing we can do anymore. You cannot escape this place. And neither can I. Our fates are bound together."

Reann's eyes darted left. Tromwen noted the mark on the bottom of the parchment and turned it over.

"Not done yet. Ah, one more name. I should hope it is someone with a very short title. I'm getting hungry."

The gathered gave yet another polite laugh.

Verick locked eyes with Reann.

There was only one more name on the list. It could be his, or it could be hers. There was only one move left to be played.

"This name is one I've never seen," Tromwen announced in a tenor voice that quavered. His eyes fixed on the page.

A rush of movement passed through the gathered Erdali nobles like wind through willows.

The question was, had Reann written her name out on the parchment, or Dorian's?

Verick's hand hovered by his sword. His jaw was set, but his eyes flickered with doubt.

Reann knew he could cut down most of the overweight middle aged nobility in the room, but not all of them. Reann put her hand on his and closed her eyes.

If anyone was to die, she would be the first.

The anticipation in the hall grew by the moment as the color drained from the magistrate's face.

Reann released Verick's hand, which went to the hilt of his saber.

"What does it say?" a voice called.

"Read it, man!" another urged.

"Behold," Tromwen announced, sounding indignant suddenly. "I read the name as it appears on the register: 'Her majesty, high princess and heiress of Erdal—Reann, daughter of Emra and Toran, conqueror and lord of the five realms.'"

Rancor spread through the group. Reann stood to acknowledge her name, one hand sweeping her skirt in front of her. With her other hand she gripped Verick's.

She moved forward and down the steps into the center of the room.

Verick followed. What courage or folly gave him the strength Reann could not imagine. She paced directly into the center of the rotunda and nodded to Tromwen.

The noise washed into a perilous silence.

Reann faced Tromwen and gave a bow, a proper curtsy, only slight as of one to an equal rank.

Tromwen looked from the paper to Reann, then back to the page, and clutched his ceremonial crimson magistrate's robe at his chest.

Reann reached out and took the paper from him. She rolled it and handed it back to Tromwen, who, though two heads taller, trembled as though she were a giant.

"I welcome you all," Reann said boldly, "to the house of my father." She reached out for Verick's hand again. He took it like a man taking a sentence from a judge. Denial was no option. But better to be on her side now than against it.

Verick gripped her hand tightly as he turned his head toward her, intending to make his intentions clear and present. But a flood of questions and answers mobbed the rotunda.

"Is she the heir?" a lady gasped.

"He meant Emra, the translator," an older noble explained to his table.

"Where has she been these many years?"

"What sort of mockery is this?" a heavy-set gentleman demanded.

"She can't prove it," another shouted, to a chorus of agreement.

Reann stepped forward, leaving Verick next to Tromwen, her back to the one man on earth who had sworn to kill her.

"There is one here who knows who I am," Reann said. "I have brought him here to witness it."

The brilliance of her plan shined like a ray of light at dawn. Reann smiled and turned to Verick.

His face was a monsoon of emotion.

"Friends," she whispered to him, in a promise, a suggestion, and a plea.

Verick paced to the center of the rotunda, where eyes like spears stabbed at him. The windows to the hall were crowded with servants. More pressed in at the main entrance.

The head butler burst through, his bald pate glinting in the light of a hundred oil lamps as he stormed into the rotunda.

"Reann! What do you think you are you doing? Come with me this instant. This behavior is beyond—"

Verick drew his sword in a flash and clotheslined the butler with a blow from the butt of his saber. The clobbered man scrambled backward as Verick aimed the point directly at his chest.

Men around the room shifted, putting hands to sword hilts.

As he backed away the head butler raised his hands to cover his head in the Erdali gesture of submission.

"I came here," Verick spoke. A chill hung on his voice, as if speaking at his own funeral, "to find the heirs of Toran."

Verick gestured with his sword point at Reann. The blade tip was within the range of a sudden thrust. "I spared no end of research, my own clues added to the notes of Toran's own cupbearer, Ranville. I had reached the zenith of my charge, my mortal duty, when I found her." He nodded at Reann.

Verick turned and faced the gathered assembly. "Rulers of Erdal and the five realms, I came here tonight expecting to be betrayed. I came expecting a fight, to bloody my sword in defense of my life." He looked at Reann. "But I was not betrayed to my death. This lady protected my identity. She gave me honor I did not deserve and robbed me of my revenge."

"Who are you?" Tromwen said boldly, stepping into his familiar role as chief judge of the Erdali court. "Speak your name, I charge you."

"I am the heir elect of the Serbani protectorate of Ruban. Among you I took the name Verick, but I was born Dorian . . . son of Dorgan."

The hall burst into an uproar. The nobles at the tables pointed and in an instant the entire assembly was leaning in for a glimpse.

"How dare you!" bellowed a hefty bearded man shaking his fist.

"My son died in that harbor," cried an aged woman. "Slain! Drowned!"

"Blood traitor!"

Verick brandished his blade with a deftness that spoke of imminent death and shouted them down. "My motives for seeking Toran's blood relatives are no mystery to any of you. My face is that of my father, the one who betrayed you and your sons. And for that, Toran's retribution was legendary." He dropped his blade into its sheath. "But

Toran didn't kill my father. Fate cursed him with disease, as it did Toran. It took them both. And so . . . I have no quarrel with his heirs."

Reann finally took a breath.

Verick's hands balled into fists. "I am cursed above all!" he bellowed. "Evil finds me wherever I go. My family name is wretched. And my vengeance is in vain." He turned and looked Reann in the eyes. "My father failed to destroy yours. And he mine. You declined to destroy me when you had that chance, and so I can do you no injustice." Verick turned, eyes wide and brave. "She is your rightful ruler! She has wisdom and kindness, with her father's diligence and her mother's gift for language. Even if she were not the heir—and she is the heir—her ascendance would be a boon to this realm. You will find none wiser and none truer to the realm."

Verick sheathed his sword, unbuckled his sword belt and handed it with one arm to Reann. "You have my sword and my pledge. My vengeance dies this day. I will restore the heirs of Toran and so seek to end my curse."

Whispers again ran through the gathered crowd.

Reann drew the sword. It was a lot heavier than Verick made it look. She inspected it, point aloft, and then slid it back into its scabbard.

"So long as you shall use it in my service, may this blade bring you honor." She handed it back and rose up on her toes to plant a delicate kiss on Verick's cheek.

Verick stood steady, though his eyes flinched at the words. He found his voice as Reann squeezed his hand once again. He bent to one knee. "I swear this day that I will, with you all as my witnesses, give my life to the cause of restoring the throne and the kingdom of Toran. If by this I may purge my father's sin, I so dedicate myself. And so I beg your mercy."

The crowd fell into an abyss of silence.

Reann was the most surprised of all.

Had he known she would do this? Had he decided already to

abandon his quest? Or was he only playing at loyalty because her trap had left him no other options.

Reann could accept only one reality.

"Let us be allies, so long as we both live," Reann said. "You have buried the dishonor of the past. I ask all my subjects to let their hatred also pass away." She had won the first battle of her life. All that remained was to get her throne—and she had no idea how she would manage that.

Verick looked up and smiled for the first time at Reann, who reflected back a rather quizzical expression. He let go of Reann's hand and turned his palm outward, indicating the young woman standing at his side.

"I give you Reann, daughter of Toran."

The swelling wave of emotion broke into a chorus.

"It cannot be."

"I say, she's a servant at the castle."

"Nay, look at her features. I see something of the man."

A voice rose from the crowd. It was an old fellow. "Listen all, to what I know."

"Hear old Dentr!" another voice shouted. "Let him speak."

The crowd paused, but their nervous bodies seethed and writhed like trapped serpents.

The man called Dentr stood as straight as his aged body would allow. Reann knew him. She had served him many times as a guest at the castle and he had always been polite to her.

He gestured at Reann. "She was born," he said solemnly, "seventeen years ago to Emra, daughter of Rembra, captain at arms. I knew Rembra. I was there in Dervan, when we fought to the last man, when the robbers fell upon us like a sandstorm and Toran fell wounded and there was no one else beside him but Rembra and his sons. Who could be more worthy to bear the seed of the king than Emra, his daughter?"

Reann's face flushed to hear her mother spoken of in such honored terms.

"I cannot say for sure Toran was her father," the man said in a solid voice that rumbled over the crowd with such passion and ferocity co-mingled. "But if she knows her father, she will bear the token of his victory there, taken from his place of hiding, which only the most loyal knew."

"I second that," Tromwen said. "We were a small band there." Tromwen's eyes drifted. "I recall it as well—a token only the heir can bear."

"What kind of token?" shouted a young noble.

The challenge was laid by this old man who showed by his scratched and scarred face to have suffered uncountable wounds in battle.

"Hear old Tromwen, too. He speaks the truth. I'll stake my fortune on it."

"Hear! Hear! Let her present the token."

"Can she show it?"

Reann's hand moved suddenly to her chest, a defensive gesture. But the eyes of the crowd tracked the motion. Reann clutched the pouch under her dress. Her heart beat against the one thing that connected her with her parents.

Verick looked to Reann, eyes wide. "You have something from Toran?"

Hands shaking terribly, Reann looked down and drew out the black pouch to a collective breath, which they each held as her small fingers opened it and reached in.

The lamp light scattered in a hundred directions as she removed the finger-sized crystal and held it aloft, its color shifting continuously in the flickering lamp light.

"Lyrium," Verick whispered.

Reann scarcely had time to register the word she had read in Toran's diary. Showing the crystal to the gathered nobles, she said, "I am the fifth child of Toran." She spoke, feeling the words come from her as if they had life of their own, "The heiress of Erdal."

"She speaks truth!" Dentr declared. "A gem from the forbidden cavern!" He raised his arms and covered his head, then dropped to one knee.

Others in the crowd followed, until all had given the sign of submission. Verick could not, for Reann clasped his hand too tightly to allow it.

As Reann lowered the crystal, a face flickered across it. Then dozens of faces spilled into the facets and a chorus of voices sounded in her head.

Shaking off the strangeness of the sight, she looked around at the crowd, heads still bowed under their arms.

A soaring feeling came over Reann. *I'm the crown princess!* But the glowing awe collapsed almost instantly into a burden that closed around her like a python's grip, the weight of a kingdom.

Reann whispered out of the corner of her mouth to Verick, "Well, neither of us died. What now?"

"They can't kneel all evening," Verick said. "Do something about it."

"Rise," she said simply.

The nobles stood.

"We all rise into a brighter future. We will strengthen the bonds of loyalty, the true strength of Erdal. From this place our renewed allegiance will reach out to our sister realms. I intend to serve you first of all, as I always have. And I intend to lead as my father did, hand in hand," she raised Verick's hand and beckoned for Tromwen to join hands with her.

"All hail the princess Reann of Erdal, heiress of Toran," commanded Dentr, the aged fellow who had challenged Reann to produce the evidence of her claim to the throne.

Immediately the room roared with a hundred voices.

"HAIL, REANN OF ERDAL!"

The power of the cheer was so loud that Reann felt it beat through her entire being.

"HAIL, THE HEIRESS OF TORAN!"

It was so loud she knew that all the eavesdropping servants had heard it as well. At the thought of it, she realized she was more scared to face them than the nobles.

Arrangements were hastily made to move Reann, and Verick at her behest, to the centermost table near the lectern.

The meal was roast pheasant, something Reann had never eaten before. But her stomach was so upset with anxiety that she could scarcely eat anything. And it was just her luck to be served by Carena, who upon seeing Reann seated at the head table and being called "Lady Reann" froze in a pose of absolute terror.

Reann looked at her. "Carena?"

She dropped the tray. Only the sound of the dishes breaking shook her from the shock. Her face continued moving from green envy to pale doubt, fear, red anger, and finally complete and total embarrassment. She gathered a jug and her tray and jetted out of the room like a chased rabbit.

"Someone you know?" Tromwen said politely.

"My roommate."

"Ah, you mean your handmaiden," he corrected.

"Uh." She looked at Verick who nodded.

"Yes," Reann said, feeling a stab of pain shoot through her middle. It felt like betrayal to leave her friends behind and, worse, to serve her. It added to the knot in her stomach.

Reann didn't see Carena the rest of the evening.

Tromwen continued the scheduled events by announcing the entertainment: singers, musicians, and dancers.

Reann was offered wine in a large goblet, which Verick graciously moved out of her reach.

Verick was already defending her.

"You should eat only shared dishes," Verick whispered. "You could be poisoned. And only take your drinks from the hand of a friend."

He offered his own water glass, which Reann sipped carefully.

"Poisoned?" she asked playfully.

"Missed my chance, I'm afraid," he said.

Reann exchanged a smile with Verick. She took a large swallow and gulped. Then it hit her.

"Verick, where am I going to sleep tonight? I can't go back to the servant's quarters . . . I just can't."

"You will sleep in my chambers," he said quietly.

"But where will you sleep? All the rooms are taken."

"I will not sleep tonight. You do not yet have guards you can trust."

Reann leaned her head against his arm. "Thank you."

"Don't worry about your friends either."

Reann nodded, but she couldn't sever thirteen years of fellowship with a thought. They were her family: Katrice, Carena—even Ret.

What would Ret say? *He'd better not say anything,* Reann determined. *Or I'll give him demerits.*

That thought made her smile.

Reann looked around the room. Eyes glared and gazed. Others peered sidelong at her. Some eyed her as they drank from their glasses. It was as though she had lived her life invisible and suddenly become real and tangible.

"Everyone is looking at me," Reann whispered.

"Don't do anything foolish then," Tromwen urged.

"You will not treat the princess like a child, sir," Verick returned. "I fear your advice borders on undeserved censure."

"You are most welcome, both of you, for your concern," Reann said quickly, hoping to defuse the tension. "Shall we have a dance?"

Reann raised her hand and nodded to the head musician who seemed to have been waiting for her cue—how long he had been waiting she didn't know. Then she offered her hand to Verick, who stood and lifted her. She stepped carefully around the table, her hand held aloft gently by Verick's. She nodded to Tromwen, who rose and gave a heartier pull to raise his much rounder wife, whose eyes made desperate protests. Reann nodded to three other nearby couples, one from each of the major counties neighboring Erdal, and the group descended again into the "dogfighting pit," as Ret called it, and began a simple three-step waltz.

Reann was not a perfect dancer and was becoming more aware of it by the moment. But Verick was as exquisite and accurate in his dance footwork as he was at his swordsmanship and made easy work of keeping her moving the right direction. It was as if time had stopped.

During a waltz, he drew her quickly to his chest and lifted her around swiftly out of the way of another waltzing couple. He set her back down as smoothly as if the dance move had been practiced.

Reann wished he hadn't had to set her back down.

"That was a close call," she breathed.

"Perhaps it's a good time to make a graceful retreat," he suggested.

Reann and Verick turned once more and ascended out of the center of the room. Other couples joined the dance in their place.

The music and dancing took Reann right out of time. The worries and fears somehow retreated into oblivion and a pure joy like nothing she had ever felt slipped into her middle and spread through her arms and legs, like being wrapped in a fuzzy, fur blanket. She clapped with the music and smiled and, around her, other smiles emerged.

Reann stood and joined in a circle dance. Verick watched this time from his dinner chair where a portion of pheasant vied for his attention.

Boys.

Reann shook many hands after the dance and made countless introductions. She knew nearly all of them—it was her job to know the guests and their likes and dislikes. She amused a table by naming each guest in turn and telling some vegetable or seasoning they didn't like or which they habitually requested.

A young noble, only a few years her senior, asked about Reann's food preferences.

She froze. It was a topic far too embarrassing to attempt to touch.

She had no answer besides "fresh table scraps," the alternative being "old scraps." So she pointed to an uneaten portion of bread pudding. "Are you going to finish that, or may I have it?"

His eyes widened in shock.

"I jest," she said with a twinkle in her eye that brought out a chorus of full-bellied laughs from bearded men at the table.

"Or, if you are finished, shall I clear your plates?"

The old men in the group, by this time well drunk, roared with laughter at a princess playing at serving tables.

"It is past my bedtime," Reann admitted. "And so I must retire."

"Not so soon," begged a gentleman with kind eyes and a bulging belly. "We haven't had so much to celebrate in thirteen years."

"Celebrate on," she said. "I insist—it is my first edict."

"More grog, then!" roared his friend, raising his glass. "More grog—Princess Reann's orders!"

The nearby tables chittered with polite laughter. Reann made her way back around to the head table, where she stood and waved her good-bye to the assemblage.

But it wasn't just Verick that escorted her back upstairs. An honor guard of soldiers with shields and halberds shepherded her up the four flights to the top story of the castle.

Verick opened the door with his room key and followed Reann inside. As the heavy door swung shut, Reann closed her eyes and breathed out a long, slow breath, letting everything that she had just experienced wash over her one more time.

She drifted to the bed and sat carefully on the corner of it—she had made up the bed that very morning. "You don't have to stay up all night," Reann offered as she sat on Verick's bed. "I can have Ret bring you some blankets."

"I have . . . a lot to think about," Verick confessed, his expression heavy, his eyes now red-lined.

Reann peeled back one of the heavy blankets and tossed it toward him. "Take this. I'll roast under all these blankets."

"Shall I call someone to help you undress?" Verick asked, facing away.

"Are you serious?" Reann laughed. "Why would I want somebody to help me undress?"

Verick lifted an eyebrow.

"Actually, on second thought, could you just pull that tie loose?" Reann looked over her shoulder at the tight knot the Furendali girls had put in the lace bodice of her dress.

"I'm not accustomed to such work," Verick admitted.

Reann tried not to giggle. "Fine, then just cut it."

Verick inclined his head. Then he whipped out his saber.

She winced.

With a swish of his blade the pressure around her middle vanished.

"I can mend it tomorrow," she said softly. "Even princesses are expected to know how to sew, right?"

"I wouldn't know, my lady."

Reann hopped onto the bed and pulled the drapes shut between the bedposts.

"And no peeking."

"Says the one who sneaks into—"

"Oh bother," Reann laughed. "Can't a princess have any peace?"

"By your leave," Verick said quietly. The chair squeaked as he sat. The sheathed saber always by his side dropped onto the stone floor with a clatter.

At that, Reann pulled the white dress over her head, draped it over the curtains of her bed, and removed the corset which came loose with a simple tug at the tie. She buried herself beneath cool cotton sheets, sheets that she had only ever felt as she folded them in the laundry.

Outside crickets chirped, the same crickets that serenaded the servants.

CHAPTER 25

Montazi Realm.

Megaliths rose and fell like hills with progressively deeper gaps and wider canyons between them. Nema's dragon Cymr flew at a bedraggled pace that mocked Terith's urgency.

Dull throbs and stabs issued from Terith's arm, leg, and ribs. He kept a salvaged Outlander sword, a bow, a clutch of arrows, and his cloak by his side. No water, no food, nothing to sustain him for any longer than his task would allow.

He led Cymr south and east through driving afternoon rain toward the extreme eastern edge of the megaliths. There, hidden beneath the ivy and the fog, Toran's trail led along the sides of sheer cliffs from the megaliths of the Montas out into the Outlands to the realm of his mother. How bitter that thought was. It was as if his blood had come pre-poisoned with some act of treason.

Again Terith recalled the strange question Tanna had asked once, not so many weeks before.

Did you ever feel like your future lies somewhere outside the Montas?

She knew. She knew! And she never told me anything.

Doubt stung his heart like scorpion's venom.

Erdali and Outlander blood, but no Montazi—yet I became a rider. I share the awakening and bond with Montazi. How can that be? It passes only from a Montazi mother to her child.

Why would Toran bear a child of a foreigner? And why did my father abandon me?

Was I . . . a mistake?

In that hollow void of doubt there moved something new, something foreign.

Fear.

Terith trembled with dread. And in the wash of panic that seized him, the Montazi connection to the awakening was obliterated.

Fear controlled his fate now, more than anything. In the darkness of dread, he was no Montazi.

Like my parents.

Son like father, his promises waited on promises unfulfilled.

Terith gripped the dragon's reins and rose up in his saddle.

So be it. If I am to fall, then I shall take many with me.

Terith lowered Nema's fruit dragon to just above the treetops. Cresting a divide, a canyon opened beneath him. To his left the Outlands ended at a sheer cliff that dropped into the swamps of the deep.

Terith blinked back fatigue and emotion and angled Cymr to glide out over the lip of the canyon. Several other dragons glided through the canyon. It was the season for hunting food for their hatchlings. Nema's yellow-green dragon was but one among many that flapped their wings in the light drizzle.

Terith let the dragon down not far from the final cliff that separated the Outlands from the Montas realm. He dismounted. The exhausted dragon ducked into the shade of a broad fern and made itself scarce.

Terith walked a dozen paces to the edge of the precipice. The dragons circling the canyon were not wild. They each bore a rider.

If these are Pert's missing riders, then . . .

Terith's eyes searched in the ivy of the opposite wall of the canyon for signs of movement. Toran's trail itself was not visible beneath the ivy and below the fog line, but perhaps passing movement would be detectable.

All at once his eyes pieced a pattern of insignificant puffs of haze rising out of the fog at intervals, blending with the fog.

Greenwood torches.

A column of soldiers was moving along the cliff just below the fog line. In a mix or horror and dismay, Terith realize the Outlanders had been on Toran's trail since at least that morning.

He looked to the gaps between the megaliths where vulnerable bridges stretched unseen across the canyon below the fog level. But small detachments of guards, crossbows drawn, were stationed on the megalith tops.

Neutat lay beyond a rise only five miles to the east.

How do I stop them?

Terith's mind spun, watching almost helplessly as the troops marched into the realm of the Montas, his realm.

Anger and fear boiled up in him. Suddenly two wingtips appeared in front of him quickly followed by the slender jaws of a velra. A gust of fire blasted him backward. Terith's eyes and face were seared through the gap in his face guard. As he fell back, his exposed skin at the gashes in his leather cried out as though it were still immersed in the blaze.

Terith forced himself to his feet, but the barrel-splintering force of the heavy tail of the dragon met him halfway, sending him back a half dozen paces. He landed on his side, reeling with sharp, new pain. Blackness gathered around him. Terith tried to stand up but couldn't find the strength in his legs nor air in his thunderstruck lungs.

Its dragon fire spent, Nema's mount Cymr beat the air as he took to the sky.

Pert dismounted from his velra and stood in front of him, solitary, arrogant, and supreme.

At a gesture from Pert, an unseen force closed on Terith, squeezing his chest and throat, lifting him from the ground.

Pert's demonic power had somehow increased, as if he were gaining strength with every life he took.

"Traitor!" Terith forced through his pinched windpipe.

"I told you I would take it all away," Pert said menacingly.

"You can't," Terith said. His feet reached helplessly for the ground a few inches away.

"You're dead. The Montas is mine. These savages will take the inlands, and nobody can stop any of it—especially you."

Pert drew his knife and put the tip to Terith's neck, slit the tie to his dragon-wing cloak, and yanked it away.

Terith tried to move his arms, but the dark awakening billowed stronger, squeezing him until the pain forced him to the edge of unconsciousness.

"You are nothing more than a flesh-eating maggot that crawled out of the scum," Pert spoke through gritted his teeth. "So back to the deep with you!"

He grabbed Terith by the throat and hurled him headlong over the edge of the cliff. Pert shrieked with pleasure, screaming at the sheer delight of finally defeating Terith.

The air rushed in Terith's ears, louder and louder. He tumbled at the edge of consciousness, the sight of his cloak drifting down far above him passed vaguely in his mind.

He collided with the cliff and then pinwheeled limply into a crush of leaves, rocks, water, and darkness.

And those words echoed as the life drained out of him.

Not the deep!

CHAPTER 26

Erdali Realm. Citadel of Toran.

The latch on the door clicked softly as of someone discretely leaving.

"Verick!" Reann called.

He had left without saying goodbye.

Reann pulled back the curtains of her bed and looked about for something to wear. There was nothing but the fancy gown she had worn the night before. Reann struggled into it, did her best to cinch the ties in the back, and put her feet into the soft and familiar leather slippers, a remnant of her former life.

Reann opened the door to find two sentries posted. Reann darted past them down the hall.

"He said she'd do that," the taller one mumbled to his fellow.

"Now what?" the other replied.

Reann hurried down the stone steps of the circular stair. Verick wasn't in the dining hall.

The stables—gotcha.

She smiled as she hurried out the great double doors of the castle and grabbed his arm as Verick rode his horse out of the stable gate.

Without a word he pulled her into the saddle in front of him.

"You left without saying anything," Reann accused.

"You were sleeping."

"As you should have been," Reann replied breathlessly. "Where do you think you're going?"

"Wherever you wish, my lady."

Reann grinned at the thought. She was a princess. She could have whatever she wanted. What she wanted most was time with Verick.

"Take me up to the quarry," Reann said, with a glint in her eye. "I want to see my kingdom."

Verick nodded and his horse trotted quickly to the gate.

"Open the portcullis," barked a sergeant. "It's the princess, Reann."

Word of Reann's revealed identity had spread quickly.

"Good morning, your highness," said the gate guard smartly. His eyes sparkled as if he had been given new life.

As Verick's horse stepped quickly through the streets of the lower village, curious villagers poked their heads out of shutters. The most nonplussed was the old cobbler who looked as though his eyes would fall out of their gaping sockets.

"You will make me some respectable boots, won't you?" Reann called as she passed. A chuckle rose in her, until both she and Verick were laughing as his horse sped to a canter toward the foothills north of the citadel.

A half hour later the horse slowed at the top of a tall hill. Reann jumped off and, lifting the edges of her dress to avoid the dirt, scampered to a lookout. Morning sunlight bathed the plains of Erdal, where the two tributaries of the great Erdal River joined near the citadel. Verick looped the reins on a pine bough and followed Reann.

"It's beautiful," she said, gazing over the green vineyards and endless fields of young wheat.

"It's yours, I suppose," Verick said.

"As far as the plains reach," Reann said. "The coastal mountains in the south belong to my adopted brother, the witch's son—I didn't tell you Toran adopted him."

"I knew you were holding something back," Verick said.

"Well your notes helped."

"Glad I could make them easy to steal."

Reann, blushing, exchanged a glance with Verick.

"He'll have his hands full with the Witch Queen," Verick said. "She's called back her merchant ships. I think she means to invade."

"My worst problem used to be dishes," Reann muttered. "Now it's her."

"What about the other heirs?" Verick asked.

"Trinah hasn't yet claimed her throne, but a document I found mentioned that the heir of the Montas realm was born on the day of Toran's victory against the Outlanders. We should be able to find him easily."

"If he survives the Outlander invasion."

"He'll survive," Reann said. *He's a son of Toran. He has to.*

Verick inclined his head conceding the point, but showing his understandable doubt. "The Montazi are strong. And what about Dervan?" Verick asked. "Is there an heir of the desert realm?"

Reann nodded.

"How will you know him?"

Reann spoke with a sureness in her voice that surprised him. "He has my father's sword."

The two strode carefully over piles of sharp rocks, broken remnants of the white rock quarried for the walls of the castle.

"Not the best location for a fortress," Verick commented, gazing down at the valley.

"What do you mean?" Reann asked.

"Out in the plain, vulnerable to marine attack—it's about the worst location you could imagine."

"It used to be up here," Reann said thoughtfully. "Before Toran moved it."

"He moved it?" Verick said, surprised. "I can't imagine why. The hill offers a longer range for catapults, no surprise attacks, access to springs, wood—it's superior in every way."

"Why does a king move his castle?" Reann wondered.

"Why does a dog bury a bone?" Verick said amicably.

"So rivals don't find it," Reann said without a second thought. She stopped, her heart suddenly pounding in her chest.

There is something under that castle.

ACKNOWLEDGMENTS

As with any novel, there are always many thanks to give. My super positive, creative wife, Amanda, is the one who convinced me I could do it. Sarah E. Starbuck, then a precious teenager and my first actual reader, got me on the right path with refined criticisms on my early work, such as "You have subject-verb agreement issues, big time."

Many thanks to my children and their voracious appetites for bedtime stories that kept me on task and thinking outside the box. To my critical readers Andrea, Megan, Mark, and Stanley for their thorough eyes and time, I can't thank you guys enough. Warm thanks to my brilliant editor Kenna Blaylock and the incredible team at Jolly Fish Press. Lastly, I credit a handwritten note on my tenth grade writing project from my English teacher Mr. McConkie. In that note he chastised me for not doing my best, forever searing it in my conscience until, ten long years later, I had the courage to write with my heart.

Dan Allen currently resides in the San Francisco Bay Area. He has designed lasers for the government that see through envelopes, lit a three-story electron accelerator on fire, chased a flying stool across a highly magnetic field zone, created nanoparticles in a radioactive lab, and failed to make a quantum computer, and he is proficient in the janitorial art of waxing floors. For fun, he invents sensors that are probably in your smartphone. For work, he is dad to his five children and husband to his drummer-artist wife. He regularly loses to his children at chess, as well as all the other games he invents, and is noted for his dedication to alleviating boredom for young people everywhere with his secret superpower: hyperactivity.

Fall of the Dragon Prince is the first novel in Dan's epic fantasy trilogy *The Forgotten Heirs*. For more fun and ideas, follow @authordanallen on Twitter and watch for forthcoming releases on JollyFishPress.com.